Abo

Georgette Heyer no
reading tastes as a tee
started when she was
to read after she had h
Filled with strong painkillers she imagined that she
could pen one, too. Many drafts later Sophia thinks she
has the perfect job writing for Mills & Boon Historical
as well as taking art tours to Europe with her husband,
who is a painter.

Regency Reputations

Regency Reputations:

Secrets and Betrayal

SOPHIA JAMES

MILLS & BOON

First Published in Great Britain 2021
By Mills & Boon, an imprint of HarperCollins*Publishers*
1 London Bridge Street, London, SE1 9GF

www.harpercollins.co.uk

HarperCollins*Publishers*
1st Floor, Watermarque Building,
Ringsend Road, Dublin 4, Ireland

REGENCY REPUTATIONS: SECRETS AND BETRAYAL
© 2021 Harlequin Books S.A.

Scars of Betrayal © 2014 Sophia James
A Secret Consequence for the Viscount © 2017 Harlequin Books S.A.

Special thanks and acknowledgement are given to Sophia James for her contribution to *The Society of Wicked Gentlemen* series.

ISBN: 978-0-263-30281-3

MIX
Paper from
responsible sources
FSC™ C007454

This book is produced from independently certified FSC™ paper to ensure responsible forest management.

For more information visit: www.harpercollins.co.uk/green

Printed and Bound in Spain using 100% Renewable electricity at CPI Black Print, Barcelona

SCARS OF BETRAYAL

Chapter One

London—June 1851

It was Nathanael Colbert walking down the wide staircase of the de Clare ballroom.

Cassandra Northrup knew it was him.

Knew it from the bottom of a rising horror and an unmitigated relief.

The same strength and height, the same dark hair, shorter now but every bit as black. She could barely take a breath, the guilt and the anger that had been stored inside and hidden for so long seeping out, winding her with its intensity.

Lord Hawkhurst, the heir to the Atherton fortune, descended beside Colbert, laughing at something Colbert had said. Disbelief made Cassie dizzy. Why would he be here in such company and dressed like an English lord? Nothing quite made sense, the wrongness of it all inviting disarray.

Shaky fingers closed around the small pottery shard

that she always wore around her neck, the heavy beat of blood in her ears making her feel sick. What could this mean for her?

Carefully, Cassie opened her fan so that it covered most of her face and turned from the trajectory the pair were taking. She had to leave before he saw her. She had to escape, but that was becoming harder as shock numbed reality. Maureen clasped her hand and she was grateful for the anchor.

'You look pale, Cassandra. Are you feeling sound?'

'Perfectly.' Even her sister did not know the exact details of what had happened in the south of France all those years ago, for she had never told another soul. A private torment, the details locked in shame.

'Well, you do not look it.'

The will to survive was flowing back, the initial jolt of shock receding under reason. She doubted Colbert would recognise her at a quick glance and resolved to leave as soon as she was able to without inciting future question.

Future. The very word made her stiffen. Could she have a future if he saw her? She felt as if she stood in the ballroom in nothing but the clothes he had once found her in, the events from almost four years ago searing into memory, all anger and fear and regret.

No. She was stronger than this. In a moment she would walk farther away, into the throng of people, carefully and quietly so as to draw no attention towards herself. She had become adept at the art of camouflage within society, the skill of obscurity in a crowd almost second nature to her now. It was how she had survived, washed back into the world she had not thought to be part of again, with its strict observance of manner and rule.

Cassie's gown mirrored her anonymity, the plain dove-grey unremarkable. All around the well-heeled young ladies bloomed like flowers, in yellows and pinks and light blue, tucks, ruffs, frills and flounces adorning their bodices, sleeves and hems. Her widow's weeds were another way to hide in full view from the notice of others.

As five seconds went past, and then ten, she started to feel safer, beguiled by the noise and movement of the very large crowd.

Everything is all right...it is still all right.

Her eyes scanned the room, but Colbert was nowhere to be seen. 'I should not have come, Reena,' she said, turning to her sister. 'You manage these things with far more acumen than I. It is simply a waste of my time to be here.'

Maureen laughed. 'I hate these functions, too, but Mr Riley was adamant about the invitation being for the both of us, Cassie, and his purse is a generous one.'

'Well, as he did not show himself I doubt he would have known if I had stayed away.' She needed to leave, needed to walk towards the door as though she did not have a care in the world. The ache inside intensified.

Once she had loved Nathanael Colbert, right from the bottom of her broken life.

The thought of what had happened next made her swallow, but she shook it gone. Not here, not now. Fixing a smile on her face, she listened to Maureen ramble

on about the beauty of the room and the dresses and
the lines of the small shaped trees set up near the band
to give the appearance of a natural grotto. A fantasy
world where anything was possible, a kinder world
away from all that was sordid and base and unclean.
All about her happy banter tinkled, the easy discourse
of people with few worries in life apart from what they
would be wearing to the next social occasion or the
generous inheritances they had garnered from the latest deceased relative.

A strange sound above caught her attention. Looking up, Cassie noticed one of the chandeliers lurch-
ing sideways, each globe spluttering with the motion.
Would the whole contraption fall? The horror of the
thought that perhaps it was about to made her mouth
dry. Had anyone else seen? To shout out would draw
the attention to herself she so wanted to avoid, but the
death of some unknowing soul would be for ever on
her conscience if she did not.

'Watch out! The light is falling.' Her raised voice
carried easily across the chatter around her, but a group
of girls to one side were not quite fast enough. With
a crash the ironwork of the leaves and flowers caught
the leg of a beautiful young blonde woman.

In the chaos Cassie hurried forward, kneeling almost at the same time as another did, bumping his arm
against hers.

Monsieur Nathanael Colbert.

Close.

A touch away, unbridled fury in his eyes. Grey eyes
with just a hint of blue. Unbalance hit and she felt

a jagged panic, her glance taking in the line of his jaw bissected with the scar she'd wrought upon him. When she had last seen this it had been opened red, blood falling across his shirt in a stream. She wanted to reach out and trace it, as if trying through touch to let him know of her sorrow. He would not welcome it, she knew, but betrayal always held two sides and this was one of them.

The sheer physical presence of him scorched at sense but as the woman's cries mounted the healer in Cassie prevailed. She could not deal with the ramifications of meeting Colbert now. Looking down, she placed her palm hard against the back of a shapely knee and the flow of blood waned, red dribbling on to her skirt, the colours mixing strangely.

'Keep still. There is a lot of bleeding and it needs to be stemmed.'

At that the young girl sobbed louder, grasping her free hand in a vice-like grip.

'Will I die?'

'No. A person is able to lose at least twenty per cent of their blood and still feel only mildly cold.'

Leached grey eyes raked across her own, no warmth whatsoever within them.

'How much would you say I have already lost?' The wounded girl's voice was breathless with panic.

Cassandra made a thorough check of the area, lifting her ankle to ascertain just what lay beneath.

'A little over half that amount so it would be wise to stay calm.'

The answering terrified shriek left her ears aching.

'I am certain that it is not so severe, Miss Forsythe.' The voice she had recalled in her dreams for so many years was measured. It was the first time she had ever heard him speak in English, the clipped and rounded vowels of privilege hanging upon every word. She hated the way her heart began to race.

'Well, as your shin has been badly cut it is most important that you...'

A shadow to one side caught her glance and then all she knew was black.

Sandrine Mercier? Speaking perfect English? Downed by the last falling remains of the chandelier and completely unconscious. The loathing he felt for her swelled in his throat. Another deceit. A further lie.

She lay on her side, her eyelashes magnified against the shining de Clare tiles, her hair shorter now, and sleeker. She was still thin, but the beauty once only promised had blossomed into a full and utter radiance.

Damn her.

He wanted to stand and turn away, but to do so would invite question and in his line of work such scrutiny was never a good thing.

Lydia Forsythe was screaming at the very top of her voice, but the bleeding from her leg had almost subsided. A doctor had scurried over as well as her distraught mother and a myriad of friends. Around Sandrine just himself and one girl lingered, an uncertain frown on her forehead and tears pooling in dark-brown eyes.

Albi de Clare, the host of the evening's entertainment, crouched down beside him. 'My God, I cannot understand how this has happened for the lights were installed only a few months ago and I was assured that they were well secured. If you can lift her, Nathaniel, there is a room leading off this one that should offer more privacy.'

Another touch. A further punishment. When Nat brought her into his arms blue-green eyes snapped open to his, horror blossoming into shock.

'I never…faint.'

'You didn't this time, either. The debris from the chandelier hit you.'

She was vibrating with panic, her head turned away. On reaching the smaller salon he placed her down upon a sofa, wishing he could leave.

'My personal physician is amongst the guests, Nathaniel, and he is examining Miss Forsythe as we speak.' Albi de Clare's tone was muted and Nat saw Sandrine's glance flicker round taking in the presence of the others who had followed them in. 'He will come to you next.'

'No.' Already she had swung her feet onto the floor and was sitting there, head in her hands. 'Please do not take the trouble to call him, my lord. I should not wish for any fuss and I already feel so very much…better.' She stood on the word and just as quickly sat down, beads of sweat garnering on her top lip.

Albi, however, was not dissuaded from seeking a medical opinion, hailing his doctor as he came into the room.

'Mr Collins, could you have a look at this injury?

The back of the patient's head has connected with the remains of the lamp.'

The old physician placed his leather satchel on a table next to the sofa before making much of extracting a pair of glasses from an outer pocket and perching them across his nose.

'Certainly, sir. Those outside intimated that you were one of the first on the scene, Lord Lindsay. Was the young lady unconscious for long after this happened?'

'Only for a few seconds,' Nat answered. 'As soon as I picked her up she seemed to regain her mind.' Plain and simple. Everything complex and twisted would come later.

Sitting, the physician held up two fingers.

'How many do you see, my dear?'

'Four.'

The woman beside Sandrine shook her head and worried eyes went quickly to her.

'Three. Two.' Guessing for all her heart's worth.

'Do you have a headache?'

'Just a small one.'

'Is your right arm numb?'

She did not answer as she dug her nails into the flesh above her elbow. So numb she did not feel it at all?

At the doorway a group of interested onlookers had gathered, though Sandrine, marked by the blood of the other victim, looked bewildered and vulnerable. She had also begun to shake. Badly. Taking off his jacket, Nathaniel tucked it about her, for shock could be as much of an enemy as injury. He hated himself for bothering.

'Warmth will help.'

For the first time he noticed the pendant at her throat, the one he had given her in Saint Estelle before she had betrayed him. The grey fabric of her bodice had drooped to reveal the roundness of one breast and the tall woman who had followed them in knelt down to pull the gown back into place, the skin on her cheeks flaming.

'Keep still, Cassie.'

Cassie? The anger in Sandrine's eyes was magnified by a deep and startling verdant green.

Albi's voice broke into his thoughts. 'If you bring Miss Cassandra this way, Nathaniel, a carriage is waiting. Miss Northrup, if you would collect her reticule and follow us?'

Northrup? Maureen and Cassandra Northrup? These were two of Lord Cowper's daughters? Hell.

A shutter had fallen across her averted eyes at the mention of her name, wariness and the cold surge of alarm evident.

'I need no extra assistance, my lords. My s...sister can help me to our conveyance.'

At that the other moved forward, pleased to be able to do something in the room with all its onlookers and the stark awkward silence.

Within a moment they were gone, both of them, only the scent of some flower he could not name left behind.

Hemlock? Foxgloves? Lily of the Valley? All poisonous and lethal.

Albi watched them go, a frown across his brow. 'The Northrup sisters may have their detractors, but it is my reasoning that with just a little time and effort they could knock the Originals from their perches. They seldom come out into society, but by all accounts their mother was beautiful, too. I think there's a third sister, married and living in Scotland. You will need to get your jacket back.'

'Perhaps.' Nat's tone was flat.

'They live in Upper Brook Street and you can't miss Avalon, the Northrup monstrosity.' Nathaniel did not wait to hear more, walking out instead to the ballroom and being instantly surrounded by the newest and most beautiful débutantes of the season.

Young women of impeccable taste and good breeding, their pasts unblemished and flawless. He smiled as he moved into their midst.

Cassie's head ached and her neck stung. She knew the wax from the candle globes had burnt her, but there had been too much to ascertain about the health of the young woman to spend time thinking about her own injuries.

Lord Lindsay.

The physician had called him that and de Clare had named him Nathaniel. Lord Nathaniel Lindsay, the heir apparent to the earldom of St Auburn. She could not believe it, could not quite take in that her dangerous rescuer in Nay with his scarred body and quick reflexes was now a dandified lord, known across all of England for his wealth and his power, with family lineage stretching back across the centuries.

Away from the stares, Cassie was feeling a lot better. The borrowed coat was warm, her shivers lessened by the touch of wool. She could smell him, too, here in the carriage, the depth of him and the strength and if her sister had not been right there beside her she might have breathed in further, allowing the colours of his beauty to explode inside, tantalising and teasing.

The scent of a man who could ruin her.

As the skin at her neck smarted beneath the heavy silk swathe of her gown, Cassie longed to take off her clothes and walk into the shallow pool at Avalon. Her mother's pool, Alysa's gown still upon the hook and her beads draped across a single gold-leafed chair. Papa had insisted on them staying.

'Lord Lindsay has only recently returned to the social scene, but I have heard tales about him.' Maureen watched her sister carefully, and Cassie knew that she was curious.

'Tales?'

'He is said to have spent some time in France. You did not meet him there, did you? I gained the impression he knew you.'

Cassandra shook her head, the truth too terrible to speak of, and she pulled the jacket in tighter.

He had remembered her, she knew he had, and under the smile she wore to keep Maureen's avid curiosity at bay she also knew she must stay as far from him as possible.

When the lights of Avalon came into view she was pleased to see them.

Nathaniel Lindsay watched the house through the night, the moon upon its burnished roof outlining the gables and the attics.

The Gothic style here in London. Even the trees had taken their cue from the stark outline of the building and dropped some of their leaves as though it were already winter.

He should not be here, of course, but memory had made him come, the calm treachery of Sandrine's voice in Perpignan as she had dispatched him into hell.

'I barely know him, but he is a soldier of France, so better to leave him alive. But do as you will, I really don't care.'

Swearing, he turned away, but not before the pale outline of a figure holding a candle moved through the second floor, down the stairs and out on to the porch, peering through the black of night.

There was no way she could have seen him, tucked into the shadow of a brick wall. But for a second before she blew out the flame the world seemed bathed in a daylight born from the candle, and she looked right into the heart of him.

Then there was only darkness and she was gone.

Sometimes his world disgorged ghosts from the past, but never ones as worrying as Sandrine Mercier. He'd been twenty when he had entered the heady enclave of espionage, his grandfather's distant demeanour a catalyst for him to become part of a close group of men who worked for the British Service.

His friend, Stephen Hawkhurst, had already been involved and when Nathaniel's grandfather, the Earl of St Auburn, had ranted and raved about his uselessness as the only son and heir, Nathaniel had joined as well.

Determining the likelihood of the rumoured marriages between the Spanish and French crowns had bought Nat into France, his expertise in both languages allowing him an easy access to the higher and lower echelons of its society.

The ties that were being forged between Britain and France were becoming strained, leaving a climate of suspicion and fear in their wake. A united block would render England isolated and make the battle for the control of Europe all that much harder to fight.

Nathaniel's mission had been to test the waters, so to speak, and to liaise with the handful of British agents who had been assimilated into the French way of life, keeping an eye on the workings of a political ally who was hard to trust.

Determining the likelihood of such an alliance had taken him to the court of Madrid. Returning across the Pyrenees to make his way up into Paris, he had been alarmed at the murder of one of his agents whilst on the road to Bayonne. Finding those culpable had led him into an enclave of French bandits near Lourdes.

And it was here he had met Sandrine.

* * *

Cassandra knew he was there, quiet and hidden in the night. It had been the same at Nay, when in the chaos the spaces around him had been full of a certain resolve, menacing and dangerous, the last afternoon light glinting in the dark of his hair as he had taken apart the minions of Anton Baudoin.

She shivered at the name and thought of Celeste. A week sooner and her cousin might have lived as well, might have been taken too, through the long night and back into warmth. She did not know Lord Lindsay was an Englishman then, dressed in the trousers of a peasant, skin sliced with the marks of war. The French bastards had not known it either, his accent from the warmer climate of the south and the musical lilt of a Provençal childhood masking all that he was.

Nathanael. He had named himself such. Monsieur Nathanael Colbert. At least part of his name had been true. His hands had been harder then, marked with the calluses of a labouring man and none of the softer lord on show. He still wore the same ring though, a gold chevron against blue, on the fourth finger of his right hand.

A movement behind made her turn.

'Ma'am, Katie is crying and Elizabeth cannot make her stop.'

One of the Northrup maids stood in the doorway, a heavy frown evident, and, forcing all the thoughts from her mind, Cassie hurried inside.

Tonight, chaos felt close and Lord Lindsay was a large part of the reason. She understood that with a heartfelt clarity as the cries of the girl took Cassie from her revelries.

Elizabeth, her maid, was in the annex at the rear of the house, the place used when women needed a bed for a night or two before being rehomed elsewhere. She was bathing the burns on thin legs, angry red scarring beneath the soft brush of cotton; another small casualty owing her injuries to London's underbelly of child trading.

'Did you make certain your hands were clean, Lizzie, before you touched the wounds?'

'I did, ma'am.'

'And you used the lime solution?'

'Just as you told me, ma'am.'

The smell of it was still in the air, sharp and strong, crawling into all the corners of the room. Alysa, Cassie's French mother, had always been a vehement supporter of cleanliness when dealing with sickness, and such teachings were ingrained within Cassie.

Soaping up her hands, she dried them and felt the child's forehead. Fever was settling in, the flush in Katie's cheeks ruddy and marked. Removing a clean apron from a hook by the door, Cassie put it on and went to stand beside Katie, the folds of the child's skin weeping and swollen. Carefully Cassie took plump shards of green from her medical cabinet and squeezed the slime into a pestle and mortar before spitting into the mixture. Mama had shown her this and the procedure took her mind back unwillingly into a different time and place.

She had been almost eighteen years old, still a girl, still hopeful, still imbued with the possibilities of life.

Completely foolish.

Utterly naive.

And painfully heartsick from the guilt of her mother's death.

Chapter Two

Nay, Languedoc-Roussillon, France—October 1846

The stranger had forced himself into stillness. She could see it as he stood, his heart and breath calmed by pure will-power as he raised his blade and stepped forward.

So many were dead or dying; such a little space of time between the living and the departed and Cassandra expected that she would be next.

A knife she had retrieved from the ground felt solid in her fist and the wind was behind her. Left handed. Always an advantage. But the rain made steel slippery as he parried and the mud under her feet finished the job. As she fell her hat spun off into the grey and her plait unfolded into silence. She saw the disbelief in his eyes, the hesitation and the puzzlement, his knife angling to miss her slender neck, pale against all else that was not.

The shot behind sounded loud, too loud, and she

could smell the flare of powder for just a second before he fell, flesh punched with lead.

He could have killed her easily, she thought, as she scrambled up and snatched back her cap, angry with herself for taking another look at his face.

Mud could not mask the beauty of him, nor could the pallor of death. She wished he might have been old and ugly, a man to forget after a second of seeing, but his lips were full and his lashes were long and in his cheek she could see the dent of a dimple.

A man who would not bring his blade in battle through the neck of a woman? Even a fallen one such as she? The shame in her budded against the futility of his gesture and she went to turn away. Once she might have cared more, might have wept for such a loss of life and beauty and goodness. But not now.

The movement of his hand astonished her.

'He is alive.' Even as she spoke she wished she had not.

'Kill the bastard, then. Finish him off.'

Her fingers felt for a pulse, strong against the beat of time, blood still coursing through a body marked with wounds. Raising the knife, she caught the interest of Baudoin behind and, moving to block his view, brought the blade down hard. The earth jarred her wrist through the thin woollen edge of his jacket and she almost cried out, but didn't.

'Take your chances.' Whispered beneath her breath, beneath the wind and the rain and the grey empty nothingness. Tonight it would snow. He would not stand a hope. Cleaning the knife against her breeches, she stood.

'You did well, *ma chère.*' Baudoin moved forward to cradle the curve of her chest, and the same anger that had been her companion for all of the last months tasted bitter in her mouth.

She knew what would come next by the flare in his eyes, knew it the moment he hit her, his sex hardened by death, blood and fear, but he had forgotten the knife in her palm and in his haste had left her fighting arm free.

A mistake. She used the brutality of his ardour as he took her to the ground, the blade slipping through the space between his ribs to enter his heart and when she rolled him off her into the mud and stood, she stomped down hard upon his fingers.

'For Celeste.' She barely recognised her voice and made an effort to tether in her panic. The snow would help her, she was sure of it; tracks could be hidden beneath the white and the winter was only just beginning.

'And...for you, too.' The sound was quiet at first, almost gone in the high keening of wind, a whisper through great pain and much effort.

Her assailant, his grey eyes bloodshot and sweat on his brow underpinning more extensive injuries. When he heaved himself up, she saw he was a big man, the muscle in his arms pressed tight against the fabric of his jacket.

'You killed him too cleanly, *mademoiselle.*' Not a compliment either as he glanced at Anton Baudoin. 'I would have made him suffer.'

He knew how much she had hated him, the prick of pity behind his eyes inflating her fury. No man would ever hold such power over her again.

'Here.' He held out a silver flask, the stopper emblazoned with a crest. 'Drink this. It will help.'

She meant to push it back at him, refusal a new capacity, but sense kept her quiet. Half a dozen days by foot to safety through mountainous land she held no measure of. Fools would perish and she was not a fool.

The spirits were warm, slung as the metal had been against his skin. The crest surprised her. Had he stolen it in some other skirmish? She could feel the unfamiliar fire of the whisky burn right down into her stomach.

'Who was he?'

'A bandit. His name was Anton Baudoin.'

'And these others?'

'His men.'

'You were alone with them?' Now his eyes only held the savage gleam of anger. For him or for her, she could not tell. Against the backdrop of a storm he looked far more dangerous than any man she had ever seen.

As if he could read her mind, he spoke. 'Stop shaking. I don't rape young girls.'

'But you often kill men?'

At that, he smiled. 'Killing is easy. It's the living that's difficult.'

Shock overtook her, all the horror of the past minutes and months robbing her of breath and sense. She was a murderer. She was a murderer with no place to run to and no hope at safety.

He was wrong. Everything was difficult. Life was

humiliating, exhausting and shameful. And now she was bound for hell.

The tall stranger took a deep swallow from the flask before replacing the lid. Then he laid his jacket on the ground, raising his shirt to see the damage. Blood dripped through a tear in the flesh above his hipbone. Baudoin's shot, she thought. It had only just missed killing him. With much care he stooped and cut a wide swathe of fabric from the shirttails of one of the dead men, slicing it into long ribbons of white.

Bandages. He had tied them together with intricate knots in seconds and without pausing began to wind the length tightly around his middle. She knew it must have hurt him to do so, but not in an expression, word or gesture did he allow her the knowledge of that, simply collecting his clothes on finishing and shrugging back into them.

Then he disappeared into the house behind, and she could hear things being pulled this way and that, the sound of crashing furniture and upturned drawers. He was looking for something, she was sure of it, though for the life of her she could not imagine what it might be. Money? Weapons?

A few moments later and he was back again, empty-handed.

'I am heading for Perpignan if you want to come.' Tucking a gun and powders into his belt, he repositioned his knife into a sheath of leather. Already the night was coming down upon them and the trees around the clearing seemed darker and more forbidding. The cart he had used to inveigle his way into the compound stood a little way off, the wares he plied meagre: pots, pans and rolls of fabric amidst sacks of flour and sugar.

She had no idea as to who he was or what he was or why he was in Nay. He could be worse than any man here ever had been or he could be like her uncle and father, honourable and decent.

A leaf fell before her, twirling in the breeze.

If it rests on its top, I will not go with him, she thought, even as the veins of the underside stilled in the mud. *And if he insists that I accompany him, I will strike out the other way.*

But he only turned into the line of bushes behind and melted into green, his cart gouging trails in the mud.

A solid indication of direction, she thought, like a sign or a portent or an omen of safety. Gathering up her small bundle of things, she followed him into the gloom.

There was no simple way to tie a neckcloth, Nathaniel thought, no easy shortcut that might allow him the time for another drink before he went out. Already the clock showed ten, and Hawk would be waiting. Catching sight of his reflection in the mirror, he frowned.

His valet had outdone himself with tonight's dress, the dizzying hues of his waistcoat clashing with the coloured silk of his cravat; a fashionable man with nothing else to occupy his mind save entertainment. People dropped their guards around men such as this. His fingers tightened against the ebony of his cane and he felt for the catch hidden beneath the rim at the back as he walked downstairs.

He had returned from France in the early months of 1847 more damaged than he allowed others to know and had subsequently been attached to the London office. For a while the change had been just what he needed, the small problems of wayward politicians or corrupt businessmen an easy task to deal with after the mayhem of Europe.

Such work barely touched him. It was simple to shadow the unscrupulous and bring them to the notice of the law, the degenerate fraudsters and those who operated outside justice effortlessly discovered.

Aye, he thought. He could have done the work with his hands tied and a blindfold on until a month ago when two women had been dragged from the Thames with their throats cut. Young women and both dressed well.

No one had known them. No one had missed them. No anxious family member had contacted the police. It was as though they had come into the river without a past and through the teeming throng of humanity around the docklands without a footprint.

The only clue Nat had been able to garner was from an urchin who had sworn he had seen a toff wiping blood from a blade beside the St Katharine Docks. A tall and well-dressed man, the boy had said, before scurrying off into the narrow backstreets.

Stephen Hawkhurst had been asked to look into the case as well, and the Venus Club rooms five roads away towards the city had caught their attention.

'The members meet here every few weeks. They are gentlemen mostly with a great appetite for the opposite sex. By all accounts they pay for dancers and singers and other women who think nothing of shedding their clothes for entertainment.'

'So it could be one of them is using the club for more dubious pursuits,' Nat expanded. 'There are a number of men whose names and faces I recognise.'

He had kept a close eye on the comings and goings from the club across the past weeks, astonished at the numerous alliances taking place. 'Any accusations would need to be carefully handled, though, for some there have genuine political and social standing.'

'Hard to get closer without causing comment, you mean?' Stephen questioned.

'Exactly. But if we joined we could blend in.'

Stephen had not believed him serious. 'I don't think belonging to the ranks of the Venus Club is the sort of distinction one would want to be known for.'

'It's a place hiding secrets, Hawk, and privacy is highly valued.'

'Well, I'm not taking part in any initiation or rites of passage.'

Each of them had laughed.

'Frank Booth is reported to be a member. I will ask him to sponsor us.'

A week later they were given a date, a time and a place, a small break in a case that was baffling. Girls were ruined all the time in London, for reasons of economics, for the want of food, for a roof over the head of a child born out of wedlock. But they were seldom so brutally hurt.

Sandrine. He remembered her ruined hand and the fear in her face when he had first met her.

The rage inside him began to build. Back then Cassandra Northrup had never given him any glimpse of an identity, though with each and every day in her company questions had woven their way into the little that she told him.

The first night had been the worst. She had cried behind him in small sobs, unstoppable over miles of walking in the dark. He had not helped her because he couldn't. The wound in his side had ached like the devil, fiery-hot and prickling, and by midnight he knew that he would have to rest.

Throwing down the few things he had taken from the cart after abandoning it many miles back, he leaned against a tree, the bark of its trunk firm behind him. Already the whirling circles of giddiness threatened, the ache at his hip sending pins and needles into his chest.

The girl sat on the other side of the small clearing, tucked into a stiff and inconsolable shape.

'You are safer than you were before. I said I would not hurt you.' He couldn't understand her weeping.

'I killed a man.'

'He was about to rape you.' Nat's heart sank at the implications of her guilt. God, how long had it been since he had felt anything remotely similar? He wished he had been the one to slide a knife into the French miscreant, for he would have gutted him and enjoyed watching him die. Slowly.

Her hands crossed her heart and her lips moved as if reciting a prayer.

Had the bullet wound not hurt as much he might have laughed, might have crossed the space between them and shaken her into sense. But he could only sit and watch and try to mitigate his pain.

'I am sure that the wrath of God takes intent into account.'

'Oh, I intended to kill him.' Honestly said. Given back in a second and no hesitation in it.

'I was thinking more of your assailant's purpose. I do not think Monsieur Baudoin would have been gentle with you.'

'Yet two wrongs do not make a right?'

He closed his eyes and felt the bloom of fatigue, irritation rising at her unreasonableness. 'If you had not killed him, I would have. One way or another he would have been dead. If it helps, pretend I did it.'

'Who are you?' The green in her eyes under moonlight matched the dark of the trees. In the daylight they were bluer, changeable.

'Nathanael Colbert. A friend.' Barked out, none of the empathy he knew she wanted held within the word. She remained silent, a small broken shape in the gloom, tucked up against bracken, the holes in the leather soles of her shoes easily seen from this angle. 'Why the hell were you there in the first place?'

He did not think she would answer as the wind came

through into the hollow, its keening sound as plaintive as her voice.

'They caught us a long time ago.' He saw her counting on her fingertips as she said it, the frown upon her brow deepening. Months? Years?

'Us?'

He had seen no other sign of captives.

'Celeste and I.'

Hell. Another girl. 'Where is she?'

'Dead.' The flat anger in her voice was cold.

'Recently?'

She nodded, her expression gleamed in sadness. She had old bruises across her cheek and new ones on her hand. In the parting of her hair when her cap had been dislodged he had seen the opaque scar of a wound that could have so easily killed her.

As damaged as he was.

Tonight he did not have the energy to know more of her story and the thin wanness was dispiriting. If they could have a drink things would be better, but the flask he had brought with him was long since empty.

'Can you hear that stream?'

She nodded.

'We need water...?'

He left the words as a question. No amount of want in the world could get him standing. He had lost too much blood and he knew it.

'Do you have the flask?'

'Here.'

When she took it and left he closed his eyes and tried to find some balance in the silence. He wanted to tend to himself, but he would need water to do that. And fire. He wondered if the young French captive would be able to follow his instructions when she returned.

He also wondered just exactly how those at Nay had gained their information on the identity and movements of a British agent who had long been a part of the fabric of French country life.

It was quiet in the trees and all the grief of losing Celeste flooded back. Her cousin's body rounded with child. Her eyes lifeless. The pain of it surged into Cassie's throat, blocking breath, and she stopped to lean against a tree. The anguish of life and death. What was it the man who sat in the clearing wrapped in bandages had said?

Killing is easy. It's the living that is difficult.

Perhaps, after all, he was right. Perhaps Celeste had known that, too, and put an end to all that she had loathed, taking the child to a place that was better but leaving her here alone.

Alone in a world where everything looked bleak. Bleaker than bleak even under the light of a small moon, the trickle of water at her feet running into the tattered remains of her boots and wetting her toes. The cold revived a little of her fight, reminded her how in the whole of those eight terrible months she had not given up, had not surrendered. She wished the stream might have been deeper so that she could have simply stripped off and washed away sin. A baptism. A renewal. A place to begin yet again and survive.

The flask in hand reminded her of purpose and she knelt to the water.

Her companion looked sick, the crusted blood beneath his nails reflected in the red upon his clothes, sodden through the layers of bandage. Without proper medicine how could he live? Water would clean the wound, but what could be done for any badness that might follow? The shape of leaves in the moonlight on the other side of the river suddenly caught her attention. Maudeline. Her mother had used this very plant in her concoctions. An astringent, she had said. A cleanser. A natural gift from the hands of a God who placed his medicines where they were most needed.

The small bank was easy to climb and, taking a handful of the plant, she stripped away the woody stems, the minty scent adding certainty to her discovery. She remembered this fresh sweet smell from Alysa's rooms and was heartened by the fact. The work of finding enough leaves and tucking them into her pocket took all her concentration, purpose giving energy. A small absolution. A task she had done many hundreds of times under the guidance of her mother.

An anchor to the familiar amidst all that was foreign. She needed this stranger in a land she held no measure of and he needed her. An equal support. It had been so long since she had felt any such worthiness.

He was asleep when she returned, though the quiet fall of her feet woke him.

'I have maudeline for your injury.' Bringing out the leaves, she began to crush them between her fingers, mixing them to a paste with the water on a smooth rock she had wiped down before using. She saw how he watched her, his grey eyes never leaving the movement of her hands.

'Are you a witch, then?'

She laughed, the sound hoarse and rough after so many months of disuse. 'No, but Mama was often thought to be.'

Again she saw the dimple in his right cheek, the deep pucker of mirth making her smile.

'Maudeline? I have not heard of it.'

'Another name for it is camphor.'

He nodded and came up on to his knees, holding his head in his hands as though a headache had suddenly blossomed.

'It hurts you?'

'No.' Squeezed out through pain.

When he stood she thought he looked unsteady, but she simply watched as he gathered sticks and set to making a fire. The tinder easily caught, the snake of smoke and then flame. Using the bigger pieces of branch he built it up until even from a distance she could feel the radiating warmth.

'The tree canopy will dissipate the smoke,' he said after a few moments. 'The low cloud will take care of the rest.'

Half an hour later flame shadow caught at his torso as he removed his shirt, the bandages following. His wound showed shattered skin, the tell-tale red lines of inflammation already radiating.

'Don't touch.' Her directive came as she saw he was about to sear the edges of skin together with a glowing stick. 'It is my belief that dirt kills a man with more certainty than a bullet and I can tell it is infected.'

Crossing to him, she wiped her hands with the spare leaves and poured water across the sap. When she touched him she knew he had the fever. Another complication. A further problem.

'I have been ill like this before and lived.' He had seen her frown.

Lots of 'befores', she mused, lines of crossed white opaque scars all over his body. The thought made her careful.

'You are a soldier?'

He only laughed.

Or a criminal, she thought, for what manner of man looked as he did? When he handed over the flask of water, she did not take a drink.

'I will heat it to clean the wound. It might hurt for it has been left a while. If you had some leather to bite down upon…?''

He broke into her offered advice. 'I will cope.'

Stephen Hawkhurst's voice made Nathaniel start, the echo around the marbled lobby disconcerting as all the years past rolled back into the present.

'You look as though you have the problems of the world upon your shoulders, Nat. Still thinking of the Northrup chit, I'd be guessing: fine eyes, a fine figure and a sense of mystery. Her uncle, Reginald Northrup, will be at the Venus Club tonight. Perhaps you can find out more about her from him.'

'Perhaps.'

'A few years ago when I was in Paris I heard a rumour about a woman who sounded remarkably like Cassandra Northrup.'

'What did it say?'

'That she was kept a prisoner in southern France and that she was not released for quite some time.'

'I see.'

'Her rescuer was also mentioned in detail.' The flint of gold in his friend's eyes was telling and there was a certain question there.

'It was you, Nat, wasn't it? And she was one of theirs?

'Whose?'

'The French. One of their agents.'

Anger sliced in a quick rod of pain. 'No, Cassandra Northrup never held loyalty to any cause save that of her own.'

'Others here might disagree with you. She is the chairwoman of the charity Daughters of the Poor.'

'Prostitutes?'

Hawk nodded, leaving Nat to ponder on how the circles of life turned around in strange patterns.

'She must have been a child then, and scared. God, even now she looks young. And you got home in one piece, after all.'

One piece? How little Stephen truly knew.

Taking his hat and cloak from the doorman, Nat

forced away his recollections and walked out into a cold and windy London night.

They were all there, myriad affluent men gathered in a room that looked much like a law chamber or a place of business. Nat was glad that Stephen stood beside him because he still felt dislocated and detached, thrown by the reappearance of a woman he had thought never to see again.

He recalled Cassandra Northrup's eyes were exactly the same as they had been, guarded in their turquoise, shuttered by care and secrets. But her hair had changed from the wild curls she had once favoured and she was far more curvaceous.

If her eyes had not given her away her left hand would have, of course, with the half-finger and the deep scar across the rest of her knuckles.

It had been a newer wound back then in the clearing, when she had reached forward and laid one cool palm across his back. He had flinched as she brought the knife she carried upwards to cut away the badness.

The pain had made him sweat, hot incandescence in the cool of night as she simply tipped the heated flask up and covered ragged open flesh.

The camphor helped, as did her hands threading through places on his spine that seemed to transfer the pain. Surprise warred with agony under her adept caresses.

The poultice was sticky and the new bandages she bound the ointment with were from the bottom of her shirt. Cleaner. Softer. He could smell her on them.

He wished that he had the whisky to dull the pain. He wished for a bed that was not on a forest floor, but some place warmer, more comfortable, some place where his heartbeat did not rattle against the cold hard of earth.

'If you sit, it should help with the drainage.'

He was shivering now, substantially, and went to drape his jacket around himself to find warmth, but she held it away and shook her head.

'You are burning up. The mind plays tricks when the fever rages and as I cannot shift you to the stream we will have to make do with the cold night air instead. I had hoped it would snow.'

Her accent was Parisian, the inflection of the drawing rooms and the society salons where anything and everything was possible. He wondered why the hell she should have been in Nay, dressed in the clothes of a lad, and when he inadvertently blurted the thought out aloud, he saw her flinch.

'I think you should sleep, Monsieur Colbert.'

His name. Not quite right. But he needed to be quiet and he needed to think. There was danger here. He wished he could have asked her who she was, what she was, but the camphor was winding its way into the quick pricks of pain and he closed his eyes to block her from him.

He would be sore in the morning if he lived. The wound or the fever could kill him, but it was the bleeding that she was most concerned about. She had not been able to stop it. Already blood pooled beneath him, more hindrance to a body struggling with survival.

Tipping up the flask, she took the last drops of water.

She was starving. She was exhausted. The embers of the fire still glowed in the dark, but outside the small light the unknown gathered.

Baudoin had not existed alone and she knew that others would follow. Oh, granted, this stranger had hidden their tracks well ever since leaving Nay, his cart discarded quite early in the piece. She had watched him set false lures into other directions, the heavy print of a foot in a stream, a broken twig snagged with the hair from her plait, but she knew it would only be a matter of time before those in France's underworld would find them.

She held far too many secrets, that was the problem. She had seen some of the documents Baudoin's brother had inadvertently left in Celeste's chamber, documents she knew had been taken from the carriage of a murdered man on the road towards Bayonne. A mistake of lust and an error that would lead to all that had happened next.

Her fault. Everything was her fault and her cousin had not even known it. The same familiar panic engulfed her, made her lean forward to catch breath, trying in the terror to hold on to the reason of why Celeste had done as she did. Cassie still felt the sticky blood across her fingers, the warmth of life giving way to cold.

Softly she began to sing, keeping herself staunch;

the 'Marseillaise' because it was fast paced and because it was in French.

> *To arms, citizens,*
> *Form your battalions,*
> *We march, we march...*

Celeste was dead. And the Baudoin brothers. How quickly circumstances changed. In a heartbeat. In a breath. She looked across to the stranger, Colbert, and determined that he was still in the land of the living before she shut her eyes.

The girl was asleep, her hat pulled down across her head and her jacket stretched over the bend of her knees. As Nathaniel looked at her in repose there was a vulnerability apparent that was not evident when she was awake. She was thin, painfully so, and dirty. On a closer inspection he saw on her clothes the handiwork of small, finely taken stitches covering rips and larger holes. Her shirt was buttoned to the throat and the jacket she wore was tightly closed. More than a few sizes too large, it held the look of a military coat without any of the braiding. He knew she still had the knife, but it was not visible anywhere. Too big for the pockets, he imagined it tucked in under her forearm or secreted in one of the boots she wore beneath loose trousers.

A child-woman lost into the vagaries of a war that could not have been kind.

He felt stronger, a surprising discovery this, given

his fever, and although the wound tugged when he shifted it did not sting like it had. Still, his vision blurred as he stood from the loss of blood or his own body's heat, he knew not which.

Camphor. Perhaps there was something in the doctoring, some healing property that would confound even the best of physicians? He resolved to use it again.

She stirred across from him, wild curls escaping from the plait and falling around her face. In sleep she looked softer, the burden of life not marking the spaces between her eyes. Her ruined left hand sat on top of the right one and fire outlined the hurt in flame. Not a little injury and not an accident either. This looked to be deliberate, a brutal act of damage that would have taken weeks to heal. It was strange to see such a battle scar on one so young. His own back was filled with the vestige of war, but he had been in the arena of secrets for some time and such damage was to be expected.

Her eyes flicked open suddenly, taking him in, fear reverting to wariness.

'How do you feel?' Even fresh from sleep she was observant.

'Better.'

Her glance at his throat read the measured beat of his heart. 'Your temperature is still high so you should be drinking as much as you can. In a moment I will fetch more water.'

A frown of concern slashed the girl's forehead, but he was tired of thinking of her as 'the girl'. 'What are you called?'

'Sandrine Mercier.'

Rolling the name on his tongue, he liked the sound of it. 'How old are you?'

'Almost eighteen.' Surprisingly forthcoming, though she did not look to have as many years as she professed.

'And your cousin?'

Moonlight caught her face as her chin lifted. 'Celeste was twenty and she loved music. She loved everything beautiful and charming and good. She played the piano and sang like an angel...' Her voice came to a halt.

Nat knew what she was doing because he had done the same himself when those close to him had died. A memory they might be, but in speech they came alive, drawn for others to know, almost living.

'Did Baudoin kill her?'

Only the quick shake of her head.

One day she will be beautiful, he thought. One day she will take men's hearts and break them. For now she was young. Too young for him. For now the stamp of grace lay in her long limbs and her boyish defiance, the promise of womanhood only hinted at.

He turned away, not wishing for her to see his regard.

He was back to being angry, his eyes the colour of a storm, not dark, not light, but the in-between shade that spoke of rain and coldness.

'Are you a part of Guy Lebansart's circle of spies?' If she found out something about him, there might be protection there.

His interest ignited. 'Spies?'

'Men who would take secrets and use them.'

'For France?'

'Or for whoever is paying the most.'

His frown deepened. 'Did you ever know any of these secrets, Sandrine?' In his words she could hear exactly what she did not want to. Interest and intrigue. Eight months in captivity had taught her every nuance in the language of deception.

'No.' She kept her voice bland and low, shaking out the truth with effort. 'I was only a prisoner.'

'Where did they keep you?'

She did not answer, moving instead to retrieve the flask. Her mattress had been in a room off Celeste and Louis's chamber, a sanctuary she tried very hard to seldom leave. Lying low, she only ever ventured out when the early hours of the morning saw each inhabitant befuddled by strong drink, her cousin included. But Celeste had made her own bargain with the devil and had won conditions to make the tenure livable. Cassie's thoughts went again to Celeste's beautiful voice and her smile. When memory was selective, everything was easier.

'I will get water and then we should leave. If others follow—'

He cut off her worry with two words.

'They won't.'

The confidence of a victor. So fragile. So absolutely flimsy. Baudoin had said no one would ever dare to challenge him and look at what had happened. Her French uncle had been certain, too, of the route west and then lost his way into peril.

Everyone could be bought for the price of pain or promise or vanity. She wondered what Monsieur Nathanael Colbert's price might be. Her own was freedom and she would never give it up again for anyone.

'When we reach the next town, hide your face with this.' He tossed her a scarf, dirtied with dust and blood. 'And tuck your hair well into the crown of your hat. If anyone asks a question of you, look stupid, for there is safeguard in a simple mind. If you could walk with more of a swagger—'

She cut him off. 'I know what to do.'

He swore at that, roundly, and began to collect his things.

Reginald Northrup was a large man, his face florid and his smile showing a mouth with at least a few teeth missing. The brandy he had hold of was in a glass as oversized as he was. The sweat on his brow reflected the light above him.

'It is a surprise to see you here, Lindsay. I hear you aided my niece the other evening at the de Clare ball?'

The man who sat near Northrup turned to hear his answer.

'Indeed. The last pieces of a falling chandelier knocked her unconscious and a doctor was called.'

'I am certain Cassandra herself could have remedied any wound she received. She has a knack for the healing and her mother was just the same.'

'Her mother was reputed to be one of society's beauties, was she not?' Hawk's question. Nat could not quite let go of the thought that he had voiced the query for his benefit.

'She was, but Alysa Northrup died a good many years ago when one of her science experiments went wrong. Had she lived a century ago she might have been burned at the stake as a witch, for there were rumblings in all quarters about her unusual endeavours and none of them was kind.'

The easygoing stance of the man hardened, giving Nat an impression of much emotion.

'She was a beautiful woman, Reg.' Lord Christopher Hanley, sitting next to Reginald, had imbibed too much strong drink, lending his speech an air of openness. 'None of the other débutantes that year could touch her in brains or beauty. I thought for a time it was you she was sweet upon until your brother snaffled her up right under your very nose and made her his wife.'

Northrup seemed out of step with such a confidence. 'Both girls are as odd as their mother was. You will do yourself a favour by staying out of the way of them, Lindsay. Indeed, most gentlemen in society have done so already.'

Hawk beside him laughed. 'I think it might be the other way around, sir, for even though they seldom venture into the social realm your nieces rebuff all interested parties with alacrity.'

'If they turn their noses up at everything, it is because their father has too little left of his wits to bid them marry. Maureen has already reached a grand old age and I fear that she will always remain a spinster.

Rodney, their brother, shall have to no doubt house them when he inherits the properties.'

By the look on Reginald Northrup's face Nathaniel judged that he was not pleased about the fact. The terms of an entailment, perhaps, that left him with little to fall back upon?

'The younger daughter was married in France, if memory serves me well? I remember it as quite a scandal at the time, Reg, and she never took on his name.' Hanley spoke again, and Nathaniel stiffened. Another ache hooking into the cold prick of betrayal. He wondered what she had done with the ring he had given her, his mother's ring, a single, pure, verdant emerald set in white gold.

'What was the story of her groom?' Nat addressed Reginald Northrup directly.

'Oh, up and gone by all accounts, for she arrived home in a melancholic state that took a good year to recover from. I doubt any new husband would have put up with such gloom for that length of time, though my brother was happy enough to have her back and never questioned the marriage. He lives in his own world of science and experiments much the same as his wife was wont to. It was this interest that drew them together in the first place, I suppose.'

The layers of truth peeled back and, within the Venus Club in a room gilded with ostentation and excess, Nat found himself disheartened. It was what had happened after that which Nathaniel failed to understand: the closeness and then the unfathomable distance. He shook away his thoughts as Hawk spoke again.

'Reginald is asking if we wish to join him at his country home for the Venus Club's August celebrations, Nat. I said we would be more than delighted to accept his offer.'

'Indeed.' The taste of bitterness in Nathaniel's mouth was strong, for nothing here made sense to him. Why had Cassandra Northrup never married again given the fragile and unorthodox legality of their nuptials?

She was beautiful. More beautiful than any other woman of the *ton*, even in the dreary guise of a widow. Aye, muted dove-grey suited the tone of her skin and the colour of her eyes and hair.

Her hair had been longer once, falling to the line of her hips in a single swathe of darkened silk as they had pulled themselves out of the river.

He had realised the danger the moment they awoke in the barn they had found in the late afternoon of the day before after walking for many miles. A sense of threat permeated the early morning air, and he was a man who had always relied on instinct.

Sandrine had stirred as he stood, straw from the beds they had fashioned still in the threads of her hair. Everything about her was delicate. Her hands, her nails, the tilt of her chin as she listened.

'Someone is here?'

'More than one. They do not know we are inside, however, or their voices would be quieter.'

He saw how she drew the knife from her sleeve and held it at the ready. Her hands were shaking.

Six of them, he determined, from the footsteps and the whicker of horses. By himself he would have taken them on, but with Sandrine to protect…?

Placing a finger to his lips he drew her to one side of the building and indicated a hole at the bottom of the boards.

'Crawl through and make for the river. If they see you keep running and jump. Stay in the middle where the water flows fastest for at least a mile. After that I will find you.'

Fear sparked in her eyes. 'I cannot swim well.'

'Just put your arms out to each side and relax…'

He did not finish because a shout interrupted them and Nat knew their tracks had been discovered.

'Go.'

A quick nod and the space where she had been was filled only with the scent of her and the sound of someone lifting the catch upon the door.

Unsheathing his knife Nat breathed out, another blade at his belt tilted so that the hilt was easily accessible. The dry straw also caught his eye. He would not make this easy for them and a fire would buy them some time. He hoped to God that Sandrine had reached the water way undetected.

She heard the commotion in the barn as flame leapt from straw, hot through the missing frame of a window.

Colbert had set the place on fire and as a diversion the plan was inspired. Already she saw two of the men retreating, their attention caught so firmly on the blaze they did not notice her as she ran past a line of weeping willows to the river bank.

Where was he? Why had he not come out after her? How long could a person breathe in the smoke and flame of straw? The quick report of a gun sent her under into the cold, down amongst the green of weed and the dirty swirl of mud. She pushed up and away, using her hands as he had told her, spread out as wings, the surface finally in sight, a faint glitter of day where only darkness had been and then she was out, air in her lungs again, a promontory cutting off any sight of the burning barn and distance-dulling noise.

Warm tears of fright ran against the chill, the quick rush of water taking her faster and faster, and the bank a good many yards from her on either side.

Had Nathanael Colbert died in the fight? The wound in his side and the remains of the fever would have sapped his strength and yet he had made sure she had the chance of safety before seeing to his own. He only knew her from her time with Baudoin, a girl marked with the horror of it and yet he had done this for her. Without question.

She wished he was here, behind her, as she was forced along in the rapid current, dragged down with the heaviness of her oversized boots.

And then he was there, reaching for her as she went under yet again, the water in her throat making her cough.

'Put your arms around my neck.'

He was solid and sturdy, the muscles in his shoulders keeping her up in the cold air. His hair had been released from the band he kept it secured with and was falling in wet strands down his back. She wondered how he could keep going as the water flow quickened and rocks appeared, the fall of the river changing and whitening into rapids.

'Don't let go,' he called over his shoulder, one hand fending off a jagged outcrop as they bounced into its path. Then they were free again, down onto a new level of river, softer and quieter.

Cassie could tell he was tiring, the gulps of air he took ragged and uneven. Blood from his wound stained the water crimson about them as damaged flesh opened to pressure. But still he did not stop, waiting until the bushes turned again to countryside before striking in for shore.

The mud under her feet was thick and deep as she gained a purchase. For a good long while they lay there, on the bank, the greyness of the sky above them promising rain. Freezing.

'Take…your clothes…off.' Even he was shivering.

The first soft drift of snow came unexpectedly, landing on her upturned face in a cold and quiet menace.

'Take your…heavier clothes off…th-then get into the base of the hedge and dig. The l-leaves will be warmer than the air and they will p-protect you.'

He made no attempt to move himself, the flakes of snow thicker now. Again red blood pooled beneath him.

She came to a decision without conscious thought. He had saved her twice and she could not leave him here to perish. Unbuttoning what was left of his shirt, she sat him forward and took away the sodden cotton. His jacket was long gone, probably discarded when he first went into the river. A chain hung at his neck, a ring secured upon it, white-gold with a large clear emerald.

Was he married? Did a woman wait at home for him, hoping? His eyes this close were ringed in dark blue, grey melting into the colour seamlessly. Watching her.

'Go.'

But she could not. Unsheathing the knife along the line of her lower arm as strength returned, she stood and cut a pile of branches. The leaves that lay at the base of a hedge she fashioned into a bed and rolled him into it, placing many more leaves and plant stems on top and using the brush as a shield to keep the snow away. Then, climbing underneath to join him, she snuggled in, jacket and shirt gone, skin touching skin.

Already the day had darkened, the dusk misting in early with the weather, more clouds on the horizon.

'Will they find us?'

'Not today. S-snow covers everything and whoever is looking will have to w-wait it out.'

Their small lair was becoming darker as the snow caught, layering and thickening. The wind, too, had lessened and heat was beginning to build. She liked it when his arms came about her, holding her close, the beat of his heart even and unhurried and his breath comforting.

For this one small moment they were safe.

She was glad when he stopped shivering, their warmth melding together to create hope.

* * *

Nat had awoken from their lair of snow beneath the bushes to a room with a fire burning bright. An older man and woman sat observing them, a youth standing near the window.

'Our dog found your tracks leading from the river and we brought you here early this morning.'

Looking about, he saw that Sandrine and he had been placed on a bed together, a thick feather down quilt across them. He knew immediately that they were both naked, for she was tucked about him as if in sleep her body had sought the warmth she so desperately needed.

'Your clothes and boots have been washed and repaired and should be dry by nightfall. The doctor said you were to stay very quiet for the wound at your side would have taken much in energy from you and could open again if you are not careful.'

A headache pounded in Nat's temples, impairing his vision, the room swimming as their words were lost into a droning noise. Sandrine was still asleep, their voices making no inroad into her consciousness.

Shaking his head, he tried to distil the blurriness, but the pain only intensified and so he desisted. He could not even move a muscle; a heavy stupor anchored him to the mattress, and a tiredness that defied description seeped through. Alarm furrowed his brow, but when the dark claimed him he no longer had the vigour to question it, demand it different.

Sandrine was awake before him when he next surfaced and she had moved a good distance away, a rough linen shift now in place across her shoulders. A grey blanket was wedged in the space between them and no one else was in the room. A fire danced in the grate.

'Madame Dortignac has just left. She brought chicken broth if you want some.'

'No.' The thought of food turned his stomach. Outside it was pitch-black and the noises of the house were stilled. Late, then? Around two, perhaps, though he had no real measure of time.

'It has rained heavily all day,' Sandrine said after a moment, 'and I heard them say that the river has come up.'

'Good.' The threads of protection began to wind in closer. 'Any sign of our presence will be long gone from the mud on the banks.'

'They brought in a priest for you. I think they were worried you might not survive.'

'When?'

'Yesterday afternoon. It has been a full two days since you last awoke.' Anxiety played in her eyes. 'He asked if we were husband and wife before he left. When I said that we were not he was displeased.'

'A result of our bedding arrangements, I suspect. They think that I have ruined you.'

'The priest tried to make me go to another room, but I felt safe here and told him that I would not.'

She looked so damn young sitting there, the dark beneath her eyes worrying him and the homespun in her shift showing up the fragility of her shoulders. Her hair had been pulled back into a loose chignon, small curls escaping around her face. Feeling the punch of her beauty Nathaniel breathed out and glanced away, angry at the effect she so easily engendered on the masculine parts of his body, even in sickness. He could not remember any woman with such sway over him.

Safe?

If he had felt better, he might have laughed at her interpretation of security. Looking around for his sword and gun, he found them next to his carefully folded clean clothes and polished boots to one side of the bed.

'Did they say who they were?

She nodded. 'Farmers. They own the land between the river and the mountains behind, a large tract that has been in their family for generations. The Catholic priest who came was certain that God was punishing us for…for….' She did not finish.

He smiled. 'Our sins of the flesh?'

A bright stain of redness began at her throat and surged up across her cheeks.

'Life or death requires sacrifices, Sandrine, and if you had not removed my clothes and kept me warm I would have perished. An omnipotent God would know that, and I thank you for it.'

A myriad of small expressions flitted across her brow: humour, puzzlement and then finally acceptance.

'Are you always so certain of things, Monsieur Colbert?'

'Yes.'

At that she laughed properly, her head thrown back and her eyes dancing. Not the pale imitation of laughter that the society ladies had perfected to an art form, but a real and honest reaction that made him laugh, too, the medicine of humour exhilarating. He could not remember ever feeling like this with another woman before, the close edge of a genuine joy pressing in and a camaraderie that was enticing.

But when he reached out to touch her fingers humour dissipated into another emotion altogether. Connection, if he might name it, or shock, the sear of her flesh burning up into the cold of his arm.

She had felt it, too—he could tell she had as she snatched her hand away and buried it into the heavy grey of the blanket. Her face was turned from his so deliberately that the corded muscle in her throat stood out with tension, a pulse beating with rhythm that belied calmness.

Nathanael Colbert was as beautiful as he was powerful and even with the fever flushing his cheeks and tearing into the strength of him he still offered her protection. Outside, the night clothed the land in silence and inside his warmth radiated towards her, the barrier of wool insubstantial.

If she had been braver, she might have reached over and removed it, so that their skin could touch again as it had done before, close and real, offering safety and something else entirely.

Urgency. Craving. A yearning that she had no experience of, but that was there in her flesh and bones, the call of something ancient and destined, an undeniable and inescapable knownness.

Shocking. Wonderful. She did not wish him to see the remnants of all she thought so she turned away, pleased when he did not demand her attention or reach out again.

An impasse in a cold and wind-filled night, the mountains of the Pyrenees filling a darkened sky and a fire measuring out the passing moments in warmth.

One and then two. Enough to regain composure and push away the thoughts of what might have been between them should they have given it a chance. An ache wormed its way across her throat and heart before settling lower. Loss could be a physical hurt, she would think much later, but right now it was a wondrous and startling surprise.

Chancing a look at him, she saw he lay back against the pillows, the sheet pulled away from the dark nakedness of his skin, muscle sculptured under the flame light. Still sick, she realised, by the sheen of sweat across his brow and the high colour in his cheeks. She wondered how the wound at his side had fared from such exertion, but did not dare to ask him, given the state of her racing heart.

'I will protect you, Sandrine. Do not worry.'

The words were quietly said.

'From everyone?'

His lips turned up, the dimple in his right cheek deepening.

'Yes.'

She did not wipe away the tear that traced down her face, but waited to feel the cold run of its passage, the blot of moisture darkening the yellowed counterpane as it fell. As his breathing evened out she knew he was asleep, his body needing the balm of rest. Turning with as little noise as possible, she watched him, his breathing shallow and fast and his dark eyelashes surprisingly long.

The past few days rushed up at her, the chaos and the hope. Baudoin and his brother had been bandits whose livelihood was made by taking the riches from aristocrats travelling the roads towards the north and west, but Guy Lebansart was a different story altogether. He boasted about working for the French Government, though Sandrine knew enough about the houses and land that he had accrued to know that more lucrative pickings had taken his fancy.

Lebansart blackmailed people and he hurt anyone who got in his way—even Anton Baudoin had been scared of him. He had been due to arrive at the compound with a good deal of gold in exchange for information found on a man Baudoin's men had killed on the highway. But Nathaniel Colbert had arrived first.

A coincidence.

Sandrine thought not.

Glancing again at the stranger, she frowned. What were his secrets? Closing her eyes, she fervently prayed that Lebansart and those who worked for him would never catch up with them.

Chapter Three

Cassandra smoothed down the wool of her pantaloons and pulled up the generous collar of her jacket. It was cold in the London wind and it had already begun to spit.

Damn, she cursed, for the sound of the rain would dull her hearing and she knew that dawn wasn't far off.

Lord Nathaniel Lindsay had returned to his town house a quarter of an hour ago, and by his gait as he descended from the carriage she knew he had been drinking.

Perfect.

The thick line of trees in the garden surprised her. She would not have imagined him to sanction such a shelter, for intruders could easily use the screen to hide behind. Making her way through the green-tinged darkness, she sidled along the undergrowth until she came to the windows.

The first sash was rock solid. The next one moved. Unsheathing her knife, she pressed it into the crack and shifted the lock. One second and it was rendered useless, clicking into access. With an intake of breath she lifted the wood, and when she perceived no threat she raised it farther.

Waiting, she listened to the sounds of the room. A single last fall of wood in the grate as the warm air greeted her, a clock in the corner marking out the hour.

She was over the barrier in a whisper, turning to the chamber and waiting as her eyes accustomed themselves.

'Shut the window and join me.'

He knew she would come for he had seen a shadow that was not normally there against the stone wall on the opposite side of the street. This window had always been loose, a trick of wet wood or poor craftsmanship, he knew not which.

To give her credit she barely acknowledged the shock. A slight hesitation, one less certain step. He wondered if she held a knife in her hand and thought perhaps he should have bothered to arm himself. But he would not have harmed her. He knew that without a doubt.

'Lord Nathaniel Lindsay, the heir to the title of St Auburn?' Her voice was tight, tinged with more than a hint of question.

'At your service, Mademoiselle Mercier. And now you are all grown up.'

'A fact that you hate?'

He laughed at that because her surprising honesty had always appealed to him, though the sound held lit-

tle humour. 'I survived, but others did not. The names
I presume you gave to Lebansart made it easy for him
to mark them off as English agents. Didier and Gilbert
Desrosiers were like lambs to the slaughter. Good men.
Men who had never wronged you in any way. Men with
allegiances to England and who had only ever wanted
to serve this country.'

The blood seemed to disappear from her face. One
moment her cheeks were rosy from the outside cold and
in the next second they were as pale as snow.

'You were a spy, too? My God, that explains why
you were there in France and in Nay in particular.'

'They call them intelligence officers now.'

'You were a spy for the English army?'

'The British Service.'

'Not just the army then, but the quiet and hidden
corridors of a clandestine and covert agency. Are you
still?'

He did not answer.

'I will take that as a yes, then.' The blood had returned to her face, and she did not waver as she went
on. 'I didn't come to offer excuses for what I did at
Perpignan, my lord, nor for exoneration.'

'Then why did you come?'

'To give you this.'

She took a ring from her pocket and he recognised
it immediately. His mother's, the emerald as green as
it had been all those years before.

'I took it and I should not have. For all the other
things that I was, I was never a thief.'

'God.' Thief of hearts, he thought. Thief of lives.

Thief of the futures of two good Englishmen caught in the crossfire of politics.

'Celeste died for nothing. At least those agents of England that you speak of perished for a cause they believed in. A righteous cause. A cause to take them into Heaven and be pardoned by our Lord for it.'

'You came tonight to tell me this?' His voice shook with bitterness.

'No. I came to say that nothing is as black and as white as it seems, and the documents I saw were there for others to see as well.'

'Yet you memorised them and gave the information back to the one person you should not have.'

'Guy Lebansart was only one man who might have wanted them dead. France was seething with those who would harm anyone with loyalties to England. Perhaps they held your name, too?'

'I doubt I was on any index of names.'

'Then you doubt wrong,' she said and turned to the window. 'From the moment you rescued me there was danger.'

And then he understood. 'So you traded our freedom for intelligence? Hell.' So many questions and so few answers. Yet something was not quite right. And then the penny dropped.

'I was the one you bargained for?'

The nod she gave him was almost imperceptible. 'Indeed, that was a part of the story, but now I need a favour, Lord Lindsay. I need the right to go on with my life without having to look behind at the chaos, waiting for it to catch up.'

'And nothing else?'

'Nothing.'

Her voice was measured. No extra emotion. No tell-tale sign of weakness or feeling. She had sacrificed the lives of others for his and she knew there was no honour in any of it. It was not thanks she had come for. Neither was it a penance. Celeste was probably more of a part of it than anyone, for Sandrine had always been like a mother lioness over any perceived tarnishing of her cousin's memory and she might have been fearful about the recount of his knowledge of her.

The complex layers of guilt and shame mixed in strangely with integrity. She had not needed to come. He hadn't further want for the ring and no explanation could absolve murder.

'You whored in exchange for my life?'

She shook away the words. 'You know nothing, Colbert.'

'Lindsay,' he corrected her with a cold and hard fury.

'If I had not traded the information, you would have been dead.'

'And instead…?'

'You lived.'

Her eyes flickered to the scar that ran across his jaw on the right side.

'Death might have been kinder.'

She raised her fist at that, the hand of ruined and knotted skin. 'You think I did not wish that, too, many times after I left you, the blood of those I'd named wrapped about the heart of my guilt? But there is no book written on the rules of war, my lord, and I was a young girl trying to exist in a world that had forsaken me. Anton Baudoin had taken the documents from a man he had murdered a few days before you came to Nay. I had no idea as to who those mentioned within it were.'

Silence filled the space between them for the time it took the clock in the corner to chime out the hour of two. It was why he had come to find the Baudoins in the first place, pointed in the direction by intelligence garnered after the agent's murder. Then she spoke again.

'You think I should have trusted you enough to make a run for it at Perpignan and believed that the impossible might be probable there with a hundred enemies at our heels and many more behind? You believed in that option of faith?'

'Yes.' Simple. Heartfelt.

Her unexpected smile was a sad one. 'On reflection you may have been correct because what happened afterwards took away all my right of choice.' There was a new note in her words now. Resignation and acceptance mixed with an undercurrent of shame.

'Merde.' The French word echoed through the dark like a gunshot. One moment a history just guessed at and the next known exactly.

'But I have made a new life here, a good life, a life that helps those whom all others have forgotten.'

'The Daughters of the Poor?'

She nodded, but in the depths of her eyes he saw the truth of what they had each found out about the other shimmering. Unspoken. The lump in his throat hitched in memory and it rested in the spaces after midnight, the weight of such knowledge making him turn away, pain lapping at all they could never say.

'I help ruined girls like me.'

He hated that pretence was no longer possible.

'Get out.' Usually he was more urbane and polished, but with her he had never been quite himself.

'Not until you agree to what I have asked.'

He did not speak because he did not trust in what he might say, but when he nodded she was gone, the whisper of the velvet curtains as they fell against the sash and a faint eddy of wind. Placing his head against the wall, he closed his eyes and cursed.

No one can get back what is lost.

That is what she had whispered then, that last time, as she had untwined his shaking fingers from around her wrist and gone with the French spymaster, her laughter on the air as rough hands wormed into the young promise of girlhood.

The sacking shield had come down as her footsteps receded, the twine it was held in place with tight at his throat. He remembered the sharp blade of a knife pressed into his ribs just below his heart.

'Sandrine, the whore.' Someone had drawled the words behind him as he had been pushed into midair and then he could remember nothing.

Cassandra was shaking so much she could barely untie her trousers and unbuckle her boots. Two good men had died because of her disclosure and Nathaniel

Lindsay hated her now as easily as she had loved him, then. A young girl of shattered dreams and endless guilt. The hero in Nathanael Colbert had beckoned like a flame and she had been burnt to a cinder.

She was so utterly aware of Lindsay; that was the problem. Even now, safe in her room, the thrum of her want for him made her body vibrate. She forced stillness and crossed to the mirror above the hearth, its rim of gold leaf scratched by age. The woman who stared back was not the one she felt inside. This woman still held on to promise and hope, her eyes dancing with passion, heated skin sending rose into pale cheeks.

He had no reason to assent to all that she asked, no obligation to the betrayal and deceit lingering beyond the limits of honour. And yet he had assented.

She thrust her hand instinctively against one breast and squeezed it hard. No joy in this, no pleasure. No reward of the flesh, but the broken promises of men.

Turning away, she swallowed, the anger of her life forming strength. It was all she had, all she could hold on to. Once, other oaths had held her spellbound in the safety of Celeste's bedroom in Perpignan, and under the light of a candle that threw the flame of curiosity on to two young faces.

'Papa said that we can all go to Barages. It has been so long since we have been anywhere, Sandrine, and taking in the waters would be something we can all enjoy.'

'Will David come, too?'

'If you are going he is bound to want to for I have seen the way my father's godson looks at you. But be warned, although he is eighteen he is also far too boring.'

Cassie blushed, hating the red that often rose in her cheeks at the mention of anything personal. She had arrived in France four months earlier, travelling from London by boat into Marseilles in the company of her mother's brother and her cousin, and the warmth of the south had seeped into her bones like a tonic.

'I want to meet someone who will take my breath away. A rich man, a good-looking man, a dangerous man.' Celeste's voice held that thread of wishfulness that Cassandra had often heard her use. 'I am so very tired of the milksop sons of my father's friends.'

'But what of Jules Durand?' Her cousin's latest swain had been at the door most days, professing his love and his intentions, a strange mix of shyness and gall.

'He is not…manly enough. He tells me too much before I want him to. He kissed my hand yesterday and all I could think of was to pull away from the wet limpness of his lips.'

All of a sudden the conversation had gone to places Cassandra did not understand, the edge of virtue tarnished by a feeling that seemed…bruised. Celeste had grown up in the year since she had seen her, the lines of her body curvy and fuller. Tonight under the bed-covers some other feeling lingered, something wrong and false.

Her cousin's blue eyes flashed. 'Do you never wish for a man's hands upon your body, finding the places that feel only magic? Do you not want to know the wonderment that all the great books talk of?'

'No.' Cassie pulled the collar of her nightgown full around her throat. Her own bedroom was down the corridor amongst the shadows and she had been scared to stay there, but this room suddenly held a fear that she could not comprehend.

'You are no longer in boring stuffy old England. Here women know the dance of love and they flaunt it.' Rising from her bed, Celeste simply pulled off her gown, standing against the flame of her lamp like a goddess.

'I want to know what it is to be passionate and wanton and brave. Only dull wits shall be for ever stuck with one boring husband for the rest of their lives and I certainly shall not be that. When we are young we should be able to know…everything.'

Cassie's eyes ran across the fat abundance of her cousin's breasts, breasts that were so different from her own. Celeste's waist had slimmed and her hips had spread and the hair between her legs had been trimmed back into the shape of a heart.

'You look beautiful.' The words came from the very depth of admiration.

'Too beautiful to be wasted on the boys that I am forever annoyed by here.' One hand cupped her breast and the other fell to the soft place between her legs. 'There is no power more durable than that of womanhood. No influence over men as strong as the desire for sex. Remember that, Cassandra, when you do finally grow up, and use it wisely.'

Draping a blanket around herself then, she smiled, turning again into the more-known cousin, the girl who would push the boundaries, but was kinder with it.

'You look shocked, Sandrine.' She began to laugh in earnest now. 'Shocked and stiff. I do not think you are made for such confessions.'

All the words fell across Cassandra. Words she had not heard before or thought of. Ideas that had been a part of a world far from her own, lost in the corruption of love. She wished she were home in England, Maureen in the chamber next door and her father not far away either. Rodney was too young to think much of right now, but even his presence would have been a relief.

'Come, let us sleep, cousin, and I promise I shall behave myself entirely. You have been ill, after all, and I should not tease you.'

In her bedroom in London all those years later Cassandra dashed away the tears that came so readily whenever she thought of Celeste. Her cousin's promise had been fulfilled in blood and in pain, the danger of Baudoin's brother Louis and the wildness within him no match for a slightly wayward French virgin steeped in the potential of adventure and romance.

'Romance.' She whispered the word into the room, and it curled into sin. Some losses were beyond comprehension and this was one of those. Some truths, too, were made mute by their sheer and utter horror.

Her truths.

No, she could never let Lord Nathaniel Lindsay

know the exact depth of any of them and after discovering today that he worked for the British Service she knew she would have to be more than careful. Just another gulf of difference between them that could never be bridged.

Lady Acacia Bellowes-Browne hung on to his arm at the Smithson ball and laughed, a soft musical sound that ran through tenseness and made Nathaniel relax.

'You said that you would come down to Bellamy for the hunting, Nat. I have held that promise for some weeks now'

'And indeed I shall,' he answered, liking the feel of her fingers on his skin, the many rings she wore decorative and colourful. He was about to speak again when Lydia Forsythe came across to the group.

'I am sorry to disturb you, Lord Lindsay, but I want to thank you for your help the other week. Mama said you were most kind in ensuring that I did not bleed to death.'

'I rather think that you would not have.'

'Well, Miss Cassandra Northrup said that I might and she is thought to be most proficient of all in the arts of medicine. When I visited her to give her my thanks she barely allowed my gratitude. Instead, she has asked for my help with her charity. Mama, of course, does not approve, but I think it is important...to remember about the plight of others, I mean...' She petered off as Acacia began to speak.

'Cassandra Northrup has lobbied us all in her pursuit of supporting those less fortunate.'

Interest sparked his question. 'You think she is too assertive in her search for patrons?'

'No, not that. She is known to delve into the shady corners of London when locating all the broken women and I think she understands neither the dangers nor the gossip associated with such an occupation. She looks as if butter would not melt in her mouth, but I have it on all accounts that she is well versed in the art of self-defence.'

'Isn't she just wonderful?' Lydia Forsythe's eyes were alight with hero worship, and the woman standing with Hawk, who Nat had not met before, also nodded her head.

A paragon and model of charitable benevolence. What would these people say if they were cognizant of the truth as he knew it? He had not told a soul about the names she had given to Lebansart. A questionable protection? A foolish guardianship? Even for England he had not betrayed her.

'She will never marry again, of course. She has made that quite plain.' Acacia's voice drifted into his thoughts.

'She won't?'

'No, my lord. The love of her life was lost in a terrible accident in Paris and she has no want to ever offer her heart to another.'

Nat's mind scrambled. Paris?

'Well, I think that it is romantic to tender thoughts for a husband long dead.' Lydia Forsythe for all her youth was most outspoken in her opinions. 'I have asked the Northrup sisters to my ball and they have promised to attend.'

'An inducement of money for the cause would no doubt bring them running,' Acacia was quick to add. 'The Daughters of the Poor is a worthwhile charity, however. I have a maid acquired from that very organisation and she has been a godsend. Cassandra Northrup's benevolent society is both efficient and organised.'

'She has a school somewhere?' Nathaniel could not believe what he was hearing.

'In Holborn. When the girl was sent to me she was well equipped with clothes and books. Miss Maureen Northrup is apparently the one who sees to that side of the business.'

Hawk began to laugh. 'They sound formidable.'

'They are. Kenyon Riley is involved in the endeavour as well.'

'I thought he had lost a leg somewhere in America?'

'Lost a leg and gained a fortune.' Hawk took up the conversation. 'And his great-uncle, the old Duke, is about to die without issue.'

'A timely inheritance, then, for the Northrups.'

'Oh, indeed,' Acacia trilled. 'And Kenyon is most besotted by them.'

Nat looked away. Cassandra Northrup had a knack of landing on her feet after adversity and using others to the very best of her own advantage.

Of all the men in the world he was the one to know that.

'Maureen Northrup has her own worries.' A wide frown marred Acacia's brow.

Now this was new.

'She does?'

'She is virtually deaf. She lip-reads, of course, and speaks in her inimitable fashion, but it is the younger sister who runs the show.'

'And the father?'

'Lord Cowper is a man who has tried to carry on the life's work of his beloved wife. Something of tiny animals we cannot see that live on our skin and make us sick.'

Nathaniel's mind went back. Sandrine had insisted upon dousing his gunshot wound in the clearing all those years ago with water and she had cleaned her hands before she had touched him. She believed in these things, too, then. Every single fact he heard about her was more astonishing than the last.

'I have read of this. Such a hypothesis is gaining in traction in scientific circles as a credible theory.'

Acacia spread out her fingers and peered at them against the light. 'Well, I can see no sign of these things of which they speak and because of the wild claims of their science there are many here in society who do not view the Northrups with much kindness. Bluestockings frighten men of little brain.'

Hawk began to laugh loudly. 'Not quite the ideal of Victorian expectation.'

'By virtue of ornamental innocence, you mean?' Acacia shook her head as she said it.

Innocence.

The word stretched across the years, and Nathaniel was back beside the river in the small cottage of the

Dortignacs, his new wife's hair spilled across the pillow like living streams of fire and gold.

Madam and Monsieur Dortignac had insisted they both be up the next morning, bathed and dressed in clothes that were remarkably formal. It was therefore no surprise when a man of the cloth had appeared an hour later, although the blood had ebbed from Sandrine's cheeks as she had grasped the intention of his visit.

'Marriage? They want us to be married now?'

'They feel as though they have fallen from grace, so to speak, by allowing us the freedoms of sharing a bed. This is their way of making amends with God.'

'But you cannot possibly want this?'

He smiled. The light caught at her hair this morning and tumbled across the soft green-blue of her eyes. 'Sometimes when people need things with as much passion as they need us to marry it does not hurt to humour them. Particularly given that they saved our lives by their actions and probably put their own at risk.'

'You think it wise, then?'

'I do.'

'Well, I should never hold you to such a farce, Monsieur Colbert,' Sandrine said. 'If we are wed by simple expedience and obligation then who should need to know of it when we leave here?'

God. You. Me. The priest. Two names in a book that make this union traceable? Nat said none of what he thought, however, as he looped the chain over his head and unhooked the clasp.

'I received this after my mother died. It belonged to her mother and her grandmother before that.'

'Then you shouldn't risk it with me.'

Ignoring her protest, he lifted her left hand, the cold smallness of it within his warmth. 'Let's try it for size.'

It did not fit her ring finger, but it nearly held on her middle one. When they reached Perpignan he would have it resized.

'It almost looks as though it could be a real emerald,' she said quietly, and he smiled as the Dortignacs and the priest came into their room. Madam Dortignac had found some winter wild flowers and she handed the straggly bouquet to Sandrine with a smile.

'For you, my dear, she said softly. 'The very last of the autumn purple crocuses.'

Much later, as Sandrine held her arm out so that the light glinted upon his mother's ring, it was impossible to clarify what he felt, the witchery of the sickness from the wound at his side still holding him prisoner, yet something else free and different.

But while his mind was ambiguous, Nat's body was not and the need in him surfaced beneath thin sheets. She had felt it, too, he thought, because she rolled over to watch him, a silent, wary question in her eyes and a hint of compliance. Her lips turned up at each end like the beginnings of a smile, a girl changing into woman right before his very eyes.

He could not help his want, nor could he rein in all that was left better unseen, the words of troth be-

tween them allowing whatever it was they might desire: warmth, relief, resolution.

Or nothing, with their sickness.

He wished he might touch her in quiet acquiescence,
but instead he turned onto his back, sense winning out.

'They were more than happy to leave us alone this
time.'

At that she laughed, joy enveloped in the dark closeness.

He remembered the feel of her in the bed when he
had awoken that first time, the contours of her body,
the thinness, the elegance. Like catching energy and
holding it.

'You were a beautiful bride, Sandrine Mercier, with
your hair let down.'

'And my bare feet. Don't forget those. But I think
green suited me.'

'Indeed. The ancient gown was particularly flattering.'

'It was our hostess's grandmother's and it was
twenty sizes too large. At least you had clothes that
fitted.'

He held his tongue and wished that they were home
at St Auburn, the English winter about them and everything familiar. When she had taken off the wedding
gown after the ceremony the lines of her ribs had been
drawn starkly on her skin.

'You are too thin.' He should not have said the
words, he knew, a piece of paper gave him no man-
date for such a criticism, but it was concern that made
him speak, not disparagement.

'I was sick. For a long time.'

'At Nay?'

'Before that even.'

'And now?'

She shrugged and looked directly at him. 'Have you ever lost someone close to you?'

He looked away.

'My whole family, apart from my grandfather.' He wondered at what had made him say it, made him confess to a hurt he had always held so very far from others.

Her fingers crawled into his, warm and true, the honesty of the connection endearing. He coughed to clear the thickness in his throat and thought with all this emotion he must be more ill than he knew.

'My own mama died fifteen months ago. It was an accident.'

She stressed the last word in an odd manner, making Nat wonder if perhaps it wasn't.

'I was there when it happened and the doctor thinks my mind became damaged. Afterwards I could not be…happy. Papa grew impatient and I was sent on the journey south with my mother's brother and his daughter to recuperate and forget.'

Cassie swallowed and held on to him even more tightly. The fever made her head swim and her vision blurry, but she knew exactly what she was saying. She needed to tell him—there was no going back because in the past few days even under the duress of hiding from those who would want to find them she had suddenly felt free. At liberty to be honest and say all that had been held bound in her mind.

'It was my fault.'

He did not even flinch. 'The accident?'

'I added some liquid to her experiment before she had asked for it to be done and the vapour from it made her sick right then and there. She died three hours later.'

'How old were you?'

'Sixteen. Old enough to wait and listen.'

'The exactness of science is sometimes over-exaggerated and the emotion of blame is the same.'

His voice was quiet, unfazed. For the first time in a long while Cassie did not feel breathless.

'Did you intend to kill her?' he asked finally.

'Of course not.' Shock jagged through her.

'But you knew that those particular elements combined might cause a problem?'

'No. I have no true understanding of all the properties of things.'

Dropping her fingers, he stretched his arms above his head, linking them under his neck so that he could watch her with more ease.

'Once, when I was small, I took a horse and rode it for hours until the steed sat down and died. My father said the horse could have stopped running with my light and small touch upon it, or thrown me off into the brush. He said the stallion did neither because he wanted to keep running. His choice. Would your mother have added the next ingredient of her experiment if you had not been there?'

'I think so.'

'Then it was her choice.'

'But I ruined our family. Papa told me so.'

'No. I think if your father blamed you, it was he who did that completely by himself.'

Perception. Skewered into truth. It was all she could do to stop the tears of a relief that felt indescribable. Someone else believed that she was not responsible even with all the facts at hand. More of the inheld tension that she always felt melted away.

Colbert had saved her in the river, she knew, the water in her throat and in her eyes, the heavy panic of exhaustion pulling her down. He had saved her, too, when he had insisted on the hole covered in leaves and branches being made on the leeward side of the bush, tucked into calm. How would she have found shelter otherwise without his knowledge of survival?

Survival was marked on his skin, in the scars of bullet and knife. On the upper side of his fighting arm she saw the blue mark of indigo. A serpent curled about a stake.

A man who had lived a hundred hard lives and come through each one. She needed this certainty and this prowess because for the first time in years hope inside began to beat again.

Not all ruined. Not all lost.

A small refrain of promise.

When she smiled at him he smiled back and Cassie felt, quite suddenly, reborn. 'How old are you?'

'Twenty-three.' He added the word *ancient* in a whisper.

'Yet you haven't married?'

'I've been busy.'

The stillness in him magnified. He never fussed, she thought, or used up energy in movements that were surplus. For a big man there was a sense of grace about him that made one look again and wonder. The danger of a panther about to strike, the liquid stretch of muscle honed with a precision that was undeniable, jeopardy tethered to a strict and unrelenting accuracy.

She had seen it in Nay in the way he fought and again at the barn by the river. Someone had trained him well. The government or an army? No amateur could have forged such expertise, but a political mercenary might have managed it. Once a man similar to Colbert had come to Baudoin's compound in the company of a French General, and had been accorded much respect and esteem.

This was Nathanael Colbert's legacy, too. No one could look at him and fail to see the menace, even when he was sick almost to death and the fever burned. Glancing away, she felt her stomach clench. To have someone like this on her side...

She shook the thought gone. One day if she was lucky she would remember back at this moment and know that just for a small time he had been hers, her husband, a ring on her finger and the simmering potential of more. She wished her body had had the curves of Celeste and that she might have met him in Paris as a woman of an impeccable reputation and virtue. They could have danced then to a waltz perhaps, her dress of spun gold matching her hair and at her throat her mother's diamonds. She could have flirted with

him, held her fan in that particular way of a coquette
and watched him through smoky eyes, the promise of
all that might happen between them so very possible.

And instead? Her ruined hand on the counterpane
caught her attention, the missing part of her forefinger and the long red scar easy to see in the moonlight.

'Could you kiss me?'

Her words were out, an entreaty in them that she had
tried so hard to hide. But the emotion of the day was
thrumming underneath everything they said and if she
parted company with him, as she knew she would, she
did not want to be left forever wondering. Or wishing.

For a moment she thought he had not heard or had
not wanted to hear and her fists clenched by her side.
But then he moved, balancing on his arm and leaning
across her, his eyes the grey of the sea at dawn just
after the sunrise.

Nathanael's lips were as she had imagined they
might be, soft at first and then harder, searching for
things that held a promise. Gentle and strong, harnessed by both power and care, his free hand caress-
ing the line of her neck and bringing her closer.

Only them in the world, only this, she thought, as
she rose up to him, her tongue meeting his and tasting.
She allowed him to force her back against the pillow,
the darkness behind her closed eyes calling for more.
She felt him turn and come across her body, the outline of his chest meeting her breasts, though his elbows
kept the bulk of his body away. The shiver of passion,
the heat of want, the memory of this day quickening as
he covered her mouth and kept her breath as his own.

A wife and her husband.

Then he broke away. 'When I am not so sick, Sandrine, I promise to take the kiss much, much further.'

Under the cover of darkness Cassie smiled because his heart was racing every bit as much as hers and when he turned away as if to quell all the thoughts his body was consumed by, she simply curled up into his warmth.

But it was a long, long while until she finally went to sleep.

They woke to the crow of a rooster outside, and inside Cassie could hear the movements of the Dortignacs preparing for a new day, the dawn only a little while off.

'We will leave with the first light,' he said as if he had been listening too. 'If Baudoin's henchmen following us find these people have been sheltering us...' There was no need for him to finish.

To the south, the mountains of the Pyrenees seemed to hold their breath, dark with the presage of rain. Another cold day. A further freezing trek towards Perpignan, many long and difficult miles to the east.

When Nathanael sat up on the side of the bed she saw the bandage across his wound was sagging. She should change it, she knew, but she did not think he would allow it and so she did not say. When he put on his clothes she understood he was in a hurry to leave and that the quiet moments of honesty between them had come to an end.

He looked healthier today. She could see it in the

way he stood, no longer favouring his right side in the way he was yesterday. She also saw in his expression a hint of the promise he had made after kissing her.

In the new day, Cassie suddenly understood the danger of a relationship. She needed to go on alone from here because she was certain Lebansart and his men could not be far behind, and if Nathanael died for her...

She shook her head.

If she struck out early across the hills, she could find a pathway and other travellers and make her way to any larger town in the vicinity.

Monsieur and Madam Colbert.

For one night of marriage only.

He had saved her so many times it was only right that she must now protect him.

Chapter Four

❧

Cassandra came across the rooftops in darkness and down into the interior of the brothel on Brown Street without being seen by anybody. An easy climb given the footholds and the balconies, but on gaining the room the note had instructed her to come to she could tell that something was wrong. Very wrong.

The chamber door was wide open and the man Cassandra had been looking for was already dead on the floor by the window. Crossing to the glass, she tested the locks, but rust inside the catches told her nobody had come this way. With care, she dropped to her knees and checked beneath the bed, knife in hand and ready to strike. Only the empty space of blackness.

She was glad for the silence in the room for it gave her a moment to think. He had not taken off any of his clothes. There had been no struggle at all and he was unmarked save for the wound at his neck. Money still lay in his pockets when she checked and an expensive leather briefcase languished in full view beside the doorway.

His right arm was bandaged, the thickness of the casing beneath his jacket belying the injury. His other arm was positioned above his head, the gold ring on his finger seen in the light.

Not a robbery then. Not a targeted wealthy man who had come to the wrong place at the wrong time and run into one of the shady characters off Whitechapel Road. Someone he knew had done this, a strike from behind without a notion that it was about to happen.

Walking to the bed, she took the bag and flicked open the buckles. Surprise made her eyes widen. Nothing lay inside, every pocket emptied and all the compartments clean. The perpetrator had been after this then, the contents of the satchel, and for such information had been willing to kill. Loud shouting made her stiffen, the sound of boots coming up the steep stairwell and voices in the night.

With only a whisper of noise she crossed from the room to the doorway and let herself out. She couldn't be found like this—in the garb of a street boy with a weapon in her belt—and she did not have the time in hand to make it up the next flight of stairs to safety without being noticed. With care she picked the lock of the room opposite and eased herself through the door. No one was in the bed and for that she was more than thankful. Dulling the noise of the closing door with the cloth in her jacket, she jimmied her foot up against the wood and flipped the latch.

* * *

Nat did not move a muscle from the alcove he stood in by the window, his breath shallow. Outside the noises were getting louder and inside the intruder stayed immobile. Was the newcomer a child? A youth of the house, perhaps, trying to escape the nefarious pursuits as best he could? The glint of a knife told him otherwise and he was across the room before the other knew it, his hand hitting out at the arm that was raised and knocking the weapon away.

He knew it was Cassandra Northrup even before she turned, the scent and the feel of her, the knowledge of each other burning bright. Bringing her against him, he felt the lines of her body even as she fought him, the fuller contours unfamiliar.

'Stop, Sandrine.' Whispered. Danger was everywhere and the discovery of a lady within the confines of such iniquity would be scandalous. Her breath was ragged, the warmth of it against his hand where he held it flat across her mouth.

She stilled, as much to listen to the noises outside the door as to obey him, her head tipped to the wood, jumping as a heavy knock sounded against it.

'Don't open it. A man is dead and I cannot be found like this.' Whispered and frightened behind his fingers, the quicksilver change into a woman startling.

'Hell.' He let her go. She filled out the boy's clothes much more generously these days, though the thinness was still there, too.

'Take everything off and get under the covers.' Already he was peeling away his own clothes, throwing each piece against a chair. Randomly. Trying to give the impression of haste and passion mixed in a room that was conducive to neither.

'Sex,' he said as he saw she was not moving. 'This place expects it.'

He pulled one dusty quilt off the bed and hung it over the other chair, hopeful in hiding the fact that female attire was missing. On a quick glance an observant onlooker would imagine them beneath.

'Open up.' A voice of authority. Probably the law.

It was enough to make her decide as her fingers flew to the buttons of her jacket and shirt, the lawn chemise beneath left on as she added her boots to the pile of clothes.

He brought those beneath the sheets with them, her body underneath his, concealed. He heard her gasp as the door opened, the correct key finally fitting the lock and giving way.

'What the hell...?' He barely needed to feign the anger as he looked around, two men in the uniform of the constabulary and the woman he had seen downstairs accompanying them. 'Get out, immediately.' He made himself sound breathless, the full blush of ardour in the words, a client in the middle of a 'paid for' assignation and surprised by the interruption. He also used his most aristocratic tones, the persona of a simple fellow disappearing into expediency. And carefully he shielded her from view.

He knew he had them as they faltered, a rush of apology. 'I am sorry, sir, but there has been a murder just reported in the house. If you could get dressed and come downstairs, we need to ask you some questions.'

Releasing a long rush of air, Nat nodded. 'Give me a few minutes and I shall be down.' No entreaty in it. Just authority.

The door closed behind them.

Silence.

Warmth.

Her skin against his own.

And then a curse. In French.

He pulled away and stood, making no attempt at hiding his body. 'Did you kill him?'

'No.'

'But you know who did?'

She shook her head.

'God.'

'Why did you help me?'

'Misguided instinct, though I am certain I shall now pay for such kindness. Is there a way out of here that does not involve going downstairs?' He reached for his clothes and began to dress.

'Yes.'

'Then I would advise you to take it.'

Already she was up, her shirt and jacket quickly donned, the boots following.

'I will expect you tomorrow.'

'Pardon?'

'At eleven p.m. Through the window of my town house to explain all this to me. Properly.'

'And if I refuse?'

'Then I will come to see you instead.'

'I will be there.'

'I thought so.'

'Will you be able to manage...everything?'

'Easily.'

She smiled. 'I always liked your certainty, Monsieur Nathanael Colbert.'

The music inherent in the way she said his name made him stiffen, and then she was gone.

His indiscretion was all over the town by midday, a lord of the first water visiting a brothel in the back streets of one of the worst areas of London and being caught out in doing so.

'You should have sent for me to come with you, Nat,' Stephen said as they sat in his library drinking brandy. 'Why the hell did you think to go there in the first place?'

'A man whom the prostitutes thought was acting strangely had been seen in the vicinity for each of the last two nights. They said he had slept at the brothel and was tall and well to do.'

'Was the dead man our murderer at the river, then?'

'No. He was short and stocky with ginger hair.'

'Memorable.'

'Exactly.'

Hawk suddenly smiled and leaned forward. 'There is something else I am missing here, Nat. It's the youngest Northrup daughter, isn't it? She was there at Whitechapel with you?'

Nathaniel ignored the query.

'The man killed at Brown Street last night was in the room opposite to mine and I heard nothing.'

'You paid for a room?'

'With a wide view of the street below. If the same man the girls spoke of was there, I would have seen him, Hawk, but I didn't.'

'Do you think the murder was related to our case?'

'Perhaps. The contents of the dead man's satchel was missing, though I found this in the corridor on my way down the stairs.' He dug into his pocket and brought out a single page of writing. 'Do you recognise the hand?'

Stephen looked carefully and then shook his head. 'Do you? It's a list for things from a chemist by the looks of it.'

'If I did, this case would already be half-solved. Will you do something for me, Hawk? Can you ask around to see if anyone saw anything? I do not want to seem interested because…'

'Because implication is only one step away from imprisonment and Cassandra Northrup's presence at Whitechapel will make everything that much harder again. Society does not seem exactly enamoured by her pursuit of the nefarious and a woman like that will only bring the old Earl's wrath down upon your head with even more than the usual vigour.'

'Remember that puppy we had at school, Hawk, the one we hid for a term in the woodcutter's shed, the one you found off the roadside on the way to Eton?'

'Springer. My God, he was the best dog I ever owned.'

'Sixteen weeks of sneaking out twice a day with the

food we had saved from the dining hall and then another jaunt for exercise. One hundred and twelve days before you could bundle him up and take him back to Atherton.'

'An unfortunate start to life, but he had the heart of a warrior till the day he died. But what is your point, Nat?'

'Cassandra Northrup is a fighter just like that dog and for some damned reason I feel compelled to help her.'

'You said she had betrayed you in France.'

'So did Springer. He bit you, remember, that time at the cliff….'

'Whilst trying to save me from falling.'

Nat drew his hand through his hair and wiped back the length of his fringe. 'What if Cassandra Northrup once did the same for me, Hawk? What if what she said she did and what she really did were two different things?'

'You are saying she might have betrayed you to save you?'

'I am.'

Cassandra had dressed carefully in a dark jacket and loose trousers, the cap she wore covering her face and her hair knotted in a bun at the back of her nape.

A caricature of Nathaniel Lindsay had appeared in the evening edition of a popular London broadsheet, one hand clinging on to the family crest and the other around the shapely ankle of a woman of the night. A poxed and toothless woman, her cheeks sunken with the mercury cure and rats scurrying from beneath the hem of her ragged skirt.

Lord Lindsay could not have been pleased; she knew this without listening to any gossip. He had also remained quiet about her involvement in this whole chaotic and sordid affair which, given the history between them, was a lot more than she might have expected.

Why he had been there in the first place she had no notion of, but he had been alone in the room waiting and completely dressed and when he had first pressed her against the door she had felt the outline of both knife and pistol.

Another thought also came. She had imagined she had been followed when she came to the boarding house in the backstreets of Whitechapel. Could it have been Lindsay watching?

The web of lies that bound them to each another was closing in, sticky with deceit, and yet here she was again, moving through his garden for a further encounter in his library. If she had any sense at all, she should be turning for home and ignoring his threats or packing her things and moving north for a while until the shock of seeing him again eased down into reason.

But she could not. Every fibre of her being could not.

He was exactly where he had been last time as she climbed through the window, his long legs out in front of the wing chair by the fire.

The only difference this time was that he had catered for her arrival, two glasses filled beside him.

'I have had a trying day,' he said as he handed one

to her, 'and as you are the reason for it I hope you will join me in a drink.'

'A celebration of your notoriety?' Even as she gave the reply she wished she had not, but he only smiled.

'Yesterday the débutantes and their mothers were pursuing me with all the wiles in the world. Today they are...fleeing.'

'Sexual deviance may appear rather daunting to any woman, no matter the size of the purse an ancient family brings.'

At that he did laugh.

'How did you know the man who was murdered?'

'I didn't.'

'Then why were you there?'

'I had word of young girls being brought in from the country.'

'And you were attempting to locate them?' Lifting his glass, he held it up and waited for her to take a sip. Cassandra hated strong drink, but, not wishing to annoy him further, she took a mouthful and swallowed. The burning bitterness reminded her of Nay and of all that she longed to forget.

'The information I received gave a location, a time and a date, but when I got there the man was already dead.'

'With a knife in the back of his neck?'

'Yes.' She did not blink.

'What else did you see?'

'A briefcase that was empty of papers.'

'Papers like this one I found in the corridor outside the murdered man's room.'

He brought out a sheet of tightly written words. He knew she recognised it by her sudden stillness. 'Your father pens articles for a science journal. The editor is a friend of mine and I spent a few hours this afternoon with him. When, by chance, he showed me Lord Cowper's latest offering the two hands appeared identical.'

'That is what the person who put this there wanted you to think, wanted the constabulary to think. My father is the one person who can stop them.'

'How?'

'He funds the Daughters of the Poor, and we are making good progress in catching those who trade the lives of young girls for work in the factories and the brothels.'

'We, meaning you. You in your boy's clothes in the dead of night risking life, limb and reputation.'

'Gone.'

'Pardon?'

'My reputation is gone. You of all people should know that.'

'The redemption of a sinner then, brazen and unmindful. I expected more of you.'

'Oh, I have ceased trying to live up to any expectations save that of my own, my lord. Now prudence rules over heroics, which in itself is a timely lesson for all who might rally against injustice.'

'Society holds you up as a saint?'

'Hardly that.'

'But not as a whore?'

The quick punch of hurt and then nothing. By the time she had come out from that hovel of a building

in Perpignan Nathanael Colbert had long been gone
and she had wiped all trace of sacrifice from her conscience since.

Just a small space of hours, blurred by pain.

She was glad he had not insisted on the removal
of her chemise last night for even in that darkened
room he would have seen and known. Her shame. She
glanced away, knowing the black anger of it would be
showing in her eyes and she did not wish for him to see.

The mark on his jaw shone opaque against the firelight, lost slightly in the growth of stubble. If he grew
a beard, it would be gone entirely. She was glad he had
not. Had he wanted to he could have erased all memory
of her for ever. As it was he must look every day into
his reflection and be reminded.

The futility of everything blended with the brandy,
a melancholy covering all she had hoped for once. He
was as beautiful as he had been then, in every way,
strong and self-assured, although the mantle of aris-
tocracy gave him an added allure.

Shallow, she knew, but it was a fact. With a man
like this she could be safe.

Sense reined in fantasy. He was all but promised
to the beautiful and clever Lady Acacia Bellowes-
Browne, a woman who would suit him exactly and
in every way. She wondered if he ever thought of the
hurried marriage in the village by the river where
Mademoiselle Sandrine Mercier had married Monsieur Nathanael Colbert, two names plucked from a
half-truth and settled in the register like impostors.

At this very moment all he looked was angry.

'Every time you come into my life, Sandrine, it seems chaos follows.'

'I am no longer Sandrine.'

'Are you not?' He came closer, the largeness of him disconcerting. England seemed full of small men with the smell of a woman about them, the indolence of life written upon their skin in softness, the bloom of ease apparent. Nathaniel Lindsay had none of these qualities. He could have been transported here from an earlier time, the menace and threat of him magnified in a room filled with books and quiet pursuits. She would be most unwise to ever think that a lord like this could offer safety after all that she had done to him.

'What other woman of the *ton* would dress as a lad and walk the back streets of hopelessness in the midnight hours? Your father must be demented to allow it.'

At that she laughed. 'The days of a man's ordinance over me are long gone, Lord Lindsay.'

'Even a husband's?'

She had wondered when he would mention it, had been expecting him to from the very outset, but the word still made her blanch, the beat of her heart hurrying with the reference.

'If our marriage was deemed to be a binding agreement, then our years apart must allow grounds for question. But given the circumstances, I should imagine it was not.'

He smiled, but the steel in his eyes hardened.

'Why were you there, at the brothel?' She needed to know if he was friend or foe.

'Two women were killed a month ago beside the

Thames in Whitechapel. I was following up a lead to find the man who did it.'

Every word he said made their relationship more dangerous. 'Do you have names?'

'No.'

'Other clues, then?'

'I am looking for a tall and well-heeled man. His hair is dark.'

'Such a one has been seen by the children we have rescued on a number of occasions.' She wondered why she told him.

'Which is why you were at the de Clare ball, no doubt. Scouting?'

'You read my intentions with too much ease for comfort of mind, Lord Lindsay.'

'Do I, Miss Northrup?' Something had changed between them in just this single second. She felt the tension in the room shift to something less certain.

'What happened after I last saw you with Guy Lebansart?'

'I grew up. I paid the debts I owed and I grew up.'

'You sacrificed others to save me? Why?' Anger creased his brow.

She felt the breath in her hollow, felt the beat of her heart flatten into some new and risky unease, and did not speak.

'I never asked that of you.' Said in the manner of a man who was not comfortable with indebtedness. 'Nor did I want it from you.'

She had had enough. 'You think that you might control everything, my lord? You think that people should only march to your drum, the drum of the morally justified? Are you now one of those men who cannot see another side of an argument, the side where good and bad mix in together to create a new word, an in-between word, that allows life?' Whirling around, she went to stand at the window. Part of her thought to slip through it into safety, but another part understood that without explanation she might never be free of him and he was dangerous. To the life she had built which depended to a large extent on her being accepted by those she mingled with.

'After leaving you I stayed in Perpignan. I was shocked by all that happened, you understand. Celeste's family needed time to know of the demise of their loved one and I needed a space to myself before...' She stopped.

'Before you returned to England?'

Jamie. Jamie. Jamie.

Under each and every word said his small and beloved face lingered and it was all she could do to hold him safe.

'I have forged a life here. My life. Once, a very long time ago, I was someone else.'

A traitor. A wife. A victim.

A woman who had used every part of her wiles to save the father of her baby. She did not flinch as he watched her. She did not think of the marks on her breast or the weeks of fever that had followed. She thought only of Jamie.

As if Nathaniel Lindsay's fingers had a mind of their

own they went to his chin and traced the damage. 'I thought that I knew you then, but now...'

'Now we are strangers travelling in different directions, my lord.'

Away from each other? Away to safety.

Turn and go now. Turn and go before he touches you and before the quiet way he gives his words makes you foolish. It is the only way that Jamie can stay safe.

With a quick snatch at the curtain, she lifted her leg across the sill and was gone.

Nat stood and watched her run, her shadow barely there against the line of trees, blending in the moonlight.

Even with Acacia he had never felt this connection, this need to protect her from all and sundry. Cassandra Northrup made him crazy, witless and sad, yet the feel of her slight body against his in the warm waters of the high pool above Bagnères-de-Bigorre lingered.

Shimmering against reason.

They had gone there by chance, a traveller's tale remembered, a small, ancient and lonely pool set amongst the mountain scrub, steam rising like God's breath from the very bowels of a restless earth.

She had forged on ahead from the little house by the river, trying to escape him, he was to understand with time, hurrying along the mountain passes without looking back, though when he had found her a good two hours later she had given no explanation and he had not wanted to ask for one.

After that they had moved with their own thoughts

across the landscape, always climbing higher. An image of Alph the sacred river running to measureless caverns and sunless seas took his imagination. Sandrine was like a sylph, light of foot and pure of heart, her hair in the grey mists the only bright and shining beacon.

His wife.

He had never been married before and the troth was surprising in its power. She was young, he knew that, but under her youth there was wisdom and discernment born from an adversity he could only wonder at.

His.

For better or for worse.

He quickened his pace. Already she was thirty feet in front of him and the slope was steepening, but to his left was the grotto he had found many years before, the steam even from this distance visible.

'There.' He pointed, and she shaded her eyes and looked, a smile rewarding his discovery.

'We can take a bath?'

He nodded and took her hand because the shale was treacherous and he did not wish for her to slip.

Later, in the cold winters of London, he would think of this time and try to remember each and every moment of it. Back then the relief of another chance at life after their sickness had made him feel exhilarated.

He could smell the sulphur as they came across the last rise, the warmth of air in the wind blowing towards them. Like an invitation, and just for a moment, he imagined them as the only people upon the entire planet, lost in the universe. He wondered if the fevers had taken his reason because he seldom thought like this, the flowery rhetoric of the Romantic poets on his tongue. Perhaps it was Sandrine who made him such but he didn't like to think of what that might mean.

Nat's side ached, and he still felt hot, but a day out amongst the clouds had revitalised and settled him.

'Will others come?' Her voice was small.

'Not now.' Already the light was falling. Another hour and it would be gone completely.

When she smiled, he smiled back, his aching bones crying out for a warm soak in a mineral pool. She dipped in her fingers, the ruined hand swallowed by opaque water, nestled in heat.

'You have been here before?'

'A long while ago.'

'Is your home near?'

This time he merely shook his head and sat down, taking off his boots and placing his socks carefully within the leather so that they did not get damp.

She was watching him, her eyes filled with delight. A joyous Sandrine was so different from the one he more usually saw, the dimples in her cheeks deep and the quiet creases of laughter charming.

'Put your clothes under mine when you have them off. That way they will stay dry.'

Within a moment he was naked, wading into the water and dipping down. She had turned away, allowing for privacy, but he did not care. Closing his eyes, he waited till she joined him.

'I cannot ever remember feeling so good.' Her words were quiet as she lay back, spreading her hair across the surface, like a mermaid or an enchantress, the colour in each strand darkened by the water. She had not pushed off from the bottom for every other part of her body save her face and neck was hidden from him.

Most women of his acquaintance would have simpered and hesitated, a lack of clothes precluding all enjoyment. But not her. She simply took what was offered with a brave determination, the mist beading her eyelashes and small drops settling on her cheeks and lips.

'It is said in these parts that this pool contains the soul of a sea sprite who lost her lover.' Another flight of ridiculous fancy. He grimaced.

'How?'

'The sprite changed him into a merman so that they might always be together, but his jealous wife threw flames upon his form and he dissolved into steam.'

'Water and steam. They still live together?'

Sandrine's hand came up from the pool and she cradled both elements. 'Legends and science. My mother would have peered into this pool to see what lived inside of each drop.'

'The new and unseen frontier of science?'

'You know of this? She looked puzzled and faintly incredulous.

'When I am not killing people I can be found reading.'

Her laughter rang across the quiet, echoing back. 'A warrior and a scholar. If you were to go to the salons of the wealthy, Nathanael Colbert, you would be besieged by women. Celeste would have been one of those had she lived.'

'How did your cousin die?'

'By her own hand. Baudoin's brother Louis was her first lover and when he was killed she had no more heart for life.'

'Difficult for you. The one left.'

She did not answer, but in her eyes there was such grief that he moved closer and took her hand, waiting till she regained composure. All the things that she did not say were written in hard anger upon her face.

'How did this happen?' His thumb traced the line of her ruined finger because he knew that to speak of such travesty would be a balm.

'Baudoin and his brother were always at odds with one another over my cousin. Once, when we first came to Nay, I tried to drag Celeste back from getting involved in an argument and Anton slashed out at me.'

Anguish solidified inside of him, and he attempted for her sake to push it down. 'I see you holding it now and then, rubbing at the finger that is missing?'

She smiled. 'It hurts sometimes, a phantom pain as if it is still there.'

The small fragility of her hand made the wound seem even more mindless. The ring of his mother's that she wore was far too big and he touched it.

'I will have it resized, Sandrine. So you do not lose it.'

Puzzlement in her eyes was tinged with surprise. 'I should not expect you to honour a marriage that was forced upon you when you were too sick to resist.'

'The church may disagree.'

Their world stood still, steam the only thing moving

between them, up into the growing blackness. Their shared night-time kiss also shimmered in the promise.

'A poor reward, no doubt, for all your endeavours to save me.' The grasp of her fingers slid about his own.

'Ah, but it could have been worse. You might have been old or ugly or had the tongue of a shrew.'

She laughed.

'No. I think on balance I was not at all hard done by.'

The lustrous colour of her hair caught at them, claiming him, binding them as one.

Alive.

She was still alive and so was he and she was pleased her attempt to escape him had come to nothing. In the silence above the world she allowed her head to rest upon his chest, listening to his heart.

The beat of vitality against her ear, the course of blood and hope and energy. It had been so long since she had been held this way, with care, like a porcelain doll shimmering in the wind. With only a small nudge she might shatter apart completely and she did not want to move. No, here she wanted to know what it felt like to breathe in the sensual and be rewarded by its promise. The lump in her throat thickened. She did not love Nathanael Colbert and he did not love her back but they were man and wife, a pair beneath the gentle hand of God, and in this, His place, a natural pool of light and water and warmth.

For so long she had been fighting alone. For all the months of Nay and then the year before that, her mother's death embedded in her sadness.

Could she not let it go for one moment on a hillside in the wilds of the Pyrenees and in the company of a man who looked at her as if she was truly beautiful?

No ties save that of a marriage that would never be real. If she survived this flight to Perpignan she would return to England, ruined by all the accounts that would follow her, she was sure of it. But would she ever again be offered the chance of this?

The skin across his arms was brown and hard, the indigo of his tattoo strangely distorted in the water. She touched it now, traced the curl of serpent with one finger and then leant her mouth to the task.

Tasting him.

He breathed in deeply, and Cassandra felt the power of which Celeste had spoken all those months before. Not a limited sovereignty or a slight one. When her fingers slipped higher to his face she outlined the features: his nose, his cheeks, the swell of his lips and the long line of his throat.

His eyes watched her, fathomless, twin mirrors of the sky and the water and the mist, but fire lurked there, too, and it was building.

'I am only a man, Sandrine. So take care that you do not cross boundaries you have no wish for me to traverse.'

'What if I do?'

There, it was said and she would not take it back, not even when the flicker of wariness crossed into grey and she saw in his soul the first thought of 'why?'.

If he asks, I shall walk straight out of this pool.

But he remained quiet and the turn of hardness, his sex, budded beneath the limed water.

It was what she needed, this truth of reaction, no whispered lies between them stating a future that could never be. For this moment she felt like a woman reborn, the girl in her pushed back by a feeling that was new, creeping into the place between her legs and into her stomach. Heavy. Languid. Damp.

Lost in the transfer of all she had suffered.

And in control of everything.

He did not speak because he was a man who understood small nuances. It was his job after all, seeking truth and finding exactly what it was those buried under the shifting tides of war needed to survive.

Sandrine needed oblivion, and he needed her to find it. It was simple. A translation of grief.

She was weightless against him, her thinness in the water disguised. He was glad he could only feel: the small mounds of her breasts, the flat plane of her stomach, her long legs draped around his waist as if they had a mind all of their own.

Opened to him. Waiting.

He wrapped the fine length of her hair about his wrist, tethering her, gentling her, the cold in the air and the heat of their bodies making light work of the joining, and when his lips came down upon her upturned mouth he did not hold back.

He was in her, tasting, her throat arched upwards and their breath mingled. He knew the moment he had her assent, for she began to shiver. In her ardency her fingers scraped down the side of his arms.

'I want to know what it is like to have a husband.' The honesty in her words undid him.

No pretentiousness, the grandiose and flowery allowances of various ladies he had known pushed aside by a simple truth. She did not play games or set rules or say one thing, but mean another. Danger and hardship had done away with all the extraneous.

Hot. He felt hot from the pool and her skin and the building need inside him. 'I would not wish to hurt you.'

She smiled at that, the dimples in her cheeks deep, and steam across the coldness of night lifting around them. 'I know that you won't. It is why I want it to be you.'

With care, his fingers dipped, the softness of woman and the heat there, and she tensed, her eyes sharpening as though pain might follow and when it didn't she urged him further, a small sigh of release and surprise.

She was tight and tense, her eyes a clear and startled turquoise as she watched him, measuring, challenging, her hips lifting to allow him in farther though her brow furrowed as he found the hard nub of her desire.

She stilled him.

'What is this?'

'You, Sandrine, the centre of you.'

Relaxing even as he spoke, she allowed him closer, the feel of her body against his, her breasts more generous than he had thought them.

'Beautiful.'

Exchanging his hand for his manhood, he pushed wide, edging inwards, filling the space of her. When her arms pulled him in he knew that he had her and, twisting his body, he came in deeper.

With the water and the bubbles and the steam about them, both lost their tapering hold on reason, the final absolution as she went to pieces, beaching waves of rigid need, and then was quiet.

He held her motionless as he took his own relief, his face held upward so that the fine mist of night cooled him, his groan of pleasure involuntary.

'God, help us.' He had never felt like this before with anyone, never wanted to start again and have her impaled upon him, for all the hours of the night and the dawn, only his.

He should have withdrawn, should have given his seed to the water where it would wither and die in the heat. And instead...

If she were fertile then a part of him would grow.

But she did not let him think. 'Take me again on the bank in the cold.' Her voice was soft and her tongue licked at the space about his chin.

A thin, brave and pale siren with no idea at all as to how much she had affected him. Lifting her into his arms, he came from the pool in a cloud of steam and laid her down in the nearly night and gazed.

'You are so very lovely.' He whispered the words, honesty in every syllable, and when she smiled he found the hidden folds between her legs and tasted her. Sandrine. Salty and sweet and young.

* * *

Much later he dressed her, carefully so that the cold did not creep into softness. He had marked her as his, the red whorls of his loving standing out on the paleness of her skin, telling the story of long and passionate hours. But already the dawn birds called across the wide mountain valleys, signalling in the light.

'I did not know it could be like that.' Her voice was guarded. 'After Nay I was not a virgin.'

The rawness of her confession grated against the new day. A confidence she did not wish to share, but had felt the need to? He frowned.

'No one could live in that hovel and remain…untouched, though Celeste soon worked out a way to protect me from them.'

'How?'

'She began a relationship with Louis Baudoin and insisted I sleep in a small room off their own.' Taking in a deep breath she continued on. 'I think she thought the accident in the carriage was her fault somehow. She had wanted to take a detour off the main road and it was there that the horses stumbled down the hill. Her father and his godson were killed and Louis Baudoin found us just before it snowed.'

'A saviour?' He hoped she would not hear the irony.

'He took us home, and Celeste was grateful.'

'And you?'

'I was grateful to her.'

When people lied they often glanced down before they did so. Their body language changed, too, the arm crossing the chest in an effort at defence. Nathaniel saw all of this in Sandrine, and when she did not answer he did not press her, but the joy of communion wilted a little in the deception and in her confessions.

With the wind behind her and the shadow of her hair across her cheeks she suddenly did not look as young as she always had before. But she was not quite finished.

'My cousin was of an age when the adventures of life are sometimes sacrificed to the safer and more conventional. I could not save her.'

Nat stood and took her hand, holding it firmly as she tried to loosen the grip.

'It is over now, Sandrine, and the past is behind us.'

But she only shook her head. 'No, Nathanael, it is here right at our heels, and if you had any sense at all you would leave immediately and escape me.'

His laughter echoed about the lonely and barren hills.

Chapter Five

Maureen confronted her the morning after she had gone to the St Auburn town house, deep marks of worry across her brow and dark eyes fixed upon her lips.

'You were so late home last night. I can hardly recognise who you have become, Cassie, and I do not think you know it yourself, either.'

Her rebuke stung. 'This is not an easy task, Reena. There are so many who need—'

'To be saved?' A question. 'And what will be your salvation when you are caught in the lad's clothes far from home and I cannot find you?'

High emotion changed a careful diction so that the words slurred together unfinished and disjointed. Realising this, Maureen reined her anger in, the hands she used so much in communication hard up against her ears, pressing, and the guilt that had been Cassandra's constant companion since the accident bloomed.

'I cannot properly hear what people say any more,

Cassie. Mama was certain that I would grow out of my affliction, but it is worsening.'

'If Mama was still here she would know what to do, but she isn't. She's gone,' Cassandra shouted back, for after an evening sparring with Nathaniel Lindsay she was heedless. 'It was all my fault that she died. I was the one who did that.'

They had seldom spoken of the day of the accident, the memory too painful for them both. Their beautiful and clever mama falling down upon the floor, her eyes wide open with surprise and pain and then nothing. Save Reena with her hands on her ears in exactly the same way she held them now, her face creased with disbelief.

The laughter was unexpected.

'Mama's science is what killed her, Cassie. Mama and her foolish insistence on having us help her.'

The shock of the words kept Cassandra still.

'Alysa only thought about her experiments. Don't you remember that? She lived in her laboratory. Her scientific discoveries were her babies so much more than we ever could be and the thought of saving the world soul by soul through uncovering unseen sicknesses was what drove her. If she had not been killed in that particular accident, then there would have been another.'

Such revelations amazed Cassie. 'You never told me this.'

'I tried to because I could see that you thought it was your fault, but you loved her too much to listen and then you got sick.'

Heartsick. Body-sick. Soul-sick.

Leached of life by guilt and then by shame.

'I should be rejoicing in my affliction in any case and not decrying it. I would have never met Kenyon otherwise for I would have heard his horse behind me and got off the path. What a loss that would have been.'

The day just kept getting stranger.

'Kenyon Riley?'

'Of course. I am getting older, old enough to imagine I should never have the chance of a family. I love him and he has asked me to marry him.'

Pieces of a puzzle clicked into place. Kenyon's presence at the school, his interest in everything that they did, his generosity and his kindness.

'You have been distracted lately, Cassie. I wanted to tell you, but you were never here. You were always dressed in your boy's clothes and out in the night, helping others.'

Mama. Maureen. Kenyon.

My God, she had missed all the signs of change.

'There is a problem, however, and I think it is only fair that you hear of it from me. There are whispers in places that say you were the woman in Lord Lindsay's bed in that whorehouse in Whitechapel, and they are gaining in traction. Kenyon has tried to douse the rumour, but it seems you were seen.'

Maureen's careful diction made the accusations sound so much worse, each rounded word ringing out the ruin.

'Tell me it is not true, Cassie, and we can refute it together. I can say you were here with me and that they were mistaken…' Her voice petered off as Cassandra shook her head and anger lit her dark eyes.

'He forced you?'

'No.'

'You wanted him?'

'No.'

'Then why?'

Because I was abused once by monsters who held no mind for a young, thin, sick and frightened girl. Because Nathanael Colbert saved me from hell and we were married under other names in a town I can barely remember. Because I betrayed others to save his life. Because I have killed men by my hand and by my words and he hates me for it all.

That is what she could have said, might have even tried to had her brother not have chosen that very second to interrupt them and come tumbling into the room with a parrot upon his shoulder.

'I was given this by a sailor in the park who had come from India and wanted to go back again without the bother of a bird. Sixpence, he charged me, and he said I was to call him "Mine".'

At the sound of his name the bird lunged from his perch on Rodney's arm up on to the gold clip in Maureen's hair, pecking at the glitter to create havoc. And Cassie knew without a single doubt that any moment of truth was well and truly lost.

'Mine. Mine. Mine', she heard them both calling as she slipped through the doorway and left.

Cassandra lay in bed that night and thought of all that Maureen had said. If the gossip about her were to become widespread, what would happen? Nathaniel Lindsay would hardly be stepping forward with an offer of his hand. Again.

Wonderful and terrible.

The day had been that. Maureen's good news balanced against her bad. The guilt felt about her mother's death lost into the wonder of Reena meeting Kenyon Riley and all because she did not hear the hoofbeats of his horse as they came from behind her. Despite everything else, Cassie smiled and rubbed at the china shard Nathanael had threaded for her in the tiny village of Saint Estelle.

They had come down into the settlement late in the afternoon, the thin sunlight slanting on to their faces as they walked in silence after their night at the pools. Cassandra had not dared to break with words the magic that danced about every part of her body.

This was what she had heard of in the ballads and in the books. This crawling, sensuous, languid warmth that sifted through everything and left her different.

She wished they might find a room somewhere, alone, and begin all over again. The punching throb of need made her groan, and he turned.

'Are you hurt?'

The redness began at her breast and crept up on to her cheeks, a wave of heat similar to that she had felt last night. Unstoppable. She was like a woman in a story book, a woman with little will of her own and a singular wish for the feelings expressed in the works of the Romantic poets Celeste and she had read under the candlelight.

Thrilling.

Please.

The word coiled inside her like a snake waiting to strike.

Please. Please. Please.

She saw the moment he understood what it was she hid, blue darkening across silver in a will all of its own.

Lust it might be for him, but for her love held on at the edges, grasping tentatively. The feel of the ring against her skin deepened it, a circle that held them together, caught in the company of each other, pledged to God.

And by flesh now, the feel of him within her, the building joy of need, the hours of play and delight so different from anything she had known at Nay.

She shook away the darkness. No. She would not think of that again.

'I will find us a room.' His voice sounded strained and unnatural.

This time the feeling was different. This time they circled each other fully dressed in a chamber that was... comfortable. Now instead of a strange world far from the one they knew, a certain familiarity crept in. The crystal of the glasses. The bed with its feather quilts. A window where the blinds had been drawn across the remains of the day; curtains of floral damask much like the ones hanging in the library room at home. Bread and wine sat upon a gilded tray on the table.

The consequences of choices already made settled in. One day she would be back in London and this would all be a memory.

She began to unbutton her shirt, but he stopped her.
'We will eat first.'

First.

She shook her head. She was not hungry for food or
wine. She did not want to wait until they had supped
and spoken, all the normal things that happened in a
relationship. This was not normal, the aching lust that
coursed through her and made her want to lunge at
him and take everything that his body could offer hers.
She wanted him inside, moving; she wanted to feel all
those things she had last night and this morning when
her mind for once had flown away from thought and
into a place that was only feeling.

No past or future, only now.

'We have time to—'

She stopped him. With her fingers across his lips.
Pressed hard.

'No.' Her other hand unbuttoned his shirt and came
inside, the warmth beguiling. Yesterday he had flicked
her nipples with his forefinger and she had liked it.
Today she did the same to him, measuring his heartbeat as it quickened.

'Tonight is by my bidding.'

The slate-grey darkened, the last light from a dying
sun slanting through a gap in the curtains and reaching the skin on his chest where she had peeled away
clothing.

'Like the daughters of Achelous?'

'The sirens?' She laughed. 'Dangerous and beautiful?' He knew the old legends of Greece and the names
of the gods. For a second she wondered just exactly

who he was, this man dressed in clothes that had seen better days, but when she kneeled to undo his trousers she forgot about such intrigue entirely.

He was her husband and he was ready for her, sprung hard against lust, nothing hidden. A gift offered without payment or coercion. Or hurt. Legal. Sanctioned. Authorised.

She laid her fingers around his shaft and brought it to her tongue, licking the ridges and the smoothness, finding the essence; and when he swore roundly she brought him in deeper.

Hell, Nathaniel thought, his world spinning in a way it never had before, the sweet feel of yearning drumming in his ears. Wild curls hid Sandrine from him, trails in gold and red, her slender shoulders bent in concentration to all that she gave. He knew she wanted control, but in another moment his restraint would break and he had to give her back more than just his own relief.

Guiding her face away from swollen flesh, he lifted her chin and she stood. He had no clothes on and she was fully dressed, small webs of repaired fabric standing out against the light. Placing his mouth across hers, he slanted the kiss, his fingers running across the fine lines of her throat and bringing her closer.

'Love me, Sandrine.' Whispered. Gentle. Allowing more than simple lust.

'I do.'

She was so light as he lifted her, a shadow of a woman, but tall with it. He brought her to the bed and sat her down, and when her hands went to the buttons at her shirt he stopped her.

'My turn.'

She did not argue.

Five buttons and one missing. Beneath the cotton was sheer lawn and lace, repaired like the rest of her clothes, but of a quality that told him of a life led before. The pad of his finger lingered on the stitching, complex, intricate, the sort of thing his mother might have worn had she lived.

The straps were thin and of satin and he slid them across her shoulders so that the chemise drooped and her breasts were there, peaked and perfect. He cupped his hand around one feeling its form, admiring the curve of skin and the unexpected smattering of freckles.

The tip-tilt of her nose as she looked at him made him smile. A girl who was the most beautiful woman in the world. The narrowness of her waist, the slender length of her arms, the elegance of neck.

This was Sandrine.

A goddess lost into the wilderness and now refound.

He traced his initials into the cream of her skin, *NL*, and she looked up in puzzlement.

'Once I was someone else,' he explained.

'And I was, too,' she responded, the rightness of their coupling underwritten by truth. 'But now all I want to be is loved well.'

He lifted her onto his knees, slipping off her trousers and socks and boots so that she sat naked and waiting.

He liked how she did not hold her legs together tightly or stiffen as his fingers came between them, exploring.

'Is this well enough?' he asked as he found the core of her in the hard nub of need. 'Is this what you want?' he added as he began to move faster and faster, the rhythm changing just as he thought she was about to come apart.

Wet for him and swollen. He could feel the throb inside and the heat.

And when she nodded he simply placed her upon his cock and drove in, the finesse transformed to something much stronger and more basic. It was not knowledge that brought them together now, but an ancient magic with no rational thought, and he cried out as her body clenched about his, taking all that he offered and more.

He took her again in the night and once in the morning when the first rays of sunshine woke them. He had not slept with a woman for so many hours in his life, his more normal caution and vigilance taking him from a bed well before they asked for more than he might want to give. But with Sandrine they spooned together in the cold and lonely hours and when they awoke their bodies called, the quick burst of need and the slow sating after relief.

Once on waking he found her looking at him, as though she wanted to remember every piece of who he was.

'Stay with me for ever.' The words were out before he knew them to be and she placed his hand upon her heart in answer.

'Here. You will always be here.'

'Do you promise?'

Nodding, she simply rolled over on top of him and all that had been magical before began again.

Cassandra awoke with tears running down her cheeks and the cold London morning bearing down. No longer in France. No longer in the place of dreams and promises, the steam bath above Bagnères-de-Bigorre and the curtained room in Saint Estelle.

Avalon. The vaulted ceilings and the shining marbled Gothic arches.

A noise made her turn, and James was at her doorway, a teddy bear held in one hand so that his furry legs dragged along the floor.

'Mummy.'

'I am here, darling.' She pulled back the sheet and waited until he came inside, tucking the warmth about him when he was settled. His small roundness pressed into her, the smell of slumber upon him.

'I dreamed we were in France.' His pale grey eyes watched her, dark hair standing on end from sleep.

'Once we were, my love. Once it was just you and I there and I knew from the very second I saw you that I should love you for ever.'

He giggled. 'You always say that.'

'And I always mean it.'

'Nigel said his daddy still lives in France. But I said mine was dead.'

The worm of dread turned. 'Well, you have so many

others who love you, sweetheart. Mummy. Maureen. Anne. Granddad. Rodney. The cook. Nigel's mummy.'

'But a daddy is special. Nigel said that they were.'

Lord Nathaniel Lindsay. More than special. She would have to tell him, she knew that she would, but not yet. Not while Jamie was still hers to love and hold like this, the secrets of the past hidden in a corner where they were unable to escape and ruin everything.

And if Nathaniel took their son away…?

She shook her head and, drawing her fingers up into the shape of a spider, began to recite a children's ditty, liking the laughter that followed.

Chapter Six

'Chris Hanley said what?'

Nat tried to curb the panic in his voice as Stephen answered.

'He said that he saw Cassandra Northrup creeping from the Brown Street boarding house as though the very devil was on her tail the night of the murder.'

'What the hell was Hanley doing there?'

Hawk began to laugh. 'He was out on the town with a group of friends, but your question precludes other more pressing ones, Nat. If, for example, your lady was not present you might have asked if he was crazy to be so mistaken? As a judge, I would infer from your words that the accusation was true.'

'Cassandra Northrup is hardly my lady.'

His mind whirled as Stephen continued to speak. 'The ruination of her reputation might only be a minor concern when stacked up against such a killing.'

'Do people believe Hanley?'

'I'd like to say no, but I think that they are beginning to. Reginald Northrup has made no attempt at silencing his friend either, which is telling. I took it on myself to find out a little of the Northrups and if Reginald himself stands to gain anything from any discrediting of the brother's family. One daughter is almost deaf, the second one is married and living in Scotland and the son is still a minor. Cassandra Northrup's ruination is irrelevant for I am certain Cowper would have made a will stating his preferred guardians for Rodney and for the trustees of his estate.'

'Is it the title he wants? From all accounts the Northrups are not as rich as he is.'

'No, not that. Just the influence, I am presuming, for the title is more than safe. Rodney is the direct heir, but there is another more pressing fact that you should know, Nathaniel, given your recent championing of the youngest Northrup daughter. Cassandra Northrup may not be the lady that you think she is. She is reputed to take many more risks than she should.'

'Risks?'

'She does not seem to give much account to her reputation. It seems she is not averse to wandering the same streets the prostitutes do in order to save some of them. Kenyon Riley was touchy when I asked him further about it.'

'You saw Riley?'

'Yesterday at White's. He bought rounds for all and sundry and I had the feeling some personal celebration was in the air. He spends a lot of time with the Northrups so perhaps he has finally decided to offer for one of the daughters.'

The wheel turned further and further. Cassandra Northrup had become the beauty Nat had predicted she would all those years before and even encumbered with two failed marriages she was…unmatched.

Swearing, he poured himself another drink.

She ransacked him with her beauty. That was the trouble. The history between them had also had a hand, their marriage, their trysts around Saint Estelle and the small villages before Perpignan, hours when he had imagined her as his forever wife safe at St Auburn and providing timely heirs for a title steeped in the tradition of first-born boys.

Lord, what groundless hopes. In every meeting thus far she had never given him an inkling that she hankered for more between them other than the safe keeping of hidden secrets arising from betrayal.

And now a further problem. She was innocent of the murder of the man at the brothel, but could he just leave her to fight the accusations herself? He knew that he could not.

'Is our membership in the Venus Club complete, Stephen?'

'Yes?'

'When do they meet again?'

'This Saturday. I thought to go there after making a showing at the Forsythe ball.'

'I will accompany you then. I would like a chat with Christopher Hanley.'

'So you will still be involving yourself with Cassandra Northrup's plight?' The laughter in his friend's eyes made Nat wary. Sometimes Stephen had a knack of finding out things from him that he did not wish to divulge.

'There may be no one else to help her.'

Hawk raised his glass. 'Then I drink to an outcome that will be of benefit to you both.' Nathaniel wondered what Stephen might have made of the fact that they had once been married and that high up on the foothills of the Pyrenees their troths had been consummated with more than just a nominal effort. He wished he might speak of it now, but there would be no point in the confidence. Sandrine had chosen her pathway and it had wound well away from his. Still, he would not want to see her made victim for a crime she had not committed.

He swallowed, for his logic made no sense. She had betrayed England and then carried on with her life with hardly a backward glance. He should not trust her.

A ring of the doorbell brought his butler into the library.

'There is a Miss Maureen Northrup here to see you, my lord. She will not come through, however, but would like a quick word in the foyer.'

Standing, Nat looked at Hawk, who lifted his glass with a smile. 'A further complication?'

Outside, the same dark-eyed girl at Albi's ball stood, her maid at her side and her hands wringing at the fabric in her skirt. Underneath a wide hat he could see her face and she looked neither happy not rested.

'Miss Northrup.'

'Thank you for seeing me, Lord Lindsay. I will be

as brief as I can be. Is there a room where we might have a moment's privacy?'

'There is.' He opened the door to his left and shepherded her into the blue salon, wondering at all the conventions being broken for an unmarried woman to be alone here. He did not shut the door.

'I wish to know what your intentions are regarding my sister, my lord?' She did not tarry with the mundane.

'I have none.'

He thought she swallowed, and she paled further at his reply.

'Then I want you to stay well away from Cassandra, sir. She does not need your dubious threats.'

'Threats? She told you I had been threatening her?'

'Not in as many words. But unless you have some hold upon her I cannot see why she would have been willingly in your bed in that house of disrepute off the Whitechapel Road for any other reason.'

This Northrup daughter was as brave as her sister, her eyes directly on his face and no blush at all upon her cheeks.

Her voice was strange, he thought, the diction so precise. Then he saw her glance upon his lips and he remembered. She was deaf. Deaf and brave, he corrected, and trying with all her might to protect her family.

'I was helping her. A man had been murdered in the room opposite and San...Cassandra would have been implicated had she been found there. I bundled her into my bed and pretended...'

He could not go on. This was the strangest conversation he had ever had with anyone before.

'Pretended...? You said "pretended"?' She mulled the word over, the light coming on in her dark eyes as she did so. 'I see, my lord. I had thought...' Again she stopped. 'Thank you for your time, Lord Lindsay. I do appreciate it.'

With that she simply glided out through the door, gesturing to her wide-eyed maid to follow and was gone, the clock in the hall ringing out the hour of one in the afternoon. The butler looked as puzzled as he did.

'If Miss Northrup returns, do you wish to know of it, sir?'

'I doubt she will be back, Haines, but if she comes send her through to me.'

Stephen still sat where Nat had left him and from the look on his face he had heard the whole thing.

'If Cassandra Northrup was with you, Nat, I should imagine your intentions are nothing like those you regaled the oldest Miss Northrup with? You have not taken a woman to bed in years.'

A reprimand. Given with the very best of intentions. He could no longer lie to Hawk.

'Once, Cassandra Northrup and I were married. In France.'

By the look in his friend's eyes this was the last confession that he had been expecting. 'Are you still?'

'It was never annulled.'

'I see.'

The silence in the room heightened, a heavy blanket of question.

'She had been captured by a group of bandits in the Languedoc region and dealt with badly. I was trying to protect her.'

'Something that you are still doing here.'

'Perhaps.'

'Then take care, Nathaniel, for society can be most intolerant to a woman who would live outside its rules. Even one who is both beautiful and clever.'

Saint Estelle had been small and run-down, a mountain town of old buildings and kind people.

In the morning after they had eaten they had walked along the river and he had found a shard of blue-green pottery at the water's edge.

'If I could buy you a tourmaline, Sandrine, I would, because that gemstone is the exactly the shade of your eyes. But as I am penniless, this will have to do.'

She took it carefully, with the hand that was not ruined, and held it up to look at. 'Gemstone pottery?' Her laughter hung in the earliness of the day and warmed his heart. 'A priceless gift that I will keep for ever.'

'For ever is a long time.' Sadness had settled in the corners of his mind. He wanted to hold her away from danger and keep her safe. He wanted to take her to St Auburn and make her understand exactly whom she had married, the coffers of the place filled with the treasure of the past in an unending array of wealth, diamonds, gold and silver and every gemstone in between. He wondered what she would make of the expectations inherent in his title and conversely what those at the castle might make of her. Especially his grandfather.

'Tonight I will find some leather and fashion a hole through the top so that you can wear it as a pendant.'

Her hair had caught the wind and the many-coloured lights of it tumbled wild with her curls, the length reaching the contour of her hips.

'Mama always insisted that one gift required another in return. She said that in the giving of a present there should also be the taking of happiness.'

He stood still as her hand came against his cheek, tracing the line of his throat downwards.

'The gift of the power of womanhood is one I could bestow upon you if you should so desire it, Nathanael.' Beneath the laughter in her words there was another cadence, full of promise. 'My cousin Celeste used to say that I should find it one day, this knowledge of the sensual, and that men would not be able to refuse such an authority from me.'

'She was right.' Gravity had crept in under humour and he could hear the steady beat of his own heart in his ears.

'So you accept?'

'I do.'

They were far from the village and he had seen no sign of others for many miles. Besides, the road out of Saint Estelle lay upon the opposite bank of the river, past the line of trees, out of sight.

Last night had been frenzied and passionate and

furious. Today a languid peace reigned, a quiet acceptance of each other's needs.

'Come.' She held out her hand and he took it, following her into the shadow of the trees until they
reached an overhang of cliff, the rocky outcrop of the
Pyrenees sheltering a little bowl of meadow. It was
noticeably warmer.

'Here, away from the wind we can love each other.'
Bringing two blankets from her bag, she laid them
down as a bed.

Within a moment she had removed her clothes,
lying on the wool without any sense of shame, burnished like an angel from one of the old religious
paintings that graced his grandfather's library.

Reaching for his fingers, she placed them upon her
right breast and leaned into the touch. His other hand
she splayed in the warmth of the space between her
legs, her thighs apart and waiting. 'I am yours for the
day, *monsieur*. I am yours until the sun lies upon the
horizon and the dusk is reached. My gift for your gift.'

Positioning the other blanket to keep out the cold,
his fingers began to move with a will of their own, up
into the warmth of her, up into the swollen wet darkness where feminine magic lingered. She did not draw
back. He slipped in farther and heard her sharp intake
of breath. Playing her tenderly and feeling the answer
of her muscles against his hand, the first tremble of
release as frenzy tightened. Taking ownership. He did
not let her move away as her whole body shuddered
into climax, roiling waves clenching skin to muscle.

She cried out, once and then again, her head arched

back so that daylight filled her, the sweat of climax dampening her skin and making her rigid with lust.

The scent of her between them, the hard erectness of nipples, the loss of self into a frenzy of feeling. Shivering need brought her arms about him, her nails gouging trails into his shoulder. Joined. For ever. Locked into union.

Moments passed in silence, the heat of her slackening to limpness.

When he brought his mouth onto the peak of her right breast, she simply clasped her hands about his head and nudged him closer. Like she might do a suckling baby, guided to the source.

Quiet. Still. Primal. The reclamation of all that had been once before and now was again. The gift of belonging. The heavy punch of sex and now the softer pull of place. Home. With Sandrine. He shut his eyes and took the offered gift, grateful and indebted.

In all of his life he had never felt as loved.

They woke to the sound of evening birdsong, the dusk across their blankets. With slow care she moved atop his manhood, filling herself with the largeness, moving in her own rhythms and refusing any help.

Her gift, she had said, and his taking. When she pinned his hands against the earth and told him that she was in charge he had allowed it, the sky above and the meadow beneath. She did not let him come until the sun had fallen almost to the horizon, the tension in him stretched to the full ache of friction, a thin hot pain of need.

And then she had taken each of his nipples between her nails and pinched. Hard. Jarring.

He had climaxed as he never had before, emptying himself into her, wave after wave, involuntary, uncontrolled. And she had taken him in, wanting his seed, drawing him up as the final gift of the day. He felt the undulating motion of her insides around him and knew without a shadow of doubt that he could love her. For ever.

On their return to Saint Estelle the tavern keeper was full of the news of a group of men who had come into the town looking for two strangers.

'The leader was a big man with dark-brown hair and a scar across his cheek. Here.' His fingers drew the shape of a crescent. 'He appeared very angry.'

Lebansart. Cassie drew in her breath and knew that Nathanael had felt her fear.

'Did they say where they were going next?'

'They didn't say and I didn't ask, but they left Saint Estelle before the noon hour and there was no talk of a return.'

'We will stay here then for a few days longer.' Nat dug into his jacket pocket and pulled out a handful of coins. 'If they should return at any time at all, I would like to be told of it.'

'Who exactly is this man, Sandrine?' The question came a few moments later when they were once again back in their chamber.

'Guy Lebansart. He was an acquaintance of Anton Baudoin.'

'What does he want?'

She shrugged her shoulders and turned away. *Me.* She almost said it, almost blurted it out before biting down on the horror. The document she should never have read shimmered in her memory.

Cassandra spent the morning at the school at Holborn. Kenyon Riley arrived around midday and walked into her office.

'Is Maureen here, Cassandra?' His voice was tinged with the accent of the Americas, and he sounded happy.

'She went to run an errand in town. I should not imagine that she will be long.'

'You look busy.'

Cassie observed the large pile of papers that littered her desk. She tried to be organised, she really did, but with the amount of work she had, such a thing was never easy.

'My sister told me the good news about your betrothal.'

'Did she? I was wondering if she would ever get around to mentioning it to anybody else.' His smile was wide.

'Reena is more contented than I have ever seen her.'

'She deserves to be.'

'I agree and I don't think she could have chosen more wisely.'

He watched her, his dark eyes perplexed. 'And what of you, Cassandra? Is there someone in your life, too?'

'You have been listening to rumour, I think?'

'More than rumours. Lord Christopher Hanley,

your uncle's friend, claims he saw you in Whitechapel with Lord Lindsay. A large section of society is heeding him.'

'Well, I have never played a big part in the life of the *ton* so it will suit me to be even more reclusive. What can they do, after all?'

'Believe me, attack is the best form of defence. Come with your sister and me to the Forsythe ball and stare the naysayers down.'

'Apart from sounding risky, did you consider the possibility you might be ousted because of your association with me?'

He laughed. 'My uncle is one of the richest men in England and he is dying. No one would chance offending the next heir to the dukedom.'

In that moment Kenyon Riley seemed more like Nathaniel Lindsay than he ever had before. Powerful. Certain. Unafraid.

Perhaps he was right. Cassie had already flouted convention with the keeping of her maiden name and no true proof of her being at Brown Street existed anywhere save with Lord Lindsay. She did not believe that Nathaniel would abandon her as she had him in Perpignan.

'Maureen is having a fitting for a new gown this afternoon. You should go with her for you have worn the shades of mourning for all the months that I have known you. Perhaps it is time to branch out and live a little?'

'You sound just like Reena.'

'If I do, it is because I care about you and because Lindsay is a good man, an honourable man.'

She nodded her head. 'I know.'

'He is also a man who would not ruin a woman's reputation lightly.'

'He didn't.'

'Good.'

When he left her office she leaned back in her chair and looked out over the street at the front of the house.

Nat was indeed much more honourable than he would think her to be, in the light of what had happened on the outskirts of Perpignan.

They had remained in Saint Estelle for almost two weeks, always putting off their leaving for yet another day so that they could walk to the hot pools above the village or to the abandoned cottage on the other side of the river and pretend that this was their house and their life. Entwined in each other's arms, the particular glow of lovers blocked out the rest of the world and the world became blurred and ill defined.

Until one morning when Cassie awoke to the knowledge that her menses had not come and her breasts felt sore and full and heavy.

Pregnant? She counted back the days and the weeks and always came up with the same conclusion. She was overdue and her body was telling her that things were changing inside.

Elation was her first thought and then caution. Caught out in the countryside in conditions that were hardly conducive for an early pregnancy she knew Nathanael would worry. So she said nothing.

In Perpignan she would see a doctor and then she would tell him. She knew the town and the people there. She felt at home in the narrow streets by the river. Her hand with the ruined finger crept to the secret she held in her stomach and she cradled the joy. Their child. A child born of love and of passion. Tears threatened, and she swallowed them away.

Five days later on the way into Perpignan she began to bleed. Only a little, but enough to make her understand that she needed to be somewhere quiet and peaceful, to simply stop and relax. Each morning for the past week she had felt sick on awakening and the nausea had not abated till the noon. She wanted a hot bath and a hot meal and a bed that she could stay in that was comfortable and safe.

She wanted a doctor's reassurance and the time to tell Nathanael that he would be a father, in a place where they were not looking over their shoulders for any sign of who followed them.

They had seen no trace of another since they had left Saint Estelle, always keeping away from the main roads and shadowing the rivers as they ran from the mountains down onto the plains below.

Perhaps they were safe now and whoever had been following them had given up completely. She knew Lebansart hailed from a place farther north. Had he realised the futility of chasing them and had returned home? She prayed that it might be so.

Taking the shaded alleys, they came into the outskirts of Perpignan at sunset and stopped on the left bank of the Basse River. The fortified walls stood before them and in the distance on a high citadel the Palace of the Kings of Mallorca sat, its limed walls pale in the last rays of sun.

Cassandra loved this place, with its warmth and its gentle winds off the sea. When first she had come she had been entranced to finally be able to speak the language of her mother and to feel the heat of the sun on her hair, the colours of this part of the world so different to the greyness of London.

Perpignan and the busy Mercier household had been a revelation, and the fact that she was only a cousin had made no difference to the generosity of her uncle. Celeste's mama, Agathe, had been dead a good two years so that was yet another thread that held the cousins together.

Another time.

A lost life.

A whole family gone.

She turned to look at Nathanael who sat leaning against a low stone wall, watching her.

'This was where I lived with Celeste's family. I came here to get well.'

'Hell!' His expletive was round as he stood. 'You never told me that. Would those at Nay have known of this?'

She shrugged, his anxiety seeping into her contentment. 'Perhaps they may have.'

'Then we cannot enter the town, Sandrine.'

'You think those who followed might find us here?'

'I know they will.'

The shadows around them moved in a way that was

suddenly dangerous, the branches taking on the outline of shapes of men in her mind. Never again. Never
again would she allow herself to be under some other
person's rule.

He must have seen her fear for he moved closer.
'We will strike north tomorrow along the coast and
find a ship to take us to Marseilles. I have friends
there.'

She shook her head. Another trek across the countryside and with the further promise of snow. The
reserves she had been storing up were suddenly no
longer there and now it was not just her life she had
to protect. She had to stop, the cramping pains in her
stomach no longer able to be denied and ignored. 'You
should leave, Nathanael. While you can. I cannot go
on.'

*It is me that they are after. Lebansart could pass
you on a street and not know your face. Thus far you
are safe.*

She wished her voice did not sound so afraid, the
cold air of an oncoming night making her shake. She
had killed Baudoin with her knife. She could not be
responsible for the death of Nathanael Colbert, too.
Not him. Breathing in, she suddenly knew just what
it was she must do. With all the effort in the world
she smiled.

'You have bought me home and it isn't as unsafe
as you imagine. Celeste's family has a position here,
a power. I can be protected.'

She should take off the marriage ring held in warm
white gold around her finger and give it back, but she

could not quite make herself do that. For the first time in a long while she felt virtuous.

'You cannot possibly think that a group of bandits whose secrets you know would stop pursuing you because of some aristocratic courtly authority? These people exist under far more brutal rule.'

Shaking her head, she placed one hand across his. She would go to the home of Celeste's father's best friend and his wife. She knew without doubt that they would keep her safe.

It all comes down to this, she thought, *his life and her child's safety. There was no room in any of it for her.*

The ache around her heart physically hurt as she gave in to all that she knew she must do.

'We have been flung together out of expedience and I thank you for the protection you have given me and for the things you have taught me, but...' She swallowed away the 'but' and began again. 'We are different in everything that we are and I want to go home, back to a life that I know. I am not used to such...a lack of luxury, you see, and eventually we would both feel embittered by our differences.'

Stifling grief, she looked directly at him, the stillness in him more worrying than any anger.

'Just like that?' he finally said, flatness in the words.

She nodded. 'It will be better for us both. I am sorry....' She could not go on, her hands spread in front of her gesticulating emptiness. Her smile was so tight it hurt the muscles in her cheeks.

They do not know you yet. They have no idea of exactly who you are.

'I have a comfortable life in Perpignan and I am tired of the squalor that we have needed to exist in.'

'I see.'

No, you do not see at all, Nathanael. You do not know what this is doing to my heart.

'We could meet sometimes, if you wish. I wouldn't be averse to that.'

'For what reasons, Sandrine? To demand my conjugal rights?'

She shook her head, his anger gathering in the storm clouds of his eyes. 'To reminisce.'

'Reminisce about all these weeks of memories that mean nothing to you or about the importance of material acquisitions? I think I shall say no.'

She could only guess at what he must think of her, one moment this and the next moment that. Disbelief flourished amongst fury as he lifted the blanket he slept on from his bag and rolled it out underneath a thick bush. 'We will talk again of this tomorrow when you have come to your senses. By then you may see the wisdom of my arguments and the half-witted nonsense in your own. The church, too, has strict and particular ideas about the sanctity of marriage.'

Then he simply turned away.

Cassandra's eyes felt heavy but she made herself stay awake, the moon much higher now and the true silence of early, early morning upon the grotto. They had made their beds on opposite sides of a small field of grass and he had not spoken to her again, but now he was asleep. She could hear it in his breathing and feel it in the way he had been so still for all of an hour.

She watched him from her place across the clearing, the strong lines of his body, the dark of his hair. She could not see his face because even in sleep he had not let go of his anger and had turned away from her, the knife on a bed of leather beside him. Readied.

He would protect her to the death. She knew this. He would give his life for her without even thinking of the payment.

Her chance. To escape. Her chance to leave him here, safe against the darkness while she attempted to creep into Perpignan alone and disappear. She did not know why she had not thought that Lebansart and his men would be waiting in the one place they guessed she might have returned to.

Stupid, she chastised herself. *You knew how dangerous they were, but you did not think and now you have placed Nathanael in danger also. Mortal danger.*

Carefully, she sat up, each fraction of movement as slow as she could make it, her breath shallow and light. Then she stood, again stopping as she came fully upright, only the wind in the trees and the far-off call of a night bird.

One step and then two, the shadows taking her beneath them, blocking out the moonlight and then an open space on the banks of the Basse, a track to a bridge across the river and the gate on the old fortified walls. Open. It had not been defended for hundreds of years, a relic of a medieval past when nothing was as safe as it was now.

She smiled at her thoughts given all that she was running from and kept to the dark side of buildings as she came into the town proper. She hadn't brought her bag because she did not want to lift it and hear the rustle of thick canvas. But she had brought her knife, tucked into her right sleeve in leather, the hilt extending from the thick fabric of her jacket.

Almost to the Rue des Vignes. Almost there.

Then a noise. Close. An arm snaked about her throat, cutting off breath, and the face of Guy Lebansart appeared next to her own.

'We thought you would come, Sandrine, although perhaps not quite so soon.'

The warmth of his palm as it caressed the line of her cheek made her skin crawl.

Nathaniel came awake to emptiness. He knew Sandrine was missing before he even looked, though her bag still stood beside her blanket.

Only a few minutes, he determined, the wool covering still slightly warm when he checked, but the wind had come up and she had used the noise from the trees to depart.

Last night they had not spoken at all after she had told him she needed to go on alone. He swore at the absurdity of everything and the nonsense of her beliefs. Did she truly think she could just fit in again to all that she had been and forget what was between them? Had all of the past days been some kind of elaborate deception to allow her passage into Perpignan, his presence a necessary one to alleviate the sense of danger? Only that?

Nat could not believe this to be true. There were other things that she had not told him, and he needed to find out exactly what they were.

Bundling all their things together, he stuffed them into an empty space between one of the bushes nearby. He would come back for them later, but it never hurt to cover your tracks, no matter how much of a hurry you were in; spying had at least taught him that.

She would have cut along the river, he was sure of it, to cross at the next bridge. From memory the Basse had more than one bridge spanning it and was swimmable in places, though he could not see her wanting to get wet. From there she would move inwards, and the town was not so big that a good search would be impossible. No. He just had to look carefully and hope like hell that she had made the place of her destination safely.

He tipped his head, listening, but there was no sound that was different from the wind on the water and the trees, no sound that alerted him to danger or compromise. Three o'clock. The quietest hour of the night. Jogging along the track until the first bridge, he then went down on his knees.

There he had it. A fresh print in the mud showing damaged soles. She had come this way. Again he tipped his head. Now there was only the noise of the water and the first spots of rain in the wind. Tracking. His forte. He had done this so many times over so many years, following so many quarries. This time, though, the stakes were raised and he knew he had to be very careful.

'What was in the document, Sandrine? The one Baudoin wanted me to see? Pierre said that he saw you reading them.'

'I do not remember.'

'Liar.' There was an unexpected laughter in Lebansart's voice as if they were playing a game that he liked. The taste of fear and panic was bitter in her throat, but there was something else again. Triumph, if she could name it. They had not mentioned Colbert at all.

Guy's voice was close as he loosened her hair. 'Perhaps you might tell me when we are alone, *ma chérie*?' His fingers digging into her arm belied his nonchalance and around him others lingered. More than a few others. Ten or twelve, she supposed, and behind them in the shadows more would be waiting.

'Silver-tongued Leb', he was called back at the compound. A man who spun a web around his prey without fuss or contretemps. He had not even drawn his own knife, leaving that to those about him, their sharp blades seen against the dimness.

She had lost. She had rolled her dice and lost. But she had kept Nathanael safe and away in the arms of sleep.

The commotion started as a low roar and then a louder clatter. The sound of a neck breaking and a knife jammed into breath and he was there, beside her, reaching out, the touch of him breaking her heart.

Nathanael. Already the others were circling behind him, quiet in the early dawn, like a pack of wolves waiting for the command to attack.

She did not let him speak; one word and they would kill him. One wrong sound and it would all be over.

Instead she got in first, swinging her left hand around to his face and opening his jaw with the sharpened edge of her marriage ring at exactly the same time another hit him from behind, the sound of metal against his skull crunching.

He bent over, shaking his head as he did so, trying to find vision.

Do not speak, Nathanael. Do not claim me.

She thought quickly. Lebansart had ties with the government that he would not wish to jeopardise. 'I have seen him before. He is a soldier of France so better to leave him alive. But do as you will, I really don't care.'

Looking away, she tipped her head towards her captor, trying to bring forth all of her womanly powers. If they killed Nathanael she would die as well, but the threat of the might of the military seemed to have done its job.

'We don't need the army after us. So blindfold him and bring him along.'

Another thump against flesh and she turned back, the blood from his jaw spilling over his shirt and his lips red raw from a wallop. He looked dazed, barely conscious. No blades though, no telltale sign of an injury that he would not recover from.

She laughed in relief, the sound bringing the attention of Lebansart back to her before he had the chance to change his mind. 'Perhaps we might find a place to speak, Guy.'

When his arm threaded round her and his hand cupped her breast she simply snuggled in.

'Sandrine, the whore.' She heard the voice of a man behind and knew that Nathanael would have known exactly what she allowed.

A whole lifetime of his years for a few moments of her shame. A tenable payment. She did not look back again as Lebansart led her away, his fingers closing in around the small shape of her ruined hand.

Nat came awake in a bed and a room, a priest at his side and the light of morning on his face.

'Finally you have woken, *monsieur*. You were found beside the river Basse six days ago and have been in and out of consciousness ever since. In truth, we did not think that you would survive, but we prayed and God has answered us our call.'

Six days.

Sandrine would be long gone.

His head ached and his sight seemed compromised. The wound on the side of his jaw smarted, and he put up his hand to feel it.

'We stitched it and it is healing.'

Sandrine. He remembered the look on her face as she had led the Frenchman away. Pleasure. Flirtation.

Relief. She had not even glanced back at him as she allowed the enemy everything.

Sandrine the whore.

He hated her, this woman who was his wife, hated her lies and her easy betrayal. He had not known her at all in the days of their flight from Nay. A stranger. A harlot. A cheat.

'There is someone waiting for you outside. He is an Englishman and he would like to talk with you. Do you feel up to this yet?'

When Nat nodded the priest rose and left. A moment later a tall man with sandy hair came through to stand beside the bed.

'I am Alan Heslop,' he said quietly, 'from the British Service, and I have come to see what you know of the Baudoin brothers. It seems you were at their compound and a fight ensued? I ask this of you because two of our agents were targeted and killed this past week, brothers whose names were on the letters taken by the Baudoins from the overturned carriage of Christian de Gennes. Letters that were known to have been in the compound.'

Didier and Gilbert Desrosiers were dead? Sandrine would have seen the documents and told of them, then. He stayed silent.

'My sources say there was a woman. A woman was reputed to have been there.'

He opened his mouth and then closed it. Even now, after all that had happened, he could not bring himself to betray her. If the British Service had word of her involvement they would hunt her to the ends of the earth. Garnering breath, he tried again.

'I saw no one. I left after Anton Baudoin shot me.' Lifting his shirt, he noticed the heightened interest of the newcomer. 'By all accounts, de Gennes's letters were at the compound, but I could find no trace of them.'

'Did you speak with Baudoin?'

'No. I was there in battle and there wasn't a chance of conversation before I killed him.'

'I see. You will start back for England next week. The Home Office has made arrangements for you to travel by ship, though I suppose you will need to answer more questions when you return.'

'Of course.'

'But for now you must rest. I will have warm broth sent in from the kitchen for you have lost a good deal of weight from the beating you received. It seems you were dropped in the river to drown, but your coat snagged on a pillar as the current took you away and a group of youths found you.'

'A lucky escape, then.'

'Perhaps.' The man's glance caught his own and without another word he left the room.

When he was gone, Nathaniel began to take stock of the wounds he had incurred. A heavily bandaged head, a broken right arm and two eyes that were so swollen it was hard to see.

Sandrine Mercier had betrayed both him and England to save herself.

Closing his eyes, he shut everything out and willed himself to survive.

On returning home, Nathaniel went straight to the family seat. His grandfather, the Earl of St Auburn, stood before him, a heavy frown upon his brow.

'A further scrape that you have no explanation for, and a newly made scar on your chin that looks like you have been in another fight. And to top it all off you have lost your grandmother's ring. An heirloom. Irreplaceable. I am almost seventy-three years old, Nathaniel, and you have never stopped disappointing me.'

Nat stood and finished his drink. It had been a bad idea to expect that William Lindsay might have welcomed him home after hard, long and lonely months abroad. Tonight, however, with the portrait of his father upon the wall above his head, Nat had had enough of such hostility.

'I shall be at Stephen Hawkhurst's for the next few weeks before going back to Europe, William.'

'Running away as usual. The St Auburn inheritance does not simply see to itself, you know. A small interest on your behalf as the one who will inherit the responsibility would not go unnoticed.'

'I am certain you are quite competent at the helm. I am also certain that any changes I made to the estate would only incense you, after all, for we have tried that track before.'

'Then take a wife, for God's sake, and settle down. You are old enough to be giving the estate some assurance of longevity, some hand into the future.'

A wife.

Nat almost laughed. He had a wife already and if he could have produced Sandrine Mercier at that moment he would have dearly loved to, if just to see the look of horror and disgust in his grandfather's eyes. But she had been lost to him in Perpignan, gone into the ether of betrayal, a woman who had not given trust a chance and who had flouted every principle of integrity.

Placing the glass carefully down on a small oak table beside him, Nathaniel tipped his head in parting and left the room.

Chapter Seven

Cassandra Northrup had come to the Forsythe town house on Chesterfield Street with her sister and Riley, just as Nathaniel had hoped she would not.

Tonight she had forsaken the colour of mourning and adorned herself in muted gold, like a flag of defiance, her eyes shining with fight. With her hair dressed and the gown complementing the sleek shades, she was the embodiment of all that Albi de Clare had once predicted.

Unmatched.

Original.

The girl in southern France only just seen through the woman she had become.

She neither fidgeted nor held on to her sister or Kenyon Riley for support, but stood there, chin up.

He doubted he had ever seen her look more beautiful than at this particular moment and when her eyes finally met his, Nathaniel knew without a shadow of doubt that the swirling rumours of a relationship between them had reached her ears.

Her sister appeared less certain, but Riley, positioned in the middle of them both, gave the impression of a cat who had just been offered a bowl of cream. Nat wanted to hit him.

'Let the games begin.' Hawk was hardly helping matters, and Reginald Northrup to one edge of the room was watching Cassie intently, as was Hanley.

Undercurrents and anticipation. Nat did not make any move towards the Northrup party whilst he waited to see what would transpire.

The older Forsythes reacted first, moving from Kenyon Riley to Maureen Northrup without a glance at the one beside them. Then Lady Sexton and her husband turned their backs. A cut direct from a woman who was known for her own dalliance was hardly lethal. But it was the next snub that did it.

Lydia Forsythe, the young hostess who had the most to thank Cassandra for given her recent brush with the chandelier, simply stood, right in front of her, the slender wine goblet she held tinkling to the ground, shattering into pieces.

The band ceased playing.

Silence descended, the inheld breath of a hundred guests slicing through movement, ruin taking the physical form of a woman in a glorious gown and sharp blue-green eyes. She stood very stiffly, the horror of all that was transpiring barely hidden upon her face, her mutilated fist tight wrapped in the folds of her golden skirt.

Despite trying not to, Nathaniel moved forward, the only motion in a room of stillness and those all around craned their necks to see just exactly what might happen next.

'Unfortunately, Miss Lydia Forsythe is a woman prone to histrionics,' he said as he reached Cassie, then he lowered his tone. 'However, if you act as if you do not care you might be able to salvage something of the evening yet.'

Cassandra was silent, dumbfounded, he supposed, by the way things had plummeted from bad to worse. Worry had furrowed a deep frown in the space between her eyes.

'The trick in it is to converse as if you have all the time in the world or at least smile. Your face at the moment suggests you believe in the ruin of your name and this is exactly what others here have come to see.'

To give Cassie her due, she did try, the glimmer of humour showing where before only a frown had etched her brow.

Her sister, however, picking up the undercurrents, began to help, droning on about the seasonal changes and the new buildings in Kew Gardens. Riley stood silent, the grin on his face infuriating.

'I always love the Palm House, of course, but I think the Water Lily House will be every bit as beautiful. They say when it is finished the giant Amazonian lily will flourish within it and that a child might sit on a leaf like a boat and not get wet at all. Imagine how huge it will be.'

Amazonian must have been a difficult word to say

for someone who could not hear properly, Nat determined, though Maureen's unusual pronunciation did have the effect of making Cassandra's lips turn upwards.

Around them the silence was beginning to change into chatter, the terrible scene that some might have hoped for fading into something unremarkable. Even Lydia Forsythe had pulled herself together, her mother signalling to the band to begin to play again and the young hostess making an overture of civility towards the Northrups in the form of a genuine smile.

A waltz. Without waiting for another moment, Nat asked Cassie for the dance and they stepped on to the floor.

'Thank you.' She held him away as they moved, a large space between them, circumspect and prudent. They did not dance as lovers might, though beneath his palms the warmth of the old Sandrine lingered. He tried to ignore it.

'Your uncle appears to welcome the demise of your name.'

'I think his enmity has something to do with his relationship with my mother.'

'It was his friend Hanley who told the world he saw us together.'

Her direct glance faltered. 'I have heard.'

'What would Reginald Northrup have to gain by discrediting you?'

She shook her head. 'Not the title, for Rodney is the heir apparent.'

He might have asked of her movements after Per-

pignan then, just to see what she might tell him, but
the colour in her cheeks was returning. Besides, the
middle of a crowded dance floor was not a place he
wanted to hear an answer in.

'He is far more wealthy than my father, so money
cannot be a factor.'

'A man with no obvious motive is more dangerous
than those who have one, and if your nocturnal wan-
derings are known to him then it would be wise to be
careful. Or cease altogether.'

She tipped her head, her expression puzzled, and his
fingers tightened around hers in a will all of their own.

He was so beautiful and so known.

The corners of Cassie's heart squeezed into pain as
he watched her, grey ringed with just a touch of dark
blue. In his arms, here in the middle of a crowded ballroom, she felt completely safeguarded, even given the
poor start to the evening. No one could touch her. No
one dared. The exhilaration was surprising.

'Come with me next time, Nathaniel. Come and
see just what it is that the Daughters of the Poor do.'

His lazy smile was lethal. 'I have already discovered some part of it in the bawd house off Whitechapel
Road.'

'No. Not that. It's the successes you need to see.'
She thought of the toddler Katie, her injuries fading
and her smile blooming again. It was these things that
she wanted him to know of. A new beginning. Another finer path away from the chaos that had once
consumed them.

'Please.' She did not wish to beg, but this moment might be her only chance to make him understand that sometimes with endeavour honour could be reinstated.

'When?'

The anger in the room and all her problems melted away with that one small question. He would allow her a chance? For the first time that night her breath was not tight and the beat of her heart quickened from something other than fear.

'As soon as I know I shall send you word.'

'Very well.'

'Wear black.'

Nothing now was the same between them as it had once been, but inside of her a bright warmth bloomed. The papers that held them together had probably long been lost and she no longer had his ring, but there it was, that same feeling from France that pulsed in every part of her body.

Love me. Love me. Love me.

Just a little. Just a bit. Just enough to allow the possibility of an understanding and forgiveness.

'How long has your charity been running for?' His question cut through all her fantasies.

'Two years now. I found two young girls wandering in Regent Street and on enquiry discovered they had been brought in from the country and then lost.'

'So you took them home?'

'Actually, no. I found out the place they had been stolen from and returned them. That was how it all began. Sometimes, though, it is not so easy. Sometimes young women are lost to us or put to work in the seedy houses of London and it is hard to recover them again. The only real chance of saving anyone is finding them before they are sold.'

'That sounds difficult.'

'It is. People do not want to know that this is happening. Here in the grand salons of London they turn the other cheek because looking would be too harsh upon their sensibilities, and if Lydia Forsythe almost swoons away on seeing me, imagine what might happen if she were to confront such a truth. It is my belief that the Victorian model of virtue strips females of the things they should be capable of knowing.'

'A fierce criticism?'

'But a true one.'

'I heard that you were in Paris after…us.'

Had he not been holding her she might have tripped, the danger of letting her guard down so very real. It was the seeing him again and gaining his help in a moment when she might have been crucified without him. Everything they had been to each other imperilled all she had become alone, and the decisions she had made after he had been dragged away by Lebansart's men influenced things again.

It was foolish to imagine they could go back to what they had once had for it was far too late for that.

'I heard that you and Acacia Bellowes-Browne have an agreement.'

The muscle in his jaw tightened. 'My grandfather's hope, no doubt. I have no wish to be married again.'

The words were underlined with a raw harshness, and Cassie had cause to believe him.

Once was enough.

The dance lost some of its appeal and she pulled back. She wished she might have been able to ask him other things, important things, things that might have led to a discussion on how he perceived her ability to look after a child. His child. She took a deep breath, smiling at her sister as she swept past them in the arms of Kenyon Riley.

'They look pleased with themselves. Riley was buying all the drinks at White's the other evening and alluding to a happy event that might be occurring in his life soon. Perhaps this is it?'

'I hope so. My sister deserves each contentment that comes her way. She is sweet and kind and true.'

'Unlike you?'

Now the gloves were off.

'If it helps at all I would do things differently if I was able to begin again.' Her eyes ran across the scar that snaked down from the side of his mouth.

Unexpectedly, he laughed. 'Do you ever think back to the days before we reached Perpignan?'

All the time. Every day. Many minutes of every day.

She stayed quiet.

'I returned to Bagnères-de-Bigorre last year when I was across the border in Spain. The high bath was still as beautiful.'

'With the witchery of steam?'

Their eyes met, etched with a memory of the place. Together, close, lost in each other's arms through all the hours of the night and day. The delight of what had been jagged through her stomach and then went lower.

'What happened to us, Sandrine?'

Loss made her look away and she was happy when the music ground down to a final halt. After shepherding her back into the company of her sister and Kenyon Riley, Nathaniel quickly left. She saw him move across to stand with Stephen Hawkhurst, interest in his friend's eyes as he glanced over towards her. It was said that Hawk was entwined with the British Service, too, and there was more in his perusal than she wanted to see.

Raising her fan, she glanced away, the balancing act of appearing all that she was not and within the company of her sister, who positively glowed with delight, taking its toll.

Acacia Bellowes-Browne was here, too, standing next to Nathaniel with her hand lightly resting upon his arm. Cassandra heard the tinkle of her laugh as she leaned closer and saw Nathaniel's answering smile.

A beautiful, clever woman with her past intact. The bright red of her gown contrasted against the dark brown of her hair. The hazel in her eyes had had poems written of them. Maureen told her that once, on returning from a weekend away at a friend's country home, and Cassie still remembered the astonishment that the eyes of a lady might incite such prose from grown men.

She was certainly using her eyes to the best of their advantage at this moment, flashing them at Nathaniel Lindsay with a coquettish flirtation and using her fan to tap him lightly on the hand as if in reprimand for some comment he had just made. Intimate. Familiar. Congenial.

Turning away from it all, Cassandra recognised with a shock that envy was eating away at her.

What happened to us, Sandrine?

Life had happened with its full quota of repayment and betrayal. Jamie had happened, too; the responsibility of a child and the overriding and untempered love that would protect him from everything and everyone. No matter what.

'Could I have the pleasure of this next dance?' Stephen Hawkhurst stood before her, his eyes probing. 'Though perhaps I should warn you I am no great mover before you give me your reply.'

'Thank you.' She liked the quiet way he spoke. 'I, too, have not had a lot of practice at these things.'

'Then we shall bumble around together. Nat was always the most proficient dancer out of the three of us at school,' he said as they took to the floor, another waltz allowing them the ease of speech.

'The three of you?'

'Lucas Clairmont was the other, but he has been in the Americas for years now making his fortune in the timber trade. None of us have families that we could count on, you see, so the connection was strong.'

He looked at her directly as he said this. 'Adversity can either pull people together or it can tear them apart, would you not agree?'

Cassie dropped her glance. Words beneath words. Nathaniel had the knack of using this technique, too.

'Indeed I would.'

'Could I give you a bit of advice, then?' He waited till she nodded.

'Sometimes in life risks can deliver the greatest of rewards, but do not be too patient about the time allotted to reap them or you may lose out altogether.'

'I am not well received in society, sir. Tonight is just a small taste of that fact. To reap anything apart from disparagement might be impossible for me.'

He laughed. 'Look around you. How many men do you see who would not take risk over the mundane, who would not say to themselves if only I hadn't played it so safe as they look in the mirror in their preparations for yet another night out in society in the company of manners and propriety?'

Cassandra breathed out hard. 'Do you know anything of what went on between Nathaniel and me at Perpignan?'

'He once told me that what you did and what you said you did were two different things.'

She shook her head.

'In that he is wrong. There were others...others who died because of the mistakes that I made.'

The names of those she had consigned to the afterlife came to mind, people planted through loyalty into a land that was not their own and then murdered for their service. Aye, the world ran red with the blood of martyrs and hers had been included in that.

Lebansart.

Silver-tongued Leb.

His knife had been sharp and his words were sharper still.

Bitch. Traitor. Murderer.

Once she had been none of those things and now she was all of them, marked for anyone to see. Her penance.

She smiled through the anger and held Hawkhurst's returning puzzlement as though it were only of a small importance, a trifling consideration.

'Do you ever think, my lord, that when the world shifts in its truths sometimes one just cannot go back?'

'Often,' he replied, 'and I believe it is a shame.' As they turned with the music, Cassandra caught the face of Nathaniel watching them, his eyes devoid of feeling.

'Cassandra Northrup is nothing like I expected her to be,' Stephen said as they stood to one side of the room beside a pillar. 'In fact, I would go as far to say that after that conversation I am half in love with her myself. But she's hiding things. Big things. You can see it in her eyes when she looks over at you, Nathaniel, and she does that often.'

Nat did not want to hear this, for the cords that had held them together had been cut so irrevocably.

'Why did she go to Paris after Perpignan, Nat? She did not arrive back in England until eighteen months after you did. Why didn't she just come home?'

Lebansart. Sandrine's face turned up to his as she had left, his hands curled into hers. He wished he did not care any more, but the days beneath the Pyrenees had defined their relationship, and he found he could not let her go.

He hadn't slept with another woman since. Not one. Just that single thought made him furious. Was he destined to be for ever trapped in his feelings from the past, unable to move on with all that was being offered now? A man for whom the holy words of matrimony meant a loyalty that remained unquestioned and unbroken.

'Well, I think it is safe to say that the youngest Northrup daughter has weathered her rocky start this evening, Nat, and I can well see why. Dressed in gold she looks like something out of a fairy tale.'

A line of young swains milled about Cassandra, though she did not seem enamoured with the fact, for her frown was noticeable even at this distance.

But Nathaniel had had enough of conjecture and, excusing himself summarily, he wound his way through the substantial crowd and out of the wide front door.

Hailing his coachman, he settled into the cushioned seats and closed his eyes. For the first time ever in his life he was at a loss as to what he should do next and he didn't like the feeling one little bit.

Cassandra Northrup threw him completely, that was the trouble. And when he had held her in the dance all he had wanted was to bring her closer. Her scent, her eyes, the feel of her skin against his.

She was a lethal concoction of beauty, brains and betrayal, but something else lingered there, too. Vulnerability, sadness and fright. What was it she was hiding? What had happened after Perpignan?

Stephen had liked her and so did Acacia. In fact, even given the collective anger of society against her earlier in the evening, he had never met a soul who did not admire her personally, apart from her uncle.

An enigma.

And she was still his wife despite all that she thought to the contrary.

He shouldn't see her again, but he knew that he would, her invitation to accompany her at night through the back streets on her charity business too tempting to turn down. What if she was hurt? She was not strong enough to rebuff a grown man who meant business, a fact he had found out in the house in Whitechapel when he had easily subdued her.

Another thought surfaced.

She had changed in four years. He could see it in her stance and in her eyes and in the way she had held the knife in the room on Brown Street in the darkness.

He had tried to teach her a few of his best tricks of attack in the final days before they had come down into Perpignan. The blade she had taken from Baudoin was a good weapon, light and comfortable in her fist.

'Grip hard and keep it upwards for this one.' He had turned her slightly, one foot away from each other. 'Position your body behind the knife, for if you lose concentration even for a moment you will be dead.'

'Like this?' She had taken to the lesson with a surprising accuracy, her footwork balanced and the line of her arm strong. Perhaps it was the legacy of months of being a captive, *never again* stamped into every movement.

'Being left-handed will give you an advantage because your attacker will not expect it so use this quickly before he has time to define it and go in under the arc of his forearm. Close contact negates skill to some extent so aim for the artery here on the outside of the leg. He will be protecting everything else.'

So far he had explained the rudiments in the slow motion of tutelage, but now he grabbed a stick that looked solid and stood before her. 'Try it on me.'

She shook her head. 'I can't.'

'Why not?'

'I might hurt you.'

He began to laugh, the sound echoing around the small clearing, and Nat thought right then and there that this is what it felt like to be happy, here, with a beautiful girl dressed as a boy in the mountain passes of the Pyrenees.

'You are a woman,' he managed to say when he finally found his breath, 'and I have been at it a while.'

'Why did you start?' She had lowered the blade and faced him, small curls of gold-red that had escaped her plait dancing in the wind.

'Belonging, I think.' He could not believe he had been so honest and that an answer to a question he had often asked himself should have been as self-evident. 'My parents died when I was young and after that...'

'You had trouble finding yourself.' Sheathing the knife, she came forward and wrapped her arms about him. Tight and warm. 'I was the same. After Mama it seemed as though I had no compass.'

'No true north,' he answered softly.

Her eyes fell to his lips and the smile she gave him held invitation as he brought his mouth across her own. They knew nothing of each other and everything, the truth of their bodies speaking in a way words never could, telling secrets, finding the honesty. They had been hurt and they had survived. Right now it was enough.

All he could do was to keep her safe.

Chapter Eight

❧❧❧

The note came on the third day after the Forsythe ball.

Tonight. 11:00 p.m. Wear black.

That was it. No directions. No meeting point. He held the letter up against the light and looked at her handwriting. Small and evenly shaped, no flourish of curve or wasted embellishment. No signature.

She would come here, he was sure of it, because there was no other place that had been mooted. Perhaps she expected trouble and to give an exact location might have exacerbated it. Black clothes indicated hiddenness and the fate of the man murdered at Brown Street came to mind.

The Daughters of the Poor seemed to be involved in more than the usual charity work of supplying funds. The faces of the women found near the Thames pointed to the dangers those antagonising the underbelly of London posed. One wrong move and Cassandra could be joining them, her throat cut from one side to the other.

Swearing, he crossed to the cupboard and unlocked his guns. He would be prepared for the same force others hadn't been and if anyone crossed his path and threatened Cassandra... For the first time in a long while he felt a sense of energy and release, and a vitality that had been lost in France. His eyes went to the clock. Almost six. Five hours to wait.

He was dressed in black from head to foot as she came through his window, the effect making him appear even more dangerous than he normally did.

'We will be back well before dawn and I do not expect trouble, but if it comes then I should probably warn you that...' She made herself stop babbling by an enormous effort of will. She was nervous, of him, of being here, of Nathaniel Lindsay looking so much like he had done in the Languedoc, the battered edge of a soldier in his clothes.

'I have nothing else planned,' he drawled and smiled, the languid, beautiful smile he had given her in Saint Estelle and in Bagnères-de-Bigorre before they had made love and she had forgotten that the world existed.

Shaking her head, Cassandra tried to clear her mind of the past. The past years had been so busy with taking care of Jamie and of trying to protect others that she had barely left a moment for herself. The woman in her ached for Nathaniel's touch, even though she knew she had long since forfeited the desire for him to care.

'I have been told of a place where young women are being kept against their will.'

'Who informed you?'

'The woman who lives in a house across the road.'

'And you can trust her?'

'As much as I can trust anybody.' She hoped he could not hear the hollow uncertainty as well as she could. Last time at Whitechapel a trap had been set and she hoped that it would not be the case again tonight.

'Are you armed?'

'Yes.' Lifting the material of her sleeve, she allowed him to see the knife in a leather sheath. He was good at hiding surprise, she determined, for not a single muscle in his face changed in reaction.

'Dangerous?'

The word had her chagrin rising. 'I am not the same person you met in France and I do not wish to be either. I shall never again be beholden to another and if you want to rescind your offer of help because of such an admission then I will understand.'

'I don't.'

Swallowing, Cassie tried to regain a lost balance. She was seldom off guard with anyone other than him, her certainty coming easily and without too much thought. 'I will be in charge.' She needed to regain the lead.

He nodded.

'Good.'

Sometimes, she mused, *I do not like who I have become, this person who is hard-hearted and tough-minded.* Her thoughts went to Acacia, the beautiful woman whose eyes had had poems written about them, and she frowned.

The crossroads in life had taken her in directions that had not all been her own choice and once she had traversed some pathways there was no going back. The burning boats of chance. Ludicrous to wish for some literary offering from a man, but there it was. She did. And not just any man, either, but the one who stood before her now, his pale grey eyes shaded, dressed entirely in black.

She gathered her words in carefully. 'I do not expect trouble, but sometimes it comes anyway. If it does, I will hold you in no account for the protection of my life.'

Nat could hardly believe the detachment she laced those words with. 'Because you no longer see me as your husband?'

The rush of red upon her cheeks surprised him before she turned away, a scarlet tide rising from her throat. Not all indifference, then. Already she had opened the window and climbed through into the cold darkness.

A carriage was waiting at the end of the street, a hackney cab with a driver who did not turn to greet them, but looked straight ahead.

'I pay him well for silence,' she clarified as they got in. 'The fewer people involved in this the better.'

'Does your sister ever help you in these night-time sojourns?'

'Of course not.' Shock was inherent in every syllable.

Suddenly he understood. 'How ruined does society imagine you to be?'

He caught the deep frown on her forehead through the gloom. 'Very. Societal judgement on the moral poverty inherent in prostitution holds a power that is difficult to fight.'

'But you are trying to?'

She shook her head. 'I help those without prospects or a place to live and most of these young women see their chosen profession in very different terms than those of wealth and power have a wont to.'

Nathaniel paused, trying to understand exactly what it was she was saying. 'You condone this activity? I thought you rescued such women.'

'The Daughters of the Poor encourages financial and social independence. Sometimes the only way of doing that is to make certain that those we aid are safe in their work.'

'You help them remain on the streets?'

'As opposed to leaving them in the throes of a fourteen-hour day inside a cold dank sweatshop run by punitive men.'

'That, I suppose, is another way to look at it.'

'The ideal of refined and protected ladies who are not only good, but who are to know nothing save for what is good is workable only for the rich, though some might say it is repression with a different face.'

At that he did laugh because he had never had a conversation quite like this with a woman. Such discourse was freeing and he wondered how far she would take her arguments.

'You are an advocate of sex for pleasure rather than for procreation? A dangerous threat to male authority?'

'Look around you, Nathaniel. Women, making their way in the world by the use of their bodies, are a highly visible aspect of our society now. The hope of the Daughters of the Poor is to keep them unharmed.'

Her use of his name was soft and familiar and when the carriage lurched to throw Cassandra against him, his arms closed around her in a movement all of their own.

Protected. Like you were not.

The scent of soft knownness was intoxicating, a small familiarity amongst everything that was changing as the carriage hurtled through the darkness of London's poorer areas.

Cassandra smiled. Nathaniel had never been a man to step back from risk—she had seen that again and again in France, and now even after a conversation of ideas that he could not have been brought up to believe in, it wasn't debate he was offering, but comfort.

A generous man. A generous lover, too. She sat up and away from him. 'You did not marry again?'

'No.'

'You did not wish to?'

He was silent.

'I thought you might be dead after Perpignan.' Cassie tried to keep the terror from her tone.

I went to Paris to look for you, to scour the streets for every face that might have been yours. I stayed there for as long as I could manage it and even as I left I looked back.

'Lebansart's men made certain I could not call for help when they dumped me by the river. When I finally awoke I was in the company of friends and taken by boat to Marseilles.'

'But you never told anyone about me?'

He shook his head.

'I am half sick of shadows,' said The Lady of Shalott.

These words went around and around Cassandra's mind, the refrain plucked from Tennyson as he balanced desire against reality. With more courage she might have told Nathaniel of Jamie and of Paris and of searching for him ever since he was lost to her. She might have reached out, too, in the darkness and simply laid his hand upon her heart so that he heard the strong beat of want and need. And reply.

But Cassie did none of these things as the carriage drew to a halt and the seedy backwater streets came into view—the call of the driver, the light rain against the cobbles making everything slick-wet and the moon far behind a bank of clouds ensuring darkness.

Her world. The mirrored shadows. And beyond that the river, sludge-grey as it ran sluggish out to a freedom at sea; neither Camelot nor any other kingdom of dreams.

'Be on your guard,' she whispered as they made their way on foot down an alleyway, the high and close buildings leaning in, every window hung with the remains of dirty washing flapping in a dirty breeze.

A woman met them almost instantly. 'There,' she said and pointed to a door, the paint peeled and the knocker broken. 'They have been here a few days and they are back now. I seen a tall man go in there a while ago and he has not come out again since.'

Nat pulled a knife from his boot.

'He were dressed well, too,' she returned. 'He will be in the room at the rear.' Taking a coin, their informant left, her shawl high up around her hair as she scurried off into the night.

Nathaniel looked around to make certain no one else was watching them. 'Stay behind me, Sandrine.' She had insisted that she would be in charge, but he was pleased to see that she obeyed instantly and moved to let him pass. A tall and well-dressed stranger who was up to some nefarious deed. Could this be the man the urchin by the river had spoken of? The corridor inside was narrow, many closed doors leading off it.

Raising his hand, Nat pointed at keys dangling in a door that was left partly ajar. These people were not expecting any company. They were also patently amateurs. His hopes faded.

He was inside in a moment and he knew without asking a question that the two youths before him were insignificant within the chain of command. Both were young and both were unarmed, the expressions on their faces frozen.

On a bed no bigger than a cot a young woman sat crying, her hat beside her and her hair unbound.

'Who the hell are you?'

'Will Fisher, sir,' the one nearest to him stammered, 'and this is my brother. He was stupid enough to believe the Lytton gang might pay him a sovereign for a girl new in from the country and he brought her here. Now that I have talked some sense into him we don't know what to do with her.'

'Is this right?' He addressed this query to the girl and she nodded. 'Did they hurt you?'

'No, sir.'

'Why did you bring her to this place?' He addressed this question to the older brother.

'Kyle Lytton uses it as a hideaway. Jack saw them here over the past few days and thought they were still about.'

'How old are you?'

All three answered at once. The brothers were seventeen and eighteen, respectively, and the girl but fourteen.

'Get out.' This was said to the brothers and they did not tarry for a moment, moving past with the look of felons unexpectedly excused from the gallows.

Cassie was already at the girl's side. 'So you are not hurt in any way?'

'No, ma'am. The coach was late and they only just brought me here. Or the younger one did. His brother was furious and arrived straight away after.' She burst into loud and noisy sobs. 'And now it's dark and I don't know where to go or what to do…and Da will be furi-

ous if I arrive back again with nothing in me hand…'
At that thought she could barely carry on.

'What is your name?'

'Sarah Milgrew, ma'am.'

'Well, Sarah, you can stay with me tonight and tomorrow we will find you a place. We have our carriage
outside on the next street.'

'I canna afford much for a room, ma'am, but I can
sew like an angel, Miss Davis says, and am quick with
it.'

'A useful trade and most sought after.'

'My sister came to London some weeks ago and
we have not heard from her again. I had hoped to try
and find her.'

Nat's mind went back to the two girls pulled from
the river. 'Did you sew for her?'

He saw Cassandra's eyes fasten on his face, a small
frown building on her forehead.

'I did, sir. She left with one of my dresses on and another in her bag. She said she would show people what
I do here and find a room for both of us. Da took her to
the coach up to London and we had no word after that.'

Both the girls from the river had been well attired,
but there was a touch of the country about them. Could
this be the lead that he was after?

'And the coach comes into…?'

'Gracechurch Street, sir. It's five hours' travelling in
good weather from Wallingford and more if it is wet.
That's where the young man met me and said he could
help, but when he brought me here I was afeared…' She

clutched her small bag tightly and looked around the room, drab and furnitureless save for the bed.

What connection could these girls have with a man who was obviously from London? Could something have happened in their home town to lead them to each other?

Wallingford was just outside Reading. He filed the name in his mind to be considered later, but right now he wondered how often Cassandra Northrup took it on herself to bring girls like this one home. Many times he surmised by the ease in which she gathered her up and showed her through the door.

In the carriage the young woman seemed to fold into herself and lean against the far corner, a pose which spoke of hopelessness, implying the difficulty of all she had been through. But at least they had arrived in time. Observing Cassandra's care, Nat knew that circumstances had not been anywhere near as lucky for her.

The same awareness that he had experienced back in France all those years before wound into the middle of his chest, and he forced it down. These thoughts were nonsensical because he had no place in her life now, nor she in his.

He felt anger as she raised her eyes to look at him, the street lamps illuminating the deep shadows of dimple in her cheeks, and was glad to see the gates of the Northrup residence when they came into sight, the fat-bodied hawks on each side swathed in vines.

As the carriage stopped the front door was thrown open and two maids hurried down the stairs to greet them. They had done this before, Nat thought, as Miss

Milgrew was dispatched without fuss or bother into their capable hands, the trio then disappearing up the wide front staircase and into the house.

Cassandra was still sitting in the carriage, but had moved on to the seat opposite, pulling the door closed in a way that suggested she required privacy.

'If your estate or town house has any need of competent staff, we have a number of girls I could recommend who could well do with a job.'

This was the last thing he thought she might say, though as he leant forward he had to stop himself from drawing closer.

'Accompany me to the Herringford ball next week, Sandrine.'

'Why?'

'Because I want you to.' And he did. Desperately.

'Acacia Bellowes-Browne may object, my lord, and the rest of society will almost certainly be astonished.'

'You would let that worry you?'

'I try to stay out of the notice of others. I have limited the occasions that I come into the public sphere and the two times I have done so lately have both been difficult.'

'Society does not quite know what to make of you, which could be a bonus if you use it wisely. I am certain that your charity would benefit.'

'I am not so sure. The Daughters of the Poor relies on the generosity of those of wealth to give donations towards ruin without ever having to confront it.'

She always surprised him, he thought, always made

him feel alive in a way he seldom had been in years. Her dimples. Her hair edging her face in curls.

'I can protect you.'

His words fell into the silence as she pushed the door open and escaped outside in one fluid movement. Once there she stopped and spoke quietly.

'I can protect myself, Nathaniel, but I thank you for your help tonight.'

But he did not leave it there. 'If a ball is too public, come to a private dinner, then, and tell me why I should make a donation to your endeavours.'

'I am certain that would be most inappropriate...'

'A hefty donation...' he added when she still hesitated.

'Very well.'

'A carriage will be sent for you the day after tomorrow at eight.'

She nodded quickly and then she was gone, pacing towards the front stairs of the Northrup mansion with the singular purpose of retreat. He watched her until the door shut and her shadow flitted briefly against the thin curtains of the downstairs salon.

My God, she should have declined his invite, she thought as she gained her room and leaned against the doorframe. She ought to be downstairs in the room off Alysa's laboratory, helping the others settle Miss Milgrew in for the night, but she could not risk letting anyone see the panic that was making her hands shake and her heart beat faster.

Nathaniel Lindsay made her careless and he made

her feel things that she should not: warm things, hopeful things, things that held her both in thrall and in fear. Running her fingers across her brow, she felt the clammy sweat of dread. None of these hopes were for her and to imagine that they were would be to simply ruin everything that was.

She had a life, a good life, a worthwhile life. In the past years she had managed to find a way through adversity and to experience...contentment.

Cassie smiled at the word. Contentment. To anyone else such an emotion might be perceived to be a bland and worthless thing. But to her it was everything; a way forward, a light after the darkness and the beacon that called her on each and every day. After Nay part of her had shrivelled up and died and after Perpignan joy was an emotion she thought never to know again. But she had known it with Jamie, holding him close against her breast in Paris where she had delivered him at night, the cold fear of aloneness failing to douse the warmth and love she was consumed with.

Jamie had allowed her a purpose, a new beginning, a way back.

And now here in London all these years later another chance was being offered. Nathaniel had held her in the carriage as if he would like to offer more than a donation, but she did not dare to believe in such a promise. Not yet. Not now. Not when anyone on seeing father and son together would realise that there was no question of paternity.

The risk of everything had her sitting, her head between her legs, trying to find the breath she had forgotten to take.

'I can protect you.'

What did Nathaniel mean when he spoke of protection? The protection of marriage? The protection of being a mistress? The protection of lust and need translated into the flesh, a transient and momentary connection that would wither as soon as he saw the marks upon her breast.

Traitor.

No man could want to make love to an embodiment of betrayal. Not even one who had seen her before, whole and beautiful.

She crossed to the mirror, making certain that the door catch was on before she undid the buttons on her shirt. The cuts stood out, dark red against pale, three long slices of agony.

Lebansart's legacy.

'Tell me what was in the documents, Sandrine. Tell me and live.'

She had recited the names without further hesitation: her child's safety or that of two faceless men whom she had never met? There was no real struggle, a fact that she was to relive over and over in nightmares that wouldn't fade. She had stood there with the blood from her breast sticky against her fingers and she had itemised all that she had seen.

He wrote her words carefully in a book with a brown leather binding and a quill whose feathers had seen better days. The ink had stained his finger with black.

Little details. Remembered. Her voice had shaken as she spoke.

'Good. Very good. You were worth the trouble.' Those were his words as he had left the room.

Leaving her to die, slowly, from a loss of blood. But he had no notion that she was her mother's daughter and that she would know exactly what to do to lessen the flow and survive. A heavy wad of sheet and two long belts wrapped tight across them before lying face down on the thick mat and willing herself out of panic.

Survival. She breathed as shallowly as she could and tried not to move at all. And then after a few more hours she began to feel less lightheaded and warmer, the quilt she had heaped upon herself an added comfort and the noon-day light at the window spilling across her.

It had taken her another hour to find the energy to leave the room and make her way into the street. A doctor on a visit to a patient had found her and bundled her into his carriage and after that she struggled with living for a very long time.

Except for Jamie. Except for the growth of a child, Nathanael's child, the only thing anchoring her to the world as everything spiralled into despair and hopelessness.

Her uncle's friend had bought her a ticket to Paris as soon as the fever left out of respect for the Mercier family. He had arranged for his small house in Montmartre to be opened for her and sent two maids and a butler along to help her in her quest for independence.

She did not mention her pregnancy and allowed

him no notion of her own family back in London. She needed to think and to plan. She needed to find Nathanael if she could and she needed to be well away from Lebansart.

The house was quiet and situated in a street not far from the Sacré-Coeur, with a view across the rooftops of the city. Even with the beauty of white marble washed in rain she was lonely and sad, shock reaching into the depths of her soul.

And then one day whilst sitting in a park, wrapped warmly against the capricious springtime winds, a colourful bird had come to sit on the branch of a shrub in front of her and her baby had moved.

Life returned. Hope blossomed. The want to survive overrode the desire to simply cease to be, and she recovered.

Rebuttoning her shirt, Cassie looked back at herself in the mirror. No longer as thin. No longer as sad. No longer hobbling into each successive hour with the burden of betrayal heavy on her shoulders. The Daughters of the Poor had given her life a purpose and Jamie had given her body a heart. She could not endure uncertainty again. If she went to Nathaniel's dinner tomorrow night she would tell him she couldn't.

It was that simple.

Chapter Nine

Nothing was simple.

Nathaniel was dressed down tonight, his clothes less formal, the unbuttoned white collar of his shirt bold against the dark of his skin, a loose garment that gave him a sense of danger and familiarity. Cassie knew that it was more than scandalous to come to his house at night and alone, but both want and need had brought her here. Shaking away doubt, she moved inside. She was not about to give in to the narrow confines of Victorian rules, and besides, in the eyes of God they were married.

'I am glad that you came.'

His house was well appointed, every piece of furniture in sight beautifully wrought. Because she was so nervous she picked up a small bowl on a side stand, admiring the colourful flowers that marched around the rim. It was the one thing that did not look eminently English.

'I remember these designs from the marketplace at Perpignan. I always liked them.'

His eyes today were the shade of well-worn slate and warmer than usual. She wished he had been plainer, less intimidating and wished, too, that she might have worn some other dress than the one she had on, the starched blue silk too grand and stiff for this occasion.

'I have a fire going in the middle salon and some white wine.'

Nodding, she followed him. The fire sounded inviting though she was determined to refuse any drink at all. *Keep your wits about you*, she said to herself, *and understand that he will want explanation of what happened in Languedoc.*

The new room was more imposing than the last. A rich floral carpet was laid on the floor, the deep colour in it matching the heavy curtains at the windows. All around every wall mirrors and pictures abounded and, as in his library, there were shelves of books stacked almost to the ceiling. A generous fireplace blazed at one end and it was here that he led her. Two leather seats had been positioned opposite each other, a small table between them with fluted glasses upon it.

The apprehension of being here was growing by the second. A portrait of a woman in full riding regalia graced the nearest wall, and when he saw her looking he smiled.

'My mother loved horses.'

'She was very beautiful.'

'Indeed.' The talk then tailed down into silence, a thousand other things to say beneath the polite banter and no way to voice them.

I love you. I never stopped loving you.

For one horrible moment Cassie thought she had blurted the words out, bare and naked in their truth, and shock crawled up her spine, caught in the gap of honesty.

'Please, do sit down.' He waited until she complied before doing so himself, pouring two drinks and placing one before her. 'How is Miss Milgrew settling in?'

A different topic completely and one she was pleased to speak of. 'Sarah has been a godsend and has begun teaching the other girls the fine art of sewing.'

'Is there any sign of the sibling?'

'No. It seems she has quite disappeared. You asked if she sewed for her sister the other night and I thought the question odd. Why was that?'

'The bodies of two young women were pulled from the Thames a month back and no one claimed them. Both were dressed in finely sewn gowns.'

'You think it could be her lost sister, then? I see.'

'Do you, Sandrine? Do you see how searching out the damaged women of London may have more consequences than you can imagine? One day you could end up in the river yourself.'

'I take every precaution...'

'And you think that is enough against an opponent who is bigger and stronger than you.' He no longer sounded as mellow. In fact, now when she caught his glance she looked away quickly, so much of Nathanael Colbert before her. The soldier. The lover. The man who had watched her betray him, blood running down his chin.

'Where is the Colbert part of your name from?'

'It is a lesser title of mine. The St Auburn earldom contains many and as the heir I have an entitlement to them.'

'A real name? Not made up?'

'Made up like Sandrine Mercier was, you mean?'

'My cousin Celeste often called me Sandrine and Mercier was her surname.'

'I know. I went back and spoke to what was left of the family. An uncle, Gilles Mercier, informed me of the demise of Celeste and her father, though he said nothing of you.'

'Celeste had that knack of making everyone around her look invisible.'

'Or you barely went out?'

This was running too close to the bone. Depression had kept her in bed for a long time, but she did not wish to recall that.

Even sitting, the breadth and height of Nathaniel Lindsay was substantial. She remembered how she had loved his largeness after the small men of Languedoc. She remembered his scent, too, an evocative mixture of plain soap and maleness.

'Your sister visited me last week. Did you know that?'

'Maureen came here?' She could not keep her astonishment at bay.

'She wanted to be assured that I was not threatening you in any way. She stood her ground and cautioned me that she would not tolerate anything that may hurt you. When I told her that I had pretended to bed you in order to help you from being discovered and compromised, she was happy.'

More unspoken words shimmered in the chasms.

Were pretence and lies all that once held us together?

Here it was harder to maintain the falsehood, even with the arguments Cassie could muster for carrying on with such a charade. She felt a choking want in the back of her throat and swallowed it down. The wine helped, a fine dry white that gave her hands something to fidget with and her mind something other than him to dwell upon. But secrets could be as damaging as any wound and her fingers tightened around the crystal glass.

All of a sudden she wished he might just reach out and take away choice. She wanted the feelings she had discovered in Saint Estelle and in Bagnères-de-Bigorre here in London, in the quiet warmth of his beautiful house, far away from others and from the responsibility of her everyday life.

Nathaniel made her believe in fantasy. That was it. He had before in southern France and he did again now, the muted sounds of the city far away and the clock showing eight-thirty in the evening. Still early. The blue in her gown shimmered as she shuffled back and sat up farther.

'My sister feels it is her duty to protect all those about her.'

'Then such obligation must run in your family.'

At that she laughed. 'Perhaps it does in Maureen, but Papa is too busy with trying to understand the complexities of science and my other sister Anne is too preoccupied with her brood of children.'

'There is also a brother?'

'Rodney. He is the youngest.'

He had told her once that he was without siblings. *Alone.* The word came with a forcefulness that made her blink. He was still like that; the solitary detachment of one who was careful not to anchor himself to another for fear of being disappointed. Oh, how well she knew that feeling.

The clock in the corner boomed out a further passage of time, and Nathanael finished his first drink and poured himself another, eyeing hers as he did so.

'You do not like the wine?' he commented.

She looked nervous and her hand shook as she made herself take a drink. Not just one sip, either, but three. Fortification. He wondered perhaps whether it had been a bad idea to invite her here because the ease that had always existed between them seemed dissipated tonight into a sheer and utter nervousness, her eyes skirting away from his and her body ramrod straight.

'Albi de Clare is of the opinion that you and Maureen are two of the most beautiful women in London.'

She smiled. 'Is his eyesight hampered, my lord?'

'Many I have spoken to would agree with him. But they also say you are prickly and distant to any advances that come your way. Most make a point of telling me that you in particular seldom venture out to partake in any of the entertainments that most are fond of.'

'There are other things that I need now more than a man, Lord Lindsay.'

He reached out and stroked a finger down the soft skin near her wrist, measuring the beat when he had finished. She often wore gloves, the left-hand fingers specially fashioned so as to show no signs of her old injury.

'Indifference requires a less rapid pulse, *Sandrine*.'

Cassie did not pull away, but watched his thumb as it moved up her arm and he had the sudden and unexpected thought that she might allow him more.

'I would like to know you again as I did once.' Firelight was reflected on the smooth skin at her throat and it was now there that his touch lingered.

'No. It cannot be as before.' She said the words slowly, enunciating each one, and he did not quite understand what she meant.

'Before?'

'Only a kiss. Nothing else.'

God. His body leapt with her words, shock warming everything. She did not turn away, but met his glance full on, the depths of burning need and pain inside them making his breath catch, for the Sandrine of old was so easily seen.

New secrets lingered there as well, he was too much of the spy not to recognise that, but they would have to wait. For now he pulled her up towards him as he stood, the length of their bodies touching. He did not wish to frighten her or make her call a halt so he was cautious. It was enough to feel her against him, will-

ingly fitting into the contours of his body and to smell
her particular and sweet scent.

Strands of hair that had loosened from the knot at
her nape lay across his arm, bright against the darkness of his clothes.

Night and day. Lost and found. Lies and truth. All
were there as he brought his mouth down across hers,
the limit of a kiss shrugged away by the blinding honesty of connection. They were back again in the hot
pools of Bagnères-de-Bigorre and in the shadowed
room at Saint Estelle, a thousand days of apartness
lost into union.

No careful kiss this, after all, but a full-blooded
connection of want. Slanting his lips, he brought her
closer, the stark heat of his body tightening with desire. Sensation washed through reserve and instead of
the judicious touch he had promised he ravished her
mouth with his tongue, trying to make her understand
the futility of boundaries and the depth of his need.
The savage movement of years of memory and betrayal
lingered there, too.

This kiss was different from any they had shared
in France, the play of anger on one edge and a trace of
hate. Once, as a girl, Cassie might have been frightened by such an emotion, but now she relished it, the
woman in her responding to their complex and circu-
itous layers of history. She wanted to punish him back,
too, for not being there when she had Jamie and for the
all the loneliness she had felt ever since; for the pain of

his birth and the cold hard hours afterwards of isolation and solitude.

A shared and desolate despondence.

Her fingers raked across the bare skin on his neck and held him closer, the breath between them hoarse and rasping. Hardly proper. Barely kind. She wished she might tell him everything even as she knew she would reveal nothing.

But for this moment Nathanael Colbert was hers. She could not think of the earldom or of society or of the duties that would drag Lord Lindsay from her as soon as they broke off their kiss.

Nothing but now, but, oh, how she yearned for more, his body moving inside her and that particular moment of release when all the world fell away to the beat of pleasure and purpose, the dark, hard power of sex mitigating everything.

When the kiss was finished, as she knew it must, she laid her head against his chest, feeling his heart pounding in her ear, like the beat of some song that was played too fast for the melody.

Their lives. Out of tune and spinning into chaos again.

Jamie.

She made herself stand alone. For now she needed the time to think. Her smile was false when she finally looked up at him—she knew it was, and yet it was all she had left.

'I do not think this was a good idea.'

He laughed. 'Then you have not had many other kisses or you would recognise the magic in it.'

She was pleased he did not comment on the anger. 'I am older now, Nathaniel, and wiser. What I think I want and what I need are now two different things. I cannot make a mistake again.'

'Come to bed with me, Sandrine. Now.'

Shocking. Enticing. Impossible.

'And if I did, what then? Can you honestly say that without reservation you have forgiven me for what happened at Perpignan?'

His smile faded and he remained silent. When he looked away she knew that she had lost him.

'I think I should go.'

One minute of silence and then two before he simply reached down and rang a small silver bell she had not noticed on a table. Footsteps outside could be heard immediately.

'You rang, sir.' The servant was all a good butler should be, circumspect and prudent.

'Miss Northrup is just leaving, Haines. Could you find her coat and see her out?'

'Yes, sir.'

Lord Nathaniel Lindsay did not move as she pushed past him and followed his man from the room.

He punched his hand against the hardness of the wall behind as she left and liked the pain that radiated up his arm.

What the hell was wrong with him? Why could he not have given her the soft words she was after, the oaths of forgiveness and absolution? Lebansart's face drifted into his mind and the anonymous visages of two men who had never known what was coming. The last words at Perpignan were there, too, as she had curled her fingers into those of his enemy.

Sandrine the whore.

He hated the truth of it, but he could not change. An impossible future moulded from an old and familiar hurt. How long had she stayed with Lebansart? It had been eighteen months later that she had returned to England according to Hawk. That long? A lifetime compared with the paltry weeks that they had been allotted. Lifting his glass, he finished the lot and his body ached with the loss of her.

Chapter Ten

'Lord Lindsay was at the Venus Club the night before last, Cassie, and according to our uncle he was enjoying all that was on offer there.'

Maureen gave her the information over the breakfast table the week after her meeting with Nathaniel, the anger in her voice lancing the words with repugnance. 'I would have thought him to have had more taste,' her sister added as she helped herself to a plate of scrambled eggs from a heated silver dish on the sideboard.

Cassandra was shocked, the shame that was still substantial from their last meeting now compounded by Lindsay's obvious lack of regard for women. He had sent a sizeable chit, too, with a servant the day after she had seen him. The bribe for the Daughters of the Poor now felt like a severance token, a way of apologising for a relationship that he did not want and could not pursue.

Nathaniel Lindsay was a bounder and a cheat; that was what he was, a man who would prey on the hard times of others and yet pretend an interest in her work with the Daughters of the Poor; a man without the courage to chance her offering of more than a kiss. She was suddenly glad that he had dismissed her from his company if this was what he had become, though anger and disappointment made her shake.

'Kenyon said he could not imagine Lindsay in such seedy places when he has all the women of society to choose from, but as Uncle Reg was adamant in his identification, I presume it must be the truth. Stephen Hawkhurst accompanied him by all accounts.' She stopped then, a worrying look in her eyes. 'I had hoped you and Lindsay might have been friends. I noticed him watching you closely at the Forsythe ball, and he was certainly helpful there.'

'Perhaps he feels responsible for me somehow. Lords of the peerage have an inflated view of duty towards others in need.' Cassandra prayed that her sister might take her explanation as an end point to the conversation, but she was disappointed.

'Kenyon thinks he is a good person. He also said that his grandfather is a mean-spirited old miser who needs a hearty talking to.'

'Your husband-to-be has strong opinions, Reena.'

'I know. Isn't he wonderful?'

Unexpectedly, Cassandra found herself laughing. Her sister had changed from a woman who often questioned masculine dominance to one who was allowing Kenyon Riley every right of persuasion. It was heartening because Maureen looked so very happy, a smile pinned on her lips almost permanently now and nothing and no one could dull it. Not even their father when he joined them in the breakfast room looking irritated.

'Reginald was here again yesterday and he is becoming more and more of an interfering and bombastic bore. I shall instruct the servants not to let him through to the laboratory again because he cannot help touching the experiments even when I ask him not to. Your mother was always exasperated by him and I can well see why.'

'I think he was after the watch Grandfather brought home with him from South Africa, Papa. He said the other week that he was certain it was supposed to be given to him.' Maureen sounded distant, as though the problems of this household were becoming less and less of a concern to her.

'The acquisition of family heirlooms is the only reason he ever comes calling and Lord knows he has more in the way of chattels than we do.'

'Why do you give him things, then?' Cassie joined in the conversation now, interested in his answer.

'Because he never loved a woman like I did or had children. Offspring. Heirs. His life is as barren as a moor and as empty. It seems he uses the clubs selling pleasure these days as a reason for living. God knows he is always trying to deter me from funding your charity.'

Cassie frowned. 'He told me at the Forsythe ball the other week that I should be placing my efforts into the marriage mart and that the frippery of charitable works would put any man off an alliance with our family.'

'And yet he himself has never entertained the idea of a bride?' Maureen's words were laced with question.

'Oh, he did once. He asked your mother to marry him and she refused. I don't think he ever forgave her for marrying me instead.'

Cassandra had heard this before from her mama. Alysa was a woman who barely spoke of the personal, but once when Uncle Reginald had come to the door she had pretended she was out and had given an explanation for the lie. Her love of science was the reason. Reginald for all his money and handsome looks could never abide a woman with a brain and if Alysa had a goal in life it was to understand the theory behind the small and unseen badness in a sick person.

'She had a lucky escape, Papa, and I am certain she knew it.'

'But it has made him mean and small-minded.'

Their father was usually far more reticent about discussing any of his feelings so Cassie determined that he must be worried about something. She had no further opportunity to ask questions, though, as he finished his breakfast and left the table. Back to the laboratory, she thought and watched as he left, a man slightly bent over by life and loss. She hoped she would not be like that in thirty years.

A few moments later a knock on the door took their attention. These days any unexpected caller had the effect of making Cassandra's heart race wildly just in case it was Nathaniel Lindsay, but when their butler showed in Elizabeth Hartley from the school, a new worry surfaced. She looked alarmed and anxious, her more usual languid demeanour disappeared beneath a flushed face and bright eyes.

'Another girl has been pulled out of the river. We have just been informed of it and we think it may be Sarah Milgrew, for she has not returned home for two nights.'

Both Cassie and Maureen stood.

'When did you last see her?'

'She said she had to go out around six the day before yesterday and never came home. She had some information of her lost sister, it seems, and was hurrying out to find her.'

'How did the word come?'

'A young boy came to the front door and asked for her by name. When I looked in her room there was no note or anything. After we heard the news this morning, though, Mrs Wilson said I was to fetch you and that you would know what to do.'

Both sisters looked at each other. 'We will come, of course,' Cassandra said. 'Where has the body been taken?'

'To the police station in Aldwych.'

'Then I need to be there. If you stay here, Maureen, until I return we will all go to the school together.'

Twenty minutes later she was pulling up in front of the Aldwych constabulary in a hired brougham. God, how she hated what she had come to do, but as there was no one else for the job she took a deep breath and stepped down from the carriage, walking right into the path of Lord Nathaniel Lindsay.

Because her mind was on the dreadful business of the discovered body it took her a second to register his presence and react. The bloom of anger and discomfort could be felt on her cheeks.

'It is Sarah Milgrew, Cassandra. I have just identified her.' His words replaced embarrassment with a deep and shocked horror. 'Her throat was cut just like the last girls'.'

He was not being careful with his facts and for that Cassie was glad. She did not wish to be treated like a woman who would need the truth filtered and sanitised. His grey eyes were filled with the sort of anger she had seen them to contain in France.

'The constabulary said that there is nothing else that they can do at the moment. I have asked them to keep me informed of any new developments, however, and they said they would send someone over if there was other information uncovered. I have my own leads, too, that I shall want to investigate.'

'You have an idea of who it might be?'

'Sarah Milgrew's home town of Wallingford might allow us some answers. I will travel across there in the morning.'

'If you could keep us up to date, too, we would be most grateful.'

'Of course. Would you like me to drop you at home?'

'If you have the wish to.' Sadness had hollowed her; sadness for Sarah and for the other girls who had died.

'My carriage is this way.' For the first time he touched her, his hand at her elbow guiding her past a group of people walking the other way; an aloof and detached touch that was discarded as soon as they reached the conveyance. Once inside he kept talking.

'Surely someone else could have been sent from the Daughters of the Poor other than you to identify the body?'

'There are no men on the pay roll, if that is what you are suggesting.'

'Older women, then. Married women.'

The barb dug deep, lancing all the hurt and anger. 'I might remind you, Lord Lindsay, that I was married even though you seem to have forgotten the fact entirely.'

'Hardly.' His eyes ran across her body in the way of a man who remembered everything.

'Well, as someone who spends his evenings in the bosom of the Venus Club you give all the impression of otherwise.' My God, she thought as soon as it was out of her mouth. What had made her say that? The sharp edge of hurt probably and the wasted loss of hope.

His laughter surprised her. 'You think I should stay at home and read instead?'

'Rumour has it the girls there are very young.'

All humour fled. 'Enough, Cassandra. You have no idea of my reasons for being there.'

'Oh, I am certain I have, my lord. Do not all men have the same purpose once they set foot in such hallowed halls?' Her temper was at full flight now, irreversible and unstoppable as years of her own loneliness and ruin came flooding in. 'I just had expected better from you, the unwise hope of one who has made choices that come back to haunt, I suppose, and your penchant for such places makes a mockery of any history between us.'

'The history of you abandoning me in Perpignan for the arms of Guy Lebansart, you mean, and staying in Paris for the whole of the next eighteen months with him?'

'Who told you that?'

'Nobody had to. I was there, remember, as you happily went off with him. A woman who looked as though she could barely wait to be in more than his arms.'

She hit him then, full across the face, the sound in the carriage terrible and absolute. But he did not pull back. Rather, he grabbed at her shaking hand and yanked her forward, his mouth coming down on hers in a single frozen angry grimace.

And he took exactly what he wanted, bearing down with a force she could not deny. One hand threaded through her hair, tethering her to him, and the other gathering both wrists, bundling retaliation into stillness. He did not hold back either, ravaging her mouth with fury, barely allowing breath. At first she fought him, and then before she knew it another feeling altogether arose and she clung to his kiss as though her very life depended on it.

With a curse, he let her go.

'I am sorry.' He didn't sound at all like he usually did, and the scar across his chin stood out in a raised white line. Neither did he look sorry. Rather he appeared as though with only the slightest of provocation he might act in the very same way yet again.

Unbridled and rampant. A lord who was used to an

easy domain over others and was trying now to find a normalcy that had never been part of their relationship together in order to survive.

'We bring out the worst in each other.' More of his words slung with insult, though a small edge of them held another emotion. Shame, if she might name it, for his behaviour and for her own, each marooned in a half place of regret.

The silence was welcomed. The clip-clop of the horses, the call of the driver, the sounds of a busy London street. Normal and proper after everything else that was not. Her lips felt rough and dry, but she did not dare to lick them in case he interpreted such an action wrongly. With eyes downcast she swallowed back tears and sat perfectly still, pleased when the horses were called to a halt and the door was opened to the Northrup town house.

The footman helped her out. Nathaniel did not touch her or look at her. It was as if three feet were a thousand miles as she climbed down onto the white pebbles.

'If I hear any other news about Sarah Milgrew I shall let you know, Miss Northrup.'

'I would be indebted, Lord Lindsay.'

The polite manners of society hung across an undercurrent of weariness and then he was gone.

White's was busy when he flung himself down on a leather wingchair opposite Hawk half an hour later and ordered himself a double shot of their strongest whisky.

'A run in with the mysterious Miss Cassandra Northrup, I presume?'

Nat ignored Hawk's jibe because the whole fiasco was just too confusing to dwell upon right now. 'Another woman has been brought out of the river.'

'Lord.' Hawk sat forward. 'Who is it this time?'

'A girl whom the Daughters of the Poor had found and given a home to. The sister of one of those dragged from the Thames last month, I am guessing.'

'Was there a meeting of the Venus Club that night?'

'No.'

'Damn.'

'But the girl had made enquiries the evening before at the Sailors Inn concerning her sister. The tavern keeper remembers her asking. I also know the name of her home town, so perhaps something happened there?'

'Bits and pieces dropping into the jigsaw. God, how I love this game.'

'I doubt the youngest Northrup daughter would see it in those terms, Stephen. She was furious to hear I had been at a meeting of the Venus Club.'

'You did not enlighten her of your true purpose?'

'And run the risk of having her poke her nose into the whole conundrum? It is getting more dangerous by the day and she seems to think she is indestructible.'

'I see your point.' Hawk leant forward and frowned. 'Have you been in a fight? Your face looks bruised.'

'Cassandra Northrup hit me. Hard.'

Stephen began to laugh. 'She makes you foolish, Nathaniel, and it's about high time that one of us found a woman who managed to do that. Besides, she is your wife.' He raised his glass and drank, his smile laconic. 'It's been years since you have given any

woman the time of day and this one...' He stopped as
though picking his words carefully. 'This one makes
you feel again.'

Anger. Wrath. Irritation. Frustration. Helplessness.
Fear. For what she was involved in and for the risks
she took. Aye, Hawk was right in his summation of
strongly feeling something. Nat stayed quiet.

'There is another matter that I have heard amongst
the whispers of gossip, Nat, and I am not sure if this
is a good time to tell you of it.'

'Something about Cassandra Northrup, you mean?'

'Yes.'

Nathaniel took a breath in because by the tone of
voice that Stephen was using he knew the news was
bad. 'What is it?'

'She has a son.'

The bottom fell out of his world in one dizzying and
frantic sort of disbelief. Of all the things he had expected Hawk to say this was not one of them.

'How old?'

'Word is that she returned from Paris with him in
tow.'

Nat's hands scraped through his hair as he tried to
recover a lost composure.

Was the child his?

Anger filtered his world with a red haze, the beat
of his heart drumming in his ears as he put down his
glass. Had Sandrine been pregnant in Perpignan and
not told him? His mind skirted back to the timings.

After his behaviour in the carriage he felt it unwise
to confront Cassandra with this new question, for the

answer she gave back would determine everything. He wished that he could have gone then and there to her and sworn that the parenthood of her son did not matter to him.

But he knew that it did. With care, he straightened in the leather seat.

'Is it yours?'

Stephen's voice came through a billowing loss and for the first time in a long while Nat found himself unable to formulate even the smallest of thoughts.

Cassie held her son close against the night and listened to his breathing, the moon coming in between the curtains of patterned velvet, illuminating the bed with its paleness.

Jamie came to her room in the night with a wail of worry, another dream disturbing slumber and leaving him upset and frightened. Often she instructed his nanny to let him come to her in the early hours before the dawn if he awoke for she liked sleeping with him.

She wondered if he remembered his time in Paris, the uncertainty, the desperation. She hoped he held no recollection of her crying out for Nathanael and searching for a face that might look like his in the Place des Vosges or the busy markets of Les Halles. She had walked the length and the breadth of the city, hoping that she might see him once in the uniform of an army officer, in the Luxembourg Gardens and the Parc du Champ de Mars opposite the L'Ecole Militaire. Just to explain. At the Hôtel des Invalides she had waited on the esplanade and searched. This face and that one.

Men ravaged by battle and memories, but none of them were Nathanael Colbert.

Today in the carriage she had hated him. No, she shook her head for that was not quite true. Even membership in a club renowned for its debauchery could not dull the hopes she harboured. His kiss had been full of anger, a savage punishing caress, but underneath the fury, passion simmered. She had felt it sliding beneath intent and taking root, anger compromised by lust.

Crying over the loss of Sarah before finally going to sleep and then being woken when Jamie had padded into her room in the small hours of the morning, Cassandra felt dislocated.

Life and death was entwined irrevocably and now, as the moon waned and the dawn called she knew that she would have to be honest no matter what the consequences. Jamie was a boy who needed a father and it was only right that she gave Nathaniel Lindsay the chance to get to know his son.

Their son. A child born from love and from passion.

Tears pooled behind her eyes. Jamie was the reason she had lived, a calling hope when everything else had been lost. He had looked like Nathaniel from the first moment he had been born, wise eyes staring up at her under a shock of black hair. And every single year the resemblance had grown.

Turning over, she looked at the ceiling and remembered the kiss in the carriage. She wanted that feeling again, pounded by strong emotion and rescued from the inertia that had made her feel so flat for all the months and years without him. But she could not blackmail him into loving her by offering their son as bait. No. She would have to let Jamie go and trust Nathaniel to be the sort of father she imagined he would be. Then she would need to step back. The realisation brought her arms in an involuntary protest around the small sleeping body and she dozed with him snuggled in beside her until the morning.

She would tell him as soon as she saw him next.

Nathaniel was waiting for her by his carriage outside the school in Holborn two mornings later and it seemed to her as if he had been there a while.

'I want to talk to you.' He did not bother with the niceties of greeting, cold grey eyes levelled at her with more than a hint of anger.

'Here?'

'Perhaps the park opposite? Could you accompany me for a walk?'

A tight request, just holding on to politeness.

'Very well.'

She was unsettled by his demeanour. She had sworn to herself she would give him the truth about Jamie and yet now the thought of actually broaching such a topic made her feel sick. Today he looked nothing like the man she had made love to in the high passes of Languedoc. No, today plain fury seemed to radiate from him.

A few words and her life might be completely different and torn apart. Jamming her teeth together, she did not say a thing, watching him as he shepherded her behind a small green hedge and turned.

'Why did you take so long to return to England? From what I have been able to gather it was almost two years before you came back.'

Her eyes snapped up to his. Something had changed. He knew of Jamie. She could see it in his face and in his stillness. He always had that, a crouching sense of both calm and danger. His silence had its own voice, too. She had known this moment would come, of course, through four long years of imaginings. How often had she sat in the dead of night and wondered how this secret would be told.

'Hawk implied you had a child in France.'

Not like this. Not like this. Not asked with anger. Not out in the open where anyone might interrupt and the time to explain was not on her side. She cursed Stephen Hawkhurst for imparting the information.

'Was there a child from our union, Sandrine?'

Ah, so easy to simply lie given his uncertainty, but she found she could not.

'There was. There is,' she amended and heard breathlessness in every syllable. 'Jamie is three years old and will be four at the end of next month. He was born in Paris at the end of July in 1847.' All the facts for him to place together, the answer hanging in any interpretation he wanted.

The quiet continued for one moment and then for two.

'He is mine.'

Cassie had never heard such a tone from Lord Lindsay; the hope was audible as was the shock, but it was the simple yearning that got to her.

'Ours.' She could not say more, the tears in her eyes welling with the relief of her admission.

'And Lebansart?'

The ugly name crept in to all that should have been beautiful. 'He never touched me in that way.'

Emotion was etched into every hard line of Nathaniel's face. 'It certainly looked like he wanted to from where I stood.'

'The names I gave him put paid to that. He was too keen to use the information I had recited to think of anything else. He left with his men ten minutes after you last saw him.'

'Did he hurt you?'

Turning her face away, she was glad not to see the question in his eyes. 'James Nathanael Colbert Northrup is our son's name. I could not think of another way to make sure you would know you were his father if anything was to happen to me.'

He breathed out loudly, a tremor in the sound, all other thoughts washed away. She was pleased for it.

'When can I see him?'

Cassie was quiet. She was, after all, not certain just what sort of a part Nathaniel wanted to play in his son's life. Or what kind of a role *she* might be placed into.

'Does he know about me?'

'He thinks that his father died in France. I thought that, too.'

With a curse, his glance took in the far horizon. Allowing himself time to take in the enormity of all that she had told him before he needed to give an answer, she supposed.

'Why was he born in Paris?'

A different tack. Beneath such a question other queries lingered.

'My uncle's best friend had a house there and allowed me the use of it. He sent servants to help me settle.'

'You did not think to come back to England?'

Shaking her head, she took his hand. 'I wanted to have Jamie first. I wanted to have our baby without the pressure of all that would transpire in London had I come home alone. I was sick for most of the pregnancy and I did not trust a sea journey. I also believed that I could find you in Paris and explain.'

His grey eyes sharpened. 'Did you know you were pregnant before Perpignan?'

Looking straight at him, she nodded.

His anger was immediate. 'You knew and yet you still left?'

'Much has happened since we were young, Nathaniel. Good things and bad. But Jamie is one of the good things and that is where our focus must lie.'

Relief filled her when he nodded. A relationship held by the smallest of threads, the past between them a broken maze of trust. Sandrine Mercier and Nathanael Colbert had been vastly different people from Cassandra Northrup and Nathaniel Lindsay. But each of them in their own way was now trying to find a direction.

'Where does this leave us, then?' She heard the tiredness in his words.

'If we were to be friends it might be a start.'

*   *   *

Friends?

Nathaniel mulled over the word, hating the limitations upon it, yet at a loss to demand more. She had borne him a son in a place far from home. Jamie. James. The word budded within him like a prayer answered.

But it was Cassandra whom he needed to think about now. In France they'd experienced lust and passion and avidity as they had made their way through the high mountain passes. Now she needed friendship. It was what she was asking of him, this quieter calm after a storm. Friendship, an emotion he held no experience of with a woman. Did it preclude touching? He moved back, for the expression on her face looked as uncertain as his, eyes shaded equally in worry and hope.

Taking a breath, he smiled as he saw her hand shake when she pushed back the curls that had escaped from beneath her bonnet. 'Does he have hair your colour or mine?'

'Yours. I am constantly amazed that my sister does not see the resemblance and comment upon it.'

'A St Auburn, then.' The words slipped from him unbidden, and she sobered instantly.

'A piece of paper all those years ago was easy to sign, but a father should be for ever. You will need to meet him first, Nathaniel, and understand what it is you offer.'

'Then let me, Sandrine. Let me get to know both of you again in a way we did not have the chance of before. In fact, let us begin right now. I can tell you something of my life as a child and then you can tell me yours.'

Her smile was tentative.

'After my parents died my grandfather found it hard to cope. He left me in the hands of a nanny and myriad servants and went to Italy for three years. When he returned home I was sent straight up to Eton. From the age of nine to the age of eighteen I barely saw him. When I did I found he was a man I couldn't like and I am sure that the feeling is mutual.'

'Where is he now?'

'At St Auburn. He rarely leaves the place and I seldom go there. Such an arrangement works for us both.'

'You never had sisters or brothers?'

'No. My mother had a difficult birth with me and could not have other babies. Perhaps that was a part of my grandfather's dislike.'

'Surely a grown man could not blame a small child for such a thing.'

His smile widened. 'My point exactly.'

With the wind in his hair and the sun on his face Nathaniel Lindsay looked to Cassandra like the epitome of a wealthy and favoured lord of the peerage. He also looked maddeningly beautiful, a fact that worried her even more than the détente that they spoke of.

She wondered if she could withstand such a thing and not give in to the feelings that swirled inside her. This time she was no *ingénue* with a hard-luck story as the unfortunate victim of crime. No, now she was the one who had betrayed honour and had the scars to prove it. With only the shedding of clothes would he see the living, breathing marks of treason branded into her right breast.

Hence she moved away. From touch. From closeness. From temptation. His confession about his relationship with his grandfather was worth more to her than all the gold and riches in the world because for the first time she saw the child who had made the man.

'I don't know what it would be like to be an only child. Through all the years of our early childhood it was my siblings' presence that made everything seem bearable.'

'You think that Jamie needs a brother or a sister?'

Despite meaning not to she laughed. 'A gentleman should not mention such a thing, Lord Lindsay.'

The dimple in his right cheek was deep and whilst he was speaking so candidly of his past she did not wish to waste the chance of knowledge. 'What is St Auburn like?'

'The house was built in the sixteenth century by a Lindsay ancestor and has been added on to ever since. It sits in the midst of rolling farmland and there is a lake it looks down upon.'

'It sounds like a home that needs to be filled with family and laughter.'

Nathaniel smiled. 'Perhaps you are right. Are you always so wise, Cassandra Northrup?'

'If I was, I doubt I would have needed to go to France in the first place. I might have recovered from my mother's death like a normal child and been a proper lady of society with all the airs and graces.'

'I like you better as you are.'

The blush began as a small warm spot near her heart and spread to the corners of her body. Out in the air in the quiet winds of late summer it was so easy to believe in such troth.

'You do not really know me at all, Nathaniel.'

'Then let me. Come to St Auburn. Bring Maureen and Kenyon Riley. Bring whomever you like to feel comfortable, and come with Jamie.'

The grey in his eyes was fathomless today, a lover who would show her only what he might think she wished to see. He was good at hiding things, she thought, the trait of a spy imposed upon everyday life. She wondered how easy that would be, to live with secrets that could result in the downfall of governments if told. Her own had been a hard enough task to keep hidden.

When a group of well-dressed ladies accompanied by their maids walked into the park they were forced to return to the road, though once there awkwardness enveloped her. On the street she saw others watching him, a well-known lord with the promise of an earldom as a mantle around his shoulders. With Nathaniel Lindsay she could not afford to make a mistake or go too lightly into the promises that he asked of her.

Jamie's welfare rested on good decisions and proper judgement. No, she would rest on his suggestions for a while until she had mulled them over.

An hour later, Nathaniel sat in his leather chair behind the large mahogany desk in his study and looked about the room without really seeing anything.

He had a son. Jamie. James Nathanael Colbert Northrup, she had said, his name sandwiched in between her own.

He should have asked Cassandra other things, should have found out what Jamie liked and what he didn't. Did he read, did he love horses, did he play with balls, did he have a pet?

Almost four years old. For a man with little contact with children the number was difficult to get his head around. What could a nearly four-year-old boy do? Sitting back against the seat, he closed his eyes.

God, he was a father. He was a father to a child conceived in the wilds of the Pyrenees above Perpignan.

He took a silver flask from the drawer and unstopped it. Cassandra had been on edge, the usual flare of awareness between them doused by responsibility and worry. Did she think he might take their son away or insist upon the legality of their marriage?

Legality.

The child was a legitimate heir to the St Auburn earldom and fortune. Nat wondered just what his grandfather, William Harper Wilson Lindsay, would say to that.

The past few days had been full of surprises. Yesterday in Wallingford he had discovered another girl had been murdered in the exact same way as those in London. He also had the name of the tall and well-dressed Londoner who had left his room at the inn the day the body had been discovered.

Scrivener Weeks.

Nat had spent a good few hours since last night

trawling through the names of all those in society, but come up with nothing.

His mind reeled with all that had happened and as he took a sip of his brandy he smiled.

Chapter Eleven

Jamie was sick, the temperature he ran more worrying by the hour, and Cassandra was increasingly beginning to panic, something she seldom did in any medical emergency.

Her mind would not be still as she imagined all the possibilities and problems that could befall her son if the fever didn't begin to abate. Maureen had helped her with the nursing for most of the day, but had gone now with Kenyon Riley to a dinner with the old duke in Belgravia. His nanny, Mrs Harris, had also been here for the past hours, but Cassie could see that she was tired and so sent her off to bed.

Hence she was alone, the weak and pain-filled moans cutting through all sense and making her as fearful as she had ever been. By eleven o'clock she had had enough. Scrawling out a note, she asked for one of the Northrup servants to deliver it immediately to the Lindsay town house and wait for an answer.

She wanted Nathaniel here. She wanted a man who

might love her son as much as she did and who could bring some sense and calm into a situation that was spiralling out of control for her. A tiny whisper that predicted Jamie might not recover was also part of the reason. If her son died, then Nathaniel would never have seen him. She shook the thought away and ordered back sanity.

It was a simple fever with a high and sudden temperature probably brought on by the dousing he had had in a rain shower in the garden. Visions of young children who went on to develop rashes and stiff necks came too, however, and she had seen enough of life in the past years to know that things did not always turn out happily.

Yesterday in the park Nathaniel had offered her the chance of reconciliation. Tonight all she wanted was his strength and his composure. She tried to regulate her breathing so that Jamie would not pick up on her panic, but found that the beat of her heart was going faster and faster, a clammy dread beginning to take over completely.

She should have called the doctor, she knew she should have, but the Northrup physician was a man who still believed in doing things in his way and even after she had stressed a number of times to him the importance of clean hands and tools he had not taken up the learning. Her father had wanted to replace him, but the traditions of the Batemans attending the Cowper family in the capacity of medical practitioners had been a difficult one to break and so he had given up. Usually Cassandra dealt with any sickness and she did it with such acumen and success they seldom asked for the physician's attendance.

Jamie was so deathly still, that was the problem, and the lukewarm water that she sponged his little body with was making no inroads to a gathering heat. She had used infusions of camphor, basil and lemon balm, angelica and hyssop, yet nothing seemed to be making any difference.

The sound of footsteps had her standing, heart in mouth, and she turned to the door as Nathaniel walked through, his shirt opened at the collar as if he had not even had the time to find a necktie, pale eyes taking in the scene before him without any sign of panic.

Cassie burst into tears, an action so unexpected and unfamiliar that she even surprised herself for having done so. He did not break a step as he gathered her into his arms and brought her with him over to the bed, his eyes hungrily taking in the features of his son.

'How long has Jamie had the fever?'

'All…day.' She swallowed, trying to make her voice sound more like it usually did.

'You have bathed him?'

'Many times, and I have used up all my remedies.'

Jamie's fit began with a twitch and a quiver, the right side of his body tensing and moving in a rigidity that spread to his legs and feet. While paralysing fear held Cassandra immobile, Nathaniel whipped off the thin sheet and spread it on the floor, lifting Jamie down to lie on his side and crouching by him.

He did not restrain him or hold him in any way, but let the shaking take its course for ten seconds and then twenty, just watching to make sure that he did not injure himself with the movement. Finally, when Cassandra thought it might never pass, Jamie relaxed, vomiting across the boots of his father.

'So this is what it is to be a parent?' Nathaniel turned towards her, his hand passing across the forehead of his son and relief evident.

Nodding, she thought that she had never loved Nathaniel more than she did at that moment, his certainty and strength edged with gentle compassion and humour.

'I had the same sort of fits when I was a child, Cassandra, and the St Auburn physician assured my mother and father that they would disappear as I grew older. Which they did. He will be fine. Better than my boots, at least.'

He leaned over to wipe the traces of moisture from his fine dark-brown Hessians, the gleam of leather a little tarnished. 'If you straighten the bed, I will lift him back up for I think the worst is over now.'

Nathaniel felt as though he were lifting treasure, his son, the small and damp body smelling of sickness and fatigue. Yet he was beautiful in the way only small boys could be, a scrape upon his left kneecap as if he had been running somewhere too fast and his colouring exactly that of a St Auburn heritage.

The same dark hair and skin tone, the same line of nose and cheek he had seen in the drawings of himself as a child. His heart turned in his chest and squeezed with a feeling that was foreign, half fear and all love, the utter storm of fatherhood beaching upon him, winding him with its intensity, fervour and suddenness.

'Thank you for calling me.'

'Thank you for coming.'

'He is beautiful.'

'I think so.' For a second a smile tweaked at the corner of her lips, the worry and fright beaten back a little, the tears drying on her cheeks.

'Is it the first time this has happened?'

'It is. Jamie is usually so well and full of energy. It was the fright of the difference, I think.'

'I had three of these fits across the space of a year when I was about his age and, according to my mother's diary, she was always as worried as you appear to be.'

Jamie suddenly opened his eyes, the pale grey confused. 'Mama?'

'I am here, darling.' Cassandra took his hand and brought it to her lips, kissing the fingers one by one. 'You have been sick, but you are getting better now.' The small face came around, questions contained within it.

'This is Nathaniel Colbert Lindsay, Jamie.'

'Nearly my name?'

'He is your—'

'Papa.' Jamie finished the sentence, and that one word sealed a lifetime of loyalty. Glancing over, Nathaniel saw Cassandra nod, and he came down on his knees beside the bed to take the offered hand of his son. Warm fingers curled into his.

For ever.

'I used to get sick like this when I was little, so I know exactly what to do and you will soon feel a lot better.'

'Did you come from France?'

'Pardon?' Was confusion a part of this sickness?

'No, Jamie. Your papa lives in London now so you may see him when you want to.'

'Can you stay here now?'

'Can I?' Nat looked over at Cassandra and smiled when she nodded. 'It seems that I can.'

'Good.' With that Jamie simply closed his eyes and went to sleep, his breathing even and the fever that had ravaged his body less than a few moments past, broken.

The silence stretched around them all, the gratitude of seeing a small child's recovery being a big part of that. His wife clasped Jamie's hand on one side of the bed and he held the other, a link of family and vigilance and concern. Outside distant bells chimed the hour of twelve, as the night softened into quiet.

'Would you like a cup of tea? I could go down to the kitchens and make it and then bring it back here.'

Tea? Nat would have far rather had a stiff brandy, but he wondered how she might feel about drinking in a child's room so he nodded at the offered drink. He felt as if he had been plunged into a different world where everything was altered and extraordinary. But right somehow. He smiled at that fact.

Left alone with his son, Nathaniel observed every feature, every part of a child who had been conceived out of love. He was sleeping now, his lashes dark against his cheeks and one arm curled beneath his head. He had slept like that, too, as a child, he remembered, and smiled as he noticed a ragged teddy bear on the floor, a well-loved companion by the looks of it. Picking it up, he tucked it beside his son. Just another one of all the small moments of a childhood he had missed, he thought, and resolved not to lose more.

When Cassandra bustled back a few moments later with a tray in hand she gestured to him to follow her into a sitting room close by and then proceeded to set out the cups, sugar and milk on a table.

'I thought if we had our tea here it would not disturb Jamie and yet we are still near enough to hear if he calls out.' She tipped her head to listen, but no noise was forthcoming. 'His nanny and the servants are all in their beds and I did not wish to wake them again so if you need something to eat…?'

'Just tea would be lovely.'

A flash of humour answered him as she understood his meaning. 'Papa does not drink at all and so our house isn't well stocked with liquor. But I will make certain that some is brought in for you next time.'

'Next time?'

'Jamie wants you in his life. Even being so sick he told you he did.'

'And what of you? Do you want me here?'

She lifted her cup carefully and looked at him directly. 'I do.'

'Then let us begin with that.'

The tea tasted like an elixir the way she made it with a dollop of milk and sugar. It was steadying after a night of emotion. He wondered why he had never taken to the brew before and resolved to instruct his staff to get this particular leaf into his house for drinking. Everything seemed heightened somehow: the scent of Cassandra's perfume, the colour of her hair. The small touch of her skin against his thumb as she had handed him the cup and the earthy aroma of tea.

Tonight lust did not rule as it usually did when they met, although in truth it simmered beneath the conversation. No, this evening a shared responsibility had engendered new emotions. Contentment. Peace. Gratitude. The quieter humours that Nat had seldom experienced before. The joy of sitting in a room with family around him and being a part of a tradition that stretched back through the ages.

'I could buy him a horse, a small one with a good temperament. One that did not kick. A safe steed.'

She smiled. 'You cannot protect him from everything, Nathaniel. What was your first horse like?'

'Wild. A real hellion. I learnt almost immediately where to stand and where not to.'

'The lessons of life. These are what Jamie needs to know from you.'

'Is it always this hard? Being a parent, I mean.'

'From the very first moment when the midwife handed him to me my heart ceased to be my own.'

'You had others there with you?'

'No.'

He swore softly so that the sound of it would not inadvertently reach the ears of his son. 'I wish I had been present.'

'I did, too, but I thought you were dead. I looked for

you in Paris and asked after you. No one had ever heard your name, of course, and you were probably already back in England. But I did not know any of that then.'

'When you came to London you did not arrive as Mrs Colbert?'

'I thought it too dangerous. I had no idea as to what had happened to Guy Lebansart and his men and I wanted to keep Jamie as safely away from them as I could. I thought placing your name within his would be enough for you to know what had happened if anything should go wrong with me and you were still alive to find him.'

'And you were condemned for not using the name of your husband because of it?'

'Oh, that was an easy sufferance for I seldom strayed into society and finally the gossip lessened.'

'If you had used Colbert I might have found you earlier.'

'Then that would be my only regret.'

'Come with me to St Auburn when Jamie is better. I can show you both the beauty of it, the solidness.'

'You said your grandfather was there.'

'Come as my family and he can meet you.'

Nathaniel wanted Jamie and her to go to St Auburn. He wanted things that she could not promise just yet with the scars at her breast and the guilt in her heart.

Tonight it had been easy to pretend with Jamie between them. Tonight he had come like a knight in shining armour through the darkness to rescue her. But tomorrow…?

Reality would creep back with the anger and then

she would be at the mercy of pity again. She needed to make sure that the feelings in France could be translated here away from any pressures before she followed him into a place that neither of them could come back from. She needed him to love her wholly with his body just as he had done once in the southern mountains and she wanted to love him back in the same way. But could she risk asking that of him? Now, after Jamie's sickness and the care he had shown, would the scars ruin everything?

The thrall of memory took her breath away. 'Do you live alone at your town house?'

'Yes.' His voice was quiet, underlaced with question.

'Then perhaps I could come there first. Just me...'

She left the rest unsaid, but he had picked up on the implications instantly.

'When?'

'Tomorrow night. At eight.' That gave her a day to make certain that Jamie was fully recovered.

'I would like that.'

'And it will only be us?'

'Yes.'

'I will need a carriage later...to bring me home before the morning.'

'It shall be at your disposal.'

'I am half sick of shadows,' said The Lady of Shalott.

Cassie just hoped that by leaving her sanctuary and following her heart into the arms of her Lancelot the result would be much happier than the one in the poem.

Out flew the web and floated wide;
The mirror crack'd from side to side;
'The curse is come upon me,' cried
The Lady of Shalott.

The three scars from Lebansart's blade burnt like hot ribbons of shame upon her breast.

After such a night Nathaniel was unable to sleep and so he sat at the desk in his office and worked on the case of the girls found near the river. Rearranging scraps of paper before him, he took away this one and replaced with that.

The list contained the names of every member of the Venus Club. The clues had to be here somewhere, he knew, the intuition that had served him so well in his years of working with the Service honed and on high alert.

Scrivener Weeks would be here somewhere hiding amongst the detail, he just had to find out where he was concealed. Removing each member who was neither tall nor dark, he was left with the names of fifteen men. Reginald Northrup's name caught his attention, but so did the name of Christopher Hanley.

Another thought occurred. It was Hanley who had told the world that he had seen Cassandra in the environs of Whitechapel Road and Hanley who had been disparaging about the role of the Daughters of the Poor trying to save every wayward girl in London. Could the existence of Cassandra's charity be threatening him in some way; threatening his preference for sexual experiences with very young women?

Placing the name in the very centre of all the others, Nat determined to find out more about his family circumstances and his night-time habits. He would visit Hanley, too. Sometimes it just took a more direct approach to flush out a guilty quarry and make them run.

Meanwhile, he would make absolutely certain that Cassandra came nowhere near the vicinity of her uncle's friend.

Chapter Twelve

Cassie could barely settle to anything for the whole of the next day, a sort of wild excitement that verged on panic underlying everything she did.

Jamie was so much better, leaving his bed and eating large plates of whatever the cook tempted him with. Maureen was astonished at how much improved he seemed, though it was another matter entirely that she quizzed Cassandra about.

'There is word you had a visitor late last night, Cassie. Lord Nathaniel Lindsay was an unexpected caller?'

Cassandra knew her sister's ways. Maureen obviously had found out a lot more about the unusual happening and was waiting for Cassandra to unravel it for her.

'Lord Lindsay looks familiar somehow. I cannot quite put my finger on how I should know him, but…?'

At that precise moment Jamie ran past playing with a small train, and it was if a shutter had suddenly been raised.

'Oh, my goodness, Lindsay is Jamie's father? Na-thanael is his second name?'

Horror stood where a humorous playfulness had lingered a moment before. 'He ruined you?'

'No. We were married, Reena. In France, almost five years ago. Everything is perfectly legal.'

'Then why…?' She could not even formulate her next question.

'One day I will tell you everything, but not at this moment. If you could keep my confidence for a little while longer, I would be most appreciative.'

'He will not break your heart again?'

'Again?' She could not quite understand what her sister alluded to.

'You came home from Paris like a half person and never looked at another male with any thoughts of in-terest although there were many good men who were offering. I knew there was someone. I just thought he was dead.'

There are worse ways to be separated than in death, Cassie thought as Jamie came over to her to demand a cuddle. Her sister's dark eyes watched carefully.

'Kenyon likes him. I do, too.'

'Who does he like?' Jamie's voice put paid to any further conversation.

In the late afternoon Cassie fussed about which gown to put on and finally decided on a dark yellow silk, a little outdated but beautifully cut. She fashioned her own hair into a bun at her nape, decorating the sides with two ornate tortoiseshell combs she had procured in the Marais. Cassie reasoned that if the night was to play out as she hoped she needed a style that would be easily unpinned and quickly redone when she left in the early hours of the next day.

Even the thought of it all made her apprehensive. Such a premeditated and deliberate choice. The hands of the clock seemed to race towards eight, and her stomach felt agitated and jittery.

She was twenty-three and she had had just one lover for only a short time. She did not count the Baudoins' rough handling of her in the first days of Nay, preferring to forget about the violence and hurt of the place. No, all she remembered now were the weeks between Saint Estelle and Perpignan, and the utter need they had felt for each other, the desire and the passion.

Breathing, she held in her hope as an aching desperateness. Could this happen again or had she ruined it with her choice of sacrificing others so that they might live?

She turned to the mirror and looked at herself. She was not a bad person or a deceitful one. She had done her best ever since the betrayal at Perpignan to make amends for the harm that she had caused. Would Nathaniel see that of her? Would he be able to look beyond the past and see a future?

'Please, God, let it be so,' she whispered and hurried to find shoes, stockings and a coat to match her gown.

Cassandra arrived on the dot of eight-fifteen, the ornate clock in the corner of the front entrance still calling out the quarter-hour. She had come. Dismissing his man, Nat went out to the carriage to open the door, the large black cape she wore hiding much, though her eyes shone through in the dark, anxious and fearful.

'Is Jamie better today?' A topic other than this want that hung between them was welcomed, and she smiled.

'He is, my lord.' She allowed the Lindsay servant to take her cloak.

'So formal, my lady.'

At that she blushed heavily, and would have tripped on the hem of her yellow gown had he not placed his hand beneath her arm. God, all he wanted to do was to snatch her up and take her to his bed, to assuage a pummelling need that was gaining more traction with every single second.

Friendship.

The word came back, loud with inherent meaning. He needed to slow down and calm down, for Cassandra Northrup deserved so much more than a quick tumble of lust, devoid of chivalry and consideration.

'Dinner is waiting in the dining room. After that I shall dismiss the servants and...' He did not finish.

'A meal sounds lovely.' She smiled at him then, as though she understood in his unfinished sentence some shared disquiet.

'The French chef from St Auburn followed me down to London and is very competent. I hope you will enjoy the fare.' Lord, why was he rambling on like this? He sounded like a green youth in the first throes of pleas-ing a girl, so he bit down for silence. He hardly recognised himself in his concern for making the right impression.

When he had visited Hawk earlier in the afternoon to tell him his worries about Hanley he had also mentioned the proposed dinner with Cassandra Northrup. With all good intentions Stephen had instructed him to smile a lot and be most attentive, but for the life of him Nat couldn't seem to make his lips curl upwards and empty compliments had never been his style.

Instead, he pulled the chair from the table and invited Cassandra to sit and then he took his own place a good few feet away. Distance made him less edgy and the procession of kitchen staff with tureens of soup and entrées turned his mind for a moment from the reason as to why she was here alone tonight.

'I don't think I thanked you properly for your help with Jamie the other night, Nathaniel. I do not normally panic.'

'I was glad that you called me, and if he is anything like me and has another fit it should be months away.'

'You only had three episodes, you said.'

'Indeed. I outgrew them exactly as the St Auburn physician had predicted that I would.'

'A family trait, then?'

'My father was prone to the same as a child. He did not have brothers or sisters, however, so I am not certain if it would have been something that ran through the whole line.'

'Well, it is reassuring to know that you recovered.' She drew a spoon of soup to her mouth and sighed.

'Onion soup. This is a taste I remember, though I have not had it since Paris.'

'You did not think to send word to your father after Perpignan and ask him to help?'

She shook her head, the red-gold catching the light from the chandelier above in a sparkling cascade of colour. 'Papa would have found the situation trying, and as a family we attempt to shelter him from anything that is difficult. After Mama died he was...brittle and I am not certain if he will ever be truly happy again.'

'So you managed alone?'

'I did.'

'You do that often.'

Her spoon hovered above the plate. 'I believe in myself more now.'

'I am glad for it.'

'I believe that atonement goes a certain way in alleviating past mistakes, and that what was, is not always the same as what will be.'

'Wise of you.'

'I have made errors, Nathaniel, big ones that I wish every single day I had not, but in the end one cannot wish life away. One has to confront it with courage and go on.'

'And you have.'

She nodded. 'For Jamie's sake, I had to.'

The strength of her washed across him. She sat there and told him that in adversity she had found a version of herself that she liked. He wanted to reach over and bring her ruined hand to his lips and kiss each finger one by one. She was no empty-headed maiden trying

to fit in with others' perceptions of her and whereas
Acacia had been hardened by the problems in her life,
Cassandra had been freed by them.

He wished he had skipped the course of soup and
gone instead for more simple fare because the hours
were running away with the task of eating and there
was still dessert. He was glad the removes of soup had
been taken away and hoped the offering of lobster,
ham and venison might disappear just as quickly. He
could not remember a meal taking quite as long as he
helped himself perfunctorily to one of the many plates
of vegetables.

Cassandra felt hot and uneasy. The food was beautifully cooked and expensive and yet she could barely
eat it. A clock in the house kept striking out the minutes
of every hour and time seemed to be racing towards
the real reason as to why she was here.

She wanted to sleep with Nathaniel Lindsay, she
did. She wanted to feel him inside her moving with the
passion only he could engender and she longed for the
quiet repose of skin against skin, their bodies speaking in a way words never did.

But the scars of Lebansart were a reminder of all
that had gone wrong between them and she dreaded
him seeing them and asking about what had happened.
She breathed out heavily and knew that he watched her
with his beautiful pale-grey eyes, the dimple in his
right cheek seen under the bright candelabras.

She would not survive again if he turned her away.
For all her bravado and independence she understood

that. The lobster felt dry in her mouth as she tried to swallow it, helping herself to a generous sip of white wine with the taste of summer in its bouquet. She seldom drank anything stronger than tea, save for in his company, where fortitude was as necessary as breath.

Cassie wished the meal would end and that the servants might disappear. She wanted him to lead her to his chamber with the minimum of chatter and undress her with the maximum of speed. She wanted to look into his eyes when he saw the scars and see acceptance or indifference, it did not matter which. It was the bewildering bloom of distaste that she hoped so fervently to avoid.

He suddenly stood. 'Perhaps we might leave the rest for later, Cassandra.' Those attending to the table stepped back and waited while he helped her from her seat.

As they reached the hall leading to the stairwell he petitioned her to tarry for a moment whilst he returned to give his instructions to the staff. She could hear his voice asking them to clean up and then retire for he would not be requiring their services further this evening. The resulting silence was full of question and speculation, but even that did not worry Cassie.

Then he was back again, taking her hand and escorting her up the wide marble staircase into the second floor of the house. His room lay at the end of a corridor, a set of French doors with an ornate gold handle and a substantial lock. As she walked through she heard him turn the key. Privacy. She was thankful for it.

His chamber was decorated in all shades of pale,

a restful luxurious interior that threw her off balance. The heavy brocades of paisley and floral at the Northrup town house looked tacky and overdone in comparison. This room was one of bleached furniture and patinas harking back to the age of a faded beauty. She wondered if he had had a hand in choosing the decor.

A whole line of leatherbound books sat on the table beside the bed. When he saw where she looked he commented, 'I read a lot.'

She remembered he had told her of that once and she had wondered. No amount of guessing could have placed him as a cultured English lord, however, with the lineage of an old family on his shoulders and a library of books at his disposal.

'You keep surprising me,' she managed to say.

At that he laughed, loudly, the first truly free emotion of the evening. A frisson of need made her stiffen. 'I could say the same, Cassandra. Few people manage to keep me as intrigued as you do and so effortlessly.'

He had come closer now. If she stepped forward she could have rested her head against his heart. With all her willpower she stopped herself doing just that.

Not yet, a voice inside her called. *He needs to understand exactly who you are.*

Her fingers came up to loosen the ties at her bodice. They were shaking in their pursuit of truth as fire began to build behind the slate of his eyes. The yellow silk had been chosen carefully. With just a few twitches of fabric it fell from her shoulders, the thin bodice of lawn the only thing now that kept his glance from her shame.

Then that was gone, too, three slices of raised red skin at the top of her right breast on show.

'I did not give the names as easily as you had imagined, Nathaniel. I paid for their lives in my own blood, too. I knew that I was pregnant, you see, and if I did not give him something he might...'

'God.' One finger reached out to trace the injuries, horror and anger on his face.

But not at her. It was Lebansart his wrath was directed at.

'The bastard did this to you?'

She nodded because suddenly she could not speak, the back of her throat closing in an aching heaviness.

'He could have killed you. Both of you.'

'I th-think he thought he had.'

'Ah, sweetheart.' His voice broke as he simply leant down and kissed the scars, one by one. Healing their ugliness, she was to think later, and dissipating their power over her. Forgiveness was a quiet and gentle emotion, the light and earnest feel of his tongue and the smooth sweep of his lips, but it held all the weight of a new beginning.

Her hand came through his hair, shorter now than it had been in France, the dark sheen of it almost blue.

'Love me, Nathaniel, and make me forget.'

In response he lifted her to him and brought her to his bed, the wide velvet counterpane beneath her as he peeled the dress and bodice away. Her stockings were next and the small slippers bought only a few days before. Then he loosened her hair from its tie and draped the length of it down beside her.

Caught in the light and in his gaze she stayed very still. 'You are even more beautiful than I remember.' His voice held reverence and awe.

He was fully dressed as he stroked one breast, smiling when the nipple puckered at his ministrations. Then his fingers fell lower, across her stomach and down into the place between her thighs, pushing into the wet warmth with a gentle insistence. And all the time his eyes never left her own, the fire within them banking and a look that said she was his. Need made her loins rise from the bed to meet him, her legs opening wider to allow him in, and she looked away because she knew that the roiling waves of release were about to come and she did not want to see his reaction to such a surrender.

Her muscles caught around his fingers, stilling the plunder and keeping him there inside her tight, and when she began to shake he pushed in farther still, eliciting a groan that held a primal relief.

She was no longer cautious or circumspect. All she could think of was the aching craving urgency in her body and the balm and ease of tension.

They belonged together, Nathaniel and she, and it had nothing to do with marriage or legality or expectations.

It was far simpler than that. It was how their skin called to each other and how the shape of his body so perfectly fitted hers. It was in the scent of him and the beauty and the strength. It was in his honesty and morality and bravery and forgiveness.

A single tear traced its way from her left eye down onto the pillow beneath. She had not expected absolution, but how she had wanted it. From him. From the only other person in all of the world who might understand what she had lost and what she had gained.

Her saviour. Now and then.

'I will love you for ever, Nathaniel.'

Cassandra's eyes were clear and her voice was strong as she said it, no half-meant troth given with a lack of honesty or intent.

'For ever?'

This time he was ready and there was no question in his reply. With care he crossed the room and opened a drawer, pulling out his mother's ring from a velvet box. The emerald glinted in the light as he walked back and he saw she was now perched on the edge of his bed, watching.

With care he bent on one knee and the smile that he had missed so much came easily to her lips.

'I never stopped loving you, Cassandra Northrup. Will you marry me?'

'I already have, Nathaniel Lindsay.' The words were wobbly and tears pooled in her eyes.

'Again then. Properly this time. With everyone around us.'

'Yes.'

Bringing her hand up, he placed the ring upon it. His mother's ring was still oversized and the ancient gold needed a good polish, but on Cassandra's finger it looked completely right.

A circle. Of life. Lost and found. He knew his mother would have loved Cassandra, loved her rarity and her honesty. The only thing she wore was a smile and this ring and she looked to him like a goddess sent from above. To heal loneliness and doubt, to bring laughter and adventure and truth.

When her hands came to the buttons on his shirt he stood still, tugging the garment off on completion and then doing the same with his trousers and boots. Life had marked them both. Inside and out. But it had also melded them together into a shape that could not withstand the world alone. He smote the candles above and the one on the stand near the bed and in the light of the fire he turned. They came together as husband and wife, his seed spilled without a care for caution.

Home. Safe. The night outside and the warmth within.

'I want as many more Jamies as you might give me,' he whispered finally when sense had returned.

'Starting tonight, Nathaniel.' The light in her eyes danced as her fingers closed around his shaft and all that had been wonderful before began again.

Much later they spoke. She leaned against him, her head upon his chest as he lifted himself to sit against the cushioned bed end.

'Lebansart left the minute after I gave him the names on the document. Louis Baudoin had already died from having allowed me to see the paper and in the end it killed Celeste, too...'

His finger came across her lips, stopping the flow

of words. 'You don't have to tell me any more if you do not wish to. It doesn't matter now.'

'But I want to. If I had not interfered, my cousin's soul may have been saved, for she died by her own hand less than a day later.'

'Guilt has as many lives as you wish to give it, Cassandra. You were young and trying to do your best to save those you loved, but it's time now to stop the blame.'

'I hated her sometimes,' she whispered, the very words so dreadful she could not give them the full power of sound.

'Celeste?'

'She made me stay there with her. I could have escaped, but she held me there with her weakness and her need. In the end she understood just how foolish she had been, but for a long while she revelled in it. The wine. Louis Baudoin. The danger. I could never trust that she would not be harmed by her lack of foresight and so I stayed.'

'To protect her?'

She nodded, the brisk anger in the movement revealing. 'And finally I could not even do that.'

'Voltaire once wrote that "no snowflake in an avalanche ever feels responsible". Perhaps you should allow your cousin more of the burden of blame.'

Cassandra mulled his words over. Celeste had grown up reprimanding everyone except herself when things went wrong and in every situation had put her own needs first.

'You think each person is accountable for their actions.'

'I do. I am the next in line for the St Auburn title and all it entails, yet the duties that came with my job in Europe were never the ones my grandfather wished for me to entertain. It was his way of life or no way of life and he harboured a resentment I could never understand.'

'Sometimes people disappoint you.'

He laughed. 'I try to allow them not to.'

Lifting her head on to her hands, she looked at him. 'Did your work in France teach you the knack of knowing what it is that others wish to hear?'

He frowned. 'Hawk and Lucas helped me more with that. You have not met Luc Clairmont yet for he is in the Americas, but without them I wouldn't have survived the loneliness of my childhood.'

She ran her finger across his chest, circling the skin around his nipple and liking the way it tightened. 'I often worried that someone might come from England and arrest me after Perpignan, and in my dreams the punishment was always death. Perhaps that was a part of the reason I didn't come home for so long. You worked for the British Service, but you never told anyone about me.'

His hand clamped down across hers. 'I couldn't. I never asked another question of that time because if I had found out you were dead....'

'You kept me safe. Us safe.'

'Then I am glad. But enough of talk, my beautiful

wife, for there are still some hours before we need to rise.'

When he rolled her beneath him she simply relaxed, opening her mouth as his lips came across her own.

He heard the birdsong at dawn but remained perfectly still. Cassandra lay against him, one leg draped across his thigh and her head tucked into the crook of his arm. Her hair cascaded around them in all the shades of gold and red, wildly tangled and curling. He lifted up one tress and felt its softness.

His wife. They had slept for much longer than she could have wanted to and for that he was pleased.

No covert sneaking back home. He did not wish for only night-time trysts. He wanted to see the sunshine play across her skin and know the ecstasy of every hour of the day in bed. Not quite the slow-building friendship she had had in mind, but then nothing about their relationship had ever been ordinary. He wondered how she might explain this night away to her family.

Her breathing changed and her eyes opened, sleep filled and disorientated, but widening as they recognised daylight at the window. Yet still she made no attempt to leave.

'You kept me up too late, sir,' she whispered, and there was a smile in her rebuke.

'Can I do so again tonight, Lady Lindsay? Or today if you should so will it?'

'I cannot think your servants would be pleased at such a prospect.' Lifting her head, she listened for a moment. 'They are at work already, yet they have not come in?'

'And rest assured that they will not, my love.'

Her left hand pushed back the heavy length of her hair and the ring of his mother glinted in the light.

'However, the grapevines of those in servitude will be ringing and my name, undoubtedly, shall be bandied around the salons in shock.'

'I'll announce our wish to marry in *The Times* tomorrow and everyone in the *ton* will recognise you as my intended. No one then would dare to criticise.'

'And your grandfather?'

'Who knows? Such a pronouncement may even bring him from St Auburn as he has hoped for such an occasion for ever. Jamie's existence will make him delirious.'

'You almost make me believe that it could be this easy for us.'

'Well, we have waited for years to be together again and that must be some kind of a miracle.'

She curled into him, holding tight. 'I have missed you. Missed this. Missed talking and loving. Missed closeness.'

He felt her breath at his throat, gentle and honest. Like his life was now with her in it. He wanted to protect her for ever and love her until they were old and grey with a million memories shared between them. The harsh and raw realities of the past faded into this new serenity, Cassandra and Jamie in the very centre of a world reformed.

Her finger traced the tattoo on his forearm. 'What does this mean?'

He smiled. 'It's one of the symbols from the healing temples of Asclepius. At the time, in the backstreets of Marseilles, I was looking for resurrection and renewal. Later on it always reminded me of the thin line between life and death.'

'Being a spy must have been dangerous work. Your body is covered in scars.'

'It's the price one pays for not carrying arms and being out of uniform. Blending into a community is not always as easy as it might sound.'

'But you have stopped?'

'Almost.'

'I am glad for it.'

'And for the first time I think I could settle at St Auburn and run the place, farm the land, sit as a judge at the country courts, grow vegetables. All the things I once would not have seen sense in.'

She laughed.

'With you and Jamie there it all feels possible.'

Cassie turned then to look at him, the light in her eyes bright and clear. He could never decide whether they were more green than blue. Today they seemed an exact mixture of both. 'I think I loved you the first moment I saw you in Nay, with your dimple...here.' She touched his cheek.

'Show me,' he returned and brought her against him, the sunlight from the new day creating a river of warmth on their bed.

* * *

They renewed their vows two days later in the chapel to one side of the Lindsay town house and it was a small and private occasion. Stephen Hawkhurst was the best man and Maureen the bridesmaid. William Lindsay, the old Earl of St Auburn, had sent a note declining his attendance. Cassandra's sister Anne had not been able to make the journey down from her home in Scotland because she was expecting her fourth child.

'You look beautiful, Cassandra,' Nathaniel said as she came down the stairs, her gown of cream silk shimmering in the new day.

'The seamstress you organised was wonderfully fast and this time around I even have shoes.'

He laughed and took her hand, but poignancy lingered beneath the humour as both thought of the small house by the river.

'Now and for ever,' he whispered, brushing his lips across her cheek despite the onlookers, and Jamie standing between them wriggled in delight.

When the clergyman called them to an altar fashioned with flowers, the three of them linked hands and walked forward, her father, brother and Kenyon Riley just behind them.

'Dearly beloved, we have come together in the presence of God to witness and bless the joining together of this man and this woman in holy matrimony...'

They looked at each other. This time they would be married under their own names, properly formed and completely legal.

* * *

A few hours later Stephen asked if he might speak to them both in the library where they would not be disturbed. After shutting the door he brought forth a leather satchel and took out a wad of documents from within.

'I have a wedding present for you both.'

Nat stepped forward, the frown on his brow giving Cassie the inkling that he might know what was held within the papers. They looked important. Her own heart began to beat fast.

'It is the official report from the British Service about the events that transpired in Perpignan after you were hurt in Languedoc, Nat.'

'God.' Her husband's curse was soft.

'It is not what you might think,' Hawk said quickly and handed him over the account. 'I have underlined the most crucial parts. Perhaps your wife might like to hear them.'

'No.' Her own voice, stiff with shock. How could Stephen Hawkhurst do this to her? She knew what would be within the letter, knew it to the bottom of her breaking heart. But Nathaniel was smiling and there was the suspicion of tears in his eyes as he began to read.

So it is concluded that on the fifth of November 1846 at about nine p.m. two masked men broke into the house of Mr Didier Desrosiers and Mr Gilbert Desrosiers in Toulouse, France, and killed each of them with two shots to the head.

Our agent in Languedoc, Nathaniel Lindsay, was also found on the right bank of the Basse River in Perpignan in the afternoon of the sixth of November 1846 with injuries to his head, stomach and right arm received by unknown enemies of England.

Despite extensive searching the perpetrators have never been brought to justice.

The fifth of November? The day before they had reached Perpignan. The day before she had told Lebansart the names. The day before she had branded herself a traitor. The day before shame had been scorched into memory.

'It was not me, after all.' The words slipped from her, tentative and unbelieving. 'They were already dead?'

'How did you know to find this?' Nat spoke now directly to Stephen, the relief in his tone evident.

'When you said you had married Cassandra Northrup in France I knew that you would not have done such a thing lightly. When you then went on to say that she had betrayed you, I realised there must be more to the affair than you had told me. At the Forsythe ball your wife made it known that there were others who died in Perpignan because of her actions and so I decided to find out exactly what it was she meant. After much searching I located this in a box that had been lost amongst others in the record room.'

'Lost?'

'Discarded, I think. Unsolved deaths. Cases closed to further enquiry.'

'But their deaths were not my fault?' The room felt farther away than it had been and a spinning lightness consumed Cassie as she groped for the chair at her side and sat down upon it. Hard. Nathaniel perched before her, taking her hands in his own.

'This is the best wedding present anyone could give us, Hawk,' he said, fingers warming her coldness. 'Cassandra was already pregnant when Guy Lebansart caught us at Perpignan. By reciting the names she had seen on the letters in the place she had been captured, she was trying to save both me and our baby.'

'But her confession and your injury took place the day after the Desrosiers died and at least a hundred miles to the south, so any information she gave was useless.'

'I didn't kill them.' Tears of deliverance fell down her cheeks. 'I didn't,' she repeated, the beauty of what the words implied washing across her like a balm.

'You have both been to hell and back on a lie. But you married her again, Nat, even knowing this?'

'When you love someone, you love them, Hawk, and there would be no argument in the world that would keep me from Cassandra. But this...this allows us peace.'

Standing up, he faced Stephen Hawkhurst. 'I should have tried to find out all that transpired after that day, but I could not. I never wanted to sift through the files and know the betrayal.'

'Yet you kept her name out of everything. I am not

certain, had it been me, that I could have done that. King, country, oaths and all.'

Nathaniel laughed. 'They are all nothing against love, my friend. Wait until you find it.'

Gathering the documents, Stephen replaced them in the book. 'If Shavvon knew I had removed these...' He left the rest unsaid. 'But if I have them back tonight he will never need to know anything of it. He sends you his best, by the way.'

Cassie looked up at her husband and wondered just exactly who this Shavvon was that they were speaking of.

'Our boss,' Nathaniel explained quietly. 'At the Service.'

'But now this case is closed. For good.' Stephen faced them both as he promised this and then he was gone, the documents in hand as the door closed behind him.

'A marriage and a reprieve,' Nat said as he drew Cassandra up against him. 'A binding and a freedom. It has been quite a day, Lady Lindsay.' She could feel his breath against her cheek, soft and known.

'Lady Lindsay. I like the sound of that.'

'My wife. An even better resonance.'

'And what of the marriage night?' she whispered, watching the flare of complicity and question in his pale eyes. 'I think we should celebrate Hawk's gift.'

'I am completely at your disposal, my beautiful *Sandrine*,' he returned, lifting her into his arms and taking her to bed.

Chapter Thirteen

The past week had been a whirlpool of activity. Maureen's delight at her news, her father's quiet pleasure at having three daughters now in advantageous unions and Jamie's thrilled disbelief that the papa he had so often spoken of was promising to buy him a horse when they arrived at St Auburn.

After their wedding Cassandra had been inundated with calling cards, every door into society now open to her, though Nathaniel seemed distracted by his own work with the Service. She confronted him about it late on the third night after their marriage when she had gone down to the library to find him surrounded by papers.

'You look busy.'

'Busy missing some clue that I am certain is right in front of me,' he returned and stood.

'It is the girls from the river and Sarah?'

He nodded. 'Have you ever heard of the name Scrivener Weeks?'

'No. He is the man who you think killed them?'

'I do. I went to Wallingford and discovered that a few months ago another young woman was murdered there. A tall, dark and well-dressed man signed into the tavern late on the night the body was found, using the name of Scrivener Weeks. He left on the London coach early the next morning. No one can truly remember what he looked like.'

'He could be anyone.'

'Not quite. I think he is a member of the Venus Club.'

'Like Uncle Reginald?' Another thought occurred. 'That is why you and Stephen Hawkhurst joined up in the first place?'

He smiled. 'It is easier to keep an eye on people at close quarters. For what it is worth I have discounted your uncle.'

'Why?'

'He was ill with some sort of a chest infection when the girls were found on the riverbank here in London. He has the same physician as Hawkhurst does and the doctor was adamant Reginald Northrup could not have left his sick bed for a fortnight.'

'How many members does the club have?'

'Sixty-eight, and I have a group of thirteen names who fit the description of Scrivener Weeks.'

'We leave for St Auburn tomorrow. Could Stephen Hawkhurst take over until we return?'

'He will. I have told him my thoughts and given him the names. Perhaps he will see something that I have not.'

'Sarah would be thankful to you for your time and effort in finding her killer.'

'I haven't yet.'

'But you will.'

At that she took his hand and led him upstairs.

Late the next afternoon Cassandra could barely believe that they were almost at the principal country seat of the Lindsays, the fields about them rolling and green.

'Will we be there soon, Papa?'

She smiled. Jamie never spoke to Nathaniel without adding on 'Papa'. He had lost four years of his father and now he was making up for it. Sitting on Nathaniel's knee, he looked at the various landmarks that were pointed out.

'I used to swim in that river when I was very young. My father made wooden boats and we would sail them in the summer. Often they got stuck so I would jump in to rescue them.'

'Can you make me a boat, Papa? We could do that, too.'

Cassandra's heart swelled as her husband looked over at her, kissing the top of Jamie's head as he did so. Maureen, Kenyon, Rodney and her father would be arriving the day after tomorrow and she was pleased to have a couple of days to settle in. The only cloud on the horizon was Nathaniel's grandfather for they had not heard a word from him.

'The first sight of the house can be seen past this rise,' Nathaniel said and lifted Jamie higher. Cassie leaned forward to see it, too, and an enormous Georgian mansion materialised out of the distance, the six pillars across the front edifice flanked by two plainer wings, sitting on a hill. The tree-lined driveway wound towards it, a lake of grand proportions to one side.

'St Auburn is beautiful.' She could not keep the worry from her words.

'And big,' Jamie added.

'It's home,' Nathaniel said and reached for her hand. 'Our home.'

He had placed three of his staff into running the ledgers for the Daughters of the Poor and with his sizeable cash donation Cassie knew that all the work she had done would be left in competent hands. She would still hold regular meetings with Elizabeth and the staff, but the night-time rambles had ended and part of her was glad. This was a new chapter of her life and one she relished.

A line of servants had come out to greet them and there at the front door was an elderly man who Cassie reasoned would be Nathaniel's grandfather. He leaned upon a stick and watched them carefully as the conveyance drew to a halt.

Jamie was out first, the sun on his hair mirroring his father's and a sense of urgency and life on show that he had inherited as well. He looked right at home here, the tall yellow walls behind him with their meticulously pointed stone and inset windows. No small task for the masons, this building would have taken years and years to construct.

The old man came forward, his face devoid of expression. 'You have come back,' he said.

'We have come home,' Jamie cried. 'This is going to be my home now with the lake and boats.'

'Indeed?'

Such curling indifference had the effect of bringing Jamie closer to Nathaniel, fingers entwined in the expensive superfine of his father's trousers.

'William, this is my wife, Cassandra, and my son, Jamie.'

Pale silvered eyes whisked across her, calculating and assessing, and then they travelled over Jamie, the first glimmer of emotion showing.

'Well, at least he looks like a St Auburn. Does he like horses?'

'I have not ever ridden one, sir.'

'Grandpa,' he corrected. 'Call me Grandpa. Your father used to.'

A rebuke coined within the softness of memory. Nathaniel's hand tightened about her own, and Cassie hoped that whatever had gone wrong between them might soon be resolved.

After being introduced to the housekeeper and butler they walked along the line of other lesser servants, each one in a crisp and spotless uniform and all with generous welcomes. Once inside the Lindsay patriarch gestured for them to join him in a salon that ran along the front of the house, a room decorated in blues and greens.

'I was surprised that you finally realised St Auburn to be a duty you could encompass in your busy life,

Nathaniel. Have you had enough of lying around in foreign taverns?'

Her husband's languid smile did not quite reflect his words. 'Protecting England from its enemies requires more than a nominal effort, William, though I do admit to a few drinks.'

Strong brandy to quell the pain of a gunshot wound in his side, but only water a few hours later as she had tried to clean it.

She wanted to say this to an old man who had much to thank his grandson for. She wanted him to see the hero in Nathaniel that she so often saw, a spy who had spent years undercover and in places that had hardly been kind. But she did not say any of this because she had no idea as to whether her husband would thank her for it or not. So she stayed quiet.

'The rooms on the first floor have been made up for you. Dinner will be at eight.'

With that he simply got up and walked away, the tap of his stick on the polished tiles becoming fainter and fainter.

'My grandfather has never been a man to show his feelings. This attitude, I suppose, was the reason my father and mother left here when I was young. They probably got the same sort of welcome we just did.'

'Does he not like us, Papa? Is he angry we are here?'

'No, he loves you, Jamie, but he is old and has gone to his quarters to have a rest.' Pulling his son up into his arms, he turned towards Cassie. 'Shall I show you to our room, my lady?'

'Certainly, my lord.' Suddenly all the politics of

family squabbles did not matter at all. Tonight they would be together in a home that was theirs for good. She couldn't wait for the evening to come.

The chamber Nathaniel led them to was beautiful, with wide French doors leading out to a substantial balcony, pots festooned with greenery and flowers. Like in France, she thought, and looked across at the view. It was majestic. The far-off hills. The lake. The trees. The farm fields that went on and on for ever.

Jamie's room was a little farther down the corridor, flanked by the smaller nanny's quarters and a maid's room. To one side of Jamie's bed a whole row of old wooden toys were arranged on low shelves.

'They were once my father's. William must have instructed the servants to bring them down from the attic.' Nathaniel looked surprised.

'Did you play with them, too?' she asked as Jamie bent to draw a wooden train along the parquet flooring.

'I did. My grandfather was never very keen on the idea, though, for he thought I might break them. Perhaps he trusts you more, Jamie.'

'I will be very careful, Papa.'

'I know you will.'

Nat thought that the smile on Cassandra's face looked tightly drawn. She was obviously shocked by his grandfather's behaviour and by St Auburn, too. Most people on first seeing the place had the same sort of disbelief, but it was one of those houses that had grown over generations and there had always been plenty of money in the coffers of the Lindsays.

Plenty of money and not a lot of love. William had seen to that. He would get Cassie and Jamie settled and then he would go and find his grandfather. It was one thing for William to be rude to him, but quite another to be contrary with his wife and son. He would simply not put up with it.

But other things began to play on his mind, too. The way the sun slanted in upon Cassie's hair and the beauty of her face in profile. Crossing the room, he brought her close.

'Thank you for coming here with me. I am not sure if I would want to face it alone.'

'I think he is sad, your grandfather. How old were your parents when they died?'

'Thirty-four and twenty-eight.'

'Young, then. Imagine what that must have been like. Did he have a wife?'

'No. Margaret Lindsay died after my father left St Auburn.'

'Two terrible losses. And then the loss of you, as well, to the British Service and the further worry of the only family left to him never coming home.'

He smiled into her hair. 'I was about to go and growl at him. Now I am not so certain I should.' Nat had seen William's lack of feeling in terms of his own grief when he had lost his parents, but with Cassie's words a different understanding dawned. Imagine if he were to lose both her and Jamie. Would he still be able to function? He doubted it. Across her shoulders his son played with his new toys and beyond that again through the window the great lands of St Auburn spread out before him.

Home.

Here.

In Cassandra's arms, the scent of violets and woman and the promise of the passionate hours of night not far off.

'If this doesn't work we don't have to stay. There are plenty of other Lindsay properties.'

'But there is only one great-grandfather, Nathaniel, and Jamie needs to know him.'

Dinner that evening was a myriad of different emotions: William's distance, Cassandra's wariness and Nathaniel's equanimity. The room itself was beautiful with its carved table and tapestried chairs. On the wall around them were paintings from ground to ceiling displaying the images of relatives long dead. Their facial expressions looked about as happy as William's did as he sat at one end of the table.

'It is strange that you did not bring your family up to meet me sooner, Nathaniel.'

'We were married in France almost five years ago, but lost one another soon after. We resaid our vows a week ago.'

That brought a light to the old Earl's eyes and for the first time that evening a gleam of interest showed.

'There was a battle and a misunderstanding. I thought Cassandra had perished and she thought that I had, too. We met again only a handful of weeks ago by chance.'

'So you did not know your son?"

'I didn't.'

'He looks exactly as you did when you were that age. I should have some likenesses that were drawn at the time somewhere if you want to see them.' This was addressed at her.

'I should love to, my lord.'

'I will have them found tomorrow. There are other things, too, that I remember, a swing and a slide and a small rocking horse. Did he enjoy the toys in his room?"

Nat cleared his throat. 'He did. Thank you for thinking of it.'

'The boy and his mother can come with me on the morrow and we will go exploring for the rest of the toys that you and your father used to play with.'

A generous allowance and the first step into a truce from the battle of wits that Nathaniel and his grandfather seemed to be playing. Cassandra hoped that there would be many more across the next few days and weeks.

Much later Nathaniel and Cassandra lay in bed, holding each other and listening to the sound of a large house settling for the night: a clock in a distant hallway ringing out the lateness, the last swish of a maid's skirt as she went by on the final errands of the evening and a log in the fire shifting into a quieter burn. Jamie was fast asleep in his room. Nathaniel had tucked him in, all the love and concern of a father who wanted to savour the small moments he had so far missed in his care.

An hour earlier Nat had lifted her up in his arms,

too, and placed her on his bed, positioning the frothy nothingness of her lacy nightgown just so.

'You cannot know how much I have longed for this moment, Cassie. To see you here at St Auburn as my wife.' He clasped her hand and turned the wedding ring that he'd had resized in London. 'We have done everything so far all the wrong way around. But from now on I mean to get it right.'

She shook her head. 'You have, my darling, all the way through. Ever since you first found me and took me out of Nay with a bullet hole in your side.'

Standing naked in the half-light of the fire, he looked like a large, strong panther, circling for all that she might give him, muscles shadowed and harsh. The tattoo stood out as did the white scars of battle. Her knight. Her hero.

Opening her arms, she brought him against her. This was the bed and the room that they would live in together for all the rest of their lives. When tears welled in her eyes and spilled down her cheeks, he pulled back in question.

'It is happiness, Nathaniel, only that.'

His forefinger came up to gently wipe away the moisture. 'I will love you for ever, Cassandra Sandrine Mercier Northrup.' The troth was given with a solemn honesty before his mouth closed down on hers.

The belltower attic was a place of wonder, a high-beamed room of generous proportion and a thousand forgotten things in it. With a new morning the old Earl seemed more fleet footed despite needing to manoeuvre around rolls of material and piles of papers. The toys were stacked on large, low shelves, numerous versions of balls and trains and soldiers and forts. One look at Jamie's face told her that they might be here a while.

'I like the big train best, Grandpa.'

The word *grandpa* seemed to sink into the deep lines of his face and flatten them out. 'I think if I look there are tracks for it somewhere.'

Cassie glanced around. 'I am sure Jamie feels as if all his Christmas days have come at once.'

'I think he may deserve it. Three years without a father is a long time.'

'Almost four,' she said quietly. 'His birthday is soon.'

They were interrupted by a squeal of delight. 'Look, Grandpa, look what it can do.' He pulled the string behind the head of a large wooden puppet and the garish mouth opened to reveal a full set of yellowing teeth.

'That used to be my favourite, too,' William replied, bringing a large white kerchief from his pocket to dab at his eyes. As Jamie continued to explore, William started to speak of the past. 'Nathaniel is very like his father was, and forgiveness is not an easily won thing. When Geoffrey died, a part of me did, too, and I lost the little piece of him that I still had left in Nathaniel. Now it might be too late to find each other again.'

Cassie shook her head. 'Family should always be forgiven no matter what happens between them, for blood is thicker than insult or misconception. It only takes honesty.'

He smiled. 'My grandson was indeed lucky to find you.'

'He rescued me from a desperate situation and he did not judge me as he could so easily have done. His job there in France was a hard and dangerous one and if he hadn't come when he did...' She stopped, the horror of what might have been evident. 'England is fortunate to have someone like your grandson protecting its interests, and you should be proud that he carries your family name with such honour. I know I am.'

'I should have known, of course, for Geoffrey was a good man, too. It was just after my wife passed on that I felt so marooned and lost, and in my sorrow the happiness of my son's family gave me no relief. I pushed them away and never got them back.'

'Nathaniel did not come here to St Auburn again?'

'Oh, indeed, he did for a time after his parents died but by then we were set in our distance from each other and we barely talked. Later he wanted to modernise the place and I was determined to leave things as they were. After a while he hardly ever came home.'

'Well, we are here to stay now, and you will have all the chance in the world to talk with him. If you told him what you have just told me...'

She stopped as he nodded his head, and Jamie came up to him with a small boat complete with sails and ropes in his hands.

'Papa spoke about this in the carriage.'

'He did?' William took the craft and turned it this

way and that. 'Your father's father made this, Jamie. If you bring it down we might be able to have a try at sailing the craft on the lake.'

'I will jump in and rescue it if it gets stuck, Grandpa.'

'Then we certainly have a deal.'

Maureen, Kenyon, Rodney and Lord Cowper arrived in the middle of the following morning, her uncle Reginald and his friend Christopher Hanley unexpectedly behind them in another conveyance. Nathaniel looked less than happy with the new arrivals as she glanced up at him. Something seemed wrong.

'I saw your father in London yesterday,' Reginald explained when the carriage stopped, 'and told him of my plans to head to the coast. When he asked if I would like to call in here at St Auburn for an hour or two, I was most grateful. I hope having Hanley here, too, will not upset anyone.'

The old earl looked about as pleased as Nathaniel did, and the arrival of Stephen Hawkhurst seemed to heighten the awkwardness yet again. Cassandra did not fail to see the look that went between her husband and his friend as they turned inside, and the tension seemed to emanate from the presence of Christopher Hanley.

Christopher Hanley sought her out an hour later as drinks and a light repast were being served in the front salon.

'You will not be so involved with your charity from now on, I suppose, Lady Lindsay? Being here should take up much of your time.'

'No, in that you are wrong. I shall be as busy with it as I ever was, and London is not far.'

'Was there ever any sign of Sarah Milgrew and her sister's killer?'

'No, nothing, though we are still hopeful of finding some clue to help us.'

'Your father continues to fund the Daughters of the Poor, then?'

'Indeed he does, and Nathaniel is involved, too. My husband has brought Stephen Hawkhurst in for added assistance.'

Hawk watched them now, Cassie saw, his eyes devouring Hanley's stance and face and a small worm of uneasiness turned in her stomach. Something wasn't right, but she could not quite put her finger upon it. She was pleased when her uncle came to claim his friend in conversation, allowing her to move away.

'You look worried.' William had joined her over by the windows. 'I knew Hanley's parents and they were not a happy couple. The father had a way with women of the night and the mother ran off with an Italian merchant and never returned to England.'

'A difficult upbringing for him, then?' Nathaniel had heard the last of the conversation as he came up behind her.

'You have had dealings with him?' William sounded interested in his grandson's answer.

'He has the unfortunate habit of poking his nose in other people's business. Suffice it to say he did Cassandra and me a favour in Whitechapel, but it could have been different.'

Uncle Reginald seemed to be making much of conversing with her father and for the first time in months Papa appeared happy. She supposed she should overlook the presence of the others here for an hour or two for it was good to see Papa smiling.

When Kenyon asked Nathaniel for a tour of the grounds of St Auburn everyone decided to go with them. Outside the sky was blue and the sun warm, and having partaken of food and drink a small exercise was desirable. Cassie was interested to see how Nathaniel shepherded Hanley, in particular, out through the front door.

Jamie was fractious though with all the excitement and so Cassie decided to stay back with him. A rest might see him through the afternoon pursuits and then he could have an early bedtime.

Bedtime.

She wished it were later already and that the hour to retire was here. Catching Nathaniel's eyes, she saw he watched her mount the stairs and she blushed with the warmth of his observance. Would there ever be a time when she could stand on the other side of a room fully dressed and in the company of others and not feel…desperate for him? She hoped not.

William, too, had decided to stay indoors because he found the heat oppressive. Concern marred Cassie's happiness. She prayed he would stay well and healthy enough to be a part of their family celebrations and outings for many years to come. They had only just found him again, after all, and underneath the gruff exterior was a man with a soft heart.

* * *

Half an hour later, sitting next to her sleeping son and thinking about her day, a new thought surfaced. Christopher Hanley had mentioned something about Sarah Milgrew, and Cassie sought to remember his words exactly.

He had asked about Sarah and her sister's killer. She sat forward, trying to pinpoint her uneasiness. The sister? Horror filled her. How had he known anything about Sarah's sister? The police themselves had not mentioned this and there had never been an identification carried out on the bodies of the earlier victims.

Oh, granted, Sarah had spoken of her sister's disappearance and Nathaniel had been interested in the gown of one of the drowned girls, but there had been no other information offered. Besides, the note that had arrived for Sarah the day she had disappeared alluded to information about knowing the whereabouts of her sibling, not the demise of her.

'My God.'

Standing, she indicated to a maid outside in the corridor to come in and sit with Jamie. Christopher Hanley was the tall, dark and well-dressed man. She was suddenly sure of it. He had been in Brown Street off Whitechapel Road when Nathaniel and she had found the body in the brothel, and the toff seen at the St Katharine Docks matched his description exactly.

Peering out the window on the stairwell, she noticed the group with Nathaniel to be perusing the formal gardens, but she could not see Christopher Hanley with them.

Fright made her heart beat faster as she hurried towards the front door. She had to get to Nathaniel to tell him what she suspected.

She had almost come into the wide hallway when a voice stopped her.

'I had a feeling I should return.' The sound came from behind and with all the effort in the world Cassandra made herself turn. She barely recognised the urbane and civilised lord, a sneer on his face and cold outrage in his eyes. Fear congealed in her throat and she could not hide her fright. 'I made a mistake talking to you earlier and I can see that you picked up on it.' Hanley's voice lacked any remorse whatsoever.

'You killed Sarah Milgrew and her sister. Why?' An explanation might buy her some moments for surely Nathaniel would be returning soon.

'They knew who I was. I thought after the first one I was safe and then the second girl turned up. I had killed their cousin in Wallingford, you see, and they remembered me.'

'And the man who was found dead at Brown Street?'

'Had come to London at the behest of their father to ask around and find out what had happened to the older sister. I couldn't let him ruin things.'

'So you tried to ruin me instead. It was you who sent the note asking me to come to the boarding house.'

'A miscalculation, I was to think later, for I did not realise that you knew Lindsay so well. Without him there, I might have succeeded. When he visited me in London the other day I knew by his questions that he suspected something.'

'Yet you still came to St Auburn?'

'To find out the lay of the land, Lady Lindsay.'

At that he moved forward and simply twisted her arm hard up behind her back. 'If you shout out, I will go straight up to your son's room and break his neck, do you understand? Like a chicken in a hen house. You or him. Make your choice.'

Fear ripped resistance into pieces. Cassie would wait till they were outside before trying to flee. Nodding, she went with him, past the first door and then the second, no servant in sight, the coast clear for his escape.

The third door was different. William Lindsay, the old Earl of St Auburn, was waiting in all readiness and with a shout he raised his cane and brought it down hard upon Hanley's head before falling.

The ungainly upending might have saved all their lives, she was to think later, for William took a sideboard full of bottles and glasses down with him and the noise was enough to wake up the dead. Blood dripped down into his closed eyes and Cassandra was certain that he had broken every bone in his body.

Hanley did not waver, finding an open window in the next salon and pushing her through it headfirst where she landed heavily onto an uneven brick wall and lost her breath.

'With you out of the way my secret will be safe and a quick escape to France will see to my own future.'

Shock had made him shake, and she felt his wrath course through her as he dragged her into the bushes surrounding the lake. Without hesitation, he pushed her into the water.

Icy coldness settled quickly.

Then his hands were about her throat, squeezing and squeezing. She tried to fight, she did, tried to stop him as the green of the water closed over her head, but already the world had begun to narrow into darkness. Sharp rocks dug into her back.

Floating. Peacefulness. The last release of bubbles as the warmth of death became brighter.

Then there was a noise, a hard punch and scream and a further whip of knuckles. The grip about her throat released and Cassie was lifted gently from the cold to be brought up into the arms of her husband where he cradled her against his warmth.

'It is all right, my love. You are safe.'

She was coughing, long, deep gasps of coughing, the air hard to find and the cold making it harder again. Her throat ached and her back had been bruised as Hanley had forced her down, but she was alive.

Alive.

Then she was crying, huge throaty sobs, her hands entwined in the fabric of his jacket.

'Your...gr-gr-grandfather tr-tried to s-save me.'

'I know, sweetheart. Don't try to talk just now. I will take you back to the house and a bath will be drawn.'

A bath. Warmth. She gritted her teeth together to try to stop the dreadful shaking and felt the heat from his skin beneath her cheek.

Nat lifted Cassie, making certain that he averted his gaze from the dark red bruises that were gouged into her throat and from the cut beneath her eye. If Hanley had not been unconscious, he would have hit him yet again. Her hair was tangled with weed from the lake, the mud at the bottom smeared across her face and shoulders.

So damn close.

Another moment and they could not have saved her. He looked over at his grandfather, worse for wear from his upending, and saw the same thoughts in the opaque eyes. With a smile, he bent his head. In homage and in gratitude. Without William's quick-thinking actions...?

He shook away the horror.

Cassie was still crying, but her sobs were softer now. Her breathing had eased a little, too, and the pale white of her skin was rosier.

Her colour was returning and her fright receding. He was glad Kenyon was there to help his grandfather walk, the back of his head already showing signs of a bruised swelling. Maureen had taken his other side and she was speaking to him in the quiet and restful tones of one who seldom panicked.

A family that would be there for each other when the times got tough. A group of people joined by blood and love. He kissed his wife's cold forehead as he strode up the steps of St Auburn and the startled servants came running.

He found his grandfather in the library an hour later, sitting and looking out of the window with a heavy bandage around his head.

'William.' Today the word did not sit upon his

tongue with the ease that it always had. 'Grandfather,' he amended and saw the old man turn.

'Is your wife recovered?'

'She is having a hot bath. The maids are with her and the warmth will stop the chills.'

'And Hanley?'

'Hawk has taken him back to London where he will be dealt with.'

'I would kill him if it were left to me.'

The sentiment made Nat smile. 'In that we are alike.'

'Are we?'

This time Nathaniel knew it was something else entirely of which William spoke. 'You never wanted my mother and father anywhere near you. You sent them from St Auburn and refused to ever see them again.'

'My Margaret had just died. I was not thinking straight and afterwards...' He hesitated. 'Afterwards it was too late. But now I see what I have missed.'

'You saved Cassandra. Without your bravery Hanley might have drowned her without a whisper.'

The earl shook his head. 'I hit him as hard as I could and it barely touched him.'

'But the noise when you fell alerted us. I owe you everything.'

His grandfather used his cane and came to stand next to Nat. 'We are both hard-headed and stubborn, Nathaniel, and we both love our wives with all our hearts.' The old eyes were watery as he placed his hand forward palm up. 'And our children.'

Pleading lay in the gesture. For family, it said, and for forgiveness, it asked.

Stepping forward, Nat brought his grandfather into his arms, tightly wrapped in an emotion that he had thought would be impossible.

'Thank you for saving her, Grandfather.'

'It was my pleasure, Nathaniel. And thank you, too, for saving me.'

Chapter Fourteen

She was wrapped in the warmth of wool and settled onto the generous blue sofa in the downstairs parlour.

Cassandra had had her hair washed and her body powdered and her feet were swathed in slippers of the finest lambswool, a present from William and one he had bought for his wife just before she had died.

She felt blessed. Jamie was cuddled into her side, and Nathaniel sat on a leather chair only a few feet away.

'If you had not been there, Grandfather, this could have all turned out far differently.' Her husband's words held a reverence and respect that was heartwarming.

'Which just goes to show that there is life in the old boy yet.' She saw William's hand rest lightly on Nathaniel's shoulder. They had spoken privately, she knew, before coming downstairs and the feud that had parted them seemed all but gone.

Reginald also had turned out to be a surprise. He had offered Cassandra a more than generous amount to be put into the coffers of the Daughters of the Poor plus the free use of a property that he owned in Aldwych as a place to set up further employment. Compensation for his poor choice of friends, he had told everyone. He had also decided to leave the Venus Club.

When Cassie glanced over at Nathaniel she saw that he was watching her closely.

'Good things come out of bad,' he said and smiled, though when his eyes settled on the marks at her throat an edge of anger was still visible.

Protection. It was so very relaxing. She closed her eyes and slept.

Much later when she awoke she found that she was back in their own chamber, but Nathaniel was not in bed with her. He stood at the window, looking over the land of the Lindsays, a moon hanging in the sky. The calmness that was so much a part of him made her smile and she simply watched.

'You cannot sleep, Nathaniel?'

The effects of the toddy the housekeeper had made for her had almost worn off now, and Cassie felt as if the shadows and mirrors she had lived with all her life had been thrown away somehow, the strong lines of hope exposed by love instead.

'I could not live if you left me, Sandrine. I could not find a way to keep on going. Today when I thought...' His voice broke, and he turned away, but not before she saw the moisture on his cheeks and the terror in his eyes. 'I never slept with another woman after Perpignan. It has always been just you.'

Pushing back the covers, she joined him at the window, winding her arms about his coldness and infusing warmth.

'Love holds no barriers, my darling. Time. Distance. Space. They are just words against love. We will always be together because we will always love.'

'Do you promise?'

'Come to bed and I will show you how I know,' she whispered, the heat of ardour rising. 'Let me take you to a place that is only ours.'

'Like the memory of the high baths above Bagnères-de-Bigorre?'

She nodded and, taking his arm, led him back to the warm nest of their bed.

As often thro' the purple night,
Below the starry clusters bright,
Some bearded meteor trailing light,
Moves over still Shalott.

* * * * *

A SECRET
CONSEQUENCE FOR
THE VISCOUNT

This book is dedicated to Linda Fildew, my
wonderful and irreplaceable editor,
who has been with me right from the start.
Thanks for knowing when to give me a push
to try new things.

Prologue

James River, Virginia—1818

He was bone-weary and cold and had been for a long time now.

He could feel it in his hands and heart and in the fury wrapped around each intake of breath, fear raw against the sound of the river.

Once he knew he had been different. Such knowledge sent a shaft of pain through him that was worse than anything else imaginable, an elusive certainty drifting on the edge of misunderstanding.

He swore as he lowered his body into the water, closing his eyes against the sting of cold. With the hand that still had feeling in it he grabbed at the rushes and steadied movement. He was here somewhere, the man who had slashed at him with a blade. He could feel his presence, close now, a shadow catching at space between darkness, barely visible. He held no weapon except for his wits, no way of protecting himself save for the years of desperation honed in distance. He couldn't remember ever feeling safe.

The voice came unexpectedly and close.

'Nicholas Bartlett? Are you there?'

The sound had him turning his head. For more or for less he knew not which. The name was familiar, its syllables distinct as they ran together into something that made a terrible and utter sense.

He wanted to stop the sudden onslaught of memories, each thread reforming itself into more, building a picture, words that pulled at the spinning void of his life and anchored him back into truth. A truth that lay above comprehension and disbelief.

More words came from the mouth of his stalker, moving before him, as he raised steel under a dull small moon.

'Vitium et Virtus.'

A prayer or a prophesy? A forecast of all that was to come or the harbinger of that which had been?

'No.' His own voice was suddenly certain as he shot out of the water to meet his fate, fury fuelling him. He hardly felt the slice of the knife against the soft bones of his face. He was fearless in his quest for life and as the curve of his assailant's neck came into his hands he understood a primal power that did away with doubt and gave him back hope. He felt the small breakage of bone and saw surprise in the dark bulging eyeballs under moonlight. The hot breath on the raised skin of his own forearm slowed and cooled as resistance changed into flaccidity. Life lost into death with barely a noise save the splash of a corpse as it was taken by the wide flowing James to sink under the blackness, a moment's disturbance and then calm, the small ridges slipping into the former patterns of the river.

He sat down on the bank in the wet grass and placed his head between his knees, both temples aching with the movement.

Vitium et Virtus.

Nicholas Bartlett.

He knew the words, knew this life, knew the name imbued into each and every part of him.

Nicholas Henry Stewart Bartlett.

Viscount Bromley.

A crest with a dragon on the dexter side and a horse on the sinister. Both in argent.

An estate in Essex.

Oliver. Frederick. Jacob.

The club of secrets.

Vitium et Virtus.

'Hell.' It all came tumbling back without any barriers. Flashes of honour, shame, disorder and excess after so very many years of nothing.

Tears welled, mixed with blood as the loss of who he now was melded against the sorrow of everything forgotten.

The young and dissolute London Lord with the world at his feet and a thousand hours of leisure and ease before him had been replaced by this person he had become, a life formed by years of endurance and hardship.

'Nicholas Bartlett.'

He turned the name on his tongue and said it quietly into the night so he might hear it truly. The tinge of the

Americas stretched long over the vowels in a cadence at odds with his English roots, though when he repeated it again he heard only the sorrow.

He searched back to the last memories held of that time, but could just think of being at Bromworth Manor in Essex with his uncle. Arguing yet again. After that there was nothing. He could not remember returning to London or getting on a ship to the Americas. He re-called pain somewhere and the vague sense of water. Perhaps he had been picked up by a boat, a stranger without memory and shanghaied aboard?

He knew he would not have disappeared willingly though his gambling debts had been rising as he had been drawn into the seedy halls of London where cheating was rife. There had been threats to pay up or else, but he had by and large managed to do so. His friends had been there to help him through the worst of the de-mands and he also had the club in Mayfair. A home. A family. A place that felt like his. He loved Jacob Huntingdon, Frederick Challenger and Oliver Gregory like the brothers he'd never had.

Shaking fingers touched the ache on his cheek near his right eye and came away with the sticky redness of oozing blood.

The eye felt strange and unfocused. The night was so dark he wondered if he had gone blind in that eye, a last gift from his pursuer. He shut the other one and tried to find an image, holding his fingers up against what little light there was on the water, and was relieved to see a blurry outline.

He did not feel up to walking back yet through the

reeds and the river path to the shade of the cottonwoods. He didn't want others to see him like this and he needed to make certain there were not more who would be trying to hurt him. A tiredness swept over everything, a grief at the loss of a life at his own hands. He had not killed before and the quickness of fear was now replaced by an ennui of guilt.

How could he ever fit in again? How could he be the lord he was supposed to be after this? Had his assailant held a family close? Had he been only doing a job he was sent to complete? The grey shadows in which he'd lived the last six years were things familiar. The sludgy silhouette of them, the blacks and whites of shining morality left as other men's choices but not available to him. Twice before in America others had tried to kill him; different men in the pay of a shadowy enemy and the mastermind at pulling the strings.

He had used so many different names as he moved on for ever, away from discovery, fleeing relationships. In the end he only brought people harm and danger. If they got to know him they were always at risk and so he had not allowed such closeness. Twice before he had felt his stalkers near.

Emily. The young daughter of the kindly reverend and his wife who had taken him in had been pushed off a cliff top. The girl had survived by clinging to the undergrowth, but he had understood that after that for him there could never be intimacy with anyone.

New towns, different jobs and a series of women with favours for sale had followed. He did not seek out decent company again, but dwelt in the underworld of secrets, squalor and shallow rapport. He understood the people who were as brutalised and damaged as himself and there was safety in the shifting unsettled disconnection of outsiders.

Peter Kingston. His name now here in the river town of Richmond, the capital of the Colony and Dominion of Virginia. He could disappear tomorrow and nobody would miss him, the man employed at the tavern of Shockoe Bottom who seldom spoke and hardly ever smiled. Stranger. Foreigner. Outsider. Murderer now. Another name added to all the ones he had gathered. A further disengagement. A shadow who had walked through the Americas with barely a footprint. Until tonight. Until now. Until his hands had fastened around the throat of his pursuer and broken the life from him.

He leant over and was neatly sick into the green heart of some poison ivy.

Leaves of three, let them be.

The ditty came of its own accord as he wiped his mouth with the frayed edge of his jacket. Had he been truly regretful he might have laid his hand across the plant and allowed its penance. As it was he merely frowned at such an idea and stood.

He would gather his few possessions and find a ship to England. Frederick, Oliver and Jacob would help him to make sense of things and then he would leave London to retire to the country in Essex. Alone. It was the only way he could see before him.

As he looked back a fog bank slid by on the flat black current of the James.

Chapter One

⁓⁓⁓

London—December 26th, 1818

It was one day past Christmas.

That thought made Nicolas smile. He had forgotten the celebration for so long in the Americas that the presence of it here in London was somehow comforting. A continued and familiar tradition, a belief that transcended all difficulty and promised hope for the likes of himself? Or would it tender despair? He could not imagine any church exonerating his sins should he be foolish enough to confess them.

The age-old music of carols could be heard as he left the narrow service alley behind the club of Vitium et Virtus in Mayfair and came around to the front door. Here the only sound was that of laughter and frivolity, a card game underway, he guessed, in the downstairs salon. High stakes and well funded. The few coins he had left in his own pocket felt paltry and he wondered for the millionth time whether he should have come at all.

The late afternoon lengthened the shadows. He could slip away still, undetected, and make his way north. Boxing Day kept most people at home enjoying the company of family. There would be few around to note his progress.

He swallowed as he looked up and saw the sky was stained in red. Blood red. Guilt red. A celestial nod to his culpability or a pardon written in colour?

Digging into his pocket, he found a silver shilling.

'Heads I stay and tails I go.' It was all he could think of at this moment, a choice that was arbitrary and random. The coin turned and as it came down into his opened palm the face of George the Third was easily visible. The thought crossed his mind that had it been tails he would have tried for the best of three.

His knuckles were against the main door before he knew it, the polished black lacquer of the portal attesting to great care and attention and a certain understated wealth.

When it opened a big man he did not know stood there, dressed in the clothes of a footman, but with the visage of one who knew his intrinsic worth.

'Can I help you, sir?'

Nicholas could feel the condescension. His clothes from the long voyage were dirty and they had not been well looked after. His beard was full and his hair uncut. He was glad there was no looking glass inside the door to reflect his image over and over again.

'Are any of the lords who own this place present inside this evening?'

He tried to round his vowels and sound at least half-way convincing. It would not take much for the man to bid those who guarded the front door to throw him out. He knew there was desperation in his eyes.

'They are, sir.'

'Could you show me through to them?'

'Indeed, sir. But may I take your hat and coat first and could you give me your name?'

'Bromley. They will know me.'

'If you would just wait here, sir.' The footman snagged Nick's attire across a series of wooden pegs carved into the shape of a man's sexual parts inside the front door. The sheer overtness of the furnishings shocked him now, where once it had not.

A further confusion. Another way in which he had changed. He swallowed and as dryness filled his mouth he wished he'd thought to bring his brandy flask.

Then there was the sound of chairs scraping against the floor and the rush of feet, a door flung back against its hinges and three faces he knew like his own before him. Astonished. Disbelieving.

'Nicholas?' It was Jacob who came forward first just as he knew it would be. Rakish and handsome, there had always been an undercurrent of kindness within him, a care for the underdog, a certainty of faith.

Oliver and Frederick followed him, each one as bewildered as the next.

'You've been gone for more than six damn years…' It was Oliver who said this, the flush of emotion visible across the light brown of his skin.

'And to turn up like this without any correspondence? Why would you not let us know where you were or how you fared at least?' Fred's voice cracked as his glance took in Nick's cheek and the bandage on his left hand holding the deep wound safe from further damage.

Twenty-five days at sea had not helped the healing. It ached so much he had taken to cradling it across his body, easing the pain and heat. He released it now and let it hang at his side, taking hope from the bare emotion of his friends even as his fingers throbbed in protest.

'Thank the Lord you are returned.' Oliver stepped towards him and wrapped his arms around all the damaged parts of his body. It had been such a very long time since someone had touched him like this that he stiffened. Then Fred was there and Jake, enveloping him so tight in an embrace he hardly knew where one of them stopped and another one started.

Safety. For the first time in years Nicholas took a breath that was not forced. Yet despite this, he himself reached out to none of them. Not yet. Not till it was over. Protecting each of them from harm was the only thing he now had left to offer.

He should not have come. He should not have been so selfish. He should have listened to his inner voice and stayed away until he knew where the danger had come from. But friendship held its own beacons and the hope of it had led him here, hurrying across the seas.

'This unexpected reunion calls for a celebration.' Fred spoke as he hauled Nicholas back into the private drawing room at the end of the corridor, the others following. A table set up for poker had been dismantled in the rush of their exit, the cards fallen and the chips scattered. Just that fact warmed him and when Oliver chose an unopened bottle from a cabinet in the corner and poured them each a drink, Nick took it gratefully.

He waited till the others filled their glasses and raised his own.

'To friendship,' he said simply.

'To the future,' Jake added.

'May the truth of what has happened to you, Nicholas, hold us together,' Fred's words were serious and when Oliver smiled the warmth in his green eyes was overlaid by question.

The cognac was smooth, creamy and strong and unlike any home-brewed liquor Nick had become so adept at dispensing in the cheap bars of the east coast of the Americas. The kick in it took his breath away. The flavour of his youth, he thought, unappreciated and imbibed in copious amounts. Today he savoured it and let it slide off the back of his tongue.

When Jacob motioned to the others to sit Nick took his place at the head of the table. This was where he had always sat, his initials carved into the dark mahogany of the chair. The first finger of his right hand ran across the marking, the ridges beneath tracing his past.

'We never erased anything of you, Nicholas. We always believed that you would be back. But why so long? Why leave it for so many years before returning?' Jacob voiced just what he imagined the others were thinking.

'I had amnesia. I could not remember who I was or where I had been. My memory only began to function again in the Americas five weeks ago after encountering a man who wanted me dead.'

'He nearly succeeded by the looks of it.'

'Nearly, but not quite. He came off worse.'

'You killed him.' The soldier in Fred asked this question and there was no room in his answer for lies.

'I did.'

'We found blood in the alley behind Vitium et Virtus the morning after you disappeared.' Jacob stood at that and walked over to the mantel to dig into a gilded box. 'This was found, too.'

His signet ring surprised him. He had always worn it, but had forgotten that he had. The burnished gold crest caught at the light above. *Servire Populo.* To serve the people. The irony in such a motto had been humorous to him once given his youthful overarching ability to only serve himself. Reaching out, he took the piece between his fingers, wincing at the dirt under his nails and the scars across his knuckles. He swallowed back the lump that was growing in his throat.

His old life offered back with such an easy grace.

'I can't remember what happened in the alley.'

'What was the last thing you remember then? Before you disappeared?'

'Arguing at Bromworth Manor with my uncle. It was hot and I was damnably drunk. It was my birthday, the fifteenth of August.'

'You disappeared the next Saturday night then, a week later. That much at least we have established.' Fred gave this information.

'Did you know that your uncle has taken over the use of the Bromley title?' Oliver leant back against the leather in his chair and raised his feet up on an engraved ottoman, his stance belying the tension in his voice. 'He wants you declared dead legally, given the number of years you have been missing. He has begun the procedure.'

'The bastard has the temerity to call himself your protector,' Jacob snarled, 'when all he wants is your inheritance and your estates.'

Nicholas took in the information with numbed indifference. Aaron Bartlett had never been easy but, as his late father's only brother, he'd had the credentials to take over the guardianship of an eight-year-old orphan. Nicholas remembered the day his uncle had walked into Bromworth Manor a week after his parents' death, both avarice and greed in his eyes.

'He's a charlatan and everyone knows it and I for one would love to be there when you throw him lock, stock and barrel out of your ancestral home.' As Oliver said this the others nodded. 'Do you think he had any part in your disappearance?'

Nicholas had wondered this himself, but without memory or proof he had no basis on which to found an opinion. Shrugging his shoulders, he finished the last of his cognac and was pleased when Jacob refilled the glass again.

He held the signet ring tight in his right hand, a small token of who he was and of what he had been. He did not want to place it on his finger again just yet because the wearing of it implied a different role and one he didn't feel up to trying to fill. He had walked under many names in the Americas, but the shadow of his persona here was as foreign to him now as those other identities he had adopted.

Jacob and Fred each wore a wedding ring. That thought shocked him out of complacency and for the first time he asked his own question.

'You are married?'

The smiles were broad and genuine, but it was Jacob who answered first.

'You have been gone a long time, Nicholas, and dissoluteness takes some effort in maintaining. There comes a day when you look elsewhere for real happiness and each of us has found that. Oliver may well be wed soon, too.'

'Then I am glad for it.'

And he was, he thought with relief. He was pleased for their newfound families, pleased that they had managed to move forward even if he had not. 'Can I meet them? Your women?'

'Tomorrow night.' Fred said. 'We have a function at my town house with all the trimmings and a guest list of about eighty. You look as though you could do with a careful introduction, Nick, and such a number would not be too daunting for a first foray back into English society.'

'You will need the services of a barber and a physician before others see you. Fred is about your size so with a tailor to iron out the differences you could get away with wearing his clothes.' Jacob watched him carefully, his blue eyes sharp on detail. When his glance ran over his face Nick knew he would have to say something, his good hand going up to the ruined cheek as though he might hide it a little.

'If someone still wishes me dead, perhaps it would

be better not to involve any of you in this. I should not want...'

Fred shook his head. 'We are involved already as your friends. There is no way you could stop any of us helping you.'

Oliver placed his hand on the table palm up in the way they had since their very first meeting and the others laid theirs on top. It took only a second's hesitation before he found his own above theirs joined in the flesh and in promise.

'In Vitium et Virtus.' They all said the words together. In *Vice and Virtue*. The motto seemed more appropriate at this second than it ever had before.

'We should retire to my town house for a drink. There is more of this cognac there and the occasion calls for further celebration. You can stay with me for as long as you need to, Nick, for I will have a room readied for you.'

Jacob's invitation was tempting. 'The offer is a kind one, but I'm reluctant to place you in danger.' He needed to say this to allow Jacob the chance of refusal at least.

'I think I can take care of myself and my family. Let's just worry about getting to the bottom of this mystery, to help you recover the final bits of memory you seem to have lost. If you can start to remember the faces of your assailants in the alley that may lead us to the perpetrator.'

'How does amnesia work, anyway?' Oliver asked this question and Fred answered.

'In the army many people lost their memories for the short term. A day or two at the most due to trauma, though I knew of a few chaps who never recovered theirs at all.'

'I don't think Nick wants to hear about those ones, Fred.' When Jacob said this they all laughed. 'At least he remembers us and the club.'

'It would be hard to forget.' Nicholas gestured to the excess and the luxury. 'But it is the friendships I recall the most.' His voice cracked on the last words and he swallowed away the emotion. He was not here for pity or sympathy. He knew he looked half the man who had left England, with his filthiness and his wounds but it was the hidden hurts that worried him the most. Could he ever trust anyone again? Was he doomed for ever to hold himself apart from others, all the shadows within him cutting him off from true intimacy?

He could see in each of his friends' eyes that they found him altered, more brittle. But the lord who had cared not a whit for social convention was long gone, too, that youth of reckless pleasure seeking debauchery and high-stakes gambling. If he met a younger version of himself now he doubted he would even like him very much.

The uncertainty in him built. He did not respect his past nor his present and his future looked less rosy than he imagined it might have on returning to England. Each of his friends had a woman now, a family, a place to live and be. His own loneliness felt more acute given the pathway they had taken. He had missed his direction and even the thought of confronting his guardian in the large and dusty halls of Bromworth Manor had become less appealing than it had been on the boat over.

Did he want it all back, the responsibility and the

problems? Did he need to be a viscount? Such a title would confine him once again to society ways and manners, things which now seemed pointless and absurd.

Even the club had lost its sheen, the dubious morality of vice and pleasure outdated and petty. The overt sexuality disturbed him. From where he sat he could see a dozen or more statues of women in various stages of undress and sensual arousal. The paintings of couplings on the wall were more brazen than he could ever remember, more distasteful.

In America he had seen the effects of prostitution on boys, girls and women in a way he had never noticed here, the thrill of the fantasy and daring dimmed under the reality. For every coin spent to purchase a dream for someone there was a nightmare hidden beneath for another.

'You seem quiet, Nicholas? Are you well?' Jacob had leant over to touch his arm and the unexpected contact made him jump and pull away. He knew they had all noticed such a reaction and struggled to hide his fury.

Everything was wrong. He was wrong to come and expect it all to have been just as it was. The headache he had been afflicted with ever since his recovery of memory chose that moment to develop into a migraine, his sight jumping between the faces of his friends and cutting them into small jagged prisms of distortion.

He wished he could just lie down here on the floor on an Aubusson rug that was thick and clean and close his eyes. He wished for darkness and silence. He hated himself as he began to shake violently and was thankful when Oliver crossed the room having found a woollen blanket, tucking it in gently around his shoulders.

Chapter Two

Lady Eleanor Huntingdon kissed her five-year-old sleeping daughter on the forehead before tiptoeing out of the bedroom.

Lucy was the very centre of her life, the shining star of a love and happiness that she had never expected to find again after...

'No'. She said the word firmly. She would not think of *him*. Not tonight when her world was soft and warm and she had a new book on the flowers of England to read from Lackington's. Tonight she would simply relax and enjoy.

Her brother Jacob was downstairs chatting to someone in his library and Rose, his wife, had retired a good half an hour ago, pleading exhaustion after a particularly frantic day.

Her own day had been busy, too, with all the celebrations, guilt and sorrow eating into her reserves as yet another Christmas went by without any sign of Lucy's father.

'No.' She said it again this time even more firmly.

She would not dwell on the past for the next few hours because the despair and wretchedness of the memory always left her with a headache. Tonight she would dream of him, she knew she would, for his face was reflected in the shape of her daughter's and this evening the resemblance had been even more apparent than usual.

She sat on the damask sofa in the small salon attached to her room and opened her book. She had already poured herself a glass of wine and had a slice of the apple pie the cook had made that night for dinner beside it. Everything she needed right there. Outside it was cold, the first snows of winter on the ground. Inside a fire roared in the hearth, the sound of it comforting.

She seldom came to the city, but she had journeyed down to be with her family in the autumn and had decided to stay for the Christmas celebrations, the food and the decorations—things that Lucy needed in her life. She would leave tomorrow with her daughter for Millbrook House, the ancestral estate of the Westmoor dukedom in Middlesex. Her home now. The place she loved the most in all the world.

Opening her book, she began to read about the new varieties of roses, a plant she enjoyed and grew there in the sheltered courtyard gardens. She could hear her brother's voice from the downstairs library more distinctly now. He must have opened the door that led into the passageway and his quiet burr filled the distance.

She stopped reading and looked up, tilting her head against the silence. The other voice sounded vaguely familiar, but she could not quite place its tone. It was not Frederick Challenger or Oliver Gregory, she knew that, but there was a familiarity there that was surprising. The click of a door shutting banished any sound back into the faraway distance, but still she felt anxious.

She was missing something. Something important. Placing the book on her small table, she stood and picked up the glass of wine, walking to the window and pulling back the curtains to look out over the roadway.

No stranger's carriage stood before the house so perhaps the newcomer had come home in her brother's conveyance from Mayfair, for she knew Jacob had been to his club.

Her eyes strayed to the clock. It was well after ten. Still early enough in London terms for an outing, but late for a private visitor on a cold and rainy evening. She stopped herself from instructing her maid to go down and enquire as to the name of the caller. This hesitancy also worried her for usually she would have no such qualms in doing such a thing.

A tremor of concern passed through her body, making her hands shake. She was twenty-four years old and the last six difficult years had fashioned such strength and independence that she now had no time for the timidity she was consumed with. If she was worried she needed to go downstairs herself and understand just where her anxieties lay.

But still she did not move as she finished her wine in a long and single swallow and poured herself another.

There was danger afoot for both herself and Lucy.

That horrible thought made her swear out loud, something she most rarely did. Cursing again under her breath, she took a decent swallow of the next glass of wine and then placed it on the mantel. The fire beneath burnt hot. She could see the red sparks of flame against the back of the chimney flaring into life and then dying out.

Soldiers.

Ralph, Jacob and herself had played games in winter with them for all the young years of their life. Her hand went to her mouth to try to contain the grief her oldest brother's death had left her with. With reverence she recited the same prayer she always did when she thought of him.

'And the dead in Christ will rise first. Then we who are alive, who are left, will be caught up together with them in the clouds...'

It was a snippet from one of the verses of Thessalonians, but the image of her and her brothers rising whole into the sky was a lovely one. Lucy would be there, of course, and Rose and Grandmama, as well, and all the other people that she loved.

She was not particularly religious, but she did believe in something—in God, she supposed, and Jesus and the Holy Family with their goodness. How else could she have got through her trials otherwise?

She was sick of her thoughts tonight, fed up with their constant return to *him*.

That damn voice was still there in her mind, too, changing itself into the tones of the man she had loved above all else and then lost.

The hidden name. The unuttered father. Although she knew Jacob suspected she had told their father, she had never told anyone at all exactly what had happened to her, because sometimes she could barely understand it herself.

For a moment she breathed in deeply to try to stop the tears that were pooling in her eyes. She would not cry, not tonight with a fire, a good book, some apple pie and French wine.

Her life had taken on some sort of pattern that felt right and she loved her daughter with all her heart.

The door downstairs was ajar again and the voices came more clearly than they had before. Her brother sounded perturbed, angry even, and she stood still to listen, opening her own door so that the words would be formed with more precision.

'You cannot possibly think that we will not help you. All of us. There is no damn way in the world that I will let you go and fight this by yourself.'

'But it is dangerous, Jake. If anything were to happen to you and your family...'

The room began to spin around Eleanor, in a terrifying and dizzying spiral. There was no up and down, only the vortex of a weightless imbalance pulling at her throat and her heart and her soul.

Nicholas Bartlett. It was his voice, lost for all these years. To her and to Lucy. To Jacob and Frederick and Oliver. Why was he down there?

He had not come to see her? He had not beaten down her door in the rush of reunion? He had not called her name from the bottom of the stairs again and again as he had stormed up to find her before taking her into his arms and kissing her as he had done once? Relentlessly. Passionately. Without thought for anyone or anything.

He had sat with her brother discussing his own needs for all the evening. Quietly. Civilly.

Perhaps he did not know she was here, but even that implied a lack of enquiring on his behalf. The man she remembered would have asked her brother immediately as to her whereabouts and moved heaven and earth to find her.

She nodded her head in order to underline such a truth.

Her own heart was beating so fast and strong she could see the motion of it beneath the thick woollen bodice of her blue-wool gown. Eleanor wondered if she might simply perish with the shock of it before she ever saw him.

Sitting down, she took a deep breath, placing her head in her hands and closing her eyes.

She needed to calm herself. This was the moment she had dreamed about for years and years and it was not supposed to be anything like this. She should be running down the stairs calling his name, joy in her voice and delight in her eyes.

Instead she stood and found her white wrap to wind it tightly about her shoulders because, whether she wanted to admit it or not, there had been a hesitancy and a withdrawal between them on the last night they had been together.

He'd seen her off, of course, in his carriage, but he had not acted then like a man who was desperate for her company.

'Thank you, Eleanor.' He had said that as he'd moved back and away from the kiss she had tried to give him, as if relieved for the space, his glance sliding to the ground.

He had not even stayed to watch her as the conveyance had departed, the emptiness reflected in her own feelings of dread.

So now, here, six years later she could not quite fathom where such an absence left her. What if she went downstairs now and saw this thought exactly on his face? Would her heart break again? Could she even withstand it?

She had to see him. She had to find in his velvet-brown eyes the truth between them. There was a mistake, a misunderstanding, a wrongness she could not quite identify.

Her feet were on the stairs before she knew it, hurrying down. A short corridor and then the library, the door closed against her. Without hesitation she pushed the portal open and strode through.

Nicholas Bartlett, Viscount Bromley, was sitting on the wing chair by the fire and he looked nothing like how she remembered him.

His clothes were dirty, his hair unshaped, but it was the long curling scar that ran from one corner of his eye almost to his mouth that she saw first.

Ruined.

His beautiful handsome face had been sliced in half.

'Eleanor.' Her brother had risen and there was delight in his expression. 'Nicholas has been returned to us safely from all his years abroad in the Americas. He will be staying here at our town house for a time.'

'The Americas...?' She could only stand and stare,

for although Nicholas Bartlett had also risen he made no effort at all to cross the floor to greet her. Rather he stood there with his brandy held by a hand that was dressed with a dirty bandage and merely tipped his head.

In formal acknowledgement. Like a stranger might do or an acquaintance. His cheeks were flushed, the eyes so much harder than she remembered them being and his countenance brittle somehow, all sureness gone.

For a second she could not quite think what to say.

'It has been a long time.' Foolish words. Words that might be construed as hanging her heart on her sleeve?

He nodded and the thought of his extreme weariness hit her next. Lifting her hand to her heart, she stayed quiet.

'Six years,' he returned as if she had not been counting, as though he needed to give her the time precisely because the duration had been lost in the interim.

Six years, seventeen weeks and six days. She knew the time almost to the very second.

'Indeed, my lord.' She swallowed then and saw her brother looking at her, puzzlement across his face, for the hard anger in her voice had been distinct.

'You welcome my best friend back only with distant words, Eleanor, when you seemed most distraught at his disappearance?'

God, she would have to touch him. She would have to put her arms around his body and pretend he was nothing and nobody. Just her brother's friend. The very thought of that made her swallow.

He had not moved at all from his place by the fire

and he had not put his glass down either. Stay away, such actions said. Stay on your side of the room and I shall stay on mine.

'I am glad to see you, Lord Bromley. I am glad that you are safe and well.'

His smile floored her, the deep dimple in his unruined cheek so very known.

'Thank you, Lady Eleanor.' He held up his injured hand. 'Altered somewhat, but still alive.'

The manner of his address made her sway and she might have fallen had she not steadied herself on the back rest of the nearby sofa. His dark brown hair was lank and loose, the sheen she remembered there gone.

'I heard you had been married to a lord in Scotland and now have a child. Your brother spoke of it. How old is your daughter?'

Terror reached out and gripped her, winding its claws into the danger of an answer.

Without hesitation she moved slightly and knocked her brother's full glass of red wine from the table upon which it sat. The liquid spilled on to the cream carpet beneath, staining the wool like blood. The glass shattered into a thousand splinters as it bounced further against the parquet flooring.

Such an action broke all thought of answering Nicholas Bartlett's question as her brother leapt forward.

'Ellie, stay back or you will cut yourself.'

Ellie? The name seared into some part of Nicholas's mind like a living flame. He knew this name well, but how could that be?

He shook his head and looked away. He knew Jacob's sister only slightly. She had been so much younger than her brother when he was here last, a green girl recently introduced into society. But she had always been attractive.

Now she was a beauty, her dark hair pulled back in a style so severe it only enhanced the shape of her face and the vivid blueness of her eyes. Eyes that cut through him in a bruised anger. He knew she had spilt the wine on purpose for he had spent enough years with duplicity to know the difference between intention and accident.

He'd asked of the age of her daughter? Was there something wrong with the child, some problem that made the answer untenable to her?

Jacob looked as puzzled as he probably did, the wine soaking into his carpet with all the appearance of never being able to be removed.

A permanent stain.

He saw Eleanor had sliced her finger in her attempt at retrieving the long stem of crystal that had once been attached to the shattered bowl. He wished she had left it for the maid who was now bustling around her feet sweeping the fragments into a metal holder.

'I need to go and see to my hand.' Eleanor's words came with a breathless relief, the red trail of blood sliding down her middle finger as she held it in the air. 'Please excuse me.'

She looked at neither of them as she scurried away.

When she was gone and the maid had departed, too, Jacob's frown deepened. 'Eleanor has been sad since the death of her husband. Widowhood weighs heavily upon her.'

'How did her husband die?'

'Badly.' The same flush of complicity he had seen on his sister's visage covered Jacob's face.

Since he had been gone the Huntingdon family had suffered many tragedies. Jacob had told him of the loss of Ralph, the oldest brother and heir, and his father in a carriage accident. In the telling of it Nicholas had gained the distinct impression that Jacob blamed himself somehow for their loss.

His friends had their demons, too. That thought softened his own sense of dislocation. The hedonistic decadence of the club had not been all encompassing. Real life had a way of grabbing one by the throat and strangling the air out of hope. Perhaps no one reached their thirties without some sort of a loss? A rite of passage, a way of growth? A bitter truth of life?

He wished Eleanor Huntingdon might have stayed and talked longer. He wished she might have come forward and welcomed him back in the way her brother had directed. With touch.

She reached her room and threw herself upon her bed, face buried in her pillow as she screamed out her grief. Six years of sorrow and loss and hope and love. For nothing.

Six years of waiting for the moment Nicholas Bartlett might return with all sorts of plausible explanations as to why he'd been away for so very long and how he had fought hard to be back at her side again, his heart laid at her feet.

The truth of tonight had a sharper edge altogether. Was he just another rake who had simply made a conquest of a young girl with foolishness in her heart? She had offered him exactly what it was he sought—the use of her body for a heady sensual interlude, a brief flirtation that had meant the world to her. Had it meant nothing at all to him?

'I. Hate. Him.'

He had looked at her like a stranger might, no inkling as to what had passed between them in his bedroom at the Bromley town house, when he had whispered things into her ear that made her turn naked into the warmth of him and allow him everything.

Swallowing hard, she thought she might be sick.

Lucy might never have the promise of a father now, a papa who would fold her in his arms and tell her she meant the world to him and that he would always protect her.

The family she'd imagined to have for years was gone, burst in the bubble of just one look from his velvet-brown eyes and his complete indifference. And the worst thing of all was that she would have to see him again and again both here in the house and at any social occasion because he was her only brother's best friend.

That thought had her sitting and swiping angrily at her eyes.

She would not waste her tears. She would confront him and tell him that to her it was as if he was dead and that she wished for no more discourse between them.

Then she would leave London for Millbrook and stay there till the hurt began to soften and the fury loosened its hold.

She would survive this. She had to for Lucy's sake. She had seen other women made foolish by the loss of love and dreams and simply throw their lives away. But not her. She was strong and resolute.

Taking in a shaky breath, she walked over to her writing desk and drew out paper. She would ask to meet him tonight in the summer house in the garden, a place they had met once before in their few heady days of courtship.

She would not be kind and filter out any of the 'what had been'. She would throw his disloyalty in his face and make him understand that such a betrayal was as loathsome to her as it was hurtful. No. Not that word. She did not wish for Nicholas Bartlett, Viscount Bromley, to know in any way that he had entirely broken her heart.

Chapter Three

He was exhausted. His migraine had dulled to a constant headache and all he wanted to do was to sleep.

Tomorrow he would clean himself up. He would have his hair cut, his beard shaved and find some clothes that were not torn and dirty. He would also see a doctor about his hand because it felt hot and throbbing and he was sure an inflammation had set in. But for now... sleep, and the bed in the chamber Jacob had given him on the second floor looked large and inviting.

A sheet of paper placed carefully on the pillow caught his attention and he walked across to lift it up.

Meet me at the summer house as the clock strikes one. It is important.
Eleanor Huntingdon

Surprise floored him. Why would she send him this? Even his own dubious moral code knew the danger in such a meeting.

Her writing was precise and evenly sloped, and she

had not used her married surname. He could smell a perfume on the paper that made him bring the sheet to his nose and breath in. Violets.

A mantel clock above the fireplace told him it was already fifteen minutes before the hour she had stated. Pulling his coat from the one bag he had brought as luggage from the Americas, he let himself quietly out of the room.

Ten minutes later he saw her coming through the drifts of dirty snow, a small figure wrapped in a thick shawl that fell almost to her knees. The moon was out and the wind had dropped and in the silence all about it was as if they were the only two people left in the world.

Her face was flushed from cold as she came in, shutting the glass door behind her. In here the chill was lessened, whether from the abundance of green plant life or just good building practice, he knew not which. When she spoke though he could see a cloud of mist after each word.

'Thank you for coming.'

'You thought I would not?'

She ignored that and rushed on. 'I was more than surprised to see you tonight. I don't know why you would wish for all those years of silence and no contact whatsoever, but—'

'It was not intentional, Lady Eleanor. My memory was lost.'

Her eyes widened at this truth and she swallowed, hard.

'I must have been hit over the head, as there was a

sizeable lump there for a good time afterwards. As a result of the injury my memory was compromised.'

She now looked plainly shocked. 'How much of it exactly? How much did you lose?'

'Everything that happened to me before I disappeared was gone for many years. A month ago I retrieved most of my history but still…there are patches.'

'Patches?'

'The week before my disappearance and a few days after have gone entirely. I cannot seem to remember any of it.'

She turned at that, away from the moonlight so that all her face was in shadow. She seemed slighter than she had done a few hours earlier. Her hands trembled as she caught them together before her.

'Everything?'

'I am hoping it will come back, but…' He stopped, because he could not know if this was a permanent state or a temporary one.

'How was your cheek scarred?'

'Someone wants me dead. They have tried three times to kill me now and I doubt that will cease until I identify the perpetrators.'

'Why? Why should you be such a target?'

'I have lived in the shadows for a long time, even before I left England, and have any number of enemies. Some I can identify, but others I can't.'

'A lonely place to be in.'

'And a dangerous one.'

'You are different now, Lord Bromley.' She gave him

those words quietly. 'More distant. A harder man. Almost unrecognisable.'

He laughed, the sound discordant, but here in the night there was a sense of honesty he had not felt in a long, long time. Even his friends had tiptoed around his new reality and tried to find the similarities with what had been before. Lady Eleanor did not attempt to be diplomatic at all as she had asked of his cheek and his circumstances and there was freedom in such truth.

He felt a pull towards her that was stronger than anything he had ever known before and stiffened, cursing beneath his breath. She was Jacob's younger sister and he could offer her nothing. He needed to be careful.

'I am less whole, I think.' His good hand gestured at his face. 'Less trusting.'

'Like me,' she returned in a whisper. 'Just the same.'

And when her blue eyes met his, he saw the tears that streamed down her cheeks, sorrow, anger and grief written all over her face.

He touched her then. He took her hand into his own to try to give the coldness some warmth. A small hand with bitten-down nails. There was a ring on the third finger, encrusted diamonds in gold.

'Was he a good man, your husband?'

'I thought so.'

'Then I am sorry for it.'

At that she snatched her fingers from his grasp and turned. She was gone before he could say another word, a shadow against the hedgerows, small and alone.

Why had she asked him here? What had she said that could not have been discussed in the breakfast salon in the morning? Why had she risked such a meeting in the very dead of night just to ask of his health?

Nothing made any sense.

Everything was now dangerous.

Nicholas being here, the desperate people who were chasing him, the new man he had become at the expense of the one he had been.

She barely recognised him inside or out. He looked different and he sounded different. Bigger. More menacing. Distant. And yet…when he had taken her hand into his she had felt the giddy rush of want and desire.

'Nicholas.' She whispered his name into the night as she sat by the fire.

'Amnesia.' She breathed the word quietly, hating the sound of it.

Lucy had been her priority for all the years of their apartness. She had risked her social standing, her family's acceptance and her future for her daughter and if there was even a slight chance that Nicholas could place her in danger then Eleanor was not prepared to take it.

He had said the perpetrators had attacked him three times already and had looked as though he expected a fourth or a fifth or a sixth. What was it she had heard him say to her brother just a few hours ago as she had over-listened to their conversation in the library?

'But it is dangerous, Jake. If anything were to happen to you or your family…'

If she told him the truth about that week before he disappeared, would he want to be back in their lives? Did she want to risk telling him of their closeness, knowing so little about him? He was a stranger to her now, so perhaps she should wait to discover what kind of man he was before revealing a secret so huge it would change all their lives for ever.

These thoughts tumbled around and around in her mind, going this way and that. If he had just looked at her for a second as he used to, she knew she would have capitulated and let him know everything. But this new Nicholas was altered and aloof, the indifference in his eyes crushing.

Lucy was now her priority. As a mother she needed to make decisions that would protect her child. She had not told another soul about her relationship with Nicholas. Jacob had been distraught from the loss of his friend and she thought he might not cope with another heartbreak and scandal. She had never seen her brother so broken.

And so she had told her family nothing of the father and lover and instead, with their help, had removed to Scotland and away from prying eyes.

Goodness, those years had been hard, she thought, and shook her head. She had been so lonely she might have simply died, there in Edinburgh in the house Jacob had set her up in waiting until she could return to Millbrook for the birth of her child. A terrible secret, a dreadful scandal and all the hope of what could have been disappeared as completely as Nicholas Bartlett had.

Blighted by her own stupidity, she'd lived in sadness until the first look at the face of her daughter had banished any regret.

On her return she found Jacob had concocted a story of a husband who had died and that she was now a grieving young widow with a small child in tow. She had become Eleanor Robertson at the stroke of a pen, the name being a common and unremarkable one, though she never thought of herself as such and used Huntingdon when signing letters to anyone she knew well. Oh, granted, she realised that many people did not believe such a fabrication, but nobody made a fuss of it either. She was a duke's daughter with land and money of her own and in the very few times she'd returned to the city she found the few friends she still did have to be generally accepting of her circumstances.

A fragile existence that only took the renewed appearance of Nicholas Bartlett to break it down completely. But this missing week seemed well established in his mind and he himself had said it had been a month since any recall had returned.

Which meant no other memories had crept back in. She did not know enough about the state of amnesia to have a certainty of anything, but tomorrow she would go to Lackington, Allen & Co. and look up the files under the medical section of the library. Knowledge would aid her.

Perhaps she could help him redefine his memory. But should she? Would her presence at his side, even in that capacity, put her own self into danger?

She needed to wait, she thought. She needed to see just how the next few days turned out in order to make an informed decision about her and Lucy's future.

He did not wear his crested ring any more. He did not

smile as he used to. She wondered if he was financially strapped with his hair and his clothes and his scuffed old boots. There had been talk of his inheritances passing on to his uncle given the number of years of his being away. Perhaps being presumed dead even negated legal rights to property?

Many *had* thought him dead, after all. She had heard it in the drawing rooms of society and in the quieter salons of the *ton*. The dashing and dissolute young Viscount Bromley's disappearance was mourned by myriad feminine hearts and the gold coins he had lost in the seedier halls of London's gambling scene had only added to his allure. He was now touted as a legend whose deeds had only been enhanced by the mystery surrounding him.

Eleanor could not even imagine him in society looking like he did now. No one would recognise him. People would pity him. The scar at his cheek, the injured hand and the uncertainty. He would be crucified within the hallowed snobbery of the *ton*!

How could she protect him?

By staying in London and being there to pick up the pieces, perhaps? By sending Lucy home to Millbrook House with her nanny and maids tomorrow until she was certain which way the dice tumbled?

Oh, God, now she was thinking at the opposite spectrum of what she had started to decide. Stay away from Nicholas entirely or try to protect him? Which was it to be? Which *should* it be?

Underneath her thoughts a small flame flared, then took and filled her whole body with gladness. These arguments were all academic because now he was alive to her again. Nicholas Bartlett, Viscount Bromley, was not dead. He was here and breathing, the past covering him like a dull shroud, but nevertheless still quick.

Everything was possible whilst life bloomed and her brother and his friends would not desert him. She knew that from what Jacob had said. Placing her hands together she prayed.

'Give thanks in all circumstances; for this is God's will for you...' Thessalonians again. She murmured the scripture into the silence with an emotion that she found both comforting and worrying.

Tonight she would dream of him just as she had done a thousand times since he had disappeared, his arms around her body and his warm lips covering her own.

But this time it would be different for he was no longer just a ghost.

Frederick's carriage collected him the next morning well before the luncheon and when he arrived at the home of the Challengers in St James's Square, Nick understood just how happy his friend was these days.

Georgiana, Fred's wife, was gracious and welcoming even with the house in an uproar as it made itself ready for the evening's entertainment.

'It is a pleasure to meet you, Lord Bromley.' A real smile touched her blue eyes and although she did not look at his scar, she did not look away from it either. 'I have heard much about you for Frederick has spoken of you so very often.'

'I hope he concentrated on my good qualities rather than the bad ones.' He tried to keep his tone light.

'The wildness of youth is never easy, I fear, and often misrepresented, but rest assured my husband has missed you.'

In such wisdom Nick detected that Georgiana's life might have had its own complexities and he wondered about her story.

Half an hour later when he and Fred were alone in the library and a drink had been poured, Nick put his head back against the leather rest of a large wing chair and took in breath.

'Your wife has the knack of making this all look easy,' he said finally. 'A house of things being both interesting and alive, but without the chaos of your upbringing? Where did you meet her?'

'I first saw her at Vitium et Virtus late one night when she was auctioning off her virginity to the highest bidder, wearing nothing more than a silk concoction that was barely decent.'

Nick laughed at that and liked the sound of it. 'And I gather that the winner of such an unusual prize was yourself?'

'Fortunately.'

They both took a drink and listened to the low rumbling noise of the busy house.

'Georgie was promised in marriage to Sir Nash Bowles and doing her level best to get out of it. It was the only plan she could think of. Unwise but spectacularly successful.' Frederick's laugh was deep.

'Bowles was there? At the club?'

'He was.' Fred had sobered now at mention of that name, the good humour of a second ago fading markedly.

'One of the last things I remember is warning him to never darken its door again, but he obviously returned.'

'My wife sees him as perverted and cruel.'

'And I would agree with her.'

'Well, the one thing I do thank him for is his threats to unmask her completely. It was only because she thought she might be shunned as a pariah when the *ton* got wind of her improper plan that she agreed to marry me.'

'A wise choice.' Nick lifted his glass and finished the brandy before placing it down on the table beside him and refusing Frederick's offer of another. 'The world you all live in has changed a lot since I have been gone.'

'And you have changed in appearance since last night. Jacob's barber is a magician, by the way.'

'The bath helped, too. The Westmoor physician also came this morning to see to my hand. He says he expects it to heal completely if I am careful.'

'Knife wounds can be difficult things.'

'The blade hit the bone at the back of the wrist, but at least it did not break.'

'Which explains the sling. If you don't want to be thrown into society so quickly by coming tonight, Nick, I will understand. After the army it was hard for me to fit straight back in.'

'Because you felt different? Out of place?'

'Yes, and because I had seen things that no one else could even imagine.'

Frederick was quiet then and Nicholas was glad of it.

'I had thought to go to ground, but if I don't come tonight it will only get harder. Better to get it over and done with. I saw Lady Eleanor yesterday, too, by the way.' He tried to keep interest out of his words though he was not certain he had succeeded as Frederick looked up. 'What is her story?'

'Jake is very tight lipped about his sister, but from what I can gather the man she married was from a well-thought-of family in Edinburgh. The Robertsons.'

'Was it the family of the Robertson boy we knew at school, then?'

'No, by all accounts he was not related to them. Douglas Robertson, Eleanor's husband, was killed falling off a horse, apparently in some hunting accident, and when Eleanor found out she was pregnant she came home to Millbrook to have her baby daughter, Lucy. And to grieve.'

Lucy. Nick stored the name inside him and thought how hard a path that must have been for a sheltered duke's daughter with all the promise in the world.

A bit like him, perhaps, although his promise had been dimming even before his absence from England. His uncle had encouraged him into the profligate and debauched underworld of the *ton* and he had gone in to welcome the inherent risks with his eyes wide open.

'Do you ever think, Fred, that maybe we were fools back then, playing so hard and fast?'

'I think you and Oliver were the ones who were the

worst of us although you held the biggest share in Vitium et Virtus and gambled away the most money.'

'It was fun until it wasn't,' he returned and stood to look out of the window. 'I will go up to Bromworth House tomorrow and see my uncle.'

'Take my carriage.'

'Oliver offered me the use of his yesterday.'

'Will you live there this time, do you think? Put down roots and stay?'

Nicholas shrugged his shoulders because he truly did not know.

'My advice would be to find a wife like mine, Nick. A woman who can be the better half of you, for without Georgiana at my side I'd still be lost.'

As I am, Nicholas thought, and felt the shiver of ghosts walk down his spine.

Frederick leant forward, swirling the brandy around in his glass. 'We can move the club on into other hands, younger ones. It's probably past time.'

'Do you have anyone in mind?'

'Half the upcoming bucks of the *ton* would jump to it in a second, but it has to be the right people. A group of friends like us maybe, people who could work together.' He smiled, his brown eyes soft. 'For so long we all feared you were dead, Nick. For so long we talked of you with sorrow and regret even as we relived your wildest exploits. It is good to have you back again and in one piece.'

'Well, perhaps not quite one piece, Frederick.' That truth settled between them.

'The bits will come back to you, but give it time and

don't force it. One day you will rise in the morning and realise life is easier and that the demons that once threatened to engulf you are more distant.'

'Less insistent?'

'Then you will also understand that life carries on, different from before maybe but still valuable, and that there are people in the world who never stopped loving you. Myself included.'

Frederick waited until he nodded before carrying on.

'But enough of this maudlin emotion and confession, for I think we now need to get down to this afternoon's business and find you some more appropriate clothes to wear.'

Thus the mundane allowed an end to the extraordinary truths of the conversation.

Nicholas could not remember ever taking this long to dress, but the Challenger valet was both insistent and persuasive and, although he had no clothes of his own to speak of, the man soon conjured up an array of cast-offs that fitted him well.

'Just a slight tuck here, my lord.' His grip was firm on the side seam of the jacket. 'You don't quite have the girth of Major Challenger. The trousers have been lengthened, but a good steam has taken care of any tell-tale signs of alteration. They give a fine impression of being your own clothes, Lord Bromley. Tailored to perfection if I might say so myself.'

'Thank you.' He gave this quietly. It had been years since he had had a servant fuss over him in such a way and it made him feel strangely odd. He had never given those who worked for the Bromley estate much thought before, but now he did. He hoped his uncle had treated them well and that there might be a few familiar faces at the Manor when he went up there on the morrow.

The luxury of London unsettled him and he fought for a touchstone. He wondered if Eleanor Huntingdon might come to Frederick's soirée with her brother. He would like to see her dressed in finery with her hair arranged to show off the colour of it. He would like to dance with her. He would like to have her near.

Frederick came into the room he had been assigned just as the valet had finished the last stitch and broken off the thread, smoothing down the fabric.

'A fine job, Masters. The Viscount looks as though he should fit in nicely.'

When the man collected all the assorted spools and left, Fred poured them each some wine in ornate cut-crystal glasses.

'For fortification,' he said and raised the tipple. 'Most of those present tonight are friends and acquaintances, but there are always the certain few outsiders who might want to rock the boat.'

'Are you warning me, Fred?'

'You've been away a long time and stories have formed around your disappearance that have no bearing on the truth.'

'For that I am glad.'

'But a word of advice. If you do not wish to be the continued censure of the gossipmongers perhaps you could think of a reason for your injuries that may be more palatable. An army wound? The sanctity of government violence goes a long way in suppressing criticism, I have always found. The Seminole Wars, perhaps? The time frame would fit.'

'You have thought about this already?'

When Frederick began to laugh he did, too.

'The legends that abound about you as the reckless and dissolute Viscount Bromley are also a protection. No one will know quite who you are.'

'Including me.' He said the words quietly and finished his drink.

Frederick's frown was deep. 'You can't do this alone any more, Nick. You have to let us all help you.'

'You are already doing that and I will be fine.'

Chapter Four

Eleanor had dressed as carefully as she ever had, her maids watching her with puzzlement on both their faces. Usually she barely cared. Normally if she went out it was only with much chagrin that she suffered even an hour of the business of 'getting ready'.

Today she had spent most of the afternoon changing her mind from this dress to that one, from a formal hair style to a far less structured one. Even her shoes had been swapped from one pair to the next.

And now with only a few moments before she needed to go downstairs and join her brother and sister-in-law she was still unsure. Was the gold of her gown a little gaudy? Did her hair, set into up-pulled ringlets, look contrived? Was the diamond choker at her throat too much of a statement for a woman of her age?

She looked away from her reflection and breathed in deeply. No more. No other changes. She was exhausted by her uncertainty.

Jacob smiled as he saw her descending the staircase.

'I have not seen you look quite as beautiful for a very long time, Ellie.'

Rose beside him looked as pleased as her brother did. 'It is going to be so lovely to have you with us at Frederick and Georgiana's, Eleanor. I wish you were with us more often in London.' Her sister-in-law was in blue tonight and her fairness made her look like an angel. Every time Eleanor saw Rose she could understand exactly what her brother had seen in her as a choice of wife. She was kind and quiet, a woman who did not push herself forward, but waited for others to come to her.

With a laugh Eleanor took the offered hand and felt immeasurably more confident, an emotion she would need if she were to be any help to Nicholas Bartlett.

'Nick has gone on already,' Jacob said. 'Frederick had a set of clothes that he needed to see if he fitted and he wanted Nicholas to meet Georgiana before this evening's function.'

'I am sure the Viscount will look well in anything he chooses. From all the accounts I have heard from my maid this morning as I was dressing he is a most handsome man.'

Rose's statement was firm and Eleanor glanced at her. She herself had not seen Nicholas Bartlett in the house all day as he had left in the mid-morning for the Challengers. She hoped he had found a barber at least to shave off his beard.

Her nerves started to make her worried again. If people were rude or worse to him she could not quite think what she would do. Her brother would hardly tolerate such behaviour, of course, but still there was a difference between being accepted for who you were and being gossiped about behind raised fans and turned heads.

'I hope Lord Bromley will enjoy himself,' she finally said and left it at that.

It was only a short ride from Chelsea to St James's Square and the rain and wind had held off enough to allow them a quiet passage into the house. After the death of her brother and father the family had been largely in mourning so it felt good to be able to go out again. The Challenger soirée would have a lot of people who were known to them attending, but it was not as formal as some of the grander balls.

Frederick and Georgiana Challenger were there to greet them after their cloaks, hats and gloves were seen to. Eleanor was, as always, struck anew at just how fine they looked together as they welcomed the newcomers.

'Oliver was unable to make it tonight, Jake, because Cecilia is not very well. Nick is inside, but the doctor wanted his hand up in a sling so we had to rearrange his shirt and jacket somewhat.'

Another problem, Eleanor thought. A further way to draw attention to his differences. She suddenly wished she had stayed home.

The large downstairs salon of the Challenger town house was completely decked out in yellow, the colour lightening the space and making it seem even bigger. Numerous people milled around the room in groups and at one end an orchestra was tuning up with a Christmas song, 'Hark the Herald Angels Sing'. Eleanor had always liked the melody.

'I thought Frederick said this was to be a small gathering,' Rose remarked. 'It seems half the *ton* is here tonight.'

Eleanor looked around trying to find the figure of Nicholas Bartlett. At six foot two his height should have had him standing a good head above many of the others, but she could not see him.

Perhaps he had cried off and left?

'There is Nicholas. Over by the pillars.' Her brother's voice penetrated her reveries as he pushed through the crowd and once the crush thinned a little she saw the Viscount surrounded by women and men all hanging on to his every word.

Her first true sight of him took her breath away. He looked completely different from yesterday. Menacing, dangerously beautiful, the boy she had known fashioned into the man before her, the harder lines of his face without the full beard suiting him in a way she had not comprehended before.

He was all in black, save for the snowy cravat at his neck, folded simply. His hair was pulled into a severe queue and she could see the sheen of dark brown picked out under the chandeliers above them.

His left hand was fastened into a sling of linen, the small vulnerability suiting him in a way she had not thought would be possible—a warrior who had been into battle and returned triumphant. She could see in his velvet eyes an apartness that left him unmatched.

Every man near him looked soft, tame and pliable. Untouched by danger and hardship.

Their party had to squeeze into the space about him and Eleanor noticed the frowns of those women who had hoped for a closer acquaintance as they were ousted back.

'You have cleaned up well, Nick. I hardly recognise you in the man we saw yesterday.' Jacob sounded relieved. 'I would like to introduce you to Rose, my wife. You did not meet her this morning before you left.'

Rose looked tiny compared to the Viscount, his darkness contrasting, too, against her light hair and eyes. Eleanor watched as Nicholas Bartlett brought up her sister-in-law's hand and kissed the back of it, his gallantry reminiscent of the younger man who had left them all those years before. A slide of anger turned inside Eleanor as he acknowledged her with a mere tip of his head and yet he made a space at his side and she came to stand there, making very sure that she did not touch him.

'I hope you slept well last night, Lady Eleanor.' He said this to her as Rose and Jacob were busy in conversation with an older lord they knew well. An allusion to their late-night meeting, she supposed. Unexpectedly she coloured and hated herself for doing so.

'I did, thank you.' In truth, she had gained about three hours' sleep and it probably showed in the darkness under her eyes. He, on the other hand, looked as if he had slept like a baby.

'Frederick said there would be dancing later in the evening. Might I petition you to save one for me?'

'I am rather out of practice, my lord.' She could not keep the surprise from her tone.

'And you think I wouldn't be?'

'I do not know. I have no idea of what sort of life you lived in the Americas.'

At that he sobered.

As the crowd about them jostled slightly Mr Alfred Dromorne and his daughter broke in on their conversation.

'Bromley. It has been a long time. May I introduce my daughter to you. She is recently out in society. Susan, this is Viscount Bromley.'

Nicholas Bartlett inclined his head at the beautiful girl standing next to her father, though his eyes were far less readable than they had been a second ago. It was as if a shutter had been placed over any true expression and the fingers she could see that were visible in the sling had curled in tension.

The vibrant red head smiled in the way only the very young and very beautiful know how to. All coquetry and cunning. Eleanor felt instantly older and a lot more dowdy than she had even a second before.

'I am pleased to meet you, Miss Dromorne.'

'And I you, my lord.' She brought her fan up and twirled it a few times, the art of flirtation both complex and simple in its execution.

'You will be going home to Bromworth Manor, no doubt, now that you are back. You might notice some changes to the place.'

Her father had taken up the conversation and his statement produced a flicker of genuine interest in Lord

Bromley's visage. Eleanor saw the eagerness even as he sought to hide it.

'In what ways do you mean?

'Your uncle has the run of the estate these days and he has made certain to stamp his authority on to the place. Last time I was there I rather thought that those still serving him were not entirely happy.'

'Large estates have their problems,' Nicholas replied, giving the distinct impression that he did not wish to discuss such personal matters with a stranger. Eleanor noticed, too, that the pulse at his throat had quickened markedly.

'You promised Lord Craybourne that you would be back to talk with him and I see he is free now, Lord Bromley. Perhaps this would be a good time.'

'It would.' With a slight bow to the Dromornes he allowed Eleanor to lead the way across the floor, though once they were out of sight she felt his hand on her arm stopping her.

She turned and saw right into his tortured soul, the lack of reserve astonishing.

'Are you ill, my lord?'

He looked away and swallowed hard. She had the distinct impression that should she leave him here in the middle of the crowded floor he might very well simply fall over.

Knowing the Challengers' town house as well as she did, she gestured to a room off to one side, glad when he followed her and the door shut behind them.

'I think you should sit down, Lord Bromley.'

He did that, immediately, and closed his eyes.

'I have been alone for a very long time. It takes some getting used to, this crush of people.'

'It was not like this in the Americas?'

'I kept away from others there.'

His words to her brother in the library last night came back. *'It is dangerous, Jake. If anything were to happen to you and your family...'*

He was trapped in his life as surely as she was.

'You think you might cause those around you harm? Even here in England?'

At that he opened his eyes and leant back. 'I know so.'

'Is it your uncle? Is it his doing?'

'He has the motivation, but...'

'You think it is another?'

For the first time in a long while Nicholas felt his intuition kick in fervently. Eleanor Huntingdon made him alive again in a way no one else did. He barely knew her, but there was something between them that felt right and strong.

'I have many other enemies. Some I probably don't even remember.'

'That sounds dangerous. To not have recall of people who might hurt you, I mean. Is Dromorne one of those enemies?'

'Perhaps. He is a friend of my uncle, Mr Aaron Bartlett, who now sets himself up in Bromworth Manor with the intention of taking both my title and inheritance.'

'Why would he introduce his daughter to you, then?

He looked as if he wished for you to take the acquaintance with his offspring a lot further.'

'To hedge his bets, perhaps. A pound on my uncle and another on me. The Bromley assets are substantial.'

'A gambling man? No true morality in him?'

'I remember that I owe Dromorne money. No doubt he will be calling upon it as soon as he can.'

There was now a dark cloud of worry in Eleanor's eyes as he told her this.

'Could I give you some advice?' He fashioned the words with care and was pleased when she nodded.

'You should probably stay well away from me, Lady Eleanor. The man I used to be was not much, but this one is even more...' Struggling for a word he gave up and left the implication hanging.

'Perilous?' Her smile surprised him as did the quick flare of anger. 'That may very well be true, but you offered me a dance a few moments ago and I shall hold you to your promise. The quadrille is my favourite, Lord Bromley.'

He felt better even looking at her, the gold of her gown picking up the sky blue of her eyes. 'I shall find you then when I hear the tune struck. And thank you.' He gazed around the room.

'My pleasure, but I think I must go now or the others will miss me.'

She had left before he could give her his response and the night dulled with her absence, but he needed the solitude, too, to recoup and recover. He hoped that there were not others here who would pounce on his memory. The medicines Jacob's physician had given him for his arm were making him feel sick. Sick in body and in mind. This evening was a lot more tiring than he had thought it would be and he was only glad that Eleanor Huntingdon had recognised the desperation in him and found him sanctuary.

He tried in earnest to bring to mind the steps of the quadrille she had mentioned, hoping that he might manage it without tipping both of them over.

The face of his uncle also hovered above him, a man whom he had never liked. Looking back, Nick knew he should have heaved him out of his life when his majority was reached, but he had been too self-destructive to even bother, his days revolving around the fast London set, Vitium et Virtus and gambling.

A mistake, he thought now, looking back. He would see his man of business and his lawyer as soon as he could to find out where he stood with his inheritance. But a day or two away in the quiet English countryside might be just what he needed and the sooner he got rid of his father's scheming younger brother from influencing any part of his future, the better.

The hours seemed to have flown by at this soirée of Frederick's. Nicholas Bartlett had not come near her again, but she had watched him across the other side of the room, ensconced in a group of admirers both female and male.

He looked much recovered, she thought, and the fact that her brother and Frederick Challenger were there beside him probably had something to do with that.

Rose, next to her, saw where she was looking. 'There

is something about Lord Bromley that makes him fascinating, do you not think? He looks both vulnerable and dangerous, a man whose history sits upon him with weight.'

'Did Jacob tell you of his time in the Americas?'

'A little. He said the Viscount was always moving to the next place of work and that he had a hard life there. I think people here are watching to find the careless dissolute lord they used to know, for the young girls certainly have their eyes on him. But he does not seem to be rising to any expectation and that is what is causing a quandary. Who is he now seems to be the general question. Did you know him well before he left, Eleanor? Can you see similarities with who he is now?'

Eleanor ignored the first question and answered the second. 'I think he was a lot less dangerous and more easily swayed perhaps.'

Nicholas Bartlett tipped his head as she said this and looked straight at her, across the distance of the room, across the music and the movement and the chatter and it was as if the tableau of everything faded. Only him. Only her. Only the memory of what had been. Her memory, but not his. She looked away and fidgeted with her reticule, hating the way her fingers shook as she reached for her fan.

'Do you ever imagine yourself marrying again, Ellie?' Rose's voice was soft.

'Why do you ask?'

'Because you are a beautiful woman with much to offer a man.'

'No.' The word burst from her very being, the truth

of such emotion worrying. Because she did not. If she could not have Nicholas Bartlett to love her again as he had done before then she did not want anyone. Ever.

'Secrets can be lonely things, Eleanor. If you wish to talk…'

Rose left it there as they both looked across to watch the orchestra tune up for their next round of songs and then the Viscount was right next to her, holding out his hand.

'You promised me a dance, Lady Eleanor, and I have come to claim it.'

'I think this one is a waltz, sir,' she clarified, hearing the tell-tale three-beat music.

'Good,' he returned, 'for I am sure I can remember those steps.'

'And your injured hand?' When she looked she saw he had taken off the sling in readiness, only the bandage left, a snowy white against the dark edge of the cuff of his jacket.

'The doctor assured me that if needs be I could remove the sling without too much harm.'

He had not danced at all that evening and she could see the interest in those around them as he made his way to the floor with her in tow. Her brother was watching, as was Rose and myriad other faces from further afield.

'One turn about the floor shall not drag you into the mire of who I am, I think. It should be safe.'

His fingers were at her side now, the other injured hand coming carefully on to hers. She could feel his breath in her hair as he counted in the steps and see up close the damage done to his face.

He did not try to hide it from her and she liked that, but the scar was substantial and recent, the reddened edges of it only just knitted.

'The wife of the owner of the tavern I worked at sewed it up for me.' He said this when he saw her observing him. 'She was an accomplished seamstress so I was lucky.'

'Lucky…' she echoed his word.

'Not to die from it. Lucky to have escaped a second blow and still live.'

'What happened to the man who did this to you?'

When he glanced at her and she saw the darkness in his eyes she knew exactly what had happened to his assailant.

A further difference. Another danger.

'Scars can be hidden, too, Lord Bromley.'

The upturn of his mouth told her he had heard her whisper even when he did not answer.

'And rest assured that in a room like this there will be people who have been hurt just as surely as you.'

'But they have not the luck to dance with the most beautiful woman in the house.'

'I think your eyesight must have suffered with your injury.'

'Gold suits you.'

She was quiet.

'So does silence.'

At that she laughed, because thus far since meeting him again she had voiced her opinion without reserve. He made her talk again. He made her take risks.

He was quickly catching on to the rhythm of the

dance and manoeuvred her easily about the room despite the number of others on the floor. She could feel hardness in his body where before there had been softness. He smelt of lemon soap and cleanliness, the lack of any other perfume refreshing.

At five foot six she was quite tall for a woman. With him she felt almost tiny, her head fitting easily into the space beneath his chin. Breathing him in, she allowed him to lead her, closing her eyes for a second just to feel what she once had at the Bromley town house the night before his disappearance. The night Lucy was conceived.

She had sent Lucy away today, back to Millbrook, just so that as a mother she might understand the road she must now travel.

Towards him or away? The quick squeeze of his fingers against hers brought her eyes up to his own, an emotion there she could not interpret.

'A lack of memory is a hard taskmaster,' he whispered, 'because sometimes I imagine…' He stopped.

'What? What do you imagine?'

'That I have danced with you before.'

She looked away and hated the lump that had formed in the back of her throat.

The night lights of the city had glowed through the large sashed windows of his town house as he had taken her into his arms and danced her to his bed.

Please remember, she thought. Please remember and love me. Then Mr Dromorne's face at the side of the floor came into view, watching with eyes that held no warmth whatsoever and as the music ran down into the final notes Nicholas escorted her back to her brother.

She did not see him again that evening, but knew he had gone into the card room because the whispers of his luck there began to float into the salon.

An hour later when Rose pleaded tiredness, Eleanor was more than grateful to accompany her home.

Nicholas sat with a whisky in his room and listened to the clock strike the hour of five. The fire in the grate was still ablaze for he had fed it for all the small hours of the early morning with the coal piled near the hearth in a shining copper holder.

Eleanor Huntingdon was asleep somewhere in the house and close. He wished they could talk again. He wished he could see her smile and hear her clever honest words.

He had paid off Dromorne with a good percentage of his takings so that was one creditor he no longer had to worry about. His skill at cards had risen directly with the practice he'd had in the Americas.

The basic strategy of the games had become like second nature to him, the running number of points holding little difficulty. He could count down a single deck to zero within ten seconds in order to know exactly where his edge lay.

A dubious talent and one that told others much about the life he had lived in the interim. He had seen Jacob and Frederick watching him with questions in their eyes. He was only glad that Jacob's sister had retired early because this acquired skill was not attractive.

He would need to leave for Bromworth Manor soon. That thought had him swallowing more of his whisky and standing to look out of the window.

The orderliness of London was what had struck him first on his return. The neat lines of houses and the straight roads. The lights added to the illusion that the city went on for ever, stretching from east to west in a long and unbroken tableau. Virginia and Georgia and the Carolinas had been wild and lonely places. Sometimes he had walked between settlements for a week or more and seen no one.

Tonight he had panicked badly in that room of Frederick's with almost a hundred people in it and Eleanor had noticed and helped him. If she had not been there he wondered what might have happened. If she had not led him to that secluded room, he had no faith in thinking he would have coped.

He did not trust himself any more to act accordingly, to function here, to blend in with the *ton* whilst he tried to understand just who it was here who meant him harm.

If it was his uncle then it would be easy to negate any danger, but Eleanor's question had set his mind running in other directions.

'You think it is another?'

His father's brother might have the motivation to see him dead in England, but he doubted the man had the drive or the contacts to send someone after him to the Americas. If it was not him, then it would need to be an enemy with a good deal of money to spare and a large axe to grind. He could think of any number of past acquaintances who might have fitted that bill given his debauched behaviour as a young viscount of means.

His sins were returning to roost. If he could only remember his missing week, he thought, he might know the perpetrator, but not one drip of recall had come through the solid curtain of mist.

He needed to sleep to be focused on his journey later that day and yet he did not seek his bed. Rather he stood and watched the moon and the sky and the cold gleam of freshly falling snow on the roadway in front of the Westmoor town house, his isolation making him shiver.

Chapter Five

Bromworth Manor was exactly as he remembered, the dark trees that ran along the drive towards it as forbidding as they always had been with their twisted limbs and branches.

The family seat stood proud before a wooded hill overlooking an ornamental lake. Built for defence in the early fourteenth century, the remains of a moat and drawbridge could still be seen to one side, the stonework on this part of the building cruder and darker than its paler, more modern counterpart.

After the onset of the Palladian style a different profile had arisen around the fortress that was more beautiful and substantial. With its pale stone, large rounded windows and double-storeyed wings, Bromworth held the semblance of grandeur, history and wealth.

His direct ancestors had lived here for hundreds of years. It was an estate that spoke of family and celebrations as well as defeats and tragedy. He remembered some of the portraits that lined the walls in the lower hall with a smile. Lovers, soldiers, keepers of the law were displayed there, each Viscount and his family afforded a position in the marching changes of history.

His own visage had not been recorded. He had been very young when his parents had died and later, when a portrait might have been commissioned, he'd wanted little to do with the place at all.

He remembered the local chaplain coming with one of the women from the church in the nearest village, their faces strained in concern as their words tumbled out, banishing his parents to another realm. A quick and final malady that had come on late one night while they were from home and left them both dead by the next. No hope to it. He was an orphan now with a guardian in the form of an uncle he barely knew.

At eight he had had a hard time of imagining the concept of 'for ever lost' though it had soon started to impress itself on all the various strands of his life and he had rebelled against his new punitive reality with every fibre of his being.

The first loss was the hardest, but there had been so many more since then. He was wearing Jacob's boots and Frederick's clothes and the winnings left over from yesterday's card game was the only money in his pocket. Oliver had lent him a carriage and driver for the journey to Essex.

He'd become a jigsaw of other people's lives, the hard, distant core of him hidden from everyone. A man alone and struggling with it.

The front portal creaked open before he had knocked and old Ramsey the butler stood there, his face showing a number of emotions before settling into a smile.

'Lord Bromley.' The man's mouth worked as he tried to say other things, but could not. In the end the servant stepped forward and grabbed his hand, the tight warmth in the shake reassuring. 'I cannot believe it is you, my lord. After all this time you are finally come home.'

'Is Mr Bartlett in, Ramsey?'

'He calls himself Lord Bromley now, my lord.' That was given with a worried glance. 'He believes you dead.'

'Where is he?'

'In bed, I should imagine. He rarely rises before the noon hour and it is not yet that.'

'Can you take me to him?'

'With pleasure, my lord.'

The man waved away a younger servant who stood behind him, stuck out his chest and walked to the large and winding staircase. 'He has your old suite of rooms, Lord Bromley.'

As they went Nicholas saw many of the paintings that lined the stairway had been changed. Dark, sombre strangers now peered down at him. After he tossed his uncle out of Bromworth Manor these would be the next things to go.

The bedchamber was dull and muted, the curtains not yet drawn. Without glancing at the bed, Nick crossed to the windows and threw the shades back. The light fell on the man resting against his pillows, older now, but still as mean spirited and bad tempered as he always had been, his face suffused by a number of changing emotions.

'You. But you are dead.'

'Not quite, Uncle, though I imagine you to have had some say in the fact that I nearly was.'

'Some say? Says who?' Aaron Bartlett threw his head back and frowned as he pushed back the covers. Both cheeks were aflame with rosacea and his jowls had markedly thickened. He looked nothing at all like his brother.

'Those who hit me in the back alley of Vitium et Virtus mentioned your name. They said it was you who had sent them.' It was a lie, of course, as Nick had no memory of any of it, but his friends had told him the story of the pool of blood and the retrieval of his signet ring so he took the gamble. 'You wanted the Bromley inheritances enough to kill for them.'

The man opposite him had his feet to the floor now and sat. The shake in his hands could be seen easily even at this distance across the room. In his white nightgown he looked both a pathetic figure and a powerless one. For the first time he also looked frightened.

'The men I sent to the alley were paid to merely scare you off. You cannot prove I meant to kill you. No court in the land would try me on that. You were out of control with your gambling and I was trying to stop you from ruining everything.'

'After encouraging me in it for all the years before?'

'The Bromley fortune, whilst rich, was not limitless and you rarely won after the first few flushes.'

'So you sent assassins after me to the Americas in order to keep what was left?'

'I dispatched no one across the ocean. Why should

I have done so? You were already gone. Drowned in the Thames.'

Such a confession sat congealing in the thick air of the chamber, a truth that held nothing in it save betrayal.

'Get your things and leave. You have my permission to use the Bromley carriage to take what you can carry away from here, but after this there will be nothing.'

Nick was furious and shocked, the numbness of his uncle's treachery creeping into coldness.

'Nothing? Nothing?' Bartlett stood now and bellowed the two words.

'Less than nothing if you argue.' His reply was quiet. 'You have half an hour. After that I will have my servants throw you out.'

'You cannot do that, for God's sake. Your father wished for me to be a figure in your life…'

'A cantankerous, avaricious greedy bastard is not what I imagine he had in mind and I owe you less than nothing. You are dead to me. A man who could have chosen a better path, but didn't.' He pointedly looked at his timepiece. 'Twenty-nine minutes now.'

At that Nick turned, ignoring the run of insults that followed him to the door as he shut it behind him and took in a breath. It was over. Aaron Bartlett was out of his life.

Exactly half an hour later his uncle stood before him, hastily dressed and furious.

'This is not the end of this, mark my words. There will be legalities to deal with and the fact that you were all but dead for so many years—'

Nicholas had had enough of his threats and, grabbing him by his shirt front, he hauled his uncle off his feet.

'If you ever darken my door again, I won't be as kind as I have been this time, do you understand? My advice would be to leave England before any creditors know you have gone, for this way you have a chance of leaving the country alive. If you stay, I will find you and deal with you as you dealt with me.'

'You were out of control and reckless...'

'Enough.'

This time Bartlett blanched white and was silent and Nick, releasing his hold, allowed the butler to show Bartlett out. A few moments later Nick heard the movement of the carriage and the call of the driver.

Gone.

He thought back to all the moments he had hated his uncle and felt no remorse at all. His guardian was a heart-dead greedy sycophant, but worse than that he was immoral. He still held the thin scars on his arms where he'd been whipped time after time as a child when he had refused direction.

The grave of the family dog his guardian had had shot was marked in the woods by all the shale and stones that Nicholas himself had buried him under, each one drenched in tears.

His uncle had made him into a young man of wildness and anger, the responsibilities of love and family lost under greed.

'Could I pour you a drink, Lord Bromley? There are some fine reds from your father's collection that we managed to hide.'

Ramsey looked both worried and relieved. 'We have been waiting for your return, you see, my lord, for the reappearance of a master who was not...so immoral, I mean. Mrs Ramsey has ham and fresh bread in the kitchens should you wish for it and the chutney this year was particularly tasty.'

'Thank you.' When Nick looked at him closely there were tears in the old butler's eyes. 'I would like that.'

Ten minutes later he was sitting in front of a roaring fire in the large kitchen, the fare of the county on the table before him and an uncorked bottle of his father's burgundy.

A row of servants stood behind him, some known and some new. All looked tense and uncertain.

'Find another few more glasses, Ramsey, and we will all partake in a toast.'

He had never once in his years at Bromworth Manor spoken so familiarly to the staff and he had never before been in this room, the very heart of the place.

He was once again lord of Bromworth Manor and lord of these lands, but there had been a shift inside him. He felt more comfortable with these people than he did with the gossiping aristocrats of the *ton*. He felt at home here, a belonging, a place to put down roots and stay.

The very feeling calmed him and made him lighter. For the first time ever he felt he was following in the footsteps of his beloved father.

The land held an ancient history, carried down by the centuries, of planting and nurturing. Perhaps it was the same with people? The rain, the soil, the forests, the hills. They were imprinted within him, known and familiar, a part of his understanding in the translation of life.

In the Americas it had all been so foreign. Different seas and rivers and plants. Foreign languages and foods that he had no understanding of or liking for.

The codes for being a Bromley had been ripped out of him, forgotten, lost in violence and circumstance. Here, the pattern reformed and carried on, the smells of the place, the sounds, the shadows and the light.

A comradeship. A rightness.

He picked up the cheese knife and looked at the crested end of it. *Servire Populo.* For the first time ever he understood exactly what it meant.

Much later he walked down to the small graveyard behind the ruined chapel, the stones of commemoration ill kept and unweeded.

He found his parents' graves side by side in one corner, the late winter sun still upon them, and he was glad for it.

His fingers traced the words that he knew by heart. Their names. The dates of their births and deaths. The epitaph was short. Chosen by his uncle, he guessed, and conveying little.

Until we meet again.

The words made him smile as he imagined his father with his hands around the throat of his brother in an eternal celestial retribution when he arrived at the heavenly gates for judgement.

Placing the wildflowers he had gathered on his mother's stone, he bowed his head.

Today he felt closer to them than he had felt in years.

'I will become a better man.' The words were out before he knew them said, slipping into the breeze, though when his good hand dug into his pocket to try to banish the cold he felt the hard outline of a set of dice. His injured hand ached with the effort of lifting Bartlett, but it was worth it.

People arrived at the place they were meant to be even if they came with a past. It was how life worked. But the past did not have to define one just as the present did not. The future was his, here in Essex, in the ancient seat of the Bromleys. It was his to nurture, grow and tend to.

Hope filled him. For Bromworth, for a new direction, for his friends and their support.

For Eleanor Huntingdon.

That name had him tensing. They barely knew one another, but she was there none the less in his mind, her smile, the way she spoke, the vivid blue of her eyes and the dark of her hair.

He would like to show her this estate. He would like to walk with her and tell her all that had happened to him, as a child, as a youth, as a man, so that she might know of the darkness inside him.

Of all the people in the world he thought she would be the one to understand.

Eleanor sat in the library at the Westmoor town house, stitching a complex tapestry of colourful nasturtiums, although her heart was not in it.

At every noise outside she stopped to listen, every sound of horses and carriage, every call of a night bird or the far-off ringing of bells.

Her brother and Rose had gone to a play at the Royal Coburg Theatre, but she knew Nicholas Bartlett was expected back from Essex tonight. She hoped it might be when the others were absent for she wanted to speak with him privately and make him an offer.

An offer. Even the words sounded impossibly difficult.

Placing down her stitching, she pulled back the fabric of her bodice and lifted up the gold chain that she always wore around her neck. The small ring brought a smile to her lips as her fingers closed about it.

Blue zircon had a charm more captivating than the sophisticated diamonds which it sometimes imitated.

They had found it in a jewellery shop in Piccadilly on the day they had visited Lackington, Allen & Co. and Nicholas had purchased the trinket because the colour matched her eyes exactly.

'Like blue starlight,' he had said and she'd laughed, because of the fancy and daydream.

She had worn it then on the third finger of her right hand, a troth, a promise, a way to the future that she could see so very easily before her.

And even when he had disappeared she could not bear to have it away from her skin and so she had fastened it to a fragile chain her father had made her a gift of on her fifteenth birthday and she had worn it there every day since.

She looked at the clock. Half past nine. Perhaps the

Viscount was not returning from Bromworth Manor tonight after all. Perhaps things had gone awry with the uncle that her brother had said Nicholas had gone to expel from the family estate. Perhaps there had been a fight or an accident on the road like her father and Ralph had had. She shook that thought away.

Jacob had told her this morning that Nicholas was almost certain his guardian had been the one to waylay him in the alley. After today there would be no more looking over one's shoulder and expecting trouble, for if he knew the perpetrator of all his problems he could deal with the man summarily. She breathed out with decided relief and was pleased for the decisions she had made last night to help Nicholas Bartlett with his lost week.

Noises came through the quiet and then there was the sound of horses and bustle, a called-out goodbye and footsteps leading up the steps. After that the front door closed behind the newcomer and his voice reached her with its deep and steady tones, hints of another land in the cadence.

Eleanor hastily tidied herself and put her needle through the next stitch needing execution. She also quietened her nerves as best she could.

'You are up still?'

He looked more relaxed then he had yesterday. The boots he wore now were Jacob's. She recognised the engraved silver buckles.

'I seldom retire before ten.' She gave this back to him and was glad when he came into the room and sat in the chair opposite.

'My brother said you went to Essex to the Brom-worth estate?'

He nodded. 'Oliver leant me his carriage and driver. With such horses it was a quick run both there and back.'

'I hope it all went well.'

At that he laughed. 'Well for me and poorly for my uncle, but I am finally shot of Mr Aaron Bartlett and his plotting so at least now I will be able to afford my own boots.' He added this in a wry tone as he stretched his legs out before him.

'I heard that you had won a substantial sum at the card tables last night?'

He frowned. 'A dubious talent in the eyes of the *ton*. Once it was losing I was better at, failure more accept-able to the doyens of good taste here.'

She smiled because what he said was the truth. She had heard the rumblings of gossip before she had left Frederick's and the strong opinion on the Viscount's new ability to fleece any other man at the table was not flattering.

'Perhaps you should pretend sometimes to be a lesser player?'

He sat up at that and looked at her directly. 'Drom-orne threatened to foreclose on his IOUs if I did not fully reimburse him last night.'

The truth of this made Eleanor place down her flow-ery craftwork. 'There was no choice for you, then?'

'None. Tonight, however, I have my title and my es-tate returned into my care. Undoubtedly there will be others who will come forward demanding payments of past debts that I have long since forgotten, but now I can manage.'

'You will open your town house again?'

'I have a man hiring staff as we speak.'

'And your memory? Has it been jogged at all with the sojourn back to Bromworth Manor?'

'No. I had thought perhaps…' He let this tail off and shook his head. 'But, no.'

Standing, she walked across to the hearth, using the mantel for support. 'Then I want to offer you a proposition, Lord Bromley.'

She stressed his title. Better to make the suggestion formally and holding no whisper of emotion.

He looked up at that, his eyes darker than they normally appeared. 'A proposition, Lady Eleanor?'

'I want to help you retrieve your memory.'

After these words he said nothing, but merely waited.

'I was with you for many of the days that you have forgotten. The days before your attack,' she qualified.

'With me?'

She was not brave enough yet to give him all the truth. 'As a friend. You were at a loose end and so I accompanied you on day trips.'

The candles against the darkness, the smell of scented wax, his skin under moonlight, her unbound hair draped across the tanned folds of his shadowed arm.

She did not speak of this.

'Where did we go?'

'The Vauxhall Gardens. Hyde Park. Bullock's Museum. Fortnum and Mason. Gunter's Tea Shop.'

'Quite the potpourri of establishments.'

'There were others as well.'

'All in less than a week? Not a little acquaintance, then?'

She smiled and spoke with more trepidation than she meant to. 'The thing is, Lord Bromley, I might be able to help you to remember by going back.'

'Recall by association, you mean?'

'Memory aided by events that are familiar. I have been reading about amnesia. Hypnosis is one treatment, but so is the quieter option of passing again across what your soul would know and hence allowing a passage for the brain to reconnect.'

She recognised in her words the text she had studied all afternoon at Lackington's.

'Why would you do this? For me?'

'You are my brother's best friend and Jacob would be more than pleased to see your memory restored.'

He could not understand her motives. One thing was for certain—they were not quite as she had admitted them, for she had blushed bright red at his question and looked away.

What was it she was saying underneath her words?

'I truly went to Gunter's Tea Shop with you?'

That brought a smile into eyes that were anxious.

'Happily, my lord. You particularly enjoyed the chocolate sorbet in a pewter mould shaped as a pineapple. But then Gunter's frozen indulgences are all particularly alluring.'

He could not ever remember laughing with a woman as he did with Eleanor Huntingdon.

'I can see why that memory has been expunged from my recall, Lady Eleanor.'

'You brought a box of the extravagant pastries home. The almond croissant was your favourite.'

'To the Bromley town house?' Had she gone there with him, too? The tea shop was a place she might have accompanied him without being exposed to scandal, but to visit him at home?

As if she had said too much, she retreated into silence.

'Very well.' He gave this quietly as she looked across at him. 'Our first destination is the tea shop on Berkeley Square. I'll pick you up at two o'clock tomorrow and we shall go and have ice cream.'

'You are not staying here this evening?'

'My town house is being readied for me and it will be good to put my head down in a bed that I know.'

The sharp flash of anger that crossed into Eleanor Huntingdon's face as he said these words were another puzzlement.

'Then I look forward to tomorrow, Lord Bromley. On the last occasion you wore a dark blue jacket and beige trousers.'

'You think the details important?'

'I do.'

'What was it you had on?'

She frowned at that as though she could not exactly remember. 'It was warm so no doubt I had on one of my summer silks.'

'In gold?'

'Pardon?'

'I liked you in gold at Frederick's.'

'I am not certain I have…'

'Anything, Eleanor. Wear anything you feel comfortable in. I was teasing.'

A further blush at the informality of his using her Christian name. Jacob's sister was beginning to confound him completely and the thought crossed his mind that he would sit anywhere opposite her just to see her blue eyes smile. Even in Gunter's Tea Shop in Berkeley Square.

Had it been the same back then?

He could not ask her. He couldn't ask Jacob either. He swore under his breath because the loss of his memory was causing havoc in every sort of way possible and Eleanor's offer was the one avenue to help him get closer to finding out the truth.

He just hoped like hell that he had not hurt her.

She watched him leave and for just a second was transported back to the night before his disappearance. They had made love and it was late, but the magic between them seemed doused and awkward as he had escorted her to the front door of the Bromley town house and to the carriage that awaited outside.

He had not kissed her. She remembered that vividly. When she had reached up that last time he had pulled away, calling to his footman to escort her home, anger and distance in his voice. He had not even stayed to wave her goodbye either, the door shut firmly so that all light was gone. She had stumbled on the steps in the darkness and almost fallen.

Falling. It felt like that again now as uncertainty clawed at truth. She did not know him any more. The man she had imagined was different from the one he had become, but she was different, too, with the responsibility of Lucy. She was also scared of allowing him in once more and being hurt because of it.

The dry ache in her throat made her breath shallow.

Chapter Six

Nicholas spent the next morning in one of the more squalid parts of the Ratcliffe Highway, asking questions that might lead to answers about his uncle's involvement in his lost years.

Once he might have felt out of place in such a location but the forces that had shaped him in the Americas were the same as those he now trawled through in the pestilent dark alleys of Stepney. Destitution, filth, poverty and overcrowding abounded here and criminal activity was a direct result of that.

The smell of the river was everywhere and the toil of those who lived by it easily seen, the scavengers and mudlarks who survived on what they could find on the bottom of the Thames when the low tide washed in various pieces of coal, rope, bones or copper nails if you were lucky. Nicholas knew this because the James River had held the same desperation and there were times, especially in the early months there, when he had wondered about crawling into the sludge himself.

Those who held the run of the docklands were

steeped in beggary and with no other means available to them were unlikely to overlook opportunities that might keep them from the workhouses.

Opportunities such as the kidnap of a viscount and his subsequent disposal. He'd had the name of a man who might have some information about such things, given to him quietly, of course, and taking the last of his gambling winnings from Frederick's soirée to obtain.

He'd dressed accordingly, but there must have been something in the lines of his face that spoke of menace and experience because walking through the mean streets of the place he had been completely unchallenged. Perhaps the scar did him a service here.

Mess with me and I will deal with you, as others have dealt with me.

The White Horse Tavern stood on the corner of East Smithfield and a smaller unnamed street, the river visible from its front portal. Those who watched him enter were miserably clad with barely a boot between them and the stench of the streets followed him inside to the bar where he recognised the look of some of the cheaper liquor he'd dispatched himself in Richmond.

A stranger approached then, a man in his forties with an eye that was patently false in its deformed socket, as well as being poorly fashioned.

'You'd be the one who has been asking about the details of a snatch in Jermyn Street some years ago?'

'I am.' Words were not things to be bandied by the starving in the same way as the *ton* was wont to. The less said the better.

'Join me over there.'

The very position of the man's seat told Nicholas two

things. He liked his back to the wall and he felt safer near a further exit. A small door was visible beside the table, three steps running down to it.

The newcomer held his hand above his belt as he sat and Nick knew there would be a knife there. There was probably another one on the outside of his right boot given that was the side he favoured as he gestured to Nick to also sit.

'Did you bring money?'

'I did, but the amount depends on what you might tell me.'

Neither of them used names. The parish constables and the Night Watch were noticeable by their absence in these parts of London, but there were other means of maintaining order. Should the need arise for violence Nick knew the man would not hesitate and there were those close undoubtedly involved in the same scam. The lad in the corner tending to the fire, the bearded fellow behind the bar, the two older patrons to one side who were stiff with focus.

He turned back and waited, his breath quiet and even, but nevertheless relieved when the contact fumbled in his pocket to bring forth a small book.

Turning over the pages to find the right entry, the glass-eyed man read quickly.

22nd August 1812
Jermyn Street, Mayfair
Viscount Bromley
Twenty pounds
Paid

The shock of the words made Nicholas's breath come shallowly. 'Who paid?'

'An older fellow named Bartlett and an arrogant toff he was, too. The mark was put into a hackney coach and thrown into the river as per instructions and then left for the tide to take.'

Or to crawl out? To be picked up? To find a ship to faraway shores?

'Did Bartlett pay again later when it was discovered that the man was still alive? Did he have someone follow Viscount Bromley abroad?'

'No. That was the end of it. A simple drowning. No amount of gold would be enough to entice those I hire out to cross the seas to hunt further.'

'But others might?'

'I have never heard even a whisper of it, but I suppose with enough gold offered it could be possible.'

Nick believed what was said and the hope of a quick resolution wilted. His uncle might have ordered his demise in the first place at the river, but when that did not eventuate another had tried to finish him off.

He put a small bag of gold on the table, the clink of it satisfying. 'If you hear anything at all about this matter I would be well pleased to learn of it. Leave word at the address inside and mark it *"Stepney"*.'

As a duke, Jacob was often receiving missives. No one would take notice of a further messenger.

A quick nod of his head and the man stood, using the small door to disappear. There was mud on his boots from the river and his cloak was torn at the hem.

As Nick rose himself the tavern owner came forward and slugged him hard on the side of his good cheek.

'In warning not to say nothing of this to anyone.' He could feel the eyes of all the others upon him as he left.

She had worn the sprigged muslin to Gunter's six years ago, Eleanor thought as she rifled through the clothes she'd brought down to London from Millbrook House. But there was nothing here remotely similar to that which her eighteen-year-old flighty self would have once favoured. Certainly apart from the one very formal gown she had worn to Frederick's, there was nothing in gold.

Hauling out a deep blue velvet, she held it up against her. The colour made her eyes bluer and she had always liked the cut.

Sighing, she stroked her fingers across the pile. Was she doing the right thing? She missed Lucy and every day she promised to help Nicholas was one less she did not have with her daughter. She wondered if she should put more of a guard up, for her protection and for Lucy's. But she wished his memories back as desperately as he himself did because only then she would know whether she could trust him to be the sort of father her daughter needed.

The demons still sat upon his shoulders and the menace that had become such a part of him now was worrying. Still, yesterday at Bromworth Manor he had discovered his uncle's part in his mysterious disappearance so that was one less concern. The debts he owed should right themselves with his newly come inheritance and things would return to normal.

Normal?

He would never be the rakish pleasure-seeking smiling Viscount she had once fallen in love with, but her older self found this dangerous, larger and quieter version even more attractive.

He was steel now, honed in fire, the pieces that had been light and reckless burned away to the bone. She could not even imagine how this Nicholas might enjoy ice cream with her at Gunter's.

Despite everything she looked forward to their next meeting. It had been the middle of August last time they were there—now hot chocolate might be more the order of the day on a cold December afternoon. All she could feel was excitement.

His carriage arrived on the dot of two and Jacob called to her as she came downstairs hoping to leave before anyone saw exactly who she had gone with.

'Tell Nick to stop in for a drink here with me afterwards.'

Eleanor smiled because there was very little her brother ever missed when it concerned his family. 'I will.'

'And make sure he takes take good care of my baby sister.'

'Hardly that. I am almost twenty-five. A matron.'

He shook his head and stood. 'Experience does not always come with the years one lives, Ellie. I don't want you hurt.'

'You think I might be?'

'After all that Rose and I endured, I am now of the opinion that no one knows better what is right for your life than you do. But a word of warning. If you are hurt, let it be your making and not that of others. He is a good person, Nick, but in a difficult situation.'

'I know.'

'And you are a bit the same, I think.'

She made no answer to this as she turned to go, but sometimes she got the distinct impression that her brother could read her more easily than she gave him credit for.

Nicholas was just walking towards the town house after speaking with his driver and he looked up when he saw her.

'The while we keep a man waiting he reflects on his shortcomings.'

She frowned at his words.

'It's an old French proverb, though I have changed the pronoun.'

His explanation made her frown. 'What are your shortcomings then, my lord?'

'I have so many I cannot remember half of them.'

When he smiled she saw a dark bruise on his left cheek, newly gathered.

'I hope no one else has decided to try to do away with you since yesterday, Lord Bromley.'

All humour evaporated and when he didn't answer Eleanor felt a growing bud of alarm.

He was dressed in his own clothes this morning. A black jacket over lighter trousers, his white shirt and cravat enhancing the tan of his skin. His hair was back in a looser queue today, allowing wisps of dark brown to frame his face in a fashion that was unusual nowadays, but one that suited him completely.

Beautiful. She had always thought him that even in the very worst of times.

But this afternoon, as he helped her into the carriage, he felt less safe than he had yesterday. She could almost imagine he might scrap the plans for the tea-shop visit and head instead to find some frightening shadow-filled tavern in which to imbibe uncut liquor in great quantities.

For years she had lived so carefully, with circumspection and quietness. She had blended into Millbrook House without incident, making sojourns to London only occasionally and always being on her very best behaviour.

She had dressed appropriately, trying not to draw any attention to herself, she had spoken solely on topics that caused no debate and in any group she had always stood back rather than pushing herself forward. She had stayed well away from the masculine gender.

Camouflage. Penance. Lucy did not need a mother of any more notoriety or shame and Eleanor had done her level best to make certain that she was exactly the type of woman others expected.

She had grown old.

That thought had all her attention.

And staid.

Another shocking truth.

She had become a woman she would not have rec-

ognised at eighteen when she had thrown away all restraint and jumped head first into the thrall of Nicholas
Bartlett.

'You seem preoccupied?' His voice came through
all introspection and shattered her resolve with ease.

'Did you like yourself when you were younger, Lord
Bromley?'

'Not much, I think, but responsibility and experience
have weathered the rough edges.'

Given that she was thinking just the opposite, she
smiled.

'I have always been careful.' She gave him this in
reply. 'So careful that perhaps...' It was hard to finish.

'Offering to help me with my memory and coming
with me to the places where I could find some recall
is not so careful? There are many here in society who
would say I am a risky man to know and stay well away
because of it.'

'And are you? Risky, I mean?'

'My uncle would swear that I am and so would
those who hold debts from me which have remained
unpaid. Society always labelled me a wild cannon and
my friends might say it, too, because in the loss of self-
knowledge there is the propensity for chaos. Sometimes
in the late of night when I cannot sleep I may even admit
it to myself. I am damaged, Eleanor, and have been for
a very long time.'

'Even before you disappeared?'

He nodded, but she could not let the subject go so
easily.

'A viscount who founded the most depraved gentlemen's club ever to grace the hallowed halls of Oxford University and then moved it to Mayfair where it became even more dissolute and scandalous? That sort of damage?'

He shook his head.

'Every act within Vitium et Virtus has always been consensual. People are there because they want to be. No one is forced.'

'A morality within the scandalous?'

'Exactly.'

And right then and there Eleanor knew what she had missed the most when he had disappeared. It was this, this conversation that was more real to her than any other thing she had ever felt. Every single part of her was more alive in his company. Her body. Her brain. Her heart. Her soul.

He made her fascinating and brave and clever. Effortlessly.

'After meeting with a few people, I don't think my uncle was the one who paid people to follow me to the Americas.'

The bubble burst. Real life rushed in like a blast of frigid cold air, enemies poised again at every bend in the road.

'How could you know this?'

He didn't speak, but she could see the answer in his eyes, on his cheek and in the guarded quiet of his posture. He had not just waited for such information to trickle slowly down to him, but had gone to actively seek out the truth. Gone presumably into the poorest parts of London that few aristocrats would feel comfortable to be. Except him.

There was a certain respect in such an action that she could not help but feel. But to pretend joy and eat ice cream?

To laugh at the fussy decorative moulds and sip at tastes inconsequential and unimportant when there was an enemy afoot who wished him harm in such magnitude?

She wanted to throw herself down on the plush leather seat of his carriage and sob because a day that had begun with such promise was now falling into complete disarray.

Damn it. He should not have said a thing about his suspicions. Now Eleanor Huntingdon was looking as though she might hurl herself out the window before the carriage stopped just to escape from his company.

He could not believe he had told her any of this. Usually he clammed up about affairs that were even remotely personal, but the laughter and ease of the conversation had been beguiling and he had let his guard slip.

There was no easy way to say that he was damaged and reduced in value, the spoiled and harmed product of years of fear and danger written inside him like a story. Any fineness he might once have had was diluted by experience, weakened by a lack of trust and diminished by an absence of honour.

Nick could still feel the stranger's neck in Shockoe Bottom breaking under his grip, the shameful truth of death by his own hand making him swallow down bile.

Like an apple in a barrel, rotten to the core. 'Please,

God, do not let me hurt Eleanor. Please, God, keep her safe.'

He recited this beneath his breath as she turned away, the sky through the window about as bleak as his mood. He needed to throw off these maudlin thoughts, or she would decide to return home. There was probably only so much of him that even an angel like Eleanor Huntingdon could take.

The anger and shame reformed into effort.

'Would you like a walk first on the square before we go in for tea? We could stroll around the pathways. Is that something we did before?'

'No.' Her voice was hesitant.

'Good. Then let us make some new memories before remembering the other ones.'

Her coat and hat looked warm and her boots sturdy. A small walk in the cold might reinvigorate them both and shake the cobwebs from their worries.

He smiled because suddenly he remembered his mother saying that to him and when Eleanor caught his glance she tentatively smiled back. He wanted to make her laugh again and talk again, her truths revealing a woman who'd been saddened by life. He wanted them both to forget what had been and to concentrate on now.

He would ask Jacob more about her dead husband when they were alone next time and if he gave back flippant answers as he had before he would confront him further.

'Virginia was a place that winter took to with a vengeance,' he said as they exited the carriage and began to amble around the small neat square. 'But the coldest region I've ever been to was Caribou in northern Maine. It's close to Lower Canada where the air sets up in Hudson Bay and is sent southwards. If you happen to be in a river valley sleeping rough you'll know well sure by the morning that you should not have been there.'

'Were you? Sleeping rough, I mean.'

'For a good week. I was on one of the trails hunting at the end of autumn and had not expected it to turn to cold so quickly.'

'A different life, then. One you would never have had if...' She stopped and he liked her confusion.

'I was probably insufferable, the man you knew before?'

She laughed at that and gave back a query of her own. 'Why would you say that?'

'My gambling debts were rising and I could see no way out. That was one of the last things I remembered before I couldn't, arguing with my uncle about the sums I owed. Hardly auspicious.'

'I agree that you were reckless and wild, but there was something else there, too. Something honest. If there hadn't been I doubt I would have stayed around to bother.'

'Perhaps you were trying to save me even then?' He said this as a jest and she hit him lightly on the arm in return before she realised it was the injured one. Then he had to stop and listen to five more minutes of apology.

'You owe the world nothing, Eleanor, and remorse should always have its limits.' He could tell she was listening as she tipped her head. 'Regret is not an easy emotion to live by and if things do not turn out quite as you expect them to, then you need to shape your world to make sure that it does.'

'Do you do that?'

'I try to. Since coming home I try to forget what once was.'

'You have reshaped your life?'

The small line between her brows was deep and because of this he gave her back something of his truths. 'Not entirely, but the pieces still lost to me will return. I know it.'

The tea shop on the south-east corner had now come into view and as expected it was half-empty, the cold driving the clients away. As they walked inside the man who met them asked if they had a preference for where they wanted to sit. Eleanor gestured to the table by the window.

'We sat here last time?' Nicholas said this as they were seated, the green and gold baize chairs small and dainty.

'A lucky thing it was, too, for a group had just moved off when we came and it was very busy. The summer view was better.'

'Yet Berkeley Square still holds its charm.'

He was careful with his words because so far none of this was in any way familiar.

'Tea for two, please.' She smiled at the waiter as she gave him back the menu.

'A simple choice. I was imagining the pineapple delicacy you told me about.'

'I was teasing you, Lord Bromley. We were only here briefly for we were en route to Bullock's Museum.'

'We shall go there tomorrow, then? I will pick you up at eleven.'

When she nodded Nick let out the breath he had not realised he was holding. Another outing. Further conversations. With the light from the window falling across her face he thought Eleanor Huntingdon was by far the most fascinating woman he had ever laid his eyes upon.

'We spoke of animals last time because there was a black spaniel sitting at that table there.' She gestured to a vacant setting over by the wall. 'You said you had had a dog most similar when you were young?'

The feeling of loss hit him so forcibly Nick thought he might have fallen off the chair had his hands not curled to the seat.

'I spoke of him?'

A frown marred her forehead. 'Are you remembering things? I think you said his name was Vic.'

The horror of what had happened to the animal made his heart beat quicken. Vic. Victor. Victory. His father had named him after the Siege of Bangalore in 1791. Another thought hit him like a sledgehammer.

'How close were we, Eleanor?' He'd never told another about the dog, its death one of the defining and terrible moments of his childhood.

Nicholas Bartlett looked at her directly as he asked his question; a question Eleanor had been expecting given the nature of her plan so she'd concocted exactly the right answer.

'We were friends.'

With a nod he looked away though she could see

anger in the line of his jaw. It had been like that last time, too, but then he had been much less adept at hiding his sorrow. Now there was only the slightest hint of it. A man with his emotions well under control, the uncertainty of a few days ago gone entirely.

For a moment she could only stare at him, this harder, more unreadable stranger wrapped in the shape of the one she had lost her heart to, but then the tea came and the moment ran again into now as she thanked the waiter for bringing the refreshments.

Twinings black tea. The very same as last time.

Today though Nicholas Bartlett used his right hand to lift the cup. Then it had been his left. She noticed he still cradled the injured hand whenever he could. In the carriage it had lain against the top of his thigh, the swollen reddened fingers curled in pain.

She didn't want to ask of this though because she knew there would be some story attached to the wound that wouldn't be an easy one. Nothing about him at the moment seemed easy.

'We talked also of your hope of a Tory victory for the Duke of Portland in the next elections. You spoke on that for a long while.'

'A topic you must have found riveting?' The irony in his tone was obvious.

'You don't follow the turning wheels of government any more?'

'Not particularly. I think I am more in favour of living life quietly.'

'At Bromworth?'

He nodded. 'The land is fertile and the work is interesting. After so long spent moving from one place to another, I would like to find a base now, a home.'

When the waiter brought them milk Nicholas thanked him. Once he would not have noticed the ministrations of a servant at all.

'I live for a good part of the year at Millbrook House in Middlesex, my lord.'

'Why?'

'The life of a widow is a solitary one.'

'But you have your daughter? The child Jake told me of?'

'Indeed I do. Is this tea to your liking, for you enjoyed it last time?'

She did not wish to discuss Lucy with him and she hoped he had not noticed her leading him on to another topic.

'It is.' As he toyed with his cup she was reminded of the quiet a panther or a lion might employ before his next strike.

'Will you come to dinner at my town house, Eleanor?'

The shock of his invitation was startling. She wanted to tell him that this was not something they had done then, but that was a lie. She had gone alone to his town house and enjoyed a meal unlike any she could remember. A meal of anticipation and sensuality and climax that had been unequalled.

'As it would be my first foray into entertaining I would like to have friends there. I will ask Jake, of course, and his wife Rose.'

Friends. She felt an ache of disappointment and of sorrow.

'That would be lovely.' The very thought of an evening at the Bromley town house on Piccadilly actually made her feel like turning to run. There had been few servants there that evening six years before as the Viscount had given much of his staff the night off, but what if anyone left recognised her? What if his memory returned in the middle of the dinner? Her brother was a man sharp on detail and nuance and so was Rose. That was a further worry.

She was swapping one set of problems for another. She was walking on a tightrope much like the artists she had once seen perform in Astley's at the Royal Grove, but without the comfort of a safety net. Recreating their 'courtship' as closely as possible was turning out to be a lot more complicated than she had thought.

Could she know Nicholas Bartlett again? Would he ever let her in? Or had the years of apartness made them into people who were too different to rediscover the core of each other.

She felt her knee brush his thigh momentarily as he moved to change position, the touch sending fingers of shock through her whole body.

Breathless.

Absolute.

Gripping her fingers as hard as she could on her lap, she felt herself slip into the flame.

Lady Eleanor Huntingdon looked flushed.

She was trying her hardest to appear normal, but her knuckles were white as she clenched her fists; the small blue artery in her throat beating at twice the usual rate.

His recent life had taught Nick to read the signs

of high emotion in people and she looked more than agitated.

It was his dinner invitation. She had been flustered ever since he had issued it. Perhaps she was regretting her decision to help him and was wondering now how she could turn him down politely and leave him in this mire of non-memory?

As he finished his tea he saw the leaves in the bottom arranged in a pattern.

'Leaves like this can be read, I think,' he said, pleased when he saw that had caught her attention. 'Once a travelling woman in Richmond told my fortune from a pile of sticks she carried. I imagine it is the same principle for the leaves.'

The corner of her mouth turned up. 'What did she say?'

'She assured me that I would be rich, famous and more than happy, though she warned there was a valley of emptiness between me and my dreams. At the time, running from town to town without a clue as to who I was or why I was there, her words meant very little, but now...'

'Your memory. A valley of emptiness? I did not expect you to be one who would put much stock in the world of the occult?'

'Amnesia does that to one, Lady Eleanor. *"There are more things in heaven and Earth, Horatio, than are dreamt of in your philosophy."'*

When she laughed out loud the tension was replaced only by warmth.

'You used not to quote Shakespeare either, Lord Bromley.'

'Another difference, then, Lady Eleanor.'

'You remember nothing of this? Of Gunter's? Of the outing?'

He shook his head and wished it were otherwise.

The bells of St Martin's could be heard in the distance counting out the night hour of eleven o'clock. Rose snuggled into her husband's side in the ducal bed as the prevailing winds came in from the south-west, shaking the fragile glass panes with their force.

'Do you think Eleanor seems changed lately, Jacob? Happier, I mean?' She whispered this into his chest and liked the way his arm curled about her, holding her close.

'She went with Nicholas for an outing today. To Gunter's. He came in his carriage and picked her up.'

Her smile came unbidden. 'The tea shop with all its fussy food is a place I can barely imagine Viscount Bromley being comfortable in.'

The shake of his chest told her that he had held the same thought.

'Perhaps my sister wants to help Nick become reacquainted with the ways of London life.'

'Like a small rabbit might aid a hungry fox, you mean?'

At that he turned, his eyes, pale in the fire flame, full of question. 'What are you saying, Rose?'

'Nicholas Bartlett gives the impression of such danger and distance that I would have imagined Eleanor to be running the other way and yet she is not. You said she has been lonely for such a very long time, but perhaps we might be hopeful for an ending to her solitude?'

Jacob laughed. 'Matchmaking is a precarious occupation, Rose.'

'I know, but they suit each other in a way that is surprising. At the ball when they danced I thought they looked completely right.'

'I doubt Nick would appreciate words on the subject from me, but I suppose a relationship could be possible.'

Rose ran her finger down across his cheek to his lips and then her touch fell lower. 'Which is exactly why we shall only watch from a distance, Jacob, but with hope in our hearts.'

He turned at that and pulled her down beneath him, his dark hair burnished by candlelight. 'You are both wise and beautiful, my love, and I thank God every day that he allowed us to find each other.'

'Show me,' she whispered and wrapped her nakedness about him. As he blew out the scented flame Rose had the distinct impression of strength tempered with gentleness, and the sheer beauty of Jacob Huntingdon, her husband, warmed her heart.

Chapter Seven

Eleanor found her grandmother in the library the next morning as she came down to breakfast.

'You look busy, Grandmama.' Her eyes fell to the large pile of books stacked in the middle of the table.

'That is because I am trying to understand the world that Nicholas Bartlett inhabited during his time away.'

Of all the things she had expected her slight and frail grandmother to say that was the very last of them.

'You have spoken with Viscount Bromley since he has been back?'

'Briefly. The first night he came home with Jacob I saw him in the hallway and he told me he had just returned from the Americas. His grandmother would have been saddened by his losses, I think, God bless her soul.'

'You knew his grandmother?'

'Anna Bartlett? Yes, she came out the same year that I did and I was glad that she died before her son and her daughter-in-law went. A terrible death and I was always glad that Jacob was Nicholas's friend when they both were sent up to Eton. You were his friend, too, if I remember rightly, Eleanor. That day in the Vauxhall Gardens just after you'd come out into society and I'd lost sight of you for a little while, I was certain he was there.'

'There?' Her heartbeat quickened.

'Watching the fireworks and speaking with you. He was always a beautiful child and he became a beautiful man even with his wild ways and a weakness for gambling. But then he was a boy. Now he is a man.'

Her words flowed around the alarm that Eleanor had felt ever since Nicholas's disappearance. Her grandmother was a woman who noticed things in a way others did not.

'I'd hoped perhaps...' She stopped, the crinkles at each eye deep.

'What? What did you hope?'

'That the happiness Anna always prayed for would be bestowed upon him. Did you know Richmond is a town in Virginia, too, Eleanor? A beautiful place by the sounds of it.'

The juxtaposition of these words and Nicholas's at the tea shop made her head spin.

Once a travelling woman in Richmond told my fortune from a pile of sticks she carried.

How much of a conversation had her grandmother held with him?

'If he returns again, my love, could you ask him if he might come and see me and have a proper visit? I would like to chat further for old time's sake.' She took a breath and turned the page on a large atlas. 'You are looking lovely today, Granddaughter. It is a relief to see the fire back in your cheeks.'

Was it just coincidence, her grandmother's chatter, or was there some other purpose underneath her words?

The Huntingdon family sorrows had overshadowed joy for such a long time now: her mother's fatal illness, her own shame with an unmarried pregnancy and a lover whom she refused to name. The more recent deaths of her father and brother had been another blow and Jacob's tendency to blame himself for everything had left them struggling.

'I hope Lucy will be back in London in time for the New Year? I miss her chatter and her laughter.'

'She is due back here tomorrow, Grandmama, for Jacob and Rose have a small family party planned for the evening of the first of January.'

'And Nicholas Bartlett will be here, too?'

'I am not sure. Why?' These words broke through restraint and caution, and were harsh and discordant.

'Because it is simply nice when the parts of one's life come together, Eleanor. The old and the new. All the pieces of it finally making sense.'

'Sense?'

'There is a time for sadness and also one for joy. It is our turn as a family to find some happiness now and to look to the future. Had your father been here he would have been saying exactly the same thing.'

'I am glad I like you so much, Grandmama.'

Kissing her grandmother on the cheek before walking away, Eleanor recited the words of Ecclesiastes under her breath.

A time to weep and a time to laugh. A time to mourn and a time to dance.

She wondered which time it was now for her.

The place was as odd as she had remembered it, she thought, as she walked through the solid Egyptian doors of Bullock's Museum in Piccadilly. The inside was even stranger, large stuffed animals in a fenced-off enclosure and trees towering above that looked as if they came from some ancient and long-lost world.

Nicholas was waiting next to a glass case, glancing not at the artefacts but at the light that spilled in through the window above him. The sight caught at Eleanor with a poignancy that made her stop still and simply watch. He looked as out of place here as he had done at Gunter's, the danger in him only thinly veiled and a sense of carefully checked distance overlaying that. He had not seen her yet, one arm held against his chest as though it was painful, the opposite hand anchoring it.

Mr William Bullock's artefacts were many after a lifetime of travelling abroad and Eleanor wondered what Nicholas Bartlett's treasure trove might look like had he gathered small tributes from all his years in the Americas.

He seemed like a man who travelled light. Her brother had said he'd had one small leather case with him when he had come straight from the ship to the door of Vitium et Virtus on Boxing Day.

He had caught sight of her now, the wounded hand replaced at his side as he walked over. It shook slightly against his thigh.

'Surely this museum brings back some memories?' She said this when he stood next to her, hoping that humour might lighten the mood. 'The naked Hottentot Venus smoking a pipe and the Polish dwarf are not sights easily forgotten, after all. If anything were to jolt your memory, it might be them.'

He laughed at her words, all the lines on his face softening. 'Did you make me laugh like this before, Eleanor?'

The world around her stopped, just slowed down and stood still because there was a look in his eyes that she recognised. A hunger that made his dark eyes darker.

'I think that perhaps I did.'

He glanced away then, a frown deepening as he moved back a pace.

His lack of memory was more irritating today than it ever had been before because he knew suddenly he would have found Lady Eleanor Huntingdon as charming and fascinating six years ago as he did at this moment and he did not know what he had done about that fact.

Had he kissed her? Had he taken it further? That thought made him step away just so that he did not reach out because he could not trust himself as to what might happen next. The memory of the women he had bedded in the Americas also sat there in the equation. He was damaged goods. Eleanor deserved a man who was exemplary in every way, not one whose life had been marred irreparably in the messy business of surviving and who still did not know if he brought danger to those he had contact with.

He needed to keep things light to allow her an escape. A sign at the doorway gave him a subject.

'Napoleon's travelling carriage is here at the museum?'

The flare in her eyes dimmed at his query.

'The French General's personal belongings have been a very popular exhibition by all accounts, my lord.'

'A gamble that has paid off, then?' He was barely thinking of Bullock as he said these words and he had the impression that she might have known this. 'The risk of the unknown to fill one's heart's desire?'

'There is also a nightgown, a set of pistols, his boots and a cloak amongst other things. With the numbers who have come to view them it's said that Bullock has made a small personal fortune from the ticket sales. Many people have been speaking of it and I have only heard interest and fascination.'

Her words ran on, one over the other, giving an impression of nerves. He thought he had never met a woman who was more fascinating. They were passing tall cabinets now which were full of more of the sort of insects he had seen before in the front room.

'Your eyes are exactly the shade of that butterfly wing, Lady Eleanor. *"Morpho paleides"*.' He read this slowly. 'One of the largest butterflies in the world apparently with wings of iridescent blue on one side and an ordinary brown on the other. It allows the insect the ability to disappear at will if you like. A camouflage against predators?'

The sort of disguise she used, he thought. At Frederick's soirée she had looked unmatched in a deep blue gown. Today she sported a coat of dull beige, an ugly hat jammed tightly over her head. Why?

'I have always been careful.' She had told him this in the carriage as they had made their way to Berkeley Square. *'So careful that perhaps...'* She had not finished.

So careful that perhaps life had passed her by? A beloved husband whom she pined for and a daughter who had kept her away from the London social scene? So careful that she saw him as only a risk?

'How old are you now, Eleanor?'

'Twenty-four. Almost twenty-five.'

She said it as if it were a great age and he smiled.

'Young then?'

'Sometimes I feel like I am a hundred.'

He swallowed because she kept doing this to him. Allowing him a small window into her soul that showed only a truth.

She had hurt him, she thought, in some way. Again. Perhaps her honesty was something he did not wish for. Perhaps in the aftermath of the lies he had lived with he now held a discomfort of the truth? Especially her truths, with all their corresponding sadness.

His hands were running across the door of Napoleon Bonaparte's carriage as if such a treasure was the only thing he wished to think about. Another couple lingering next to the conveyance watched him with interest and the man spoke suddenly.

'Bromley. My God, I had heard that you were back from the dead. David Wilshire.'

Nicholas looked at him for a second as if trying to place him. Finally he seemed able to. 'You knew Nash Bowles if I remember rightly and I beat you in a card game which you did not take kindly to?'

'I used to take losing more seriously than I do now,' the man said, 'though Bowles has not forgiven you. He still proclaims weekly that he is no friend of yours.'

'There are many more who might claim that honour, Mr Wilshire.' Nicholas's voice was tight, the tone in it hard.

'You are meaning those to whom you owe large debts at the gambling table, I suppose, though it is said now you are more proficient at winning than you once were.'

'Word travels fast in London. Did you also hear I suffer fools less gladly?'

Wilshire frowned and stepped back, tipping his hat in leave and dragging the woman he was with from the room. The Viscount looked after them with a frown.

'At school there were those students who were bullies, cheats and troublemakers and he was one of them. I doubt he has changed.'

'Who is Nash Bowles?'

'A miscreant who wanted to be a partner in Vitium et Virtus in the early days and who was not pleased to be turned down.'

'By you all.'

'By me, in particular.'

Eleanor had the impression he was not telling the

whole story, but she did not feel comfortable to press further, so she was surprised when he continued talking.

'Some of the men who hate me probably have good reason as there's only a certain amount of arrogance people can stomach before the bile begins to work.'

'People like Bowles?'

'No. Not him. His animosity comes from a whole different place altogether.'

There it was again, that uncompromising anger, that hard flash of steel in him that was so much different from the man he had been. But if she was truthful that same resoluteness was also a part of her character now. She and Nicholas Bartlett had been transformed in a way that was similar, hardened by life but still trying to live.

She liked the way he took her arm, after they exited Bullock's, and helped her across the road as they walked towards Green Park, though once on the other side he let her go.

'Did we walk much, then?' There was now decided interest in his words.

She wanted to say that they hadn't had time, particularly after the first few days when all they looked for were secluded and quiet areas to be alone together, to whisper and to touch.

To kiss for the first time in the back room at Lackington's when Nicholas had simply leaned over the dusty scientific tomes nobody ever looked at and taken her mouth beneath his.

A pure pain of shock ran through her at such a reminiscence. He had been slender then, softer. Just a youth. What would it be like to kiss this man he had become?

Could she risk taking him there tomorrow? To Lackington's? Part of her wanted to, but the other part felt only fear. What if he remembered and then scorned her? What if this new Nicholas wanted nothing to do with a woman who had thrown herself into his bed after only four days of knowing each other and had conceived an illegitimate child in the process?

'You seem quiet.'

'Oh, I am often that now, my lord.'

Love me, Nicholas, my love. Love me until we both die from the feeling.

She'd said that to him at the Bromley town house. Said other things, too, full of girly pathos and rampant exaggeration. She'd laid her heart on her sleeve and told him every little thought, every sorrow and hurt.

Now she could barely admit to anything because in the tiniest clue he might guess it all. Glancing across at him, she saw he looked full of thought, though he began to speak again after the short silence.

'For the first five weeks after I got to the Americas I lay in a poor house in Boston with fever until a reverend took me home and fattened up both my body and soul.' When he shrugged she could see the line of tension in his shoulders. 'That was the only time in all the six years I was away that I thought I was safe.'

She was astonished by such honesty.

'I tell you this because I am still not safe and that if you should wish to reconsider your kindness I will understand why.'

'My kindness?' She didn't quite know what he meant.

'Squiring me through these events that I have long forgotten. Truth be told, perhaps they are better left unremembered.' The flatness in his eyes was familiar and dragged at Eleanor's own protected sorrow.

'I used to think that after my mother died, my lord. I wished for no recall of her whatsoever because I had been hurt too much. Now, I struggle to remember her face, her voice, her smell and the irony is that I would give anything to have her visage back again.'

'Jake talked of her all the time at the club in the months after her death. You were lucky with such a mother.'

'How old were you when your own died?'

'Eight. Young enough to forget some things and old enough to remember others.'

'Seventeen was no better, I assure you.' She still remembered the shock and grief as if it were yesterday.

'My mother had hair exactly the colour of your own. In the sunshine there were threads of gold amongst the brown just like yours.' He smiled as he said this.

'I will take such words as a compliment, Lord Bromley.'

'Nicholas. Or Nick. And it was meant as one.'

There it was again, the difference in him that she could not quite pin down. He was less evasive than he had been once and much more to the point. The flowery rhetoric of the past was well gone and in its place sat an honesty that was borne from adversity. She wished she might be brave enough to simply step forward and lay her hand upon his chest and tell him everything, but a vendor of hot chestnuts called out to them from further afield and her own sense of place and time was re-gathered.

'Are you hungry?' He looked altogether younger as he asked this of her. 'In New York they sold chestnuts, too, but they never tasted quite right. And now I know why. They are different from the ones here in England.'

Perhaps confessing past problems had been good for them both because she was starving and even from this distance the smell of the roasted nuts was delicious.

'Give me a moment, then.'

As he walked away to procure the treat another man coming through the park stopped before her. Swarthy and thickset, he had the look of a gentleman out of sorts with his world.

'You are Lady Eleanor Robertson, the Duke of Westmoor's sister, are you not?'

Flustered, Eleanor nodded.

'I was introduced to you once at a ball in Chelsea and I seldom forget a face, particularly one as beautiful as your own.'

The slight lisp he had was as disconcerting as his words. She looked over towards Nicholas Bartlett, but his back was to her.

As the newcomer followed her glance, he, too, registered Lord Bromley's presence and the blood simply drained from his face to leave him decidedly pale.

'You are with Bartlett?'

Nodding, she looked away, certain that he must now move on and surprised when his hand covered her own.

'Gossip has it you are an experienced and generous

woman and he is a cad and a spendthrift. If you would like to pass some time in my company, I am certain you would not regret it.'

Snatching back her hand, she stepped away. Was this person mentally sick? Could he hurt her? Should she run? Nicholas was back now and her first thought was that he had not waited to collect their chestnuts. Her second was more along the lines of amazement. He looked nothing at all like he usually did, the disdain in his face showing every feeling.

'Get away from her, Bowles.'

Nicholas's hand was in his pocket now and Eleanor had the impression that he might have held a weapon there. In the mood he was in she was more than certain he would use it should this stranger be difficult.

The fury in Bowles was magnified as he spat out his words. 'Bromley. I had heard you were back, of course, but I scarcely believed it. Back from the dead like a cat with nine lives, though I have to say your appearance is altered for the worst. More contretemps in America? The result of your arrogance and your reckless testing of boundaries?'

'Stay away from me and from my friends. If you decide not to take this advice, then expect retribution.' Nicholas spoke quietly but there was a threat in every single syllable that was unmistakable, the echoes of an old hatred more than evident. He'd gained control of himself now, a stillness in him that was decidedly menacing and any emotions upon his face well hidden.

All fight seemed to go from Bowles and he turned

on his heels and left them, the tap of his shoe plates distinct against the stones on the ground.

Nicholas bit back a curse. What the hell was Nash Bowles doing talking with Eleanor? He didn't want that crawling amoral mongrel anywhere near her, his mind returning to the woman he'd found the bastard with in a back room of Vitium et Virtus just before he had disappeared all those years ago.

Nick had seen exactly what a madman was capable of then, the lines of carefully placed cuts on the girl's bottom weeping blood.

'It's a place of fantasy,' Bowles had shouted, his fists flying. 'And you have no business being in here and spoiling it. She's a serving maid, for God's sake, and will be well pleased with the trinket I shall leave with her as payment. Besides, the pleasure of pain is underrated.'

His victim's face told him exactly the opposite.

'Is that true?' As he'd asked the small dark girl this question she had simply shaken her head and burst into tears, trying to pull her clothes up to cover her shame in the process. There were more wounds on her fingers.

Without another thought Nicholas had picked up a much thinner Bowles by the scruff of his neck and thrown him out the front door, uncaring of his lack of dress and his plethora of threats. He fell in an untidy heap on to the pavement below.

'Never come back. If you do I will kill you slowly with as much pain as I can administer.'

'You will regret this, Bromley,' he had replied. 'See if you don't.'

Nick had laughed at that and lifting the small knife that the other had dropped threw it in an arc so that it landed within an inch of Nash Bowles's right hand.

'The only thing I might regret is not aiming that blade squarely into the space between your legs.'

That day long ago morphed into this one as Nicholas felt a warm hand tuck into the crook of his arm, his mind brought abruptly back from the past to the present.

The wind had risen and the grasses under the trees were being tossed in a silky blanket.

'I thought he might even have tried to drag me off with him.' Eleanor sounded breathless. 'I think he is deranged.'

'I am sorry. He won't hurt you.'

'He has hurt others?'

'Many, probably.'

'Then what is it he wants from you?'

'Revenge or the promise of silence? He is a bully and a coward and as he was interested in a stake of Vitium et Virtus for himself he was always hanging around the club.'

Her teeth were worrying her top lip. 'He would be a horrible person there, for there is something frightening about him, something broken.'

'You are right and I have first-hand knowledge that he does not truly comprehend the notion of a line between yes and no. He was an only child and more than spoilt so he imagines the world should be exactly as he should want it.' Nick breathed in deeply, trying to disperse the alarm he had felt when he saw Eleanor with Bowles. If she were to be hurt because of his past...?

'Will you play a part in the club's running now you are back?'

'No. I'm thinking of giving my share to the others if they want it.'

'I doubt Rose would like to see my brother more involved. The same might go for Georgiana and Cecilia.'

At that he laughed, the worry of the past few moments dwindling as he saw her smile. 'For a club steeped in secrecy there are now many who know the names of its founders.'

'Frederick's youngest brother keeps harping at them all for the chance of it, too. He is just finishing at university and is as wild as the rest of the chaotic and out-of-control Challengers. You might consider him? He'd undoubtedly be perfect.'

As she moved closer it was as if everything in the world was better. He liked her near. He liked the way it felt when her thigh came into contact with his own as they walked across the grass.

He liked her questions and her truth. He liked how she had put all the facts of things together to come up with a portrait of now. He liked how she made him happy.

If he had Eleanor Huntingdon in his bed he would feel as if he could conquer the world.

He cursed under his breath and decided such invented fantasies might rival any thought up in the passion of the moment at Vitium et Virtus.

* * *

She felt him withdraw, just as he had done every other time they had come closer. Did he think she might deceive him in some way or harry him into making a decision he would come to regret.

Nash Bowles had riled him and yet it was more than that. Nicholas Bartlett's touch was tight as he took her arm and turned towards the road, chestnuts forgotten in his haste to be away. He also vibrated with an anger that was unfathomable.

'What did he do to you? This Bowles?'

He needed to talk so when silence was his only answer she kept on speaking.

'In the times that I thought the world was landing on my shoulders I realised confiding in someone trusted is often a helpful thing.'

His glance came around to her, wary and suspicious, full of the ghosts she could only guess at. The damage on his face today was so very easily seen in this light. She could imagine the force of the blade that had come down upon him and the pain he must have endured afterwards.

'Jacob was my confidant and he was a good one, too, because he mostly listened. As you are. To me, I mean. Listening.' Now she was flustered, his very presence warming her insides. It was confusing, this strength he had, this power to make her unsettled. She could not remember it before.

Finally, a smile curled at the end of his lips. 'I doubt some of my stories would allow you to sleep at night, Eleanor, were I to unburden myself of the past. You might be well pleased never to hear them.'

But she did not allow him that excuse. 'After being ill in the home of the Reverend in Boston, where did you go?'

'South.' The word was flat and quiet.

'Because you had to leave?'

'The Reverend had a daughter. A small child called Emily. When I was walking along the cliffs one day she followed me and was hurt.' He swallowed and she could see the strength of emotion in the grinding action of the muscles in his jaw. 'She was pushed,' he finally uttered.

'So you went south to protect them? To draw off the one who had pushed her. Was it the same man who hurt your arm and face?'

'I hope so because he is dead. I killed him.'

He looked at her directly as he said this, refusing to allow for misinterpretation, ensuring her understanding in a way he had not when they had talked during the waltz at Frederick Challenger's party. There was no line of apology or uncertainty anywhere. She could imagine a weapon in the ruined fingers of his left hand raised against evil. She hoped the death had been quick. Nicholas Bartlett was a warrior wrought from the softer bones of an English aristocrat. How different would he feel from each and every other coddled lord of the *ton*? A man who had been places not one of them would have the misfortune to venture or the endurance to see himself safe. She could not quite leave it at that, though.

'Would he have killed you?'

'Pardon?'

'The man who hurt you. Would you have been dead had you not fought back?'

He nodded.

'Then my opinion is that evil does not deserve to win out under any circumstance and he warranted his fate.' Her words held that certain conviction she heard herself use in some of her dealings with her daughter. An unequivocal truth. An unarguable logic.

She watched him run his hand carefully through his hair, pushing the long and untidy fringe from his face. 'I am glad, Eleanor, that you have been safe here in England.'

Safe? Six years of the cutting words of others. Six years of pretence. Six years of lonely isolation. Six years of carefulness tempered by politeness and manners. She was so safe she could scream with the cloying breathlessness of it. Better a cut like his to the very bone and then an ending. Quick. Final. Though in all honesty it seemed that the wolves might still be circling.

A small summer house hidden amongst the trees to the left of the path suddenly caught her attention. They had come here once in their effort to find quiet and out-of-the-way places and although the green shields of the summer trees were no longer in place the park was also far less peopled in winter than it had been back then.

'I want to show you something,' she said and was pleased when he followed her over the grass and came up the steps to the circular platform which sat above the Serpentine.

Greyness surrounded them. The sky. The water. The trees with their mottled winter bark.

Nicholas had to duck as he came beneath the boarding around the roof and she smiled at him even as she shivered with the cold.

'This whole winter has been freezing.'

She felt him there next to her, touching warmth along the length of their arms. A small intimacy in a large landscape and a connection that felt so right and true she made no attempt at all to pull away.

She was shaking.

He wanted to bring her full into his warmth, but he also did not wish to frighten her.

'I should have remembered the chestnuts,' he said and liked the way she laughed. 'But I do have this.'

Pulling his flask from a pocket, he screwed open the top. 'It will warm you up at least.'

When she took it she sniffed at the top of it in a way that told him she did not quite trust what was inside.

'Is it strong?'

Before he could answer she took a swallow and began to cough, the purity of the liquor making her hand the flask back.

'Scottish whisky and the best my uncle could buy.'

'I have heard it said that Aaron Bartlett has left the country having taken money from the Bromley coffers.'

'In truth I don't care what he took, it's only good to be rid of him. Bromworth Manor is being cleaned of his presence, just as the town house was, and soon there will be nothing left of his legacy there at all. His son has followed him by all accounts so there is another worry gone.'

He tried to keep the bitterness from his words, but did not think he had succeeded when Eleanor looked at him with sorrow in her big blue eyes.

'How was your guardian related to you?'

'He was my father's brother and I hated him right from the start. He was never a kind man or a good one and young children, for all their innocence, easily recognise duplicity when confronted with it.'

There it was again, a truth he had given to very few others. His hand tightened on the wooden handrail that he leant upon, but he liked how her warmth fastened him to goodness and hope. An anchor to a world he had been gone from for so long.

With Eleanor the shadows lightened and the demons that rode on his shoulders daily were less heavy. Frowning at his flowery thoughts, he scuffed at a broken baton at his feet.

'Do you have any family left now? Anyone at all?' She looked stricken as she asked her question.

'None.' The word was bare of emotion. He no longer craved the tie of blood as he once had as a child and even as a youth.

'You could share mine, then. Grandmama is most adamant that she needs to keep an eye on you and you have always been Jacob's best friend.'

The sweetness of her offer astonished Nick, though he did wonder where she herself stood on the spectrum. He suddenly wanted to kiss her, to bring her into his arms and take her mouth in a hard stamp of ownership and possession. The feeling was so strong he turned and moved away, a flurry of freezing cold wind and rain aiding his want to escape.

'Come, Eleanor, I think I should take you home.'

Chapter Eight

⁓

The town house was cloying. Nick thought that as he wandered the environs of his library later that same day, picking up this and that as he went.

A racing broadsheet. A book on sexual positions from the East. A lewd statue of the female form made of ebony. He truly could not remember buying this even with the return of his memory. Had he actually paid money for such a thing and liked it?

His servants had emptied the rooms of his uncle's possessions and taken out all the objects that Aaron Bartlett had brought into the house.

What was left was surprisingly meagre. There were barely any books to read and the numerous gambling dices, cards and tokens lying on various shelves reminded him exactly where his interest in life had mostly lain.

And he had been so bad at it, too. To put all that effort into something that he had so little aptitude for amazed him.

A small bracelet plaited of coloured thread inside a

box on the mantel held his attention because it was so out of place. Why would this be here? He measured the strands against his own wrist and worked out it must have been the possession of a female he had known. This puzzled him more than anything.

His taste in women had been eclectic and varied, but he had usually escorted well-connected young ladies of the *ton* or the high-flying courtesans from Vitium et Virtus. All these ladies he knew preferred diamonds.

Lifting the small circle to his nose, he took in breath. A faint smell of violets. A wave of heat hit him forcibly. Lady Eleanor Huntingdon?

Nothing made sense and yet everything did. He could feel her here through the fog, laughing at him, egging him on, sitting with him before the fire, her hands firmly entwined in his own.

Was this a hope or a reality? He could not grasp the essence of it and his damned headache was worsening just as it always seemed to when he tried to force memory.

Voices outside had him turning, the small plaited bracelet tucked carefully into his trousers pocket.

'Mr Gregory, sir.'

Oliver came in, a broad smile on his face.

'I missed you at Fred's the other night, Nick, and thought perhaps we could catch up now for a drink. I also brought back a book you'd leant me just before you disappeared.'

Defoe's *Robinson Crusoe* was in his hands, the burgundy-leather cover familiar.

'At least I had one tome in my possession that was worth reading. I remember this.'

'So the whole of your memory is back?'

'Not quite all of it.'

'Jake said you are certain it was not your uncle who had followed you to America and that you had been out looking for clues as to who else held a motive. Is that where you got the bruise on your cheek?'

Oliver had always been the one to notice if things were not quite as they should be. 'Bartlett didn't send anyone overseas. I know that much, though he did mean to drown me in the Thames. He is a man of small vision like his son. I doubt if he could have come up with a plan that encompassed searching for me across years and oceans. If I can remember the last week before I disappeared, then perhaps I might remember other men...'

'I saw you on one of those days with Jacob's sister outside Fortnum and Mason's in Piccadilly. She might have some ideas to help you.'

'She is already.'

'Is what?'

'Helping me retrace the moments.'

'Does Jake know of this?'

'I'm not hiding anything.'

Oliver frowned. 'Eleanor was broken completely when she returned from the Highlands.'

'I thought she had resided in Edinburgh.'

'No. Her husband was some sort of a northern laird up by the western coast. He was drowned apparently in a boating accident in the autumn a year or so after you left and Eleanor returned home to Millbrook House. She has a young daughter so we do not see her much in London now, which is a shame. There was also some talk that she never married the fellow at all though Jacob soon put paid to such gossip.'

Such a varying account floored Nicholas, for it was nothing at all like the facts Frederick had regaled him with. All this supposition was quite patently hearsay and Nick wondered at the true story. Still, if Jacob had not told Frederick or Oliver of it he doubted it would suddenly be related to him.

But why the secrecy?

His hand slipped into his right pocket and he felt the threads of the bracelet and its beads beneath the pads of his fingers. Tomorrow he was taking Eleanor to Lackington, Allen & Co. in Finsbury Square and he'd always liked the look of the façade of the place. She'd seemed tense when he had asked her of their next destination and he had wondered if anything had happened there between them to make her feel this way.

Oliver raised his glass towards him as he took a seat on the leather sofa by the windows.

'Here's to your return and to the future.' His smile was wide and honest. 'You were my first true friend here in England and it's good to have you back.'

'It's good to be here, Oliver.'

'God, Nick, I was such a green boy back then, wasn't I? One day at a new school and they were already teasing me about my Indian background and the colour of my skin and of the different way I spoke, until you showed up.'

'With my ire up and fists flying. I'd been practising my boxing skills at Bromworth Manor that summer holiday if I remember correctly and wanted to put them into practice.'

Oliver shook his head. 'It was much more than that, I would say. There were two of us and ten of them and you had a split lip and a black eye for weeks after and a broken wrist to boot. But they never bothered me again.' He twirled the crystal stem of his wineglass in hand before glancing up. 'I used to think of that after you had gone and for years I combed the city for you and paid agents to try and understand what had happened in the back alley of Vitium et Virtus. Even when people said that there was no hope left I always held out for some...' He stopped and took a drink. 'So here is to our friendship, Nick, and to brotherhood and to finding the bastard who did this to you. We are all in this you know. We all have your back.'

'I do know and I thank you for it and when I have need of help I will let you know. Coming back again has been a revelation, all the differences and the changes. I have never seen you look quite so happy. Where did you meet Cecilia?'

Oliver stretched his long legs out before him as he took his time to answer. 'In Paris. She was at the time employed in a gentlemen's club and went under the name of Madame Coquette. She was quite famous.' The laughter in his eyes made it known the story was not exactly as he said it.

Nick drank deeply before answering, 'Here's to

women who are not boring, then, and who know how to please a man.'

'Oh, a good woman is much more than that, Nicholas. To be with someone you love is about the warmth of friendship and the certainty of a future. There's a comfort, too, in the complete absence of lies and after living a life like mine that is more than a relief.'

'By the sound of things you have all found women with as many secrets as your own. Perhaps that is the trick of happiness?'

'I think fate plays a hand, too, and timing.'

'I'll drink to that.' But all Nick could think of as he smiled was the lost week that Eleanor Huntingdon was doing her best to try to make him remember.

'Eleanor Huntingdon is helping Nicholas retrieve his memory.' Oliver said this to Cecilia when he returned home for she was waiting up for him in the morning room.

'Is he recalling anything else leading up to his disappearance?'

'Seems he is not, but Jake's sister is squiring him around town, trying her hardest to facilitate his memory.'

'Were they close? Before this happened, I mean?'

'I can't remember. I didn't think so, but...'

'I hear all sorts of accounts of Lord Bromley wherever I go. He was somewhat wild, I gather, and seldom seen out of the company of women.'

'He was lonely. Like me.' Pulling her from the wing

chair, he sat down himself and settled her on his lap. 'You are warm and comfortable, my love.'

She laughed at that. 'Like an old slipper?'

'Warm and comfortable and sensual as hell,' he amended and kissed her.

'That's better.' She leaned back against him, her rich brown hair released from its pins and clips burnished in the firelight. 'Eleanor Huntingdon is strong and sensible and I have liked her a lot each time I have met her. She is not a lightweight woman, yet she holds secrets and they worry her.'

'Such intuition is not to be trifled with. I concur with your conclusions.'

'Perhaps Nick is the man to help her, then? The way you speak of him, Oliver, gives me the impression that he was never afraid of anything.'

'The attraction of opposites, you mean?'

'Well, if he was reckless and dissolute you also said that he wasn't a man who was unfair. And if he is lonely…?'

'Perhaps they might find solace in one another?'

He was now laughing so much he could barely kiss her although he tried. 'Are you by any chance lending your hand to that dubious art of matchmaking, sweetheart?'

'If I invited them for afternoon tea, would you promise to be circumspect, Oliver? We could then test the waters, so to speak.'

'Let's go to bed right now and I will show you just how circumspect I can be.'

Oliver lifted her up then and their reflection caught

in the window, light against dark, and he wondered anew as to how he had been lucky enough to find such contentment.

Happy chance and good fortune. The two blessings had been largely missing in his life before he had met Cecilia. He hoped with all his heart that Nick might finally find the same.

After Oliver left Nick retired to his bedchamber, the blues on the walls restful and mellow. He'd loved this room and coming in here as a young boy to curl up on the enormous bed with his parents and talk.

The same slice of regret ran over him, far more remote than it had once been, but still there none the less. Their deaths were the point where his life had begun to spin out of control, a wildness growing that became unchecked and complete.

The clock on the mantel chimed one. It was late and yet the night felt alive. With ideas and thoughts and hopes.

Cecilia was pregnant. Oliver had told Nicholas that under the threat of confidentiality. A new life. Another generation and the responsibility of guiding and teaching a child about what it was to live well.

As Eleanor had taught her daughter?

'Lucy.' He said the name out loud, liking the sound of it. A little girl. He wondered if she looked like her mother. He hoped she had Eleanor Huntingdon's vivid blue eyes and brave spirit.

His glance fell on the piano in the far corner of the room and he walked over to pull out the seat. He had not played in years and he wondered why the instrument had been left here in this room when piano playing was so much outside his uncle's endeavour or intention.

Setting his fingers above the keys, he began to beat out the *Moonlight Sonata* by Beethoven. He recalled so much more of his early years when he played. That's why he had stopped in the first place, he supposed, out of pure sorrow. It was also why he could never quite abandon it.

He did not know when he'd started thinking about the music instead of hearing the notes. It was after his parents had died and he'd returned in the holidays to the cold unwelcoming Bromworth Manor. It was in loneliness that he'd gained the nuances of the pedal and had started to notice that silences, too, could be shaped by emotion.

He did this now even after all these years of awayness. He rode the edge of the beauty between easy and hard, and was absorbed in the sweet and powerful truth of the notes.

He'd never played for anyone, not even Jacob or Frederick or Oliver. He doubted they even knew he could hold down a tune. No, the music was his alone, his and his parents. A connection. Him on one side and them on the other. After his conversation with Eleanor today such a realisation was enlightening.

Lack of sleep made Nick feel wary though in those brief moments it had found him, his dreams had been strange amorphous ones full of ghosts and dead people.

It was the piano, he supposed, and the music that

had wrapped around his regret and brought his parents closer. Jacob's older brother Ralph had been there, too, with surprise on his visage at his newfound demise, blood still at his temple. The world they inhabited had been full of clouds and mist and fireworks.

That thought brought a frown because his mother had always hated the noise of them.

Eleanor was waiting for him outside Lackington, Allen & Co., a blue bonnet tied firmly under her chin and in a coat the colour of a churning winter ocean. He thought for a moment she had never looked more beautiful or more vulnerable.

'You are early?' He said the words as a question, stopping himself from reaching out and taking her hand again. It was a good ten minutes before the hour she had allotted as their meeting point yesterday.

'Last time I was early, too.'

She did not look at him directly as she said this, her glance sliding away and a hitch in her voice. The façade of the Temple of the Muses was shining, whether from the recent rains or from the lightness of the clouds he could not tell.

'You once told me that you had bought the book *Robinson Crusoe* from here and read it in a day.' She said this as they walked up the stairs into the main room with its imposing galleried dome.

'One of the few I ever purchased, then, according to the state of my library.' He liked her soft laughter. 'Actually Oliver Gregory returned the Defoe copy to me last night when he dropped in for a drink. He also said he'd seen us outside Fortnum and Mason a few days before I disappeared. What was it we were doing there?'

'Buying wine as a celebration.'

'What were we celebrating?'

'I can't really remember.' Her cheeks flamed and the memory of something was so firmly written on her face that Nick knew she lied.

The wine was a celebration of our first kiss here at Lackington, Allen & Co. at Finsbury Square.

It had been summer and the day had been hot and so they had gone to find chilled wine and a small hamper of food for a picnic by the Serpentine.

Then, he had looked at her as if she was the most beautiful woman he could imagine. Now he only appeared perplexed. At her poorly formed falsity probably and her reddened cheeks. She had not blushed in six years and now she was doing so on an hourly basis.

Well, it had to stop. She was no longer eighteen and foolish and Nicholas Bartlett was hardly going to take her hand and run laughing through the streets in search of sweet treats and then kiss the dusted sugar off each finger as she ate them.

The sheer absurdity of it made her smile.

She noticed that everyone watched him, covertly, his sheer presence now impossible to miss. At six foot two he had to bend at the portal, yet he filled the room with such a masculine grace and power that it took her breath away.

'I visit the library every time I come down from Millbrook House to London.'

'And is that often?'

'As little as I can possibly manage it, truth be told. Usually only at Christmas.'

'The life of a widow is a quiet one, then? Tell me, where did your husband hail from?'

'Scotland.'

'Fred Challenger says he was from Edinburgh and Oliver Gregory swears it was the Highlands. There is a difference?'

She felt suddenly sick and a sheen of sweat built on her top lip. 'You have been asking about me?' He was a man who could discover facts about her past that few others could. If he put the timings of her return together and the birth of Lucy...

'Only in passing, but I am sorry for your tragedy, Eleanor. It must have been hard to be so alone.'

'I have my daughter.'

'And I am glad of it.'

He did not patronise her or give unwanted advice. He spoke only in words that were simple and true.

It must have been hard to be so alone.

Because he had been lonely, too, she thought. In childhood on the death of his parents and in the wild dangerous antics of his youth. In the card rooms of London when the numbers never added up and he was left with a handful of debtors shouting for payment and an uncle who was withholding his inheritance. Certainly in his restless years abroad when he had shifted from place to place with an unknown killer on his tail and a memory that gave him no recall of peril.

Even here now, in the over-stacked salons of Lackington's, he looked unapproachable and out of place.

For a second she wondered if she had the heart to climb the steps to the small scientific reading room they had visited last time and find the quiet spot at the end of a row of shelves. Could it ever be again like it was, that young unbridled love, breathless with passion? Giddy with the thrall?

Now she was shy of him in a way she had not once been for she'd seen the glances every woman had thrown his way no matter where they went. Desire had that certain raw and hungry look she hoped could not be discerned on her own face.

'Penny for your thoughts, Eleanor?'

She smiled at his question and gestured to him to follow her.

Every leather-bound tome looked as if it had not been touched for years, the dust settled in the interim. The view was a fine one, however, and he went to the window to peer over London.

'When I arrived here I thought everything looked so neat. The houses, the streets, the people.'

'America is more wild, I suppose. Less ordered.'

'It is in parts, but there is a sort of beauty in that. Perhaps it was the same for you in Scotland?'

'Scotland?'

'Where you lived with your husband?'

'Oh, yes, it was.'

Digging into his pocket, he felt the small plaited bracelet and brought it out on his palm to show her.

'Is this yours, Eleanor? I found it in a wooden box on the mantelpiece in my library.'

She began crying just like that, one moment shocked and the next inconsolable, large tears running down her cheeks even as her hands came to wipe them away.

Crossing the room, he took her in his arms and liked how her head fitted exactly beneath his chin, the warmth and softness of her astonishingly right. She smelt of violets and freshness. He knew the moment she gained control because she stiffened and pulled away.

'I am sorry.'

He noticed that she held the colourful circle of thread tightly in her fist as though she might never let it go.

'It is valuable?'

'To me? Yes.'

Eleanor could feel her bottom lip still quivering and knew her eyes were red. When he gave her his kerchief she blew into it and then began to worry because she did not quite know whether to hand it back to him or tuck it into her sleeve to wash later.

These huge swings of emotion were something she had not felt with Nicholas six years ago in the happy haze of their new love. Then it had been easy and light.

Now everything weighed heavily upon them. Their past and their future and the present, too, because there was a danger close that she could not quite decipher.

She had given him her bracelet after he had made love to her. A circle of threads plaited for her by her mother from her tapestry basket and beaded at the end in the colours of primrose, green, cerulean-blue and *coquelicot*-red. When she'd explained how important it was he had held the gift and looked as though she had given him the world.

Today the limp gaudy bracelet had appeared tired and out of place between his thumb and forefinger, fingers that gave no impression at all of being that of a cosseted lord. There were small thin white scars across his knuckles now.

The hand of a fighter, the hand of one who had endured much hardship. A tougher hand altogether.

And yet when he had held her in his arms a few minutes ago all those elements of danger, menace, toughness and peril had only made her feel safe.

'I did not sleep well last night, my lord, and I am sorry for such an outburst.' She felt she needed to explain.

'Did I give you anything back in return?'

'Pardon?'

'When you gave me the bracelet, did I find something of mine for you?'

Another kiss. She nearly said it.

Instead she shook her head and simply looked at him, at the small gold chips at the outer edges of his brown eyes, at the wound on his cheek which today seemed lessened and a part of him, another way of how his time in the Americas had been imprinted into now.

He was even more handsome than he had been, the hard and thinner planes of his face melding into high cheekbones and a strong chin. Not in the manner of the Greek gods, unmarred and perfect, but following in the fashion of a Norse one, scarred by battle and war and the fighting arts held dear by the Viking marauders.

He could protect Lucy and her. From everything.

He had kissed her right here last time in the slant of sunbeams coming in from the window. He had taken her hand and pulled her into him, slowly, never looking away, and with his fingers in the nape of her hair his mouth had come down upon her own, allowing no escape as he had deepened the connection and taken her heart.

Unforgettable.

Eleanor stood there in the dim winter light and wished with everything she had that he might remember.

Something had happened here in this room last time. He could see the shadow of it in eyes remote with memory. He touched her lightly.

'The scent in the bracelet is violets. Your scent. Why did you give it to me?'

'You had told me of how you had lost your parents and I wished to make you happy again.'

'My parents?'

'You said you played the piano sometimes to remember them. You said you felt them close just there on the other side of the music.'

Shock tore through his equilibrium.

'You said sometimes when you could not sleep you played the *Moonlight Sonata* by Ludwig van Beethoven to try and reach them and you felt you did.'

His sudden loud curse shocked her.

'Are you ill?' Worry clawed into her words as he held on to the table, his knuckles white.

'It's just a headache. The same one I have had ever since…' He stopped.

His emotions since the incident at Richmond had been more distant than he remembered them. But now the sharp edges of feeling returned forcibly and all he wanted to be was alone.

At the Bromley town house an hour later he poured himself a stiff whisky. He could not work out what was happening, for the threads of the conversation between himself and Eleanor were as entwined and complicated as the pattern in the bracelet. Triple stranded and double braided.

Why should he have told her of his secrets when he had not even confided in Jacob, Oliver or Frederick?

The answer, of course, was simple.

He had known her far better than she'd ever admitted, not just as her brother's friend, as she'd said, but as something more important. He'd hurried her home to Chelsea from Lackington's with all the speed of someone on the verge of a collapse.

He swore roundly and hated the shake in his hands. He'd been an irresponsible and pleasure-seeking youth, distracted by both gambling and women. He could not even imagine how the Eleanor he knew now might have tolerated such weaknesses.

He hoped she had not known of his mounting debts and of the ugly characters from London's underbelly who had frequently come knocking at his door. He prayed he had not tried to sleep with her.

Jacob's voice interrupted his reveries.

'Good to find you home, Nick, because a message came for you this morning and the one who delivered it said it was urgent. A poorly dressed man by the sounds of it and a fellow who my butler said he would not like to meet in the darkness? A colleague of yours?'

'Have a drink, Jake.'

He was glad when his friend sat down.

'Remember I told you of my uncle's involvement in my disappearance? Well, the information on the payment to those who cornered me in the alley behind Vitium et Virtus came from a man in a tavern in the docklands. He runs a protection racket, but seems to have extended his area of business into the art of kidnapping for a generous sum of money.'

'And Aaron Bartlett paid it?'

'He did. He'd had designs on my title and inheritance since the beginning and given the scandals surrounding the club he used his chance to have me gone.'

'And this new message?'

'I asked the ringmaster to put his ear to the ground to see whether he could find any trace of those who had followed me to the Americas. He was certain it was someone different from my uncle, someone with a lot more money.'

'And you think he has found this person?' Jacob handed over the sheet of paper sealed with wax.

When Nicholas broke it open he read out the message. 'Perhaps. He wants to see me again this evening.'

'I will come with you.'

'No. He will only meet me.'

'So you are still hell bent on doing this alone?'

'For now, Jacob. Until I need help.'

'Very well, but Eleanor said you were feeling unwell at Lackington's. She looked worried. She also said that none of your lost memories seem to have returned.'

'Did she say anything else?'

'No. Should she have? It's good that she's helping you. She is lonely and has lived a long time under the cloud of widowhood.'

'Where did she meet her husband?'

'I think you should ask her that.'

'Oliver said he lived in the Highlands and Fred was adamant Edinburgh was his abode.'

'They don't know anything about her marriage.'

'It seems nobody does. When was Lucy born?'

'After Lucy's father died. She was born at Millbrook House.'

'I see.' He felt a pang of sadness that the small daughter was not his.

'If you hurt Ellie, Nick, I will make you regret it. She's been hurt enough already. But I did not come here to issue threats. Tomorrow is New Year's Day and I have come with an invitation to a small family gathering. Lucy, Eleanor's daughter, has arrived from Millbrook and I am certain you will enjoy meeting her. Grandmama especially has impressed it again and again upon me that she would very much like you there. Your grandmother, by all accounts, was a good friend of hers and as such she feels some responsibility in ensuring your happiness.'

Family. In the light of his conversation on the topic with Eleanor that thought had him swallowing the rest of his brandy.

'Thank you. I should like to come.' As he gave his acceptance he was taken by the idea that for a moment Jacob looked worried.

Chapter Nine

The tavern was darker than last time, the weather dull and ominous. He'd brought his knife with him tucked into his right boot just in case. The sling he'd discarded because it didn't pay to show the slightest bit of vulnerability in places like this one.

He knew that to the core of his being.

The ringmaster did not appear to be present yet, but that did not faze Nicholas. Ordering a drink as he came in the door, he strode over to sit at the same table as last time, making sure to leave the seat against the wall free.

His ale arrived, the barkeeper who had given him the bruised cheek last time looking belligerent.

'He'll be here soon.'

Nick did not answer.

Over in one corner a group of four men were playing cards. In the other a single occupant appeared to be almost asleep over his glass.

Such careful acts of staging were not new to him. For a while in the Americas before he perfected his methods at cards he'd used his other skill: his fists. It had been many a man he had thrown drunk from the tavern where he worked when they failed to see his role in the keeping of order by noticing all the small signs of discontent.

After ten or so moments the little door to the left opened.

'Do you have the payment?' The glass eye of the ringmaster glittered from the small light at the door.

'It depends what you've brought to show me.'

As the man sat he placed a card on the table.

'Vitium et Virtus.'

'What is this?'

'It's the name he paid with, a well-spoken lord who set the mark on Viscount Bromley over the seas. A goodly sum, too, it was, by the accounts of my source, and all in gold. I keep every bit of paper clients give me, just to be safe, you understand. Toffs believe people like me to be reckless and illiterate, but I was never that. I make careful notes of people and keep tight records. They come in handy sometimes.'

'Like now?'

The silence between them settled until the other broke it.

'I imagine that you have many enemies, to do a job that brings you out to places such as these ones.'

When Nick nodded, he continued on. 'Perhaps you believed in something once. Believed enough for others to want you hurt for it and now vengeance drives you?'

Such a warning from a street philosopher was all the more surprising because it was true. He had believed in Vitium et Virtus because it was like the home he had never had, a place away from his uncle and with as few rules as he wanted. A place where he could lose himself in fine wine, good women and high-stakes gambling, and be happy for a fleeting moment. Should he begin there in his search?

The well-spoken lord who set the mark on you. The sum was paid in gold. More clues. Someone of his own social standing, then? The ringmaster would not know of his own title for Nick had disguised his voice each time they met and worn clothes that fitted exactly into the setting of the docks. Here he was believed to be a thief-taker operating in the shadowy world between criminals and the law and caught in its complicated web.

With care he extracted his coins and placed them on the table.

'We will not meet again, I think,' the other said, 'but I wish you luck.'

The money was gone in the blink of an eye and as the barman crossed the floor to collect the empty glass Nick's fingers settled on the shaft of his knife.

Glancing down, the man cocked his head.

'We don't kill our own,' he said, leaving Nicholas to wonder just who he had become in the eyes of these thieves.

He wandered the river on the way home, mindful of those who watched him, but not afraid. This sort of place had been his home, too, once and the dirt and the smell of it was almost comfortable. Before the Americas the man he was would have been fearful to venture anywhere near such poverty.

He would call a meeting between Jacob, Frederick and Oliver and between them they could try to think just who the perpetrator could be. It was time he was honest with them and time to ask for their help.

The youngest Challenger was waiting at the Bromley town house when he returned, scrambling up from the seat his butler had assigned him in the library. He was dressed well.

'I am sorry, sir,' he said as Nick walked in. 'I am Frederick's brother Christian Challenger. I should have perhaps come back another time, but there is an important matter I wish to discuss with you and so I elected to wait.'

When his eyes saw the workman's clothing Nick was wearing they widened. 'There are so many stories of who you are now, Lord Bromley, and how you walk in the East End of London without fear and often in disguise. You are a legend, sir, to all of those young men who come after you. No one ever truly knew quite who you were then or are now and if we could be half the man that you—'

Nick interrupted him. 'What's the important matter?'

'Vitium et Virtus. Myself and a group of friends are wondering if perhaps you might sell your share in it to us.'

'Why?'

That question made Christian Challenger frown and yet to give him his due he answered.

'We'd like the chance to continue the club in the august tradition of friendship that you began, sir.'

A good retort. Perhaps Frederick himself had tutored the young man in an appropriate response. God, Nick suddenly felt every one of his twenty-nine years.

'When do you require an answer?'

'Oh, there is no hurry, Lord Bromley. It is just the promise of an affirmative endorsement in the future that we would like.'

'How old are you?'

'Nearly twenty.'

'Do you gamble?'

'Yes, sir.'

'And drink?'

'Copiously, my lord.'

A younger version of himself would have no doubt asked about the lad's bedding habits but the older one was tired of such debauchery.

'We will discuss it.'

'I am most grateful for such a consideration. I am also thrilled to be in your company, my lord, and wondered if you are by any chance going to the New Year's Eve party at the Jacksons tonight?'

'I wasn't thinking of it.'

'The wine is from France and the gambling tables are very rich.'

Nick did not feel like being alone again this evening. He felt restless and ornery, the anger in him over his visit to the river today growing. Perhaps if he went out it would help?

'Is your brother attending?'

'He said he might call in.'

'Wait until I change and I will join you. Help yourself to a drink.'

* * *

Once this would have been fun. Once he would have been the one to call for more wine and to set up games of chance that he had very little hope of winning. Once he would have had a woman on each arm and the promise of others all about him. Even now in the corner as far from the dance floor as he could manage he could see them observing him.

'Bromley? Is that you?' A particularly beautiful blonde came forward with a little entourage of more women of the same ilk. He felt like one of the sweetmeats he and Eleanor had probably fawned over in Fortnum and Masons all those years before.

Eleanor. He wished she was here with her wise eyes and laughter. He wanted her beside him more than he had ever wanted anything in his whole life.

'You must remember me, my lord. Diane Kennings. Now Mrs Diane Morningside.' If she could have added unfortunately without causing scandal he thought she might have. Nick had a slight recall of her visage through the drunken haze of sotted twenty-three-year-old eyes.

'We have heard such stories of your time away, Lord Bromley, and you have returned looking like a pirate.' The others giggled, but there was an undercurrent of anxiety.

The two men beside him whom he knew only vaguely looked on with interest, waiting for the start of a new scandal, he supposed. Once he would have enjoyed the challenge. Now he just wished fervently that young Christian Challenger might return forthwith, Frederick in tow.

'I don't think you can believe all you hear, Mrs Morningside. Mine is a fairly sedentary tale.'

'They say you got rich at the game of cards and that you are every bit as reckless as you always were, my lord?'

The implication was clear as the woman flicked her fan this way and that.

'Age mellows one and a seat at the gaming tables has palled in its excitement. If I could give you any idea of my future intentions, I would probably have them as being a simple farmer.'

'At Bromworth Manor? Such a beautiful property, my lord. One of the finest in Essex, it is said.'

God, where the hell was Frederick? Nick looked around to see others glancing their way with as much interest on their faces as Diane Morningside seemed to have on hers.

How could he have possibly liked this, then? How could he not have seen the shallow amorality of such pointless conquests? He wished he did not remember all the many faces of his paramours, all the tears and pleading and the futile awful hope for so much more than he could give them.

Then Frederick was there and with a slight tip of his head Nick excused himself from the party and took him aside.

'I am leaving. Now.'

'I will come with you. You can drop me home.'

* * *

In the carriage five minutes later Nicholas leaned back against the leather cushion and began to laugh.

'Was it always like that?'

'As far as I can remember it was.'

'And we liked it?'

'Once we did.'

'Your brother Christian and his friends want to buy out my share of Vitium et Virtus. As far as I am concerned he can have it for free.'

'You've changed, Nick.'

'I know.'

'You seem happier.'

That wiped the smile off his face because he was happier and the person who was making him so was Eleanor Huntingdon.

'When you met Georgiana, how did you know she was the one that you wanted as a wife?'

'I could not stop thinking about her. She drove me so damn crazy I thought I would go mad.'

Hyde Park to one side was dark and cold as they passed it, small shadows in the undergrowth attesting to those who would sleep rough tonight. He was lucky with his friends and his house and his title. But he needed to protect himself and all those about him whom he loved.

'I'd like your help with something. Is there any chance of a meeting at Vitium et Virtus tomorrow at around noon? I'll ask Jacob and Oliver to be there as well.'

'It sounds serious.'

'It is, but it will be easier if we all put our heads together.'

'I'm glad you asked. Count me in.'

'I saw Nicholas earlier this evening.'

Georgiana Challenger looked up from her place on the thick rug at her husband's feet. The fire before them in their bedchamber was warm and inviting and Frederick had opened a bottle of fine wine to share.

'At the Jacksons' town house?'

'He asked me how I knew you were the one I wanted as a wife.'

At that she turned to kneel. 'He is in love?'

'Why would you say that?'

'It is a known fact that every young and worried husband-to-be asks exactly that question of his good friends.'

'How is it known? I have never heard of this truism.'

She placed her fingers against the line of his cheek, liking the way he smiled.

'Because it is a feminine knowledge. Who was he with there?'

'No one, although there were many female hearts a-fluttering.'

'I will ask Rose tomorrow. Perhaps she has some idea. Oh, I do hope I like her.'

Fred laughed. 'Only a woman would say something as ridiculous as that.'

'And only a man would not know exactly why Nicholas Bartlett was asking in the first place. What did you tell him in answer, anyway?'

'I said you drove me mad because I could not stop thinking about you.'

'Do I still do that? Drive you mad with desire?'

'Every single moment.'

'Frederick?'

'Yes.'

'I love you.'

Chapter Ten

Eleanor sat at her dressing table and peered at herself in the mirror. She looked older and more tired than she had ever been, lines of worry marring her forehead.

Lucy was back in London and she had spent the evening with her for she'd missed her daughter's laughter and hugs. She breathed out in worry for Jacob had asked Nicholas to their small family gathering tomorrow night and that definitely posed a problem.

Did Lucy look like him? Could the others possibly see the resemblance that she herself most certainly could? Would her daughter tell him how old she was in a passing conversation and if she did, was that something that he might consider and calculate? *'Five and nearly three-quarters.'* Children were never vague about their age.

No wonder she had lines on her forehead. Eleanor shut her eyes just to find a quiet that was missing inside every single thought she had.

It was Grandmama's fault. She had insisted on Nicholas Bartlett being there and for what reason Eleanor could hardly fathom. Something about promising his grandmother that she would watch over her grandson as the older woman was dying.

Eleanor wished her mother could have been standing behind her and running her soft hands across her hair, telling her that everything would work out fine and that worrying was just 'borrowing trouble'.

But it had not worked out fine at all when Mama had succumbed to the sickness of the lungs so quickly and had gone from them before anyone could even say goodbye.

Borrowing trouble? She inhaled slowly, one breath and then another. It was a trick she had perfected when Nicholas had disappeared and she had found out that she carried his child, when her whole world had shattered at her feet.

The calm came back and her glance fell to the small bracelet sitting beside her mother's silver brush.

She wished he had kept her token. She shook her head at that thought and wondered if in the six years of apartness she had learnt anything at all.

Nicholas had not kissed her. He had not remembered. Oh, granted he had held her with sensitivity after she had burst into tears, but he had let her go soon enough and gone back to the Bromley town house. With relief, she thought, if she'd read the look in his eyes properly.

She pulled her ring out from the neckline of the nightgown and stroked it.

'Please, please, God, let him love me.'

A knock at the door made her start and Rose appeared, her long blonde hair tied in a rough knot.

'I heard you talking and wondered who was in here.'

'Ghosts,' Eleanor replied. 'And deities.'

At that her sister-in-law came in and shut the door behind her to sit down on her bed.

'You have seemed busy lately? Jacob said you were helping Viscount Bromley retrieve his memory.'

'Well, it's not working.' She knew this sounded petulant, but it was good to speak to someone other than herself on the subject.

'What do you wish he would remember, Ellie?'

She turned at that to look at her sister-in-law and saw concern in the soft blue eyes.

'How much do you know of my past, Rose?'

'Very little, I think. I do understand that you have been lonely for all the time I have known you.'

God, was she meant to be near tears for ever today? She swallowed back hurt.

'I was never married. Not to the Highland Laird who died from a horse accident nor to the landowner in Edinburgh lost in a storm at sea nor, even, to any man in Scotland.' There, she had said it, just spat it out into the world for another to hear. Even Jacob and she had never been as honest on the subject. Rose, however, was perfectly pragmatic and blatantly unshocked.

'Well, it is nobody's business but your own, Eleanor, and I for one would never judge you.'

At that Eleanor smiled. 'I know.'

'And if this lack of a husband has anything to do with Nicholas Bartlett's disappearance then that is a conversation for the two of you only. But it is one you need to have.'

'How did you get so very wise?'

'A lifetime of adversity and hard work. Your brother has a lot to do with it, too. When you love someone beyond all else and they feel the same, every difficulty is lessened. Remember that.'

'Thank you, Rose.'

'You are most welcome, Eleanor. And I promise I will not say a word of any of this to Jacob until you say I can.'

Nick walked along the small alley behind the garden of Vitium et Virtus and imagined his younger self being ambushed here and dragged away. It was strange to have a knowledge of something, but no real memory. Jacob at his side slowed a little.

'Here.' He pointed to a spot beneath a spindly hedge. In summer it must have been thicker and greener. 'We found the blood right at this spot.'

'The ring we retrieved from over there beside that pile of stones. I had the impression you may have taken it off yourself to leave as a clue for us to find. If whoever did this to you had removed it, I think they would have recognised its value and kept the piece and it would never have surfaced again. Fred, Oliver and I searched the town for you the next day and when you hadn't turned up we went to Bromworth Manor. Your uncle said he hadn't seen you in a week.'

'I imagine he said that with a smile on his face.'

'If we knew then what we do now, we would have knocked the man's head off. The Night Watch got involved the following day, but no one had seen anything of you though one of the neighbours was sure he had heard a hackney cab careening in the area at around eleven.

'A month later we acknowledged the fact that you may be dead although in all the years since we never accepted it.' Jacob's frown was heavy. 'Perhaps we should have looked further afield, Nick, and searched for you in other places outside England.'

Nicholas shook his head. 'America is a big land and it is a long way from here. It would have taken a miracle to come across me there given I'd no idea of who I was anyway.'

'I can't help the feeling, Nick, that you would never have given up on us.'

'Lives are led, Jacob, and time passes. To rally against all the choices you could have made only leads to melancholy. You did what you could and in my book you did enough. Today is the first day of the New Year. Let's look forward now instead of back.'

1819… Nicholas only wanted it to be a happy year. He'd wished for bigger things each new year when he was younger. More money. More parties. More women. In America he had never had the inclination for any dreams whatsoever. Now all he wanted was contentment.

And Eleanor. This thought had him breathing faster and he was glad Jacob, at his side, could not divine his thoughts.

The club appeared different in the light it was now in. Less new. More settled into its own skin. Familiar.

'We have had a good run here, haven't we? On the

boat back from Boston I could see the place in my mind's eye looking exactly like this.'

'Rose was working here as a maid when I met her. Did you know that?'

He laughed. 'Every time one of you tells me something about your unusual women it surprises me.'

'Nothing is at it seems, Nicholas. You would do well to remember that.'

He did not have the time to dwell on such a cryptic remark because Oliver came down the steps to meet them and then Frederick arrived from the other direction. Both looked happy to see him, a smile on each of their faces, and Nick had the feeling that almost everything was right in his world. Breathing in and out deeply, he walked into the only true home he had ever had since losing his parents.

Inside they repaired to the private drawing room where he had first found them again, a high-stakes game of cards in play. Only six days ago? It seemed like a lot longer. When they were seated and the wine poured Nick brought the meeting to order.

'I have had word that the person who paid to have me murdered in the Americas was or is a member of this club.' He brought out the card the ringmaster had given him and laid it down. 'I was reliably informed that the gentleman who paid for the mark did so in gold and that he spoke like a lord.'

'You don't think it's any of us, do you?' Oliver asked this, shock in his eyes.

'Of course not. That's why I asked you here to help me catch him. If we could make a list of those who have a grudge against the club or even suffered a loss at one of the bigger card games, perhaps we might narrow the list down.'

Frederick answered that question fairly quickly, giving Nick the impression that membership was his domain. 'We have two hundred fully paid-up members now and a few who have left. But those who are accepted in usually end up staying.'

'Who have withdrawn?'

'Only a handful. Lance Grayson for financial reasons. Tony Shelkirk, because his wife insisted upon it. Frank Davis. Keith McNair. Nash Bowles, though he was kicked out.'

Nick's attention snapped in. Had he never told anyone of the man's perversion with the maid? 'Why?'

'Because he was a slimy perverted degenerate whom we could no longer stomach.'

'When did this happen?'

Frederick spoke then. 'About two weeks ago, after an altercation with Oliver.'

Nicholas cursed and was about to explain about encountering Bowles with the maid, when Fred carried on.

'But if he is on your list of suspects, Nick, there is a big difference between being a degenerate coward and an out-and-out killer. He's more of a nuisance, I think. Irritating and ineffective. He is also a cousin of Georgiana's stepmother.'

'All right. Who else?'

'David Wilshire. He issued you a death threat when Lady Hannah Goode kissed you in front of him, remember. He thought she had a *tendre* for him and then took umbrage when you won a large sum of money at cards from him a few hours later.'

'I met him a few days ago in Bullock's Museum. He is still unpleasant.'

'He was always a bit unbalanced at school, I thought. A boy one needed to be careful of.' Jacob pointed this out as he poured them all some more of the wine.

'What of your uncle's friend, Vince Matthews? He promised to see all of us in our graves for our poor behaviour and even wrote us a letter stating it.' Oliver frowned as he tried to recite exactly what had been in the missive. 'He said we were heathens who would be punished. He also warned us to watch our backs on dark and lonely nights.'

'But his was a more general warning to us all. It's specific threats we need, to Nick in particular.' Jacob stated this and the others agreed.

Half an hour later they had a dozen names.

'The club has a reputation for passion and temper. You have to expect these contretemps for it comes with the territory. It's like the army where there are always two sides to any argument and everyone wants to have their say.' When Frederick said this they all laughed. 'But it is good to be working together, to be sitting here and discussing problems and solving them again.'

Jacob lifted his glass to that and drank. 'Has there been any word of your guardian, Nicholas, since he left Bromworth Manor?'

'None. I understand he has gone to the Continent with what he could take of the family money. If he manages to stack away a reasonable amount and not spend it he might be able to stay away for ever. I won't be chasing him. As far as I am concerned he's dead and gone.'

'What of his son? He was a member here, if I recall, although I have not seen him lately.'

'I caught sight of him a month or so ago in town and he looked as angry as he usually does.' Oliver gave this reply.

'He would have the motivation to see you dead. Isn't he the next in line for the family fortune?'

'Unless I produce an heir, but it is rumoured that he has followed his father to the Continent.'

The realisation that more than one person wanted him dead made him feel vulnerable and sad. His life here had been fast lived and careless, so fast that he had numerous enemies waiting for their chance to strike.

Did Eleanor know of this animosity? Perhaps she had pulled back from him all those years ago because of it? The waste of living his life on the angry edge of a debauched underbelly made him see for the first time just how cunningly his uncle had encouraged him into such behaviour. His foolish recklessness had allowed Aaron Bartlett to manoeuvre himself into a stronger position financially in the taking of control of his inheritances. Hindsight was a fine thing, but he could barely believe he had not thought of this when he was younger.

'I don't believe Bartlett's son would be a threat anyway. He was always too much of a coward from the start.'

'Be thankful then for it. You could do with a few

spineless adversaries, Nick.' The humour in Jacob's words was welcomed.

'Well, whoever it is will show their hand again and now that I have a better idea of who my opponent might be I will be ready for them.'

'We will all be ready for them.' Frederick laid down his hand and the others followed.

'In vitium et virtus.'

Nick only hoped it would be virtue that might win out.

Chapter Eleven

It was a small New Year's gathering, but Eleanor felt more nervous than she could ever remember being. Lucy was playing with her new china doll and her dolls' house, the front piece opened so that the rooms could be easily viewed as she sat at her chair and table to one side of the fire. On the other side on two large sofas her first cousin Frank Rogerson and his wife, Ilona, were in a lively conversation with Jacob.

Grandmama was asking Lucy about what was inside the rooms and Eleanor's daughter was giving her a running commentary on even the tiniest pieces of furniture.

'It's the smallest table in the world, Grammy, but it still has four legs and there are cups and plates that can sit on the top, see. If I pressed down hard I would squash it all to pieces like a giant.'

When did people lose that love of words, Eleanor thought as she watched her daughter, that uninhibited joy in all that was around them? She prayed that Nicholas might like Lucy. She also prayed that Lucy might like him.

* * *

The evening light was just fading as the Viscount arrived, shown into the front drawing room by the butler. As soon as he saw her he smiled, the dimple on his un-ruined cheek deeply etched in the light.

'Lady Eleanor.'

'Lord Bromley.'

They were formal here, polite and most correct, but she felt the thrill of his notice even as she stood and introduced her daughter.

'This is Lucy, my lord. She has just come back to London from Millbrook House.'

She could see the interest in his face. 'You look just like your mother.'

'That's 'cos I have the same colour hair, but mine's not so long.' Small hands brought her plait around to show him. 'But I like my red ribbon. I got it for Christmas from Mama. It has sparkles.'

When he nodded Eleanor could tell he had not been around children much, his face a picture of uncertainty and a kind of fright. So she helped him.

'Lucy was most fortunate this season and got a dolls' house and another dolly as a present. Would you like to show the house to Lord Bromley? I am sure he would love to see it.'

The thought hit her then just how much the Viscount's appearance contrasted so forcibly with their daughter, her child's soft perfectness balanced against his wounded hand in its sling and the terrible slash across his cheek. And yet in the way they held their heads and watched people there was a decided similarity. Her eyes were exactly his colour.

'You can play with the dolls if you want to. You can have the baby one because I don't like her clothes as much as the other new one,' Lucy chatted on as she found the swaddled china figure and held it out to him.

Without another option she saw Nicholas square his shoulders and walk forward to kneel to the side of the dolls' house.

Looking away, she caught her brother's glance upon her and flushed. Jacob was looking at her strangely and she could tell that he thought something was amiss.

She was not as small as he had thought she might be, this child of Eleanor's, but she was beautiful in the way of all little girls. He smiled at this because in truth he'd hardly had any contact with children in any part of his life.

Except Emily.

The name brought a cold rush of air into the warmth and his fingers shook as he held out his hand to receive a tiny china baby doll all wrapped in white cloth.

'You can put her to sleep if you like.' Up close he could see Lucy's eyes were not blue, but a warm golden brown.

'In here?' A miniature bed was in the room on the top-left storey and it seemed to be this she was pointing to.

'No, silly. That's a baby. She needs to go in the cradle, not the big girl's bed.'

Her hands found an even smaller piece of furniture,

pink ribbons festooned in every corner and rockers beneath it.

'It even lifts up and down, see.'

And it did. The sides had been fashioned so that a lever could be pushed and the wood collapsed in on itself. With all the care in the world he placed the baby doll in its cradle and looked at Lucy for what to do next.

'Now we have to tuck her in. Here.'

A minuscule quilted pink blanket was then placed in his hands and he brought it over the doll, her fingers touching his as she finished the job for him.

She had dimples. Deep dimples on each cheek.

'Do you have a little girl, too?'

He shook his head.

'Mama only has me and I have her and Uncle Jacob and Aunty Rose and Grammy and Aunty Ilona and Uncle Frank and Vic.'

'Vic?'

'My dog. Vic is what we call him, but his long name is Victory. He is black and he always licks us, but Mama does not like that very much. He is this big.'

Little hands were held out as far as her arms could go, but Nick looked past this to Eleanor and saw the horror in her eyes. And the truth.

He cursed beneath his breath as the whole world dropped out of sight and he understood all that Eleanor Huntingdon had tried to hide from him.

Lucy was his. Theirs. Their daughter. Even without any memory he knew that she was. Her eyes. Her dimples. Her age. Her hair.

'How old are you, Lucy?'

'I am five years and three-quarters of months. My birthday is in May on the seventh and then I will be six. I know how to write my name and read, too. I can count to lots and lots. Do you want to hear how I can?'

As she began to count Nicholas's mind calculated the number of months between a week after August the fifteenth and May the seventh.

Nine months, give or take a few days. His vision lightened and his heart beat so fast in his temples he could not hear the spaces in between.

She had his eyes. That thought came through the shock. It was like looking at his own in the mirror, gold shards on the edge of brown. Her cheeks were his, too, high boned and broad. His gaze took in other parts of her greedily, desperately, trying to see everything at once and all that he had missed for so very long. She was perfect and flawless and splendid. He wanted to wrap his arms about her and never let her go.

Rose Huntingdon had bustled in and must have caught Lucy's recounting of her age because, suddenly, Rose was full of chatter. 'Oh, how lovely that you could come and have a supper with us, Lord Bromley, but you look a bit pale. I hope you are not catching a cold.'

Jacob began to rise with anger from his place near the fire and Rose peered at him sharply. 'Georgiana's cousin has been taken to bed for a month with an ailment of the chest and it is most important to consider one's actions carefully in the light of such information.'

Underneath the words Nick could hear a breathlessness and a warning and he wondered at Jacob's wife's strategies. Her fingers were tightly held before her, the reddened crescent of nails clearly visible on the soft white skin on each hand.

His daughter had risen at her words, her hand reaching out for Eleanor. Small hands still slightly rounded from babyhood. Every tiny detail of her was a joy to him.

'Dinner is served, so if you will follow me in. Grandmama, perhaps you could bring the Viscount. Ilona, you, of course, should accompany Frank. Lucy, as a special treat you can take Uncle Jacob's hand and sit with us for a little while before your nanny comes to fetch you. Eleanor, perhaps you and I could bring up the rear.'

Rose's voice was hard to hear through the rush of noise in his ears.

Eleanor felt cold with shock, though Rose's fingers against hers squeezed so tightly it brought her back with a desperate whisper.

'Get through the meal, Ellie, and then have your conversation. I will arrange it. But for now...'

Nodding, she took in a fearful breath. Frank and Ilona were lovely, but both were great gossips and she needed to hold on to her secrets until she could explain them properly. To Nicholas.

Rose had come into the room and heard Lucy, she was sure of it, for she had never seen her sister-in-law become quite so effusively shallow or overtly bossy. Even Grandmama was looking at her strangely. For such a deliverance Eleanor could only be eternally grateful.

Nicholas was seated as far away from her as Rose could manage, between Frank and his wife and opposite Grandmama, Lucy and she were at the other end of the table, Jacob and Rose between them. Everyone, save Lucy and the Rogersons, looked less than comfortable.

Eleanor could feel the Viscount's gaze upon her and Lucy, but didn't look up. She did not know how she might make it through a whole meal with the emotions that raced through her rendering her mouth dry and her pulse quickened. The grand clock in the corner showed only the hour of five forty-one.

She was glad for the wine that the footman poured and when Jacob finished his toast for the New Year she drank down a good portion of her glass. A temporary buttress, a provisional support. She waited as the footman topped it up again.

'Can I have some wine, too, Mama?' Her daughter's voice carried on the air and Nicholas Bartlett turned to listen to her answer.

'You may have some lemonade, sweetheart, but only a little as it is nearly bedtime.'

She was amazed her voice sounded so normal, so sensible, so very parental. The footman behind them half-filled her daughter's glass and then stood back.

'London suits you, Eleanor.' Ilona said this and her husband nodded his head. 'I said to Frank this afternoon how very relaxed and content you look. I think you are losing years rather than gaining them.'

'It must be the Christmas season then, Ilona.' Her smile was tight and false. 'I always enjoy it.'

'It's a Huntingdon tradition to treasure family gath-

erings for the connections and discoveries they foster.'
The darkness in Jacob's voice made Eleanor stiffen.

'We all of us enjoy it.' Rose added this quickly in
a completely strained tone and the way she sat up so
straight gave a clue as to how tense she really was.

'Jacob was informing us before your arrival this evening of your recent return from the Americas. Did you
celebrate the Yule season abroad, Lord Bromley?'

'I lived mostly in the country, Mrs Rogerson. Christmas did not have a big presence there.'

'But you have been away a very long time?' The implication in Ilona's voice told Eleanor that her cousin's
wife knew a lot more about his absence than she was
letting on. Another problem. She was certain that the
gossip of the Viscount's return had been as damaging
and false as that of the talk of her own mysterious husband's death, embellished so much that even she had
sometimes found the tales amusing.

'Too long, it seems.' Nicholas Bartlett's voice held a
harshness she'd never heard from him before.

She felt a further rush of red come to her cheeks and
caught the Viscount's glance at exactly that moment,
the anger in his eyes clearly visible.

Anger. Of course he would be furious, but she had
not even thought of that. She'd imagined questions or
even joy. Such rage had her straightening in her seat
and taking a breath. Two could play at this game and if
he thought it had been easy for her all these years to be
the sole parent of a child without a father then he had
another think coming.

She would not cower.

So when Frank told a funny story about one of his childhood Christmases she made sure to laugh loudly and look as if she was enjoying the tale immensely. The wine helped, of course, and she was on her fourth glass before she saw her brother shake his head at the footman who came to refill it.

There was a bottle already left on the table of a fine red so she helped herself to the rest of that instead.

It was becoming easier, this charade, as time marched on and when Lucy's nanny came to retrieve her for bedtime at seven Eleanor made a show of kissing her daughter on the forehead and looking like the most congenial of parents.

'Say goodnight to everyone, darling.'

She had expected Lucy to simply bid the table adieu and was surprised to see her cross to each person and kiss them on the cheek. When she came to Nicholas she hesitated.

'Goodnight, Lucy.' He said the words quietly, the deepness of his voice filled with regret. Whether it was this or the wounds that he carried, but her daughter simply fell into his arms and kissed him twice.

'That one is for your hand to get better and that one is for your face. Mama always kisses my hurts better.'

'Thank you.'

Shame flooded her. Her small five-year-old daughter had acted with more grace than she had and as sorrow began to take over from false animation, all Eleanor felt was an endless tiredness.

She was careful to place her glass down on the table

before standing, the wobble in her voice presumably as noticeable as that in her gait. 'I think I should probably retire as well, as I have drunk far, far too much, so I wish you all a good evening.' She made a point not to look in Nicholas's direction at all.

Then she was free, walking out into the lobby and up the stairs, following her daughter to the nursery.

She could not talk to Nicholas tonight. Not like this. She needed to understand what she might say, needed to know just what she wanted from him as a father and as a man.

'He was nice, wasn't he, Mama? The man who came last. The one who played dolls with me.'

'He was, darling.'

Well, at least she had the answer to one of the questions she had posed herself earlier in the evening.

Her daughter liked Nicholas a lot.

Nick ate the cheese and figs and swallowed the last of his wine. When he looked at the clock it was just past nine and he knew he could not stay much longer, for more hours of smiling and pretence would simply do him in. His eyes went to the dolls' house Lucy had played with, the front of the edifice shut now and the dolls inside.

He loved her. He did. He loved his daughter so fiercely that it hurt his heart.

They had all lied to him. That thought was what had kept him rooted to the seat when Eleanor pleaded tiredness and excused herself. Jacob fidgeted in the way he always did when he was worried and Rose looked more and more desperate.

Only Grandmama kept smiling at him, her dark eyes watchful.

'Your grandmother would be pleased with how you have turned out, Lord Bromley, especially given your antics as a youth after the loss of your parents.'

He inwardly groaned. Was there nothing in this family that was off limits, no notice of that which was awkward or uncomfortable?

'You knew her well?' It was all he could think to say to try to divert her attention.

'Like a sister. We came out together and I was her bridesmaid when she married your grandfather. She was a strong woman just like Eleanor is with her own opinions and certainty.'

He suddenly understood where this was heading. My God, did the whole entire family know what he had not? When he looked across at Jacob he saw the apprehension on his face was reflected in his wife's.

If Eleanor had not seemed more than a little intoxicated he might have demanded to see her right there and then, but Frank and Ilona Rogerson were patently not in on the family secret and he did not wish to make a fuss in front of them.

So he did the next thing he could think of. He finished off his wine and stood to take his leave, insisting Jacob stay at the table with his cousin and that he would let himself out.

A moment later he signalled to his driver and waited till the Bromley conveyance came to a halt beside him.

'The town house, please, Thackeray.'

It wasn't a long drive and as the horses gained speed he leaned back and expelled his breath. He would return in the morning and demand to see Eleanor Huntingdon, that much he was certain of, for she and her brother had lied to him about everything. The implications of that rebounded in his head. How many others knew of Lucy's parentage? Were they ever going to tell him? Was there some test he needed to pass before they considered him worthy?

A sudden noise caught his attention, the shout of strangers and the stoppage of the horses. Outside Nick saw two men running along the side of the carriage, their faces masked in cloth, weapons in their hands.

He was off his seat before he realised it, opening the door and jumping. He rolled up to a stand, not even feeling the heavy thump of the road in his anger, his arm shooting out and taking one of the hidden faces with his fist. When the man went down the second was already upon him and he felt the crunch of his nose as the man made a wild swing at him, the blood running thickly down the back of his throat.

Turning, he ripped the mask from his attacker's face. A snub-nosed stranger stared back at him, surprise about the only thing registering before he tore himself away and disappeared into the night, the iron bar he held clanking down on the street. When Nick looked around the other attacker was running, too, for a side alley a few yards up the road.

Panting with exertion, he came down on his haunches, trying to catch a breath, his left arm hurting like hell and his nose feeling painful and swollen. Then Thackeray was there, his voice unsteady.

'Shall I call somebody, sir.'

Nick stood. 'No. They have gone. Just take me home.'

Chapter Twelve

Eleanor had watched Nicholas Bartlett leave the Westmoor town house, his hat in hand and a heavy coat shrugged on in the winter chill of the night. She had been waiting for him to go ever since she had said goodnight to Lucy, not to hail or shout to, but just to observe.

He'd looked tired, his fingers threading through the hair at his temple, and she thought of the headaches he had told her of.

His hand was again cradled over his chest in the way he always held it if he thought no one was looking. Jacob had said the wound was substantial. A blade, he had intimated, that had cut the flesh to the bone.

The same blade that had glanced his cheek, perhaps? She wondered whether he would go home tonight as it was still early or whether he would head out again to enjoy the frivolity of the London night life.

If she knew exactly what it was she wanted from him, she would have run after him or waited downstairs to catch him as he left. But she did not even know that.

She had badly miscalculated the effects of being so secretive. Lucy did deserve to know him and Nicholas also needed to understand what had happened between them all those years ago so that he might make a decision based on facts.

The wine from dinner now sat in her stomach, souring her mood. The start of another year and here she was, in the place she had been for the past six of them, worrying again about her future and caught in a limbo.

Well, it would not do at all. She would go and see Nicholas Bartlett and explain her reasoning for such a subterfuge. Fear. Uncertainty. Years of making decisions about her and Lucy's life that had been entirely her domain.

Eleanor wondered whether the shock of understanding that he was indeed Lucy's father might have jogged other memories.

The heat of summer. The gauzy thin layers of cotton sheeting on his bed. The sound of her heartbeat as he had leaned down to take one nipple in his mouth.

Her breast rose even now at the memory and she castigated herself for being so shallow, so very bent on the sensual. Last time she had let her heart rule and not her head and look what had happened.

She would go and see Viscount Bromley in the morning before anyone here realised she was gone and she would lay her cards on the table with as much honesty as she might muster. She hoped that it would be enough.

On arriving home Nick went straight to his library to pour himself a straight whisky. The shock of Lucy's parentage added to the attack in the carriage had left him shaken and exhausted and he needed to understand just how much of a threat these assailants could be to Eleanor and his daughter, let alone to him. This uncertainty needed to end. He needed now to reclaim his own life, all of it, so that the past and the present could lead to a future that was decent and sustainable.

So he spent the rest of the evening sifting through names on the list that he and the others had drawn up in Vitium et Virtus. He wrote down every single thing he remembered about the two attackers he had met tonight.

Both had carried weapons and had been dark haired. He'd scratched the first assailant on his cheek and the mark would undoubtedly last a while before it disappeared. If he could find this man before that happened…

But how?

Looking through the names, he kept returning to Bowles and Wilshire. Taking another page of paper, he drew a line down the centre and scrawled a list of any interaction he had ever had with either man. Bowles was the one who seemed to have more of a motive to hate him and yet Nick could not imagine why he would want to pay assailants over so many years to try to see him dead.

Unless…

What was it Eleanor had said of him? *There is something frightening about him.*

The incident at Vitium et Virtus had shown him that, the maid Bowles had hurt with his small sharp knife shaking in fear and pain. What might have happened if he had not chanced upon the pair when he did? Could Nash Bowles have taken things even further? If he had been hanging around the club, perhaps the others might have noticed other situations that were similar?

Nick's head was starting to ache with all the possibilities and he leaned back against the soft leather and watched the fire.

Flame had always calmed him. He'd spent a month in a cold, hard-floored jail outside New York after being accused of cheating in a card game by a man who was later found dead. It was winter and he had nearly frozen to death by the time they let him out, the charges dropped altogether when witnesses to the murder and the actual culprit had come forward.

After that he had gone into the wilderness and built a fire at his campsite every night right through to the springtime.

Taking a sip of his whisky, he felt the warmth of it slide downwards as the clock on the mantel chimed the hour of three.

Another thought struck him. At Bullock's Museum the other day when he had met David Wilshire, the man had informed him that Nash Bowles had not forgiven him, a fact alluding to strong feelings especially after six years of absence.

Why would that be? Surely Bowles would have realised his actions at Vitium et Virtus were despicable at the least and moved on?

Outside the moon passed behind a cloud and the room darkened. Nicholas seldom sat up at night with a light on, save for that of the fire. Years of hiding had taught him the shadows were safer places in which to dwell and to be hidden.

He wished Eleanor were here to talk to for only with her did his sadness lift and disperse and he yearned to know more of the little daughter that they had made together.

Lucy. He wondered if she had been given a middle name.

A pile of notebooks he had taken from Vitium et Virtus sat on the table beside him, tomes that described some of the day-to-day happenings at the club that had been kept as a reference by Jacob, Frederick and Oliver ever since he had left. He flipped over the first page of the top book and smiled as he slanted it to firelight. Jacob presumably had drawn a couple in full mask at a ball. The notes below described the night in detail— those who had attended and those who had won or lost at the card tables.

The rest of the book was in the same vein, he saw, as he kept on turning the pages, though towards the end a passage from two weeks ago caught his whole attention.

'Nash Bowles has been harassing a number of the patrons with his particular kind of unsuitable lust and when confronted by Oliver he asked if we believed Nick to be dead. Oliver's hand was injured by Bowles's blade and he told him to forget Nicholas for it was no business of his anyway.'

Nicholas could almost hear Oliver giving the warning in his direct manner. But why would Bowles even ask such a question?

He could well have been killed a number of times in the Americas, but it was too far-fetched to imagine Nash Bowles paying for someone to stalk him thousands of miles from home.

Yet Nicholas felt as though he was missing things. It was late and he was tired and the stamina he might have had in his early twenties was wilted at almost thirty. His searing headache probably did not help, nor the throbbing pain in his left hand and fingers. Stretching out, he grimaced as a shot of white heat buried into the bone at his wrist without warning and did not relent.

He'd been hurt so very often. The gunshot at his thigh. The more recent knife wound to his face and hand and the strips of scarring on his back from the jail in Boston. But this time everything was different for he did not want to be shunted on to another location to find safety. This was where he must stand up and meet the one that wished him harm, head on and with determination. He had the help of his friends and the resources of the Bromley fortune. He had the motivation and he also had the fury.

His eyes went across the darkened stains of blood on the breast of his jacket and the dried brownness of it on his fingers. He should wash, he knew, but somehow such stains gave him strength and courage. A badge of resolve and tenacity, his vehemence harnessed by something more than just himself now. He had a daughter to protect and he had Eleanor. It was time to bring the fight out into the open and end it once and for all.

Leaning back in fatigue, he gave consideration to the fact that it was now the second day of the new year.

A sign. A direction. He closed his eyes and dozed.

The doorbell rang before the hour of ten in the morning, waking Nick with a start for he wondered just who on earth would come to see him this early.

'Lady Eleanor, my lord.'

She was there in his library even as his man stopped speaking, pushing in behind him and coming into the room.

'Thank you, Browne. That will be all.' He tried to keep the surprise at seeing her from his eyes, but he was disorientated and cold and his arm hurt like hell. Last night's soiled clothes were still upon him although he hoped he had washed all the blood off his face.

'You have not slept?'

Her words were laced in question.

'Did you?' He made a point of looking across at the time.

'No. I lay awake all night and wondered what I should do.'

'Honesty,' he drawled, 'may have come a little late for me, Eleanor.' Her eyes were ringed in the same darkness he knew his own would be.

'There is no good time to tell a man you have not seen in six years, and who cannot remember you at all, that he is now the father of your child.'

He laughed at that because the words were so quintessentially Eleanor.

'Were you going to enlighten me if I had failed to

guess the truth or made no progress in regaining my memory?'

When she lifted her left hand to her temple in a gesture of complete worry he saw she wore her small braided bracelet with the colourful beads around her thin wrist and the fight went out of him just like that.

'I want to know you, Eleanor. I want to remember you.'

The blue in her eyes blazed.

'Well, I am running out of days to try and help your recall. After tonight—the sixth day we spent together—I do not know what happened next, for it was the last time I saw you.'

'What happened the last time I saw you, Eleanor?'

'You asked me for dinner at your town house.'

'Here? Alone? Just us?'

She stood stock still and quiet against the backdrop of his dimly lit library. Her lips were pursed and her hair was jammed under another of her horrible hats. There was a pin in the felt, enamelled in the colour of the butterfly wing he had seen in Bullock's Museum, the one that had exactly matched the blue of her eyes.

'I was young and foolish and my mother had just died and I was lost in thrall to you, lost in the hope of something I had no knowledge of. That is why I came here, then.'

A tear ran down her cheek, the splash of it darkening the lighter collar of her cloak, but she made no attempt at wiping it away, merely watching him through the awful horror of truth. She looked beaten and some hard-formed part of him broke with her distress as he stood to move forward.

'It was not your fault, Eleanor. It was all mine. I was older than you and arrogant, and what I desired I took. I am sure that that was how it was and it should not have been so.'

But she spoke then with the utter conviction of the damned.

'No. When you kissed me that first time at Lackington's I wanted it all, more, everything that you knew. Two days later I peeled away my bodice even as you tried to stop me in your bedchamber and by then it was far too late for the both of us. I had not worn undergarments, you see.'

'Hell.' He did see. The most beautiful woman in all the world offering her naked body to him without conditions or reservation. Even a saint would have had a hard job denying such a gift and he had never been one.

Had he said he loved her? Had he at least given her that to hold on to as a troth in the many years of his absence? He could not ask because a negative answer would lessen everything. He needed to make things right. He needed to court her in the way the sister of a duke would expect to be. He needed to reinstate her absolute value.

'Come to dinner tonight, Eleanor. Here. With me.'

For a moment he thought she might not answer him at all, but then she did.

'Why?'

'I want for you to understand that it was not all a lie, our past. That the truth was there, too.'

'What time should I come?'

'Eight o'clock.'

He breathed out because the relief was so great.

'I am not sure of who I was six years ago, but I was not the man I should have been and I am sorry for it.'

She smiled at that. 'Perhaps I was different, too. Sillier. More unwise.'

He shook his head. 'I cannot even imagine you as that, Eleanor.'

'Immature then. Impossibly romantic.'

She could sense his closeness and his urgency and the stretched want of him and she knew a madness that had been there before in her. Uncloaked again. Let free.

Touch me and we shall both burn down to ashes.

She wanted to warn him as she had not, then. She wanted to shout such concern out loud here in the quiet of his library in the dulled light of a grey morning.

But she didn't because every single part of her tingled with the need to feel him against her. She had never met another like him. Then and now. But especially now with his strength and his distance and a hardness that had risen from all that was softer.

'May I kiss you, Eleanor?'

'Yes.' The word tangled in her throat even as she whispered it when he came closer. An elemental knowledge. The shivers chased each other across her skin and pulled up her spine.

Yet she didn't go lightly into his embrace, for she was no young girl any more, the tears from before dried salt upon her cheeks. No, she went with hesitation across the few footfalls and came up against warmth; the quiet silence between them full of sound, breath and heartbeat.

Her defences were breached and broken, every reason she knew she should not be here drowned by the arguments that she should. Her arms came around him and she closed her eyes against the moment, only feeling. With trepidation she took in a breath and waited.

One finger touched the line of her cheek, feather-light. 'You are so very beautiful, Eleanor. More beautiful than any woman I have ever known and you are brave, too, which I thank you for.' She looked at him then, directly, as his hand travelled upwards tracing the tip-tilt of her nose and the shape of one eye and then threaded through her hair at the temple, all the time the pressure building.

His mouth came across her own, sealing intimacy, the heat of his flesh and the push of his tongue. He was greedy in what he took, shaking away her small offering and coming in further. His good hand cradled her head so that the kiss could deepen and he could know every part of her, her whole body bound up in his own. Wanting.

And then the dam broke, the gentleness replaced by only need and the hot savage touch of his lips against hers. She pushed against the tautness in her own desperation.

Do not make this gentle, Nicholas. Do not kiss me as if I might break. Please.

As though he understood he suddenly brought his mouth in from a different angle and took her without restraint, a demanding kiss that promised everything. Sensation scorched through her body, in her stomach and between her legs and in the tight pull of her nipples against the lawn of her petticoat.

This is what she had dreamed of for all those years. Exactly this. And her release came with barely a warning, the edges of lust opening and beaching across the shattered pieces of her soul.

Only him. Only her.

She clung to him as if he was the last salvation between her and eternity.

He could feel her release, strong and then stronger, the clutching waves of passion making her throw back her head and groan. No longer a duke's sister. No longer the careful Eleanor Huntingdon who seldom showed her colours either. Here with him she was somebody else. Dangerous. Vulnerable. Recklessly unsafe. The sting of her fingernails carved small troughs down the side of his neck.

He knew now that he could take her, that he could simply lift her up and carry her to his bed. The old Nicholas would have done exactly that and without compunction, but something inside him had changed and instead he drew her close to his body and held her, the hard ache at his groin pressed into her cloak.

Not like this, he thought. Not again.

But his heart thumped with the shock of her and the want, for all the shadows of who he had been were pushed into a corner by her light.

With Eleanor he could live again. With her he could

be healed of bitterness and of loss. The smell of violets made him smile into her hair, soft curls of brown and gold tumbling under his chin.

She was so fragile in her honesty that it frightened him.

Take it slow, he thought. Let her get used to you and know you. Let her understand that this was a mutual want and that they had all the time in the world to understand it.

'I am sorry.' Her words, hot against the skin at his throat.

'For allowing me to kiss you?'

Her head shook. 'For being so...wanton.'

He laughed at that and his grip strengthened. 'You think I might want a milk-sop girl who hardly moves or breathes, but simply stands there as I kiss her?'

'I do not know.'

And she didn't. She had made love to him for one night all that time ago and then been thrown into the lonely winter of widowhood for six long years until tonight. Until now.

'You are perfect, Eleanor. In every way possible.'

She stilled and pulled back, looking up at him as if he was giving her an untruth.

'Tonight I will show you exactly how I mean it.'

'The dinner?'

'And more if you will allow me. Much more if you stay with me.'

The beat of his heart was heavy as he offered her himself.

He would remember this moment, this second scrawled

into faulty memory. In the reds of the fire and the warmth of her skin. In the grey of the morning and the silence in the room, save for breath between them, ragged in need.

He'd been trapped in time for so long and to suddenly be released to feel again, to walk and love and laugh, was overwhelming. The joy of her filled him, overflowing, her fierceness and her beauty, the grace of rediscovery, the benediction of touch. He let her go when she pulled away because he wanted to do nothing to frighten her.

'I will see you tonight, Nicholas.'

It was the first time she had called him by his Christian name and he was heartened by the fact. Then she readjusted her hat and was gone.

Eleanor lay down upon her bed when she got home and buried her head in a pillow.

My God, had that just happened? Had she truly been so very shameless? He had known what had transpired inside her for he had said as much and yet he'd stood there, composed and collected, watching on as she simply went to pieces.

Even now the echoes of what she had felt gripped her insides, sliding their treachery into the heated folds of her skin.

In penance or in vindication, she knew not which.

All she did know was that for years she had felt nothing, wanted no one, the emptiness and void of her life without Nicholas welcoming oblivion.

It was for Lucy that she had kept going, kept breathing, kept imagining that he would come back, alive and whole and loving.

Well, here he was, offering her his bed and his touch and his body. Not the love words yet, she thought with a frown, and remembered how distant he had been last time after she had allowed him everything.

She rolled over and looked up at the ceiling. Tonight she would go to his bed and know him again. Her hand came over her mouth, in both worry and in delight. But she would not falter, not now, when the world was being offered back to her, without condition.

She was twenty-four years old, soon to be twenty-five, and she had slept with only one man for one night in all her life. Him.

She felt breathless and light headed and slightly sick.

She had been thinner then, more girlish, but the long lines of eighteen had formed into softer curves at twenty-four. Would he like the change? Would he notice the small white marks of motherhood that had appeared across her stomach, muted, she knew, but nevertheless there?

She sat up, her hands held tight across her middle as the worry inside her grew. What if he did not love her in the same way? What if she got pregnant again and he left, this time for greener pastures and more beautiful women?

But the night was like a treasure offered, a place to start again, a way of reconnection that was as absolute as the desperation she felt for him. She would not give the chance of it up for anything.

Crossing to the mirror at her dressing table, she sat at the stool there. The woman who looked back at her was a stranger, for excitement pooled in her eyes and the streak of animation on her face made her look so completely different. Almost beautiful. When she moved, her smile ran into the rainbow edges of the glass and she saw herself a dozen times or more, stretching back into the distance.

Multiplied. Proliferate. That was how Nicholas Bartlett had made her feel right from the very first second of meeting him.

A small sound at the doorway alerted her to the presence of another and she turned to see her daughter there, three dolls all tucked in a basket that she held.

Opening her arms, she waited until Lucy was within them and turned to the mirror again, her child on her lap.

'What do you see, Lucy?'

'Me and my mama. You are smiling a lot, but your hair looks messy.'

'I see my beautiful daughter and her three small friends.'

'I see rainbows there—' little fingers touched the bevelled edges '—and here I see your eyes. They are bright blue and mine are brown. Where does eye colour come from?'

'From your mama and your papa.'

'But mine is gone.'

'No.' Eleanor squeezed tight and looked at Lucy through the glass. 'No, he is not gone for good, my darling, and one day soon you shall meet him and he will love you.'

'All the way to heaven and back?'

'That's a very long way, but, yes, all that way and more.'

Chapter Thirteen

An hour later Eleanor rummaged in her wardrobe to try to find a newer version of the same dress she had worn before at the Bromley town house. A dark primrose gown, with embroidery around the bodice and the bottom of the sleeves.

The décolletage was low, but she heightened it with a swathe of ivory Brussels lace that had been her mother's. Today she needed courage and conviction. After this morning it was time to face the ghosts of the past whether Nicholas remembered what had happened or not.

He had been ill shaven when she had visited him and the jacket he'd worn had been covered with bloodstains. Another contretemps, she thought. A further recklessness.

Was his life going to be blighted by such violence for ever? Today he had not looked angry, only sad. That had thrown her more than the fury.

It was not his fault he had been shanghaied into a journey to the Americas and yet…

It was not her fault she had fallen in love with him so quickly and allowed him everything and yet…

They were both to blame for what had happened six years ago. There was only the desires of the present in all that they had done, the thrill of the flesh and the forbidden.

She had just lost her mother then and Nicholas's uncle was becoming more and more impossible. Each to the other was a way out, a way to forget.

But now…

She liked him more as a man.

Stay here with me.

She swallowed hard and stood to look out the window into the winter. She knew what she wanted. Last time they had laid together it had been in the summer warmth. Now it was cold, but if they could find a path back to each other the spring came next and then new life. The smaller niggle of uncertainty also crept back again. He had never said that he loved her.

There was a knock on the door and Jacob's head appeared.

'Can I come in?'

'Of course.' She knew her brother would want to have a conversation after the events of last evening.

'Nick thinks Lucy is his, Ellie. I can see it in his eyes.' Jacob did not beat about the bush and, given his lack of addressing her pregnancy this directly before, she was shocked because it was a statement more than a question. After her conversation with Rose she knew she owed him at least the truth.

'He wants to talk to me tonight. At Bromley House.'

'Is it true, Eleanor? Is he the father?'

'Yes. We slept together once the night before he disappeared.'

'Why didn't you tell me?'

'Because you were too sad. Because you had just lost him and I knew that you would not be able to bear hearing his name everywhere in our house and in the tragedy of what had happened to me.'

'Nicholas will marry you. I know he will. It is his responsibility and his duty.'

She smiled. Another honourable man. Her brother.

'It is not quite as easy as that, Jacob. He has changed and so have I. We are different people from those that we were.'

'You are parents of a little girl who needs a mother and a father.'

'And you think I do not understand that? You think I don't wonder about this every single moment?' Her ire had built and Jacob raised his hands.

'I am of the belief that every problem well discussed can be solved.'

The truth of that advice comforted her, made her calmer.

'Which is the reason I am going there to see him tonight.'

With that he moved forward to kiss her on the cheek. 'Then the carriage will be at your disposal and Rose will watch over Lucy. I will leave it to you to give the driver his instructions. Whatever you choose those instructions to be, they will be no one's business save your own. If you are not home tonight, then I will see you on the morrow. I have every faith that you can make this right.' Then he was gone.

Nicholas moved a pile of books from one desk to the next in his upstairs sitting room.

He had a roaring fire and good wine. Dinner would be served in an hour on the small table here. For the only time in his life he had asked the cook if he could peruse the menu.

He was nervous. He admitted this to himself as he paced the room. If this went badly...

'No.' He shook his head and caught sight of his reflection in the mirror above the fireplace. The scar blazed red on his cheek and his nose was swollen from the carriage incident last night.

A noise from further afield told him Eleanor had arrived. He could hear her voice through the silence and then footsteps coming up the staircase. Tonight he had given all the servants, save for a few, the night off.

'Lady Eleanor Huntingdon, my lord.' Browne was the soul of discretion and formality.

She stood very still in her cloak, a dark woollen sheath that enveloped her completely. She did not speak at all as the door closed, but simply stayed there looking at him.

'Thank you for coming.'

She nodded at that, both hands tightly clasping the brocaded edges of her apparel.

'It is warm in here,' he said. 'Perhaps I could take your cloak?'

Her eyes went to the fire and she tugged at the fastening at her neck. Tonight she was in yellow, a dark yellow that picked up the lighter strands in her hair and the curve of her figure. The frothy cream lace at her throat suited her as did the way she had done her hair. It was not fussy. She had pulled the mass of it into a loose pile at the back of her head, the curls that had escaped making her look younger. More uncertain. Beautiful.

The kiss from this morning still simmered in the air around them and he made sure he did not touch her, not yet, not until they had spoken of their daughter for there was so very much he wanted to know.

'We need to talk, Eleanor. About Lucy.' When she nodded he waited.

'I am sorry for the way you found out about her existence. It was unacceptable.' The crisp sound of the word rolled from her tongue in a way that only she could say it.

Unacceptable. To her?

The frown line between her eyes was deep, her lips pursed in on each other in consternation.

'In my defence I might say that your coming back was indeed a surprise and that I was caught in uncertainty.'

'Does Lucy know that I am her father?'

'No.' He saw her swallow back emotion and saw her flinch, too, when he used her name.

Turning away, he poured them each a drink, handing a glass to her with care.

He wished he had not asked the question so baldly. He wished he could take it back and say it differently.

She had been here only a few moments and already the barriers between them were rising.

'I bought her something today.' Crossing the room, he took out a small burgundy box and then placed it in Eleanor's outstretched palm.

'For Christmas?'

'No. For ever.'

At that she half-smiled and, opening the lid, brought out the small gold locket in the shape of a heart that he had purchased from the jewellers Rundell, Bridge & Rundell in the early afternoon.

'Perhaps it is not something a small girl might want…' He stopped.

'She will love it.'

Her hand reached out to touch his arm in reassurance and he felt the heat of it physically, the same punch of lust he was becoming used to in her company.

Go slow, his mind warned. Do not frighten her. He held his want in such check that he trembled with the effort and was glad when the small cuckoo clock chose that moment to beat out the hour, breaking the pressure into fragments that were less sharp and more manageable.

'It's never worked properly.' His words, falling into the silence. 'My grandmother bought it for me years ago.'

'Ten minutes late is not too late, I should imagine.'

He swallowed away thickness. She often phrased her words like no one else did.

An image of the piano came, her fingers across his

and tears in her eyes. And then left. The suddenness of it was shocking.

Bits. Pieces. Nothing.

Putting down his glass, he ran one hand through his hair, trying to soothe the ache that was building in his temples, trying to right the imbalance.

'It was here we slept together?' He could hear the truth of it in his own question.

'Only once.' Her answer.

And once had been enough. Lucy. Eleanor's enforced widowhood and years away from the *ton*. She had been eighteen and alone, the kind and obedient only daughter of a duke when he had come into her life. One night had demanded a large payment.

'Was anyone with you for the birth?'

'Grandmama. Lucy was born at Millbrook.'

'I should have been beside you.'

'The midwife was a great believer in the idea of men being nowhere near a birthing room.'

'Was Jacob at the manor?'

'Yes.'

A stab of jealousy pierced his equanimity.

'My papa was there, too, and he thought Lucy a miracle. Mama had died the year before and his sadness was lessened by her coming. A new life, I suppose, and new hope for the future, despite the circumstances.'

'Was she a little baby?'

Eleanor nodded. 'Small and perfect. She had blonde hair and then it turned darker on the ends so that she looked like a porcupine with its quills sticking out.'

He drank up such words like a man who had been lost in the desert for days without water, imagining.

'She walked when she was ten months. She simply stood up and took six steps. Two weeks later she was almost running.'

'Clever girl.'

'Her first word was "dog". Then she said "Mama" and she has never stopped talking since. She is learning the piano. She loves to dance. She puts on shows for us and we all buy little tickets to watch. Vic is one of her main players.'

Nervousness always made Eleanor talk and he smiled, liking every single thing he learned.

The silence re-gathered.

'Does she have a middle name?'

'Christine. After my mother.'

Please, God, do not let me cry.

Eleanor could see his eagerness and his loss, the poignancy of all those missed years written in every line of his face.

The golden heart was warm in her hand. When she flipped the necklace over she saw the Bromley family crest had been engraved on the back of it. Another effort that told her of his hopes.

His hair was wet, the curls falling with loose dampness upon the white of his collar and the jacket he wore was tight enough to define the muscle beneath the fabric.

How easy it would be to simply move forward and

fall into his arms. With hope. But she had to know him first, had to understand what it was he wanted of them.

Was Lucy the only thing that held them together now? Just the promise of her? Eleanor drank the wine and liked the feeling of how it bolstered her courage. Ever since he had come back she had drunk much more than she had before.

Another difference. She struggled for a further topic, but he spoke before she could.

'How did we meet, Eleanor? I remember you only as the much younger sister of Jacob whom I seldom saw?'

'I had gone to the Vauxhall Pleasure Gardens with my grandmother and her friends to see the fireworks and you were watching me. When Grandmama was busy, we spoke.'

'Just spoke?'

'You touched me.'

And I thought I had been burned by flame.

'How?' He had moved closer now.

'You took my hand and kissed the inside of my palm. The darkness allowed it. I knew you, of course, but at first you did not know me. The orchestra was playing Handel and when it was supper I escaped to eat it with you. Cold meats and cheese and puddings. You held a silver pass for the season and pots of beautiful red and blue flowers hung from every tree above our heads. The air smelt of fireworks.'

'You remember details.'

Every single one of them, she felt like saying, but didn't.

* * *

He wanted to remember so badly.

'Did I kiss you?' His finger reached out to touch her lips softly.

'Not properly.' She blushed bright red as she said this and he thought such reticence did not sound like him. When he desired something he had usually taken it without worrying about consequences. Then.

'You kissed my hand and my wrist. Just there. Then Grandmama came to find me and you disappeared.'

Interrupted as he would not be tonight.

'Can I try again? Now?'

Staying just where she was, she lifted her hand and he turned it over, his thumb stroking the patterns there carefully.

He could feel her draw in a shaky breath and was glad when her eyes came up to meet his, the blue in them as startling as he always found it.

'And then you say I kissed it?'

She nodded, fear overwritten by something else entirely.

'Like this?'

She tasted of lemon and salt and woman. His tongue drew along the same pathway his thumb had just left and he could smell the violets imbued in her skin.

The yellow gown was long sleeved so he pushed away the fabric to measure the pulse there with his lips. Fast and shallow. His own was probably much the same.

The first salvo was fired and, releasing her hand, he took his wine from the table nearby and held it out to her.

'To beauty and to memory, Eleanor. And to Lucy, our daughter.'

She drank to that, her lips leaving a mark on the glass that he then covered with his own.

He was a thousand times more dangerous than the man she used to know, the light playfulness gone and in its place a scorching sensual certainty. He was also promising her nothing save for this one night.

Her worry increased. What if his memory was suddenly jogged back and he recalled how he had pulled away last time? A lover who thought she had not quite been enough? A man who had sampled all that she'd offered and decided it wasn't for him?

A hundred thoughts whirled around in her mind, a vulnerability that had been so complete six years ago she had barely survived and one that she was only just now beginning to recover from. Could she chance it all again or should she leave?

Her heart sank at such a thought.

Tonight he had allowed her the space to come to terms with what he wanted, but he would not be denied. She knew that to the very core of her soul.

The wine was an interlude to be enjoyed, but that was all. The stories that she had heard of him through the gossip mills of the *ton* had been running around for years, but the living and breathing reality was so much more overwhelming.

She ought to call a halt to what he was proposing, cry enough and leave before she lost any will to say no. On his terms. Again.

'I think perhaps I should eat. The wine is strong.' She sounded like her grandmother, the rigid tones of sense discordant after the softer ones of lust.

His smile sent her heart into further spasm. Sensing her fear, he rang the bell on the small table beside him and instructed the man who came to serve the dinner immediately.

'Can I show you to your seat?'

When his hand came up under her arm she felt the spark of connection like a shock.

It was a small table and they sat close. As the creamy chicken soup was served she saw the footman did not tarry, but rather closed the door behind himself and left them alone. When Nicholas locked it she was glad. Without interruption she could speak to him properly.

'It was not my intention to deceive you about Lucy for I thought you were dead.'

'To an extent I was. Deception is an emotion I have had lots of practice in, for when you do not know who you are you can be anything at all and make others believe it, too.'

She smiled at that because she understood the concept entirely. 'And who were you? Then?'

'A traveller. A businessman. A tramp. A card player. An outsider. It depended on the time of year and the places I was in. Summer usually found me in the back country far away from anyone. In winter I had to return to civilisation and shelter.'

'A hard life for a lord?'

'At first it seemed worse because, I suppose, I was softer.'

She could imagine him as a twenty-three-year-old without memory thrown into the chaos of a new country, without money, without a name.

'Who were you there? How did you call yourself?'

The brown of his eyes was full of harsh memory.

'A variety of different names all cobbled together by expediency. I was Peter Kingston when the man who did this found me in the town of Richmond tending a bar.' His good hand gestured to his bad one and at his face.

'It had been a while since I had moved so I was feeling safer and it was a shock when he tried to kill me as I was gathering wood for the fire from a shed by the river.'

'Did you know him?'

'No. But I did not know the others, either.'

This truth nearly broke her heart because in those few words she could imagine exactly just what his life there had been like.

As if he thought he had said too much he raised his wine glass, struggling for a lost ease.

'But tonight I am in the company of beauty, grace and honesty, so here's to the future, Eleanor. And here's to faith.'

'Faith?'

'In that future. Faith to decide how we go on from now.'

'Where do you want us to go?' The words came unbidden, tumbling out over the top of her more normal caution.

'I'd like to do away with your Scottish husband for a start.'

She could see naked desire scrawled across his face and the thick soup of chicken, veal and almonds became dry in her mouth. She was also far too hot. With care she removed her lace fichu, squaring her shoulders so that the bodice was not quite as revealing as it might have otherwise been.

'The story of my marriage was Jacob's idea. A way to protect me from the censure of society.'

'And I thank him for it.'

'But I promise that I never gave Lucy the same lie.'

He looked up at that, the gold chips on the edge of his irises caught in the firelight. 'What did you tell her?'

'That her father loved her. That one day he would be back because I…'

She stopped.

Loved him.

How easy it would be to simply move forward and fall into his arms.

The muscle along the side of his jaw moved, the scar on his cheek standing out further because of it. 'I am grateful, Eleanor.'

And just like that she was back again, back six years sitting opposite him in front of the fireplace in his room.

I am grateful, Eleanor.

His words then, when they had dressed finally and he had got ready to return her home. She had sensed his distance then, but it was different now. Could the wasteland of the years lost finally end in salvation?

She laid her hand gently down across his damaged hand, feeling the ridge of bandages end under the fabric of his sleeve.

'Once, I hoped that you loved me.'

There, it was said and she did not wish to take it back. If she was to trust him, she needed to have faith.

His other hand came down over hers, warm and solid.

'Hoped?'

'You did not say it, but…'

He swore softly, their fingers intertwined. 'Sometimes I barely even like the man that I was and I should not have—'

She didn't let him finish.

'Being together was a mutual decision and if you didn't say the words then—'

He placed his finger on her lips to stop her from admitting more.

She was frightened. He saw that her whole body shook with it. She had given her eighteen-year-old self to him, then he had disappeared and ever since…?

He was still dangerous to her, the attack from the early hours of yesterday morning leaving him agitated and on edge. He should make her go home to her brother and to safety, but in her words there were things he could no longer ignore. Nicholas had to tread carefully for it seemed that last time he had not.

'Our daughter looks like you, but her eyes are mine.'

He could see her listening. Lucy was the centre of her world and it was a way in.

'She has dimples, too.'

That brought a nod.

'Could I meet her as her father, Eleanor? I would very much like to do that.'

He was gentle with his request. He took nothing for

granted with his rights to see his daughter. It was her decision alone to allow it…or not.

'Yes,' she whispered, her eyes meeting his exactly and the fright there eased.

The soup was finished now and he knew he should open the door and ask for the next course to be brought in, but he couldn't move.

One finger ran across the length of her thumb and across to the forefinger. She had freckles on the bridge of her nose and he looked at the smattering with a smile.

'How could I forget this, Eleanor? How could I forget you?'

His whole mind struggled for a glimpse of her from back then, at Gunter's or Lackington's or here, but there was nothing save the ache of the trying for recall in his temples.

'Last time we were here it was summer and the candles were warm because there were so many. After the dinner you loosened my hair…'

He stood at that and drew her up with him, their bodies almost touching as his hands rose to the pins she had tied it back with and he carefully drew them away. The brown curls fell in a curtain down to her waist, unravelling into silk.

Unravelling like his caution and his ever-present distance.

The floor tilted as he pulled her to him and took her mouth, not with softness but with a hard and desperate need, his hands at her nape as he slanted the kiss.

'Eleanor.' Her name was groaned in a broken whisper as he brought her closer.

He kissed her completely differently now. Before he'd left England he had been more careful and softer, but now he held a scorching sensuality that made her head spin.

She clung to his heat and took the offered breath as he seized what he wanted, quick and desperate. She heard the guttural sounds she made, but could not stop them, her breath slowed into only desire, her body melting into need.

'Nicholas?' Breathed out as his tongue came around the fullness of her lips, the feel of it shocking.

Her own mouth opened and she let him in to taste and to savour. There was no reason in their kisses now, logic lost beneath feeling until he turned her abruptly and his teeth fastened on the skin of her throat. She keened into the silence and pressed into him with demand.

Every touch he gave her left her more naked in spirit than the one before. She was stripped down into an intensity that held no fight whatsoever.

He could do as he wanted with her and he knew it. She could see it in the velvet brownness of his eyes which were so like her daughter's.

'Let me make love to you, Eleanor.'

When she nodded he took her up into his arms, striding towards a door at the far end of the chamber and opening it.

His room was filled with blueness, the same wallpaper as before with its patterned cut flock. The bed was a different one, however, the coverlet now a patched quilt of mismatched fabrics.

It was here he placed her before crouching down at her feet so that their heads were level.

'This time it is your choice, Eleanor, and I need you to be sure…'

'I want you.' She gave him her answer without thought because she did. She was certain in a way she had never been before.

'And if I never retrieve my memory?'

'Then we will make new ones. Together.'

'Starting now?'

She reached out to run her hand across his cheek, the skin rough beneath the pads of her fingers. 'I wish I had been there for you when this happened.'

'And I thank the God above that you were not.'

Tipping his forehead down against her own, he sucked in breath.

'I have slept with other women, Eleanor, both here and in America, and while I have not been a saint I promise from now on it will only be you in my bed. For ever. Is that enough for you? To take all the parts of me that are damaged and still want what is left?'

His voice shook and she knew the depth of all he was saying, his years of lostness marked in sorrow. And, now, honesty.

She had loved him as a boy, but she loved him twenty times more over as this man. Strong. True. Hurt. Dangerous.

Her hand dipped into her bodice and she showed him the ring that hung at the bottom of her chain.

'You gave me this one of the last times we were together and I have not taken it off since.'

The gold caught the flame in the fire and she saw the flash of it in his eyes, his pupils distending and tightened into brown as he looked away.

It was like turning a key in a lock and the door finally opening. He remembered. He remembered laughing with her as he had bought the ring from a small shop in Piccadilly after their kiss at Lackington's. It was a celebration gift to go with the wine and hamper from Fortnum and Mason.

Her blue eyes had matched the stones and she had loved them. Zircons, the man had called them. Imitation diamonds.

And with that small crack in memory other walls began to teeter and fall and it all came tumbling in, his lost days and weeks.

He cursed as his hands flew to his head because colour slammed into his temples, not quite painful, but almost. Rushing words and images and the noise of voices. And there in the very centre of everything was Eleanor, laughing, crying, lying there beneath him with love in her eyes.

'I saw you at the Vauxhall Gardens. You were with your grandmother and we met in front of the rococo Turkish tent.'

'You remember?'

'It was evening for the lights had just been turned on and you had dropped your coin purse as I passed you and I bent to pick it up.'

Her blush surprised him.

'You told me your name was Antoinette? Why?'

'I'd recognised you and yet you did not seem to know me and with all the stories that circulated about your exploits I thought I should be a more interesting acquaintance if my name was exotic.'

'You spoke with a French accent?'

'An accent and name which you knew as false in the first moment of conversation.'

He began to laugh. 'Your grandmama called to you to come back to her and you grabbed my hand and ran.'

'I was fresh out of the schoolroom and it was said by everyone in society that you were reckless and fascinating. It was my chance for an adventure and I took it.'

'Six days?'

'Pardon.'

'We were here six days later. At Bromley House in bed together.'

'Are you shocked I was so shameless?' Her teeth sat on the fullness of her bottom lip.

'No. I thank the lord that you were.' Frowning he sought for another recall. 'Ellie? I called you that, didn't I?'

'Yes.'

'And you were a virgin.' He sobered. 'And it was my fault. If you had never been at the Vauxhall Gardens you may have been spared.'

'Spared?'

'Of all that came next. It was my arrogance that led to the incident in the alley behind Vitium et Virtus. If you had not met me…'

He stopped because he could not quite say it.

You were the Duke of Westmoor's only daughter with

all the possibilities in life that such a position implied.
And I took that away.

He saw her swallow and find her answer. 'If I had
not met you then we would not have Lucy?'

'I want you, Eleanor. I promised myself that I would
go slowly and let you choose the time and the place. I
told myself that I could wait and court you, do it properly this time, with good food and the finest wine and
music. But I can't. I swear I can't.'

Her hands came up to both sides of his face and she
brought him in. 'Then that is a good thing, for I do not
wish any more to love a ghost.'

Love? The word vibrated on the end of his tongue,
in question and in relief, but the heat that lay between
them was building, a desperateness that held no mind
of circumstance or propriety.

He wanted to claim her as his own, keep her here in
his bed so that she might never leave him. He wanted to
know every part of her as well as he knew his own body.

His mouth came down across hers in a single movement, her lips opening to his own, so that he could come
inside and taste. Her sweetness and her fear.

'I will not hurt you, Eleanor.' He whispered this
against the alabaster of her cheek.

'I know.'

He should be careful, he should be gentle and tender, but he could be none of those things. He kissed
her as though she had always been his. His. To keep
and to hold.

His hands were on the long row of tiny buttons now

at the back of her gown, fumbling, shaking. He could not recall a time he'd been so desperate or so clumsy.

And then the fabric gaped, exposing the lawn below and the skin beneath. Her breasts were round and pink tipped, the stuff of dreams and hope.

'My God,' he said quietly, as she simply stood there naked to the waist, watching him. 'You are so very lovely.' One finger trailed along the fullness to the nipple and he quickened the movement to run back and forward so that it tightened into hardness. She stretched, taken unawares, and his mouth fell to the corded elegance of her throat.

She was breathing hard now, the sound of it loud in the room, as she melted into acquiescence, shivers chasing each other across her skin. Undoing the gown further, he was pleased when the yellow wool pooled at her feet and the lawn of her petticoat covered only the thin lace of her drawers.

The chill of the room came across her bareness, her skin alight with the flame of the fire and the heat inside.

He was careful as he dealt with the last of her clothes and then she was naked before him, save for the silk stockings with the garters pulled up by pink ribbons and the soft silver slippers on her feet.

'Eleanor.' He moaned this, the breath of him reaching across the small distance between them and he knew only pain as he bent to lift her into his arms, close against his chest, because if he hurt her again he would never forgive himself.

Chapter Fourteen

He was fully dressed and she wore almost nothing, yet Eleanor understood the truth of all that she had imagined. Her legs opened and his hand rested in the junction of her thighs before slipping lower, into the place that was hidden and wet with her want of him.

He looked at her without blinking, the movement of his fingers deepening and quickening, like a maestro or a magician, and she pressed back into the patched quilt and only felt. The rush of lust, the dislocation of time, the wet warmth of her and the thick need of him.

Higher and higher she went as he came on to the bed above her, his swollen manhood replacing his fingers, the smooth sheath of it penetrating deep and then deeper.

Filling up the loneliness and despair.

When he tilted her with one arm beneath her waist her eyes flew open and she kept him there tight with her muscles, regulating movement, in wildness and in ecstasy. When he changed the rhythm of it there was a loosening, the spiralling lack of control sliding over an edge into the realm where everything impossible could happen, where life was changed into before and after, where her whole body jolted to the beat of the music he made. There was no question in it but certainty, clawed together in the chant of a melody that was eternal, a fine unbearable pain cleaving them into another world, as she reached for all that was offered.

She felt the waves of release and rode them, on and on into the nothingness and the light, her heart beating along with his, their breath melded in the heat. Bound by something neither of them could forget.

Afterwards they lay together on the bed and listened to the crackle of the fire and the wind at the shutters and the rain on the glass. Her head was tucked into his shoulders and his arm lay heavy across her, the smell of sex and sweat in the air and exhilaration, too, a memory that had not been faulty, a known pleasure that filled her heart with joy.

'It was just like the last time...?'

His half-question was filled with such awe it made her heart's blood sing.

Her reply held the same wonder. 'Almost, but even better.'

The counterpane was across them now, the stitchery rough and frayed. Like their lives, patched from bits, making a new whole pattern from all the pieces of what had been.

She smiled and his eyebrows raised up.

'What are you thinking?'

'I was wondering where this quilt came from.'

'Remember I told you of the reverend in Boston?' He waited until she nodded. 'His wife made this for me and

it represented hope for a long while after. But now...'
His voice tailed off into the silence and he began again.
'Now my hope is here with you.'

He pulled her across him, his bare chest tickling her.
He had removed her stockings and the remainder of his
own clothes after they had made love and settled her
against him so that they might understand more of each
other in the closeness.

'If you had not returned, Nicholas...'

He stopped her. 'I am here and I shall never go again.'

'You promise?'

He lifted his hand and removed his signet ring, the
gold of it heavy in the light.

'For you, my love, in troth.' He fitted it across her
thumb and the crest of the Bromleys was easily seen
in the fire flame. She covered the piece with her other
hand so that it was tucked into warmth.

But the magic had seeped in again between them,
the enchantment and the need as he sat her above him
and came into her centre, without warning, watching
her all the time.

'I like looking at you when you are breathless and
I like the way your hair hangs like a curtain hiding us
from the world.'

'Can we stay here for ever? Just the two of us? Like
this.'

He'd begun to push in further, lifting her with the
movement, her knees on each side of him steadying balance and his hand tightening around one breast.

'Come with me, sweetheart. Come with me to the
edge of reason and beyond.'

She laughed at that, though the sound was not simple. Rather it was layered with lust and passion and desire.

Later she awoke to hear bells pealing out the hour of three, soft in the winds of winter.

Nicholas was not in the bed. He was sitting at the window with a blanket about his nakedness and his long hair loose, one curtain drawn back so that he might look out into the night.

A fierce night, she thought, with the raindrops hitting hard against glass and the stripped branches of bare-leaved trees swaying in the force of breeze.

The fire was banked now, only embers, small flares of occasional orange banishing back darkness. Suddenly she was afraid for them both, unreasonably and forcibly.

As if he knew what she was feeling, he turned, the scar on his cheek in the moonlight raised in a relief so that the shadow of the wound enveloped the whole of one side of his face.

He had remembered other things in the night as he sat at the window, darker things and less ordered. He recalled feeling full of shame and regret the first time they had made love because he knew that he was not worthy of Eleanor and yet he had taken her virginity without a backward glance. She made him hopeful and foolish for things that might never come to pass, good things, proper things in a lifetime that had been remarkably dissolute and disordered.

Once he'd had nothing much to forfeit, but now…

'If I ever lost you again, Eleanor…' He stopped,

unable to carry on. He did not hold back his honesty though he wished there was more warmth to his words instead of a bleakness, empty of belonging, devoid of hope.

He had never had someone stay in his life. Not since his mother had kissed him goodbye and told him she would be home before he knew it, the mis-truth in her words still there in his mind. Love did not conquer fear at all, it amplified it and made it stronger, the loss a hundred thousand times worse because the promise had sounded so very sweet.

Eleanor had risen, the quilt draped about her. 'You won't. You won't lose me again.'

His heart was beating so fast at her words he wondered if she might hear it and when she came against him he opened the blanket and she sat upon his knee, all warmth and softness and violets. He pulled the quilt tightly in about her, banishing any drafts. She felt the tension in him, rippling through his body.

'You are cold?'

'No, not cold, but fearful.'

'For us?' she questioned and he nodded, because her confession of love was still ringing in his blood.

'If anything happens to you because of me...'

Her hands came around him, sealing off the loneliness. He felt a finger reach out and take his nipple in a hard grasp and with a start he leaned back.

'I liked it when you did this. Is it the same with you?'

Her other finger flicked the opposite nipple and it was suddenly harder to concentrate on the yawning desolation inside him.

'If we have only now, Nicholas, we should use it wisely.'

There was a tone in her voice he had never heard there before, the tone of a courtesan, perhaps, who knew that even a moment of pleasure took care of every other doubt.

'Wisely?'

Her hand trailed downwards and she cradled his growing hardness between her fingers.

'You are ready and so am I.'

'For an untutored lover, Eleanor, you are surprisingly bold.'

'When you have society's very best teacher, is there any wonder to it?'

He laughed then and the sadness was pushed back further, quick desire left in its place.

'This time let me show you another way of loving.' He removed the quilt and the blanket and stood her before him, kneeling in front of her and parting her thighs, pleased as the skin he could see rose up into goosebumps of delight.

She could not believe such a thing was possible, his lips against her femininity and his tongue penetrating the place between her legs.

She'd wanted to give him comfort and instead... Every thought flew from her mind as other feelings began to build and her hands moved down to hold him there.

'Don't stop.' Her voice was harsh as she opened to him further. 'Don't ever stop.'

She was wicked and wanton and shameless as she

called his name and rose again over the top of pleasure and into the realms of the gods Eros and Aphrodite, their voices calling only for her.

When it was finished he stood, his mouth coming over her own and she tasted herself on his tongue and liked it. Musky. Salty. Sweet. All the hues of desire and wanting and needing.

'Love me, Nicholas. Love me for ever.'

'I do, Eleanor. And I will.'

She was dressed when he awoke next and she insisted on going home alone before the dawn broke properly and London awoke into a new day.

'Lucy will know I am missing if I stay and I don't want her to think...'

'Her mother has spent the night loving her father?' His question broke over her words, but there was a warm note of teasing in his voice. 'Meet me again to-night. Here.'

When she nodded it was as if everything in his world was right and he kissed her, softly this time and with intent.

'Don't come down with me, Nicholas. Let me re-member you here, warm from sleep and naked.'

Without his clothes on he could do nothing but watch her open the door.

'You asked for the Westmoor carriage to come back for you at this hour?'

'I did.'

He smiled because the arrangement was so much like her, unusual and different.

'Tell your brother I will call on him at one o'clock in the afternoon.'

She nodded and then she was gone.

The note came to the Bromley town house at nine-thirty in the morning and was delivered by Browne.

'This came especially by one of the Duke of Westmoor's servants, my lord. The message accompanying it stressed the fact that the Duke thought it might be important and you were to be made aware of it immediately.'

'Thank you.'

When Nicholas looked at the writing on the missive he knew a momentary failing of hope. The same hand as the spymaster in the docklands. A new lead. Another pressing difficulty.

Meet me at noon. I have some new information that will interest you. Come alone.

The game had begun again then, he thought. It was just as it always had been in the Americas. Let your guard down for a moment and the demons would pounce.

They had in Boston and in Philadelphia and in Richmond. They had here in London, too, after the New Year's dinner at Jacob's when his carriage had been attacked.

Had someone been watching the house? Could they have seen Eleanor leave? Had they been observing him as he had visited Gunter's and Lackington's and the

Bullock's Museum with her at his side, laughing, listening.

Could they learn about Lucy, too? An innocent five-year-old child whose only crime was that she was his daughter.

The world began to spin and Nick sat down, trying with all his might to remember what had happened after he had been hit on the head in the alley behind Vitium et Virtus for any clue that might aid him. He'd already ruled out his uncle's involvement, but having his full memory return was of utmost importance to Nick. If he could remember this part of his past then it might unlock other memories.

Two men had been waiting, crouched in the bushes just in the place his ring was found. They'd said something of collecting a gambling debt, he remembered that, as they had bashed him across his head. He had gone down heavily before getting up again to try to fight his way out of it. But the dizziness had been all consuming and although he managed a few more punches it had not been long until those who wanted him hurt had got the upper hand.

He remembered the moment he had twisted his ring off and thrown it into the bushes, a slow motioned arc that was then cut short by another heavy thud of wood over his head.

Then all he knew was water and running and the shout of voices, the dark of night and a boat turning on an outward tide, a gangplank, a ship's captain who took him to a small dank cabin and left him there.

All these thoughts turned in the chaos.

He had run himself, away from a life he could no longer fathom, reasoning that safety lay in the need for flight.

Instinctive. Elemental. Spontaneous.

The deep chasm of his life flowed in again, the danger, the shadows, the people who had been hurt in the Americas only because they knew him.

The ringmaster was already there this time even as some church bells chimed twelve. There were two ales on the table and beside him a thin dark man sat.

'Tell him,' the older man instructed the stranger as Nick also took his seat. 'Tell him what you told me and don't you leave nothing out, mind.'

The man paled and cleared his throat, his voice shaky and nervous as he started into the tale. 'It is said that there is a new mark out on Viscount Bromley and the bagging of the prize is rich. A hundred pound for those who can take him.'

Nicholas's blood had frozen at his name, but in company such as this it did not pay to give too much away.

'He is a toff. He was the one who they had followed to America, only this time he's here in London and there is no need to cross the ocean to kill him.'

'Who gave the orders?'

'The secret man. No one has seen him, but the gold he deals with is real.'

'And why are you telling me this?' Nicholas stressed the personal pronoun with a flourish.

''Cos it is said that your pay is almost as good and a lot less dangerous, guv. My wife insists that I have to abide by the law from now on if I am to be any use to her, but if I can pick up a bob here or there on the way, well, whose to know the difference?'

'Have you heard anything of a plan?'

'It's a snatch from what I hear, at night. Maybe at his town house or the place of his lovebird.'

'Lovebird?'

'That was mentioned in the note. A woman who is a lady.'

Nicholas schooled his fury and his absolute and utter shock. All he showed was the interest a thief-taker might, distant and unattached as he dug into his pocket and handed over twenty pieces of gold.

He did not hedge his bets this time. No, this time he revealed his hand in all its rich glory. Let there be no question as to whether or not he would reward well for more information along the same lines.

The ringmaster gathered the coins, allowing the thin man one third of the pieces and himself the rest. The art of intelligence was never cheap or easy, every pimp knew that.

'Find me a name and you will be able to leave London and buy land for yourself on the reward. I promise it.'

Both men now looked at him, their jaws slack and their eyes wide, and it was he who left the room first this time, the tavern-keeper tipping his head to him as he left.

He could not visit Eleanor again. He could not be seen with her. He had to stay his distance to keep her and their daughter safe, whatever the cost.

The well-spoken lord with the gold was watching him. Watching them. Only in cunning could he outwit the fellow, but he had to start his campaign right now. This minute.

The gall stuck in his throat as he understood exactly what he must do.

Three hours after Nicholas was supposed to have been there he sent a note. Even her brother looked worried at the missive.

'If Nick is hurt, it will serve him right for not asking any of us to help him.'

But the world had begun to fade for Eleanor, the tunnel of light darkening as she read the words, scrawled in his upright hand with black ink on white paper.

I am sorry. I can't. Forgive me.

It was happening again, only this time he was doing it himself, without excuse.

She tried to grab at the chair beside her but the world had shrunk and with only the barest of sighs she sank down into the oblivion that was claiming her.

She came awake with both Jacob and Rose kneeling around her, their faces full of shock and disbelief.

'If this means what I think it does, I am going to damned well knock Bartlett's head right off his shoulders.' Her brother's voice was harsh and Rose was trying to calm him, but her other hand was shaking as she sought Eleanor's.

'There must be a mistake.'

'No mistake. I know Nick's writing and it is his hand.' Jacob roared this out.

'Did you have an argument?' Her sister-in-law's words were whispered, almost unhearable.

'An argument?' Eleanor could not understand what she meant.

'For Viscount Bromley to break it off like this and after you returned in the early hours this morning?'

Shaking her head, Eleanor swallowed, a retch of sickness threatening at the back of her throat.

She could not believe it. She had let herself trust Nicholas Bartlett only to be abandoned summarily and completely and left to deal with the consequences all over again.

My God, how foolish could she be? How gullible? How very duped?

And yet even now, lying here with the smelling salts under her nose and sweat upon her brow, she could not understand how it was all a lie. And that was the worst of it. Her belief in him. Her never-ending absolution, the mercy of the damned.

She felt both broken and repaired even as she thought it, her own heart hardening around the softness she had admitted to him, relegating it to a lesser place, resolve filling in around the cracks.

It was over this time. She would never trust him again and she was only glad he had not become better acquainted with Lucy and that the secret between them would not now impact on the very happiness of their daughter.

'Don't hurt him, Jacob.' She took his hand and held it close. 'You have to promise me you will not hurt him.'

Much later she crept into the room of her sleeping child and sat on the chair beside the bed, simply watching her breathe. They had been on their own for years and survived, just the two of them. They had not needed another to make their lives whole and good and they most certainly did not need Nicholas's interference confusing matters.

They would survive.

As she pulled the blankets back into place over the sleeping form, Lucy's eyes opened, looking straight at her in that particular place that lies between sleep and wakefulness.

'I love you, Mama, for ever and ever.'

'Till a million years,' Eleanor said back in the way they had done ever since she could recall.

'And then one more,' Lucy returned, the smile on her face fading as her eyes closed.

Always one more, Eleanor thought. Eternity and one more. One more chance. One more night in his bed. One more betrayal. The tears that she had been holding on to all evening fell then in wet runnels down her cheeks and she simply sat in the light of the banked fire and did nothing at all to stop them.

Chapter Fifteen

Rose came in as Eleanor was eating lunch the next day and she was bristling with news that she wanted to share.

'Oliver is to be married tomorrow afternoon to Cecilia Lockhart at Vitium et Virtus. The ceremony will be performed under a special licence and we are all invited.'

'All?'

'Jacob and I. Frederick and Georgiana. Nicholas Bartlett and you. Jacob has promised to behave himself, but I am not certain what may happen when he sees Nicholas.'

Eleanor's heart sank. 'No. I won't go. Not yet.' The words fell out in a whisper.

'And you think that is wise?'

'Pardon?'

'To refuse to attend when the people you hurt by such an absence had nothing at all to do with any of it? Cecilia specifically asked for you to be there.'

'I barely know her.'

'She likes you. She admires your fortitude. She has told me this over and over again. The wedding is a small one and if you do not come people might also wonder why and any gossip can be damaging.'

'I cannot see him, Rose. I just cannot.'

'There are always two sides to every story, Eleanor. What if Nicholas Bartlett is scared of commitment because he is running from something we cannot even begin to comprehend? There are so many questions about Lord Bromley. His disappearance. His scars. His hurt and his danger.'

Eleanor shook her head. 'But he will not let me help him, Rose. I get closer and then he moves away.'

'Which is exactly what happened between Jacob and I. Should I have just given up on your brother when I was let go from the household? Should I have left my heart there at his feet to never see him again and gone to hide in shame and sadness all on a mistake? If I had, where would I be now?'

Eleanor smiled, for she could see exactly where Rose was going with this.

'You think I should fight for him?'

'I do. Because a man who is worth such emotion is also the one who could keep your broken heart safe.'

'And if it does not work out?'

'Then you will have done what you could and will have no regrets whatsoever. It's a tiny wedding. The only guests there are our friends. It will be the easiest place to see Nicholas Bartlett again with all the celebrations going on about you.'

'If I agree, I need to be able to leave when I want to. I am not staying if...'

She did not go on and was glad when Rose nodded at her condition.

She saw him the first moment she came into the main room of the club. He was standing with Frederick Challenger and Oliver Gregory in one corner, dressed in dark blue and beige, the tan of his face made deeper by the whiteness of his neckcloth.

The last time she had seen him he had been naked in bed, flushed by the exertion of sex. Almost as if he could hear her thoughts he looked up, eyes unreadable and a new stiffness in the set of his shoulders and head.

Her brother beside her swore underneath his breath and she understood at that moment this occasion was every bit as difficult for him as it was for her. The undercurrents of friendship, betrayal and enforced joviality hung over Jacob's face as she stole a glance at him, the sort of emotions that were probably as clearly visible on her own.

Cecilia was laughing on the other side of the room with Georgiana Challenger and as they went over to join them she saw Jacob carry on stiffly towards the men.

She felt like the bad apple who had brought the rot into a barrel, distance amongst good friends, uncertainty to a group who had managed thus far to triumph over every adversity sent their way.

Nicholas had not even once caught her glance and her brother's stance was sure to be noticed by Frederick and Oliver.

Shaking her head at self-blame, she refused to harbour such nonsense. It was not she after all who had taken what was offered and thrown it all away.

'Thank you for being here, Eleanor.' Cecilia took her hand and held it. 'I only wanted a very small wedding, but I was adamant that it should include women who might be to me like Jacob, Fred and Nicholas have been to Oliver and I have always admired the way you have lived your life exactly in the way you might want it.'

Such words were so unexpectedly sweet, Eleanor simply nodded. Cecilia Lockhart had had her detractors, but she had not ever let them sway them from her cause. Her life had not always been easy, either, for the gossip was rife when any beautiful and mysterious newcomer graced the hallowed halls of the *ton*.

'I am very honoured to be asked today, Cecilia. Oliver has been a fixture in the life of the Huntingdons for a long time now.'

The compliment, however, did make her braver and she was glad for the light pink gown she had donned which suited both her figure and her colouring and was one of her favourite dresses. Her hair had been fashioned with only the minimum of fuss and, in an embroidered half-cape to keep out the cold, she knew she looked her best which was important to her today.

A woman with a thousand other pathways to choose. Boudica, the warrior of the Iceni tribe, Ethelfleda, Queen of Mercia, or Gwenllian Gruffydd of Wales. Strength filled Eleanor where doubt had otherwise lingered and she lifted her chin. The power of womanhood could shine as brightly in adversity as it ever did in triumph.

As Frederick called for them all to gather closer and a minister she had not noticed before took his place, she made her way to the large windows at one end of the room. A bower of paper roses had been placed there with streams of cream ribbon and green holly. Appropriate and beautiful for a New Year wedding in a venue that had been important to both Cecilia and Oliver.

Of a sudden her own worries were pushed aside and she felt the delight of a couple who were well suited and about to be joined in holy matrimony.

Nicholas was the best man. This fact surprised her as he came to stand next to Oliver, a ring box in hand. Frederick and Jacob were right next to him, a group of four men who had been close friends since childhood. Each had a sprig of winter jasmine in their lapel and there was a large vase of the same perfumed flower on a table behind the bower. Jacob still looked out of sorts, but less so than he had done on first entering the club. Perhaps he had had a word with Nicholas? She hoped so.

'We are gathered here today for the marriage of…'

The words of the minister sounded out over silence and it was then that Nicholas Bartlett truly looked at her, his velvet brown eyes locking into her own with a sort of pained desperation.

Shock tore down Eleanor's spine, for everything she could see on his face was the exact opposite of the words that had been in the note.

She could not take her eyes from his and for a good ten seconds they looked into each other's souls and then away. Her heart was beating so fast and hard she felt slightly sick.

Disorientated. Dizzy. Gritting her teeth together, she concentrated on the wedding.

Cecilia looked radiant and Oliver looked… She could not quite describe how he looked. He was a very handsome man who had set the *ton* on fire with his charm and grace, but he had never seemed quite relaxed. Today he did, his smile wide and his eyes bright with love. Their hands were joined tightly together, the white of his knuckles easily seen from where she stood.

They were perfect.

And, God, she wanted that for herself, the melding of one person to the other so that the whole was better than the two halves.

Swallowing twice, she tried to catch on to a failing fortitude. She had known such perfection as she had lain in the heat of Nicholas's bed and loved him.

Her cheeks burned as the minister glanced her way and then the rings were exchanged, Cecilia's a small white-gold circle with diamonds and Oliver's a wider plain gold band.

Nicholas looked thankful that this part of the service was over. Would he make a speech?

She heard Rose sigh beside her and looked at her sister-in-law who was dabbing her brimming eyes.

'Weddings always make me cry,' she explained. 'It's the hope in them, I think, and the promise.'

Her own lack of true participation made her feel guilty. She had been so preoccupied with seeing what Nicholas looked like up there that she had hardly spared a thought for either the bride or the groom. When she was called up to the front to sign the marriage papers as a witness she was shocked for she would have to stand right next to Nicholas Bartlett and look him in the eye whilst acting as if she was neither devastated nor heartbroken.

The pretence of it was almost too much to bear.

Rose's elbow came against her, urging movement, and smiling, even though it was the last thing she wished to do, she stepped forward.

Nicholas Henry Stewart Bartlett. He was left handed. She had not known that, but he used his damaged arm to sign his name, with the bandage just visible under the dark cuff of his jacket.

And when he had finished he turned and gave her the pen, his fingers touching hers at the transfer.

'You need to place your name beneath mine.' Today the accent of the Americas could be heard squarely in his words. A further separation. Another distance.

With care she bent to add her name to the document, although all she could concentrate on was the feel of him at her side.

He had never said 'I love you' when she had been in his bed at the Bromley town house. In the throes of desire and lust he had promised her a lot less than she had promised him and yet he had not been dishonest. He had asked for her consent and she had given it. But he had never spoken of his love.

Now as he stood next to her speaking with Jacob and Frederick and with six inches between them, all she wanted to do was to move closer and touch him.

* * *

Eleanor had barely looked at him save for one glance just before the ceremony began. She was smiling at Cecilia now, a smile that gave the impression that every single thing in her world was exactly as she would want it, his defection a trifling thing, a small inconvenience only.

Eleanor's middle name was Christine. Like her mother's. Like their daughter's.

Eleanor Christine Elise Huntingdon. He consigned her full name to memory.

He was glad that Jacob and Frederick and Oliver were here. It made the day safer somehow with them around. Eleanor would also accompany her brother and sister-in-law home afterwards. A further protection. For the next twelve hours he would not need to worry about her at all.

The thought of that made him smile and as he turned he caught her eye. She smiled back. And the world simply stopped. Just her and him in a room full of winter sunlight and flowers.

The ache of sorrow inside him nearly brought him to his knees, there in the blue salon of Vitium et Virtus, for after the joy of Oliver's happiness his own seemed compromised beyond recognition and there was nothing now that he could do to make it different if she was to stay safe.

I will always love you.

God, had he just said that? Relief filled him when he realised the words were in his head, although Jacob was looking at him oddly, a sort of shared understanding in his eyes that made no sense whatsoever.

He was pleased when Frederick called him away to help with the wine that had to be brought up from below because it allowed him an excuse to leave her side and regain his sense.

Once in the cellar Frederick turned on him. 'What the hell are you doing, Nick? Eleanor looks as though you have just stabbed her through the very heart and Jacob has all the appearance of a man who wants to kill you.'

'My memory is back, Fred, and Eleanor Huntingdon and I were close once.'

'How close is close?'

'We were together just before I disappeared.'

'God,' he said as his hand slid through his hair, sweeping it back. Such blasphemy in a man usually so very articulate worried Nick further.

'And now? It's Oliver's wedding, for God's sake. Even he is starting to realise that things are not quite right.'

'Someone wants to do her harm, Frederick, because of me.'

His friend put down the bottles he had gathered and took in a deep breath. 'Another note?'

He shook his head. 'A meeting this time. The informant told me Eleanor was being watched.'

'So you think to put distance between you. To fool the one who wants to harm you?'

'If it looks as though I am interested in others I think he will only target me. With my history...'

Fred swore again and took the cork from a bottle of wine before finding two glasses and handing him one. 'I think we need this more than anyone above does.'

There was silence for a moment before Nick began to speak.

'I'm the father of her child, Fred. We slept together again two nights ago and the next day I discovered that she was a target, too, because of it. If anything happens to her...' He could not go on.

'You love her? My God, you do.' A smile covered his friend's face, broad and surprised. 'You never do things by half, Nick, I had forgotten that about you. You couldn't just tell her?'

'That someone still wants to kill me and that if she's in the way she will be hurt, too? She'd never let me out of her sight.'

'I see your point, for Georgiana would be exactly the same. Jacob has to know, though, so that he can make sure Eleanor stays safe when in his care.'

'You're right.'

'And Oliver is part of it, too.'

'Tell them today for me after I have left, Fred, when you think the time is right.'

'And what will you do?'

'Keep looking for some clue as to who it is who hates me so much and then deal with him.'

Nicholas raised his glass, calling the small crowd before him to order, and Eleanor turned to listen. She had not spoken to him again after the signing of their names as witnesses, but instead looked about the room, seeing the club through the eyes of someone who had never been in this type of place before.

She'd been astonished by the large array of books on the shelves and if the statues and pictures were more than racy, then that, too, added to the character.

Nicholas looked at home here, she thought, the stuffy strictures of the *ton* disappearing completely and there was a freedom inherent in the place that was beguiling.

Cecilia and Oliver were now standing next to him and he smiled at each of them before beginning to speak.

'I've had no true experience with marriage and what it entails, but it seems that love conquers all difficulties and any problems. It moves people on from one place to a better one where together they can solve life's problems. It makes them stronger, more whole, more accepting, bolder. So here's to adventure and courage and to faith in the future. Here's to Cecilia and Oliver Gregory. To a long life together and a happy one.'

Faith in the future? He'd used those same words before they had slept together and look where they had got her. The wine tasted like dry vinegar in her mouth as she raised her glass along with the others. Another few moments and she would be able to slip away from such lies and go home to Lucy. Tomorrow she would make her preparations for returning to Millbrook. Away from Nicholas. Away from heartbreak.

'They look so good together, don't they?' Rose's words came through a tunnel and she nodded. 'Bromley, however, looks like a brick has hit him, though.

He keeps glancing your way when he is sure you are not looking.'

'Guilt, I suppose.' She ground the words out quietly even as Rose laughed.

'His words on marriage are surprising for a man so frightened of commitment. Your brother looks less angered by him, too. I wonder if they have spoken?'

Without giving a reply, Eleanor tipped up the glass with the rest of her wine and finished the lot.

Chapter Sixteen

He needed to be seen. He needed to be available. He needed to wait until they pounced and then… He would deal with them as easily as he had the others in the Americas who had threatened him.

He was no longer the man that they thought him and he would use this to his advantage.

Every light was on in his town house and he had given most of the servants the night off. To set the scene and make certain that whoever watched the house was also made aware of the chance to strike.

Yesterday he had squired a dozen ladies along the pathways of Hyde Park, making sure to appear animated and entertained. Last night he had done the same at the Fielders' party, chatting to this woman and then that one, giving an impression of being most available and distinctly single. The effort of it all had exhausted him. Even this morning in town he had stopped to speak with the small groups of acquaintances he met, garnering invite after invite to all the celebrations of the *ton*.

He had not caught any sight at all of Eleanor Huntingdon and for that he was glad. Priming his duelling pistol, he slipped his knife down into the leather holder of his boot and took in a breath.

The soft London Lord was long gone. He had killed before and would do again to protect his own. It was both simple and sad because to admit to being such a menace without missing a heartbeat put him in a place that was neither honourable nor decent.

After this he could not go back and live as he had once imagined he might. If he ended a man's life here tonight, he would be outcast for ever. But Eleanor and Lucy would be safe. That thought overrode every other one.

A movement on the street caught his attention and then Frederick Challenger was there at his door, dressed in black from head to foot. He looked nothing like the second son of an earl and all of the soldier.

'I have come to help you, Nick.' His eyes took in the gun on the table primed and ready. 'It will be here?'

'From what I suspect, yes.'

Another noise out at the front garnered their attention to the doorway, the knock surprising them. This time it was Oliver, dressed in the same sort of fashion as Frederick.

'You shouldn't be here. You have just been married.'

'Let's sort this out first, Nick. It would be hard to enjoy being away on a bridal tour knowing you were battling for your life in London and Cecilia agrees with me. Jake is out the front, too, watching for any movement.'

Nicholas could only stare at Oliver and Frederick in wonder. He was no longer alone. It wasn't just he who had to deal with this peril now. There was a chance for him to still survive and live.

An hour later Jacob came inside, too, though he barely looked at Nick, the tension between them palpable.

'Eleanor is in danger because of me, Jake, it's why I sent the note. I need to see her safe. If she is hurt in any way at all…' He didn't continue.

'You could not tell her of your plan?'

'Would you have told Rose?'

'So you thought to take this on alone without telling any of us a word about it? Would you be there if we were in trouble, Nick?'

'Of course.'

'Then I rest my case. But I warn you, at the end of all this, if you don't damned well marry my sister I will kill you myself.'

'Agreed.'

'No more lies, Nick, for it's killing us all. This time we face it together and end it.'

By the morning they doubted anyone at all was coming. Perhaps they had been warned off by the appearance of the others or perhaps the heavy rain had persuaded them to wait for another night, a better chance.

Whatever the reason they locked the front door and drew the curtains, stoking the fire into a life it had not enjoyed before and sitting down near it to feel the warmth.

'This reminds me of the time the Night Watch came

to the club to question us about that girl they had found by the river who had been killed. We had a roaring fire when they knocked and it was a filthy night which was odd for the start of September.'

Oliver said this as he picked at the bread, cheese and pickles Nicholas had had brought up from the kitchens. It was the first Nicholas had heard of the murder and he wondered out aloud just why the Watch would come to Vitium et Virtus to question its owners.

'The girl was a maid who had worked for us. She disappeared a few weeks after she quit the job and moved in with a new lover.'

'Did the lover kill her?' Nick's attention was caught by the story.

'No, he was absolved because he had been drinking at a tavern close by and her body was found miles away down by the Isle of Dogs.'

Jacob continued with the recount now. 'You might have known the girl, Nick, for it was the month after you disappeared that this all happened. She was slight and dark and from the country. Cornwall, I think. Sally was her name. The strange thing was the way she had been murdered. There were rows of distinct cuts all over her body, cuts that were precisely placed in every sensual zone. She'd bled to death, it was determined, and the constables named it as a sexual crime. They wondered if there was anyone at Vitium et Virtus who might have known her well enough to want her dead, though they never caught the perpetrator.'

'My God.' Nicholas stood now, his whole body

shocked by such a revelation. 'I know who did it. It was Bowles who killed her.'

'Nash Bowles?' The others looked at him as though he had just lost his mind.

'I had found him doing exactly the same thing to exactly the same girl a week before I lost my memory. He said he had paid her handsomely for such a service even as I threw him out of the club by the scruff of his neck. He had a little knife in his hand and there was a look on his face that was…deranged is the closest I can come to naming it. I didn't have the time to tell you all of it before I was taken.'

No one spoke for a second as they tried to understand the sense of it all.

'It's why he wants you dead, then. This secret.' Oliver said this, the truth of his words undeniable. 'He figured out you could put it together like you just have and identify him. When you arrived home here again every part of his life was compromised.'

'It was only a matter of time and he knew it. That is why he had your carriage attacked.' Jacob stood and hit his hand hard against the mantel. 'The bastard. I never liked him. Where the hell does he live now?'

'We'd have to go to the club and get the files,' Fred said. 'I heard he had moved earlier last year, but he was still somewhere here in the city.'

Within a second they were all ready to leave, jackets and hats on and each of them bristling with anger.

Eleanor needed to get out even for an hour, her chamber squeezing in on her with all its memories and spilled tears. Lucy was tired, too, a broken night's sleep leaving her irritable. Jacob had not come home at all, she found that out as she'd met Rose at breakfast, her face tense and strained by the fact.

'Where did he go?' Eleanor asked the question, a growing alarm building.

'He just said out. When I questioned him he told me to go to sleep and he would be back by dawn. He wasn't.'

'My God, if this has anything at all to do with Nicholas...'

'I would say it has everything to do with him, Ellie. The note. Your sadness. Jacob's friendship with a man who has betrayed you. He was gone most of the afternoon yesterday, too.'

'I will visit Nicholas Bartlett.'

'Do you think that wise?'

'I don't know any more but to just sit here...?'

'Take Lucy for a walk in the park first to get rid of some of your energy. After that either Jacob will be home and be able to tell you the news himself or you can go to Bartlett, but in a better frame of mind.'

The plan sounded like a good one and Ellie went upstairs to find her warm cloak hat and gloves before calling for her daughter to do exactly the same.

Half an hour later she did feel better. The rain had held off and the wind had lessened and although she was cold she was also less wound up.

'Will we go home soon, Mama? Back to Millbrook House?'

'I am not certain, sweetheart. There are a few things here in London still left for me to do.'

'Is Papa one of those things?'

She stopped and looked at her daughter. 'Why do you ask that, Lucy?'

'Because you have seemed sad and lonely and you said I would see Papa soon. I wish I could.' Lucy was holding her hand as they walked to head back to their carriage when another conveyance drew up closely beside them.

'Get in,' the man inside said as the door opened and her heart hit the bottom of her stomach in a horrible jolt of surprise. She pushed Lucy behind her, fearing that the gun Nash Bowles held in his hand was about to go off.

'I will shoot twice if you do not get in, Lady Eleanor, for I have absolutely nothing left to lose. I will allow you only the one warning.'

The new address of Nash Bowles proved more elusive to find than they hoped it would be.

'I know he left town for a while a few months back for he got in trouble with a gambling debt and went into hiding somewhere in the English countryside. But when he returned, I thought we had some sort of an address for him.' Frederick was now crouched at a cupboard full of paper and rifling through it.

'Keep looking. It must be here somewhere.' Jacob emptied another drawer on the desk and was sorting through the sheets of information carefully when a messenger arrived.

Frederick took it from the man it had been sent with and handed it over.

'It's for you, Nick.'

The missive was sealed by dark scented wax and tied with two strands of equally dark ribbon. Not recognising the handwriting, Nicholas tore it open and read the message inside.

If you want to see your lover and her daughter again, meet me on the north-west corner of Hampstead Heath before the hour is up. Come alone.

Fury consumed him, the red-hot waves of hatred that ran through him making his whole body shake.

'He has Eleanor and Lucy. He's taken her to Hampstead Heath.'

'Who has her?' Oliver asked this.

'Bowles. The note's from him.' Nick handed it across to Jacob, who swore roundly, and he could barely breathe as he strode to the door, leaving the note there in the unbelieving hands of his friends.

'Wait, Nick, we will come, too.'

But the violence and savagery had taken over completely now and he was a man who only wanted his guns in hand and a horse beneath him, the red-hot waves of intensity fuelling the savage need for vengeance.

He hailed a passing cabriole and made for the Heath, leaving the others there in his wake to do as they wished.

He would kill Nash Bowles if the man had even touched one hair on either Eleanor's or Lucy's head. If he had done more, it would be a slow death and no clemency in it. He did not have a moment to waste.

If Bowles used his little knife on an inch of her skin... He pushed that thought aside and concentrated instead on calming himself for what he needed to do to deal with one such as Bowles.

She knew Nicholas would come as soon as she sat in the carriage that was now parked on the edge of Hampstead Heath. Bowles had exited the conveyance a few moments ago, striding into the undergrowth behind them and telling her to stay absolutely still and quiet.

Lucy was finally speaking again and for that one small normality Eleanor was eternally grateful. Her daughter had spent the entire trip from Hyde Park to Hampstead Heath cowering behind her skirts and crying, her shaking body the one moving point in an otherwise still carriage.

Nash Bowles was demented, she was sure of it, his eyes unfocused and wide. He hadn't spoken much, but he had written a note and given it to a messenger as they had pulled over at the side of the road in the city. A ransom demand, perhaps? When Nicholas received it he would be furious and he would come for them.

'Your papa will be here soon, my darling, to take us home.'

That information made her daughter stop sniffling as nothing else would.

'My papa is coming...?' Light shone from eyes that looked exactly the colour of Nicholas's.

'He is, sweetheart. He will be collecting his things and coming to get us.'

'Things?'

'His present for you.' She felt in the pocket of her skirt for the small outline of the box from Rundells. She had not wanted to give Lucy the necklace after what had happened, but now she used it as a carrot on the end of a long and difficult stick.

'Wait until you see it, for I know you will love it, darling. Let us think of all the lovely things it could possibly be.'

'A pony?' her daughter guessed. 'A princess. A new baby doll for the others I have. I need a mummy doll with twins next time.'

Outside Eleanor could see Bowles now standing beside a tree about twenty yards away. He had warned her not to pull the curtain in the carriage and not to move away from his sight in any way. If she tricked him, he had threatened to begin shooting and she would not risk a stray bullet with her daughter so close.

Make things normal, her mind shouted. Make things relatable to the everyday in Lucy's life. Avoid conflict and anger and excess. Smile. She lifted her lips into a dreadful parody of humour, feeling the stretch of her cheeks even as she wanted to scream.

Her calm manner seemed to finally be pacifying Lucy for she even yawned in tiredness and asked when they might be able to go home.

A good half an hour had passed since Bowles had sent Nicholas his note.

'He has an hour,' Bowles had said in a voice that

hinted of darker things that might happen if the Viscount did not materialise.

She had thought to deny knowing Nicholas that well, but the day she had met Bowles in the park when buying chestnuts had probably done away with that lie. Instead she stayed very quiet, trying not to annoy him in any shape or form and watching for a chance to escape.

Nicholas suddenly appeared across the grass to one side of the conveyance and Eleanor moved in front of her daughter so that she would not notice the proceedings outside.

He looked furious and dangerous, but it was the menacing stillness of him that she noticed the most. Here was a man who had cheated death a number of times and instead of panicking he looked calm and certain. She searched his hands for weapons, but could not see any.

Nash Bowles met him as he came out of the shadows, a pistol in hand and a sneer across his face.

'Put the gun down.' Nicholas's voice came across the wind. 'Put the gun down and we will talk.'

Eleanor could see his glance coming over to the carriage and he swallowed as he saw her face in the window.

'There is nothing at all to be gained here by violence, Bowles.'

The other laughed. 'In that you are wrong, Bartlett, for there is everything to be won in my case and everything to be lost in yours.'

'Let the woman and child go and deal with me. They have nothing at all to do with what is between us.'

The answer back was given with venom. 'With the Duke's sister here you will do exactly as I ask and if you don't...' He turned then and pointed the pistol straight at the carriage and all Eleanor could do was to wrap her body around her daughter in an effort to protect her.

'No.' Nick felt the tightness in his throat as he said the word, but he did not shout it. The man was crazy enough in his threats without adding any pressure to it. 'Shoot me, Bowles. I am the one you want. I am the one you had followed to the Americas, although I could never quite work out why you should do that.'

Bowles had turned back to him now, his lips tight in a sneer of fury.

'Throw down your weapon, Bromley. I know you'll have one there somewhere. Take your jacket off and your belt, too. Do it.'

Nick complied, glad at least that Bowles's attention no longer dwelt on the carriage, though he made a point to come closer. The gun he'd kept in his belt was gone, but he had a knife strapped to his ankle. Soon he would be well in range to use it.

'Let me help you, Bowles. Put down the gun and there will be all the help that you need. I promise.'

'Liar.' The gun went off and Nick felt the bullet sear along the skin of the thigh that was already scarred. He dropped to his knees and breathed hard, willing the pain at bay as he stood again. If he lost consciousness he would be no help at all to Eleanor and Lucy.

He could hear Eleanor crying now in the carriage

and prayed that she might stop. Attracting any sort of attention with a madman around was dangerous.

Bowles had another pistol in his hands now, primed and ready, the first one thrown down upon the grass, the smoke from the shot curling up into the air before him.

Nicholas cursed. He could not run at Bowles with his leg burning up in pain and he was still too far away to throw his knife with any accuracy. For the moment he thought it was better to keep him speaking.

'If you talk about what you want changed, I may be able to help.'

'Talk? Why? You never liked me, none of you did with your fancy names and your tight-knit friendship. All those years of trying to be a part of your group, of currying favour at Vitium et Virtus while you laughed behind my back. Did you think I would not know? I watched you that night you disappeared from the alley behind the club. I saw the henchman beat you over the head with the wooden baton as you fell to the ground. I followed you to the river where they threw you in and I hoped that the current would take you under, so that all breath was gone. But it didn't. When the hackney cab left you crawled out again and I saw fear there on your face where before had lain only arrogance and I laughed at the way you ran like a stray dog for the docks, the grip of hell itself wrapped around your very neck.'

'But you could not leave it there? You needed to make sure I was gone. In Boston and Philadelphia and Richmond?' Keep him talking, Nick thought, for in the distance he could see the outline of Frederick behind the trees and he knew Jacob and Oliver would be close behind.

'You had seen me, seen me with her, the foolish maid from your club, and do not pretend you fail to remember that. How was I to know she had some sort of a disease that meant the bleeding would not stop? How was that my fault? She died with your name on her lips, cursing me with all her life was worth, and I knew right then that you were a danger to me and I needed to see that you never returned to England.'

He had begun to shout louder now as he advanced upon him, the gun still in his hand but shaking, more perilous than it had been even a few seconds before.

'It's over, Bowles. Give it up. Take your punishment like a man.'

'You had everything, don't you see? You had every single thing that I never did. The friends. The women. The money. The looks. But now I will take it from you because I can.'

'Get out.' Nash Bowles shouted this to the carriage behind and when the door opened Eleanor stepped down with her hands held up, Lucy at her side. Nicholas made a point of not looking at them, all the worry and guilt wrapped about his heart.

'Very well—' Bowles's voice had become more flat now '—I will grant you one thing, Viscount Bromley. You alone can choose who I save and who I kill.'

The choice of the devil. Nicholas stood stock still and raised his hands high.

'Kill me. I am the one you want. No one knows anything about the maid from the club. Your secret dies with me.'

The agonising scream from Eleanor distracted them both and it was in this moment that Nick pounced, simply leaping at the man without any fear for himself, the gun Bowles held going off and the bullet whistling within inches from his head to slam into the wide hard bulk of the trunk of an oak.

His leg ached like hell, but he had Nash Bowles, twisting his arm up behind his back. Part of him wanted to finish the job, but he shook his head and reclaimed logic even as Frederick rushed in, grabbing the other arm as Oliver got his feet.

Jacob was with Eleanor and Lucy, his voice coming through the space between them in a soft quiet whisper. They were safe. They were safe. The words beat against Nicholas's breath in a litany, but then the tunnel of light that he'd fought off began to close around him.

Blood loss, he supposed, for he had felt this before. The rush of sound in his ears, the dizziness, the feeling that his mind was somehow disconnecting from his body and going some place entirely on its own.

Eleanor ran forward, grabbing at his hands from where he lay on the wet cold grass, the rain falling in his face.

'I...am...sorry.'

He mouthed the words rather than said them. The shaking was getting worse and he was cold, far colder than he had ever been in his life. Colder even than in the Caribou Valley in the north of Maine. It was his fault that Eleanor was here having to deal with this danger and fright, his demons clawing at the ordered and gentle world that she was a part of.

Her tears of fright washed across him, hot against all that was freezing, and he tried to lift his arm, but he could not. Then all he knew was darkness.

Chapter Seventeen

He woke to pain. He woke to memory and dreams and a half-world he could not quite decipher.

He knew he was thirsty, but he was finding it hard to speak for the shivers ran through him in a constant stream of movement. A wet warm flannel came across his brow and he closed his eyes against the feel of it.

'You are in the ducal town house, Nicholas, and you have been very sick. It is a week since the accident and we thought…' Eleanor's voice faltered and stopped.

'That… I…would…die.' Every word was difficult to get his tongue around. He felt as if he had a mouth full of cotton and so he swallowed and tried again.

'Lucy?'

'Is in her bed fast asleep and dreaming of the bravery of a father who came to save her.'

Save her? The words stuck dry in his throat. Save her from the danger he had placed them in in the first place? If he had not returned, none of this would have ever happened. He wanted to ask of Bowles, but didn't, the effort too much to muster.

'My…leg?'

'The bullet punctured an artery and you were lucky to escape with your life. Frederick had seen the same thing on the battlefields of Europe and tied his neck-cloth around the top of your leg.'

'Useful…knowing a…soldier.'

She laughed at that and the sound warmed him as nothing else could have done.

'You nearly lost your life for us, Nicholas.'

'Worth…it.'

Then he closed his eyes and slept.

Next time he awoke he felt much better, more level headed, less dizzy.

Eleanor was still there by his bed, but dressed in other clothes now and the afternoon sun was coming in through the windows. How could that be? A few moments ago it had been night time. He lay perfectly still and watched her. Her eyes were closed and the pins in her hair loosened. One curl had slipped from its mooring and settled across the line of her breasts.

She was so beautiful she simply broke his heart.

As if she felt his gaze her eyes opened. Would he ever get used to the startling shade of blueness? he wondered, only to decide that it was very unlikely.

'Hello.' Her voice was soft with sleep. 'How are you feeling?'

'Better.'

'Would you like a drink?'

He nodded and she brought a glass of lemonade to

his lips, her hand behind his neck to help him as he leaned forward.

'That is good.' The liquid was like ambrosia to his dried mouth though she did not let him have too much.

'The physician said that we were to offer this to you, but that I had to be careful about what you took.'

'Physician…?'

'He is retained by the Westmoors and has been earning his year's stipend over the past week.'

Nicholas wiggled his toes just to make sure that the leg was still there, that he had not had the thing amputated or cut into whilst he had been asleep, but everything seemed in order save the sharp ache the movement brought forth.

'You lost a lot of blood and there had been another injury in the same place which complicated things. But he says you should be able to start getting up after the next few days for the fever at least has gone.'

'Fever?'

'You burned with it for three days and nights.'

She had thought he would die as his temperature had soared. She imagined that a man could not last with such a sickness, the redness across his cheeks and his body building into rash.

She had been shocked by the scars he wore beneath his clothes for in the hard light of day they were far more extensive than she had thought them. Myriad injuries that crossed his back and his front, the worst of it being on the same thigh the bullet had passed through.

A history of violence written in flesh. She hated

Nash Bowles with even more intensity than she had before. Sometimes she wondered just who she had become.

Were another threat to stalk Nicholas here in his vulnerable state she would have had no compunction but to squeeze out the life from any assailant. She wondered where the kindly polite sister of a duke had disappeared to in the face of all that had happened.

'Where is... Bowles?'

'In jail and he will be for a very long time. Oliver and Frederick took him to the constabulary after they had seen to you. Jacob stayed here and waited with me for the doctor.'

'He is sick, I think...in the head.'

'He wished he was like you. He wanted to run Vitium et Virtus. He kept yelling that out all the way across the park even as they took him away.'

When Nicholas nodded Eleanor thought he looked tired and she stopped speaking. He had been distant since the shooting, with an edge of anger. Did he blame her in some way for endangering Lucy?

As his eyes closed she brushed away the tears that had pooled in her eyes and threatened to fall down across her cheeks.

It was later the next day when Nick felt well enough to haul himself into a sitting position and dangle his legs off the side of the bed. At the beginning his heart hammered against his temples, but then it subsided. Perhaps he would not stand just yet, he thought, looking at the thick bandage wrapped tightly about his thigh.

A small noise at the doorway alerted him to the fact that he had a visitor.

'Lucy?'

The child came further into the room. Not so close that she could not turn and run if she needed to, but closer than he held any right to expect.

'Are you better?' Her voice was tense. He could hear the vestige of fright from the incident at Hampstead Heath in what she said.

'Nearly.' His eyes went to the doll she carried and it had a sizeable bandage around its head.

'Did your doll get hurt, too?'

'Yes. By a speeding bullet. Mama says that for every three bullets that miss there is one that will find its mark.'

'I am glad it didn't find its mark with me, then.'

She smiled. 'But it did.'

'Not badly, at all,' he replied, liking how she watched him, taking him in, tossing up whether or not he was worth the fuss as a father. 'A leg is much better than a head or the chest to get hit in. Poor doll.'

At that she moved forward and set the doll down on his bed, removing the bandage deftly and retying it around a thin china leg.

'Now she is just like you and getting better. Did you know Mama cries a lot when you are not looking?'

The truth of the words had him taking in breath.

'I think she thought it was her fault that we were shot.'

'I don't think the fault was anyone's except the man with the gun.'

'Bowles. That was his name. Nasty Bowles.'

The words took him by surprise and he smiled. 'You have named him well.'

'And you are my papa. I have always wanted one. Everyone else has one and I never did.'

Again he smiled. Lucy had the same habit as her mother had of setting words down in a way that was unusual. He was glad of it.

'When you are better would you like to play dolls with me again? I could show you how to dress them, too, and feed them. I could even bring the dolls' house in here if you would want me to.'

'I would.'

At that she smiled, a full real smile that lit her eyes and brought out her dimples.

A woman then came to the door, her face furrowed with a frown. 'I have been looking everywhere for you, Lucy. I am sorry, Lord Bromley, I hope she has not been disturbing your rest.'

He watched as Lucy followed the woman out of the room and thought his daughter was every bit as beautiful as her mother.

He saw that she was wearing his locket around her neck.

Did you know Mama cries a lot when you are not looking?

Lucy's words sliced right through him. It was well past time to let her see exactly who he was and wasn't.

Eleanor came to see him just as the sun was setting. She had been in and out for small pieces of time, but always in the company of others, once with the doctor and then again with Jacob. The third time when she brought her grandmama to visit Nicholas wondered if she did not wish to be alone with him.

He could understand her reasoning. She had a daughter to see safe and so far all he seemed to have brought her was heartache and fear.

He had lived in the shadows for so long that he was now unfit to inhabit a better world, a brighter place. His presence in other good people's lives was a dark influence, a grimy dimness that invited in danger and jeopardy.

Jacob had been civil but distant after the incident in the park. As the head of the Westmoor family he could probably see the foolishness of closer relations with someone who was tainted irreparably by such chaos.

That evening Nicholas had insisted on wearing his own day clothes instead of the nightgown and he felt more like himself with each passing moment. Stronger. Less like an invalid for he knew he needed to be gone from here as soon as he was able.

Tonight Eleanor was dressed in a soft blue, the fabric picking up the colour of her eyes, but also the dark shadows beneath them.

'You look almost returned to normal?' her words more a question as she stood against the mantel, the candle there lighting up all the shades in her hair.

'The physician said that I should be able to go back to the Bromley town house tomorrow. At the end of the week I will go north to Bromworth Manor and I am not certain when I shall be back.'

'I see.' A frown lingered now and she bit her lip.

'Eleanor…'

'Nicholas…'

Their words collided and she smiled shakily before she bade him to go first.

'I cannot be with you, Eleanor. If anything were to happen to you or Lucy because of me I would never forgive myself. There is no way I can foresee the future, but if the past is anything to go by, you would be well rid of me.'

'And Lucy? You are saying she should forget her papa when she has only just found him?'

'I am saying she needs to be safe. If there are more like Bowles out there then I will need to be wary and there are many others with their own reasons for seeing me gone. When we were searching for the culprit who was threatening me your brother and I made a list at Vitium et Virtus and there was more than a small amount of names there who held grudges against me. I cannot guarantee they will not come next, with their sharpened knives and loaded guns. It's who I am, don't you see? Tainted. Ruined. Perilous.'

He held his hand out as she began to speak because now that he was started he could not seem to stop.

'It's why I left after we…made love. It's why I sent the note to tell you that I couldn't and that I was sorry but… I will provide for you both financially for ever, but I think you should not tell anyone outside of the family that Lucy is my daughter. Who knows what other perils are lurking unbidden? The world is a far more dangerous place than you realise, Eleanor. Without me there might be a chance for safety. If I stay well away from you and from Lucy the gossip will die down and people might forget.'

Her eyes were full of tears as she stepped forward. 'I love you, Nicholas, and so does Lucy.' There was no hesitation in her promise.

He shook his head, hard. 'No. You can't say that.'

She kept coming closer, one hand placed across his arm now, her fingers holding on with all that she was worth. 'I have loved you since the first moment I ever really saw you at the Vauxhall Gardens and I've loved you more and more each day since.'

He swallowed and placed his thumb across her lips to stop the words from coming.

'I can only hurt you, don't you see?'

'You can hurt me by staying away, by believing that you are this person that you are not. We belong together, you and I and Lucy, and if there are challenges in the future we can meet them.'

'Sometimes I dream of blood.' His words held a flatness and a finality that made the back of his throat thicken. But he needed to say what he was, what he had been, what he had done. 'The blood of the man whose neck I broke by the James River. Just a quick twist and he was gone into the water though his eyes watched me as he went. The blood of others I have hurt, too, in fights and in arguments, with knives and glass and wood. This is who I am, Eleanor. You must have seen the marks on me in the sickbed. In each and every one of those scars lies the ghost of fury or fear or just plain ordinary temper.'

'Or the badge of honour? The bullet you took at Hampstead was in lieu of me and Lucy. You were trying to save us, Nicholas, by offering up your own life. I could see that in your face as you tried to draw Bowles away from the carriage.'

'I should have shot him through the head when I had the chance. And I did have that chance. I had seen him through the trees when I first arrived at the Heath. It would have been so very easy to skirt around and come up behind him to take a shot at close range. Instead I left you and Lucy in danger and it could have turned out so very differently.'

'No, don't you see?' Eleanor's voice was stern. 'Instead you tried to talk Bowles out of a course of action that was impossible. Even in danger you tried to help him, tried to defuse the situation so that he might come out of it alive. You are not a killer, Nicholas, and you never have been, but you have had to fight for your life, too, and there is no shame at all in that.'

Nicholas took in a breath at her words because he heard a truth in them that was undeniable and sweet.

'You are free now to live how you want. There is no one else ready to spring out and hurt you. Please, Nicholas, please believe it is possible.'

She could see the terror in his eyes, but she could also see the beginnings of something else. Hope, if she might name it, and faith.

With his limp and his scars and his left arm still in a bandage, with all the old hurts beneath his clothes and a belief inside himself that he was damaged and dangerous and unknowable, Nicholas still looked beautiful to her. More than that, though, he was beginning to look as if he was realising it, too. Realising that she knew the worst about him and was still here, that no matter what he threw at her she would not be shifted in her belief in him and that the words she had given him, words of love, could even possibly be true.

'You would want me like this, Eleanor? After Hampstead Heath and being in all that danger? After knowing who I am? Who I truly was?'

'I want you for ever. I want to grow old with you and have more children with you and know what it is like to have years and years in each other's company. That is what I want.'

She moved closer, only the smallest distance separating their bodies from what was and what could be.

'If you love me, Nicholas, you will want that, too.'

Nicholas swore and his dam suddenly broke, she could see it in his eyes and on his face and in the way his body enveloped her own, his arms about her, drawing her in, his breath in her hair as he held her against the heavy beat of his heart. 'I love you, Eleanor, but I cannot believe I deserve you.'

'How much do you love me?' She was smiling now, the joy in him chasing away the shadows.

'With every fibre of my body, with every thought in my mind. With my heart and my breath and my soul I love you, sweetheart. And more.'

'Take me to bed again at your town house. I promise I will be gentle with all your wounds.'

When he laughed she heard the sound of freedom and she knew that a healing had begun.

'Perhaps we should be married first?'

She smiled at his question and nodded.

'Is your brother home tonight?'

'Yes. He is in his library.'

'Stay here, then. I won't be long at all. Don't move.'

He got down the stairs on the wings of elation for this time everything would be done in the correct order. This time he would not fail Eleanor as he had before. This time he wanted everything to be exactly as it should be.

Jacob was reading in his old leather armchair by the fire.

'Nicholas.'

The restraint that had been a part of their relationship since he had sent the note separating himself from Eleanor could be easily heard in his name.

'I need to ask you something, Jacob, but I also need to tell you things that you might not wish to know.'

Jacob stood and crossed to pour them both a drink, holding a glass out to Nick after he had done so and pulling another chair closer to the fire, gesturing for him to sit.

When he did so he felt at odds as to where to begin, but was pleased as the brandy fortified his resolve.

'I love your sister, Jake, and I want to marry her. I want to care for her and protect her and Lucy. I want to make certain that they are always safe.'

'And the part I might not wish to know?'

'I have killed a man, and done things in the Americas

and here that I have no reason to be proud of. Bowles perhaps was a part of that, too, along with an arrogance and recklessness that came back to haunt me.'

'You have always been the most dissolute of the four of us, Nicholas, but then I always knew, too, that you had a good heart. I still do know that. Rose says you are like a plant, untended and wild, and that Eleanor with all her gardening skills will make certain that you grow in a way that is perfect.'

'I like your wife, Jake.'

'I like her, too.'

'Will you give your blessing on our marriage? I haven't asked your sister yet because this time I need to do things properly and I know Eleanor would like her family's support.'

Jacob stood as Nicholas did.

'More than a blessing, Nick. I want to be your best man. But right now you had better let me help you back upstairs to bed for you look as though you might keel over.'

It was late and the fire in the hearth was well banked.

They had been married for six hours and the ring on Eleanor's finger shone in the light of the flame, where two unmatched diamonds sat in a clasp of rose gold.

'It is the most beautiful piece of jewellery I have ever seen, my love,' she whispered, her cheeks flushed from their recent lovemaking and desire.

'The large one is for you and the smaller one is for Lucy. The two jewels of my heart.'

They were lying on his patched quilt in front of the

fire, as naked as the day they were born. The bandage on his leg had been removed yesterday and she traced the thick red line on his thigh with care.

'Does it still hurt?'

'Only a little,' he returned, his fingers coming across the fullness of her breast, 'and not a bit when I touch you.'

The edges of his mouth were turned up, his hair soft around his face but his eyes held only an unsated need of her body and spoke a language that heralded no words at all.

Today in the tiny chapel in Mayfair they had sworn a troth to each other in front of their family and close friends. Tonight they were sealing the promise in flesh.

'Let me love you, sweetheart,' he whispered and she opened her legs to his touch, the wetness there attesting to his other ministrations and endless want.

He came in slowly this time, none of the desperation of the first hours apparent, but a quiet and languid joining. And he watched her with his velvet eyes and his smile, watched as she was pushed over the edge of reason on to the slippery slope of passion and down and down to the river of release.

This was love. This was life. This is what she had dreamed of in all the years of her sadness.

'Love me for ever, Nicholas,' she finally whispered when her breath was back.

'I will, my darling. I promise.'

Epilogue

Christmas Eve, 1819

The main salon at the ducal town house was filled with Christmas.

There were stars cut in gold paper and silk fabric scattered across the trestle tables which were heavy with the fare of the season. Rosemary, bay, holly and laurel had been brought inside this morning as it was unlucky to have it displayed until Christmas Eve. A roaring fire in the hearth warmed the room, the crackle of the Yule log competing with the excited chatter of Lucy, who was using this evening to give out her own special gift with all the aplomb that a six-year-old was able to manage.

'This is for you, Papa,' she said and sidled up on to Nicholas's knee. The present he opened was embellished with the sparkly red ribbon that Eleanor had given her the year before.

The year before.

So much had happened in a year, she thought, looking around the room at her brother and Rose, who was four months pregnant, and then at Oliver and Cecilia sitting together on the sofa by the fire. In Cecilia's arms was a baby who was the spitting image of his father right down to his light green eyes and coffee-coloured skin.

Frederick and Georgiana sat in the two leather arm chairs, a sleeping child in the bassinet at their feet. At six months old Harriet looked to be finally settled and her parents were enjoying a moment's respite, though Grandmama was watching closely for any sign of wakefulness in order that she might have a hold.

Nicholas's present was now revealed and Eleanor had to smile. Lucy had made him a painting for his library which she had framed in rainbows and kisses. The image showed the three of them at Bromworth Manor with their arms around each other. Victor was seated next to them, almost as large as they were, his pink tongue lolling.

'I shall hang this family portrait above my desk,' Nicholas was saying. 'Right where I can see it when I sit down to work.'

'You really like it, Papa?' There was a shy hopefulness in Lucy's voice. She always addressed him as Papa whenever she was able to. A vestige of five years without him, perhaps, that now translated into a need of constant ownership?

'I love it,' Nick was saying, her arms coming tightly around his neck in reply as he kissed her on the forehead.

'I want one for my library, Lucy,' Jacob said. 'Can I commission you?'

'Comm...ishin? What does that mean, Uncle Jacob?'

'It means he will pay you money for a portrait of him and Rose and the new baby when it comes. Make sure it's a goodly sum for he can certainly afford it.' Nick was smiling as he explained this and Lucy nodded.

'I think we should all have one, Lucy, of each family.' Oliver's voice was serious. 'It can become a new tradition.'

'Because the old ones are seeming more and more irrelevant?' Frederick laughed and his hand slid into Cecilia's. 'I don't think that Christian and his friends know quite what they are inheriting with their acquisition of Vitium et Virtus.'

'A monster?' Oliver smiled.

'A way of life that is fleeting,' Jacob amended, 'and yet…look what it had brought us. I wouldn't have met Rose had I not found her at the club late one night trying on one of the performer's dresses.'

Rose shook her head. 'The fabric was so beautiful I couldn't resist pretending for a moment that instead of being the maid I was a high-born lady dancing with a handsome gentleman.'

Lucy clapped her hands at the story and Rose blew her a kiss. 'Dream big, Lucy,' she said, 'just like I did.'

'Here's to Vitium et Virtus,' Oliver spoke next. 'And to the beautiful Madame Coquette who came my way because of it.' He lifted his glass to Cecilia, who smiled back at him, her brown eyes alight with tenderness.

'If you had not come to Paris on business for the club…' Her voice tailed off in worry.

'I would have met you somewhere, my love. Trust me on that.'

Frederick stood now with a toast. 'To Georgiana with her perfect but foolish plan at avoiding an arranged marriage. Vitium et Virtus was the venue for her fall into notoriety and that in turn brought her straight to me.'

'There is a silver lining, Frederick, in every cloud of hopelessness.' Georgiana raised her own glass and drank.

That left only Nicholas to give the others his memory of meeting her at the club. Only they hadn't met there in any shape or form, his pool of blood discovered in the alley behind the day after he had disappeared.

'For me Vitium et Virtus was always about a family I never had. It was about friendship and freedom and if the place encouraged excess and recklessness then it also helped me to understand what I truly wanted my life to be like. Here's to you, Eleanor and Lucy. My jewels. My home. My family. The virtue to my vice.'

Frederick lifted his glass. 'To family then and to friendship. Christian told me as I left tonight that he hoped we enjoyed our one last party at the club. He has opened the cellar and given the entertainers the evening off. He said tomorrow they shall all be back and heaven help anyone who thought Vitium et Virtus had become proper.'

'He sounds like us, back then when we were young.' Nick laughed as he stated this.

'Well, it's in safe hands at least.' Oliver's voice held a good deal of the same humour. 'He has not paid us for all the bottles of liquor stored in the cellar after all, so we need to be sure to drink up deeply.'

'Can I come with you, Papa? Can I go to the club, too?'

'No, you may not, Lucy, until you are at least twenty years older and hopefully not even then.' Nicholas sounded like a protective father, his tone all that of a man who had never had a wild and reckless youth. 'It's bed for you in order to be up early for all the celebrations. But your mama, on the other hand, is most welcome to dance just with me until the morning.'

His eyes were bright with love, the wary distance gone now to be replaced by joy. A family man, a man of the land, a man who had discovered his place in life and in her heart.

Eleanor raised her own glass.

'Here's to the Christmases past and all those to come, for blessed is the season that makes the whole world love.'

And under her breath she thanked God for the best Christmas present she had ever received, the first fluttering of a new life quiet in her womb.

Tonight she would tell Nicholas when they were alone, tucked in their bed under the patched quilt on the second floor of the Bromley town house, a waxing Yuletide moon outside.

Breathing in, she looked over at her husband and when his glance caught hers she tipped her head and he tipped his back, a secret smile across his face.

Perhaps he already knew?

Her world was so full of promise and hope that she felt her own mother and father close.

You would have loved Nicholas, she thought, just as the Yuletide log suddenly flared.

They were watching with Ralph, she knew they were,

from up above. Tonight of all nights she understood the eternity of family as she had not before as somewhere close the strains of a Christmas song could be heard on the wind.

> *Hark! the herald angels sing*
> *Glory to the newborn king!*
> *Peace on earth, and mercy mild*
> *God and sinners reconciled*

* * * * *